LINDA LAEL MILLER

I'll Be Home for Christmas

and stories by
CATHERINE MULVANY
JULIE LETO • ROXANNE ST. CLAIRE

POCKET BOOKS
New York London Toronto Sydney

Pocket Books
A Division of Simon & Schuster, Inc.
1230 Avenue of the Americas
New York, NY 10020

This book is a work of fiction. Names, characters, places, and incidents either are products of the author's imagination or are used fictitiously. Any resemblance to actual events or locales or persons, living or dead, is entirely coincidental.

This Pocket Books paperback edition November 2010

POCKET and colophon are registered trademarks of Simon & Schuster, Inc.

For information about special discounts for bulk purchases, please contact Simon & Schuster Special Sales at 1-866-506-1949 or business@simonandschuster.com.

The Simon & Schuster Speakers Bureau can bring authors to your live event. For more information or to book an event contact the Simon & Schuster Speakers Bureau at 1-866-248-3049 or visit our website at www.simonspeakers.com.

Illustration by Alan Ayers; Design by Min Choi
Interior design by Davina Mock

Manufactured in the United States of America

10 9 8 7 6 5 4 3 2

ISBN 978-1-4516-0940-0
ISBN 978-1-4165-4834-8 (ebook)

Contents

Christmas of the Red Chiefs

❄❄❄❄❄

Linda Lael Miller

To my Uncle Harry,
who was the best Santa Claus Northport ever had.

I wish to acknowledge the talent, insight, patience, and skill of my longtime editor, Amy Pierpont. Thanks, Amy. I learned so much from you.

Chapter One

❄ ❄ ❄

The bus door opened with a pneumatic *whoosh,* alongside the Mega-Pumper gas station, and expelled my twelve-year-old stepdaughter Marlie and me on the exhale. Marlie juggled her backpack and fashionably tiny purse while I schlepped a weekender and my tote bag.

We were the last two passengers, arriving in a place where neither of us wanted to be—my hometown of Bent Tree Creek, California—and as we stood there on the asphalt, our ears stinging from a snow-laced breeze and our most recent scathing argument, my heart attempted a swan dive and belly flopped instead.

"It so seriously sucks that we don't even have a car," Marlie said. Toes curled over the edge of the precipice between childhood and raging adolescence, she'd recently morphed from a sweet and very girly girl into the reigning mistress of hormonal contempt.

I raised the collar of my too-thin coat against the bitter cold and stifled a sigh. These days Marlie did enough sighing for both of us, but it wasn't as if she didn't have reason. Her dad and my husband, Craig Wagner, had been killed in the crash of a small private plane eighteen months before. Since then, we'd lost a lot—the beach bungalow in San Diego, the family printing business, two cars, and a lot of illusions.

At least *I'd* lost my illusions. Marlie was still clinging to hers, and who could blame her? She was so very young, and the world she'd known before Craig's death had collapsed around her.

Her Real Mother—recently, Marlie had taken to capitalizing the words every time she uttered them, lest I think for one moment she was talking about me, mama non grata—worked as a pole dancer in some second-rate club in Reno, when she wasn't in rehab for alcohol and/or drugs. Brenda, stage name: Bambi, was a subject we mostly avoided.

"Yes," I agreed, remembering my vintage MG roadster with a pang. "It sucks that we don't have a car." My eyes burned, but it wasn't an opportune time to cry. I had two rules about shedding tears: I had to be alone, and I had five minutes to feel sorry for myself, max. At first, when I'd found out Craig had let all but one of his life insurance policies lapse, lied to me about our financial situation in general, and left us with a pile of debt, I'd actually set one of those little electronic kitchen timers to make sure I didn't go over the time limit for helpless weeping.

Of course there had been good times with Craig— he'd been handsome, funny, and full of life, but now those things seemed more like half-forgotten dreams than reality.

While the bus driver unloaded the rest of our earthly

belongings—stuffed into four large suitcases and two moving boxes sealed with copious amounts of duct tape—Marlie took in her new surroundings.

It was 4:30 on a late-November afternoon, and Bent Tree Creek wasn't exactly the western version of a Norman Rockwell village, the way I remembered it. The town is rimmed by pine forests on three sides, but between the exhaust fumes from the bus and the gasoline odor from the Mega-Pumper, I couldn't catch even a whiff of evergreen.

"Is somebody coming to get us or are we just going to stand here all night?" Marlie pressed, peevish. I knew she was tired, hungry, and scared, and I wanted to reassure her, not let her see that I was pretty much in the same uncertain place at the moment.

I moved to touch her shoulder, but then thought better of the gesture. Seven years before, when Craig and I got married, following a too-short courtship, Marlie was only five, a gawky little thing with moppet eyes and a lisp. After an initial and entirely natural period of wariness, she'd accepted me as an understudy for the role of Mom, but now I wasn't even in the running for the part.

Don't call us, we'll call you.

Lately, it seemed she blamed me for everything, from the federal deficit to our present situation. Oh, yes. If it hadn't been for me, Marlie Rose Wagner would be living the perfect life.

"I want to go to Reno and move in with Mom," Marlie said.

I bit my lower lip and refrained from pointing out the obvious flaws in that fantasy. Brenda/Bambi had abandoned Marlie when she was two—Craig had come home to find his daughter wailing in a playpen in their apartment, wearing a soggy diaper and waving a long-empty bottle. Brenda hadn't been back since, and except for the odd email, phone call, birthday card, or box of Christmas candy, she never initiated any sort of contact.

Emotionally, I was on the ragged edge. Once I'd been so sure of myself—singing all the time and indulging in one of my favorite hobbies, trying new recipes. Converting standard comfort foods to low-fat, low-calorie versions, much to the delight of my friends, who were all busy career women on diets.

Where had those friends gone?

Where had the joy gone?

When had I stopped singing?

"You know you can't go to Reno," I said, bringing myself firmly back into the present moment, difficult as it was, and with hard-won moderation. It would have been easier to point out that Bambi wasn't exactly in the running for Mother of the Year, or offer the kid a ticket and wish her a good trip, but in the first place, I loved Marlie, even if she wasn't particularly fond of me, and in the second, we both knew it was a spindly threat. Brenda was too busy being Bambi to bother with a twelve-year-old.

The bus pulled out, flinging back a biting spray of slush.

Cars came and went from the Mega-Pumper.

Families strolled in and out of Roy's Café, across the street. Old-fashioned bulb lights edged the windows at Roy's, and maybe it's an indication of my state of mind that I noticed several of them were burned out.

I began to wonder if Delores had forgotten we were coming.

Delores Sullivan was my dad's only sister, and my sole living blood relative, but she and I weren't exactly close. When she'd called in a panic just a week before and asked if I'd come back to Bent Tree Creek and help her run Barrels of Carols, I'd reluctantly agreed. My latest dead-end job had just fizzled and I didn't have another one on the line—plus, all my friends had either left Southern California or dived into new relationships, leaving me with just acquaintances, so I was at loose ends in more ways than one. Marlie and I had been camping out in a neighbor's guest house while the family was in Europe, but now the Brittons were back, with a couple of exchange students in tow, and they needed the space.

Meanwhile, back here in the Present Moment, it was getting colder, and darker.

I got out my paid-in-advance cellphone, the last vestige of my old life, and struggled to remember Delores's number. Like I said, we weren't close.

The little panel read *No service.*

I hoped that wasn't a metaphor—an omen for the way things would go between Delores and me.

"We ought to at least move our stuff," Marlie said, as the snow began to come down in earnest.

"Good idea," I answered, injecting a lot of false cheer into my voice, and moved to pick up one of the big suitcases. I tend to think in allegories, and just then, those Vuitton knockoffs seemed like more than containers for my clothes. They were symbols of my personal baggage. I'd gone to college. I'd fallen in love with a man and built a life, made friends. Refined my cooking skills and sung in a community choir.

How could it all have come down to *this?*

The largest of the bags didn't have wheels and lifting it was out of the question. I was just starting to drag the thing toward the door of the Mega-Pumper when a blue van whipped into the lot and came to a stop about three feet in front of Marlie and me.

The window on the driver's side whirred down.

A square-jawed man with ebony eyes and dark hair pulled back into a ponytail looked me over pensively. I felt a visceral *zap* when our gazes connected and immediately took an inner leap back. Once I'd trusted my instincts, but no more. Craig had cured me of that.

I motioned for Marlie to stay behind me.

"Are you Sarah?" asked the van man. There was something tender and knowing in his eyes, but I saw caution there, too.

I nodded. "Yes."

Nothing could have prepared me for the sudden flash of his grin. Like a supernova, it transformed his whole face and set something quivering deep inside me. He shoved open the van door and bounded out, one hand extended. Lean and muscular, with an air of controlled power, he wore jeans, a polo shirt, and a battered leather jacket.

"Joe Courtland," he said. "Delores sent me to pick you up."

I hesitated, then shook his hand.

He looked past me, grinned at Marlie.

Inside the van, a dog barked, and the faces of two

small boys appeared in the window, curious and some-how hopeful.

"Are you a serial killer?" Marlie asked.

"No," Joe Courtland answered, suppressing another nuclear-powered grin. "I'm a music teacher."

Serial killers and music teachers weren't necessarily exclusive, I reasoned, and he was, after all, driving a van. Plus, there was the electricity, a sort of invisible charge in the air that made me want to chase after the departing bus, get back on, and keep going.

"Where's Delores?" I asked. There might have been some suspicion in my voice. Like I said, my aunt and I hadn't exactly bonded. I barely knew her, and when I needed her most, she'd shuffled me out of her life so fast it took my breath away.

Joe looked me over thoughtfully, as though taking my measure and finding me a few light-years short of what-ever standard he'd had in mind, then rounded the van and pulled open the rear doors. "She broke her ankle yesterday," he said, tight-jawed, returning and gripping the handles of the two large suitcases. "Then there was a crisis with one of the carolers."

Delores provided singers for malls, hospitals, office parties, and the like. It was a thriving operation, as I un-derstood it, and with Thanksgiving only a few days away, the heat was probably on. I knew she auditioned people, had them fitted for Victorian costumes, and rented them out. Though the performances were seasonal, the crew rehearsed year-round.

I almost said, "I used to sing."

"I see," I said instead, with a corresponding twinge of

sympathetic pain in my own ankle. Not to mention my heart. I wondered what Delores had told him about me.

Joe came back for the boxes, one by one.

"I guess if he were a serial killer," Marlie speculated, whispering, "he wouldn't have a couple of kids and a dog in his van."

"Probably not," I replied.

And so it was decided. We would risk life and limb by accepting a ride.

I sat in front, while Marlie climbed into the back, buckling in beside a German shepherd. The kids, identical twin boys about eight years old, looked nothing like their father. They had thick red hair, copious freckles, and both of them wore glasses.

"My sons," Joe explained, after getting behind the wheel again. "Ryan and Sam. The furry one with his tongue hanging out is Dodger. He won't bite, though I can't make the same promise where the boys are concerned."

The heat spilling from the vents in the van's dashboard was bliss. I wondered distractedly where Joe's wife was and if the kids took after her. Maybe she was home baking pumpkin pies or thawing out a turkey. For some reason, the image made my throat tighten.

"I'm Marlie," my stepdaughter piped up, evidently speaking to the twins, "and that's Sarah. She was my dad's wife until the Cessna he was riding in collided with the side of a mountain."

A thick silence fell in the backseat and Joe slanted a look in my direction. "Marlie likes to shock people," I said quietly, after an involuntary wince. If Delores and Joe were good enough friends that she could ask him to fetch a pair of shirttail relatives just spilled out of a bus at the Mega-Pumper, then he probably knew about Craig's death. Delores had sent a sympathy card, but she hadn't come to the funeral.

"It's the truth," Marlie said.

I leaned back in the seat and closed my eyes, weary to the marrow.

"Our mom died, too," one of the twins remarked as Joe pulled the van out into the kind of light traffic you might expect in a town that size. Bent Tree Creek is far enough from Sacramento to be semirural, and close enough that it's rapidly becoming a bedroom community. "She got sick and then she turned purple."

This time, I was the one slanting the look.

"Hepatitis C," Joe explained. He must have caught my glance out of the corner of his eye, but he was looking straight ahead. All traces of the grin were gone; the planes of his face seemed grim and angular and I noticed a slight stoop in his broad shoulders.

"I'm sorry," I told him.

"Me, too," he answered simply.

"My mother had hepatitis once," Marlie said.

Yeah, I thought uncharitably, from a needle.

Fortunately, it wasn't far to Delores's two-story house.

My aunt was waiting on the covered porch when we pulled into the driveway, leaning on her crutches and looking as though the last thing on earth she wanted was company. Her gray hair was cut in a slanted bob and she wore a bulky pullover top and sweatpants with the right leg cut open to accommodate her cast. Even from a distance, I could see that the plaster had been much-autographed.

15

Delores had always had a lot of friends.

I just hadn't been one of them.

She stumped as far as the steps, which looked icy.

"Stay where you are," Joe ordered cordially, standing on the running board to address her over the roof of the van. "One broken ankle is manageable. Two will put you on bed rest for the whole season."

Delores conceded the point with a nod and watched warily as I opened the passenger door and climbed out. Marlie followed, in no hurry.

"Cold enough for you?" Delores called. We'd always found it hard to talk to each other, and when we did speak, it was usually in clichés. Keep it superficial; that was the unspoken rule.

I tried to be philosophical. She'd offered me a job and she was taking Marlie and me into her home, and who knew where we'd be if she hadn't. "Cold as a banker's heart," I said, keeping up the tradition.

Even though he'd been occupied unloading the luggage and now carried a suitcase in each hand, Joe still managed to get to the gate in the picket fence before Marlie and I did. He set one bag down to reach over and work the latch and stood back to let us go first.

"Interesting house," Marlie murmured. It was the first positive thing she'd said since we'd left San Diego a day and a half before, and I was encouraged.

I looked up at the familiar frame structure.

Both Dad and Delores had grown up in that house, and when I was sixteen, and the latest in a long line of stepmothers had just cleaned out the family bank account, Dad and I moved in. My mother died when I was four and I don't remember anything about her except that she cried a lot and smelled like freshly laundered sheets drying in the sun.

We lived happily in Bent Tree Creek for a couple of years. I went to school, studied hard, and sang with Barrels of Carols—second soprano.

Then it all collapsed. I was a senior, basically just marking time until graduation, since I'd already earned all the necessary credits. Delores and I were getting along, considering the usual teenage stuff.

Then, suddenly, Dad had a heart attack and died. Delores collected the insurance money, handed it over, and sent me off to college early.

I'd come back to visit, once or twice, and Delores was kind to me, in her busy, distracted way, but I didn't belong. I was obviously in the way, though she'd never said so outright, and I'd been too uncomfortable to stay long.

"Come inside where it's warm," Delores urged quietly, snapping me back from the sentimental journey. "And you must be Marlie Rose," she said, summoning up a smile for my stepdaughter. "It will surely be nice to have a young person around again."

"We're young persons," one of the twins pointed out. They'd both materialized on the porch, along with the dog.

Delores ruffled the boys' hair fondly. "Yes," she said, "you are. But you live across the street, so I naturally don't get to see as much of you as I'd like, and Marlie will be right under this roof."

I should have been glad she was making Marlie welcome. Instead, I just felt shut out.

"If you people would move," Joe said, with affable

frustration, from the base of the ice-glazed steps, "I could bring in these bags."

We all trooped into the house, Delores first, hobbling on her crutches, then Marlie, the dog, and the boys. I followed, pausing on the threshold to look back over one shoulder at Joe. Then I raised my eyes to the large but modest house on the other side of the road.

When I lowered my gaze, it collided with Joe's. Something sparked, then sizzled, and we both looked away quickly.

Chapter Two

﹡ ❄ ﹡

Delores's old-fashioned kitchen, with its outdated appliances and worn linoleum floor, was just as I remembered it. Her familiar discount-store perfume hung wisplike in the air, and the scent of something savory, baking in the oven, made my stomach growl. I was starving after nearly two days of grabbing whatever was available, whatever was cheap, at whatever bus stop we rolled into along the lengthy, diverse, and winding roads between San Diego and Bent Tree Creek.

Delores had set the table with three places, so I guessed Joe and the twins weren't staying for supper. Oddly, I was both relieved and disappointed. There was something disturbing about Joe. He looked more like the leader of a renegade rock band than a schoolteacher, and I sensed a depth in him that I'd never encountered in another man, certainly not Craig.

For all his charm, Craig had been about as deep as a puddle.

"Take off those coats," Delores ordered.

I peeled out of mine and so did Marlie. I took them

both and hung them on the familiar peg next to the back door.

Joe popped in, got the attention of the boys and the dog with a low whistle through his teeth. "Time to go," he said. "Homework."

"Thanks for making the bus run, Joe," Delores told him.

"We thought he was a serial killer," Marlie put in, plopping into a chair at the table.

I blushed.

Joe laughed. "Now," he said, "I've heard it all." He directed his gaze to Delores, fond and full of humor. "If you need anything else, give me a call."

Delores nodded. "Carolers' meeting tomorrow morning at ten," she reminded him.

Joe, the boys, and the dog left in a flurry of noise.

"Sit down," I told Delores when she started toward the wall oven.

She sat, landing in her chair with a relieved sigh.

"Don't mind if I do," she said.

I washed my hands at the sink, scouted up a couple of pot holders, and pulled the casserole from the oven. The smell was delicious. Someone cares, it said. There is still reason to hope.

Don't go down that road, I warned myself silently. You'll be ambushed for sure.

"My dad died in a plane crash," Marlie told Delores while I set supper in the middle of the table, along with a serving spoon. Marlie injected some version of that statement into the conversation every time she encountered someone new; I think, in a strange way, she was trying to make herself believe it. To accept the unacceptable.

Delores patted her hand. "I heard," she said with gentle practicality. "It's pretty awful."

Marlie nodded, scooped up a plateful of chicken spaghetti, and started shoveling it in. "Do you have a bathtub? I hate showers, especially when I'm cold. Do I get my own room or do I have to share with Sarah?"

"You get your own room," Delores replied. "It's small, but it's all yours. And the bathtub is big enough to swim in."

I passed Delores a cautious glance as I waited for her to help herself to supper. When she had, I spooned up a healthy portion for myself.

What was she up to anyway? Why, after years of silence, had she suddenly asked me to come back to Bent Tree Creek? Was there more to it than just needing help running Barrels of Carols?

"My mom," Marlie confided, between bites, "is a dancer."

"Isn't that nice?" Delores said.

I kept my eyes on my plate.

"Can I sign your cast?" Marlie asked.

"Sure," Delores replied.

After supper, Marlie cleared the table without being asked—something I'd never been able to get her to do at home, or a least since we'd moved into the guest house—found a pen, and crouched to autograph the plaster casing around Delores's right foot with a decided flourish.

"Thanks," Delores said.

Marlie yawned. "Which room is mine?" she asked Delores.

"Top of the stairs, first door on the right. The bathroom is at the end of the hall."

Marlie nodded and left the room.

I sighed with relief.

"Maybe you'd better get to bed early tonight, too," Delores told me. "You must be just about done-in, with all that's happened, and a bus trip on top of it."

I suddenly wanted to cry, but waited stoically until the urge passed.

"I appreciate your taking us in," I said, when I thought I could trust myself to speak without blubbering. "I promise we won't stay long."

"We'll see how it goes," Delores said.

I didn't know how to respond, so I didn't.

"Still skittish as cold water sprinkled on a hot griddle," Delores commented. "There's a lot of your daddy in you—always ready to light out before somebody can send you packing."

Like you, for instance, I thought. My aunt had shoved a check into my hand and basically run me out of town three days after Dad's funeral, but the time didn't seem right to bring that up.

She leaned forward in her chair, studying me. "What are you thinking?"

I swallowed. Looked away, then back. "About the day you drove me to college, with all my stuff. As soon as we'd unloaded it in the dorm, you were out of there." I'd wanted to run behind her car, though I wasn't about to say so, of course.

"Sarah Jane," Delores said, still watching me closely, "that school is forty miles from here, not four hundred, and you could have visited whenever you wanted. You make it sound as though I dropped you off the edge of the earth. I was short-handed at the time and I had to get back to work. Keep things going."

I nodded. My brain understood, but my heart was way back there on the front steps of the dorm, adrift among surges of cheerful strangers who all seemed to know each other, watching Delores's station wagon disappear around the bend.

The loneliness of that moment echoed within me still.

I'd buckled down, kept to myself, studied hard.

I'd gone to Chicago after earning my liberal arts degree and worked as a receptionist in an art gallery. After that, I'd landed in Houston, managing a bookstore, and then in Los Angeles, selling radio ads. I never stayed in any one place very long and my friendships were all disposable, and not just on my side.

Then I'd met Craig, with his young daughter.

Instant family. Port in the emotional storm.

Craig made me laugh. He bought me flowers.

It never occurred to me that his feelings might not run as deep as mine.

I'd been all over the whole love-and-marriage thing like a kudzu vine. Now, in unguarded moments, I wasn't sure I'd ever loved Craig for himself, not just his child and the home he could give me, and I had all kinds of guilt because of it.

"What's really going on here, Delores?" I blurted, because I couldn't hold the question in any longer.

"I told you on the phone," my aunt answered briskly, avoiding my eyes. "I need help with the company."

"Why? You've gotten along just fine all these years—" Without me.

Delores looked thoughtful and a little grim. She stared into a corner of the room. "I'm getting older. Slowing down." At last, she looked directly into my face. "When I started Barrels of Carols, there was nothing like it. Now there's a big company operating out of Los Angeles, undercutting my prices and trying to steal my clients. I can't fight them alone."

"What about Joe? Can't he help?"

"Joe's busy."

A surge of indignation swelled inside me. *I* wasn't busy, though. To Delores, evidently, I was a cardboard figure, standing idle and forgotten in some closet—until she needed me.

"If you didn't want to come, Sarah Jane," she told me, "you should have said so."

I hadn't really had a choice, with no job and no place to live, but I was too proud to admit it. "I'm here now," I said evenly. "What exactly do you want me to do?"

"Sing," Delores said.

I stared at her. "Sing?"

"You've got one of the best voices I've ever heard," Delores told me flatly and with no indication of admiration. "It's a shame you never did anything with it."

I opened my mouth. Closed it again.

One of the best voices she'd ever heard? It was news to me.

Besides, the day Craig died, I'd stopped singing. Once I'd been full of music—it had sustained me during the lonely times as nothing else could have done—but now it was gone. Dried up and blown away.

"I can't," I said.

Delores arched a skeptical eyebrow. "Well, that's a fine

how-do-you-do. I asked you here so you could take over for my best soprano. She moved to Albuquerque."

"You told me you needed help running the business," I pointed out.

"That, too," Delores said with a dismissive wave.

I closed my eyes. Sighed.

The legs of Delores's chair scraped the linoleum floor as she stood. "You need a place to live. I need a soprano who can double as a referee. Sounds like a fair deal to me, Sarah Jane. But if you're not up to it, maybe you'd better get on the next bus and go back to LaLa Land."

I couldn't speak. If I'd tried, it would have come out as a pathetic croak. So I just drew a deep, shaky breath and held it until Delores finally gave up and left the kitchen, shaking her head as she went.

When I was alone, I checked the clock and allowed the tears to come.

Five minutes' worth. No more.

Marlie was curled up in the spare-room bed when I got upstairs, snoring softly, wearing mismatched pajamas and hugging her childhood teddy bear. She must have resurrected the toy from some secret hiding place around the time Craig was killed, without my knowing. Seeing it again, clutched in her arms, even in sleep, bruised my heart.

I loved Marlie, but, as she constantly reminded me, I wasn't her mother.

How was I going to help her when I couldn't even help myself?

We were both lost and it should have been a comfort, having each other. Instead, my stepdaughter and I were like a couple of strangers, huddled in the same life raft. We were surviving, but not living.

Heartsick, I backed into the hallway, softly closed the door of her room.

My own room looked pretty much the same as it had the last time I saw it, long, long ago.

I walked past my suitcase, yet to be unpacked, and over to the window. Snow drifted lazily through glowing golden cones cast by the streetlights.

Joe Courtland's house, directly across the street, looked like the front of a Christmas card. As I watched, the front door opened and Joe came out, with Dodger. I almost stepped back when he glanced up, our gazes connecting like two bare wires, but I waved instead.

He waved back.

The dog sniffed the snowy ground, circled the base of a bare-limbed maple tree, and lifted his leg against the trunk.

Joe spread his hands, as if to say, "What can you do?"

I smiled.

He and Dodger went back inside.

I turned away, retrieved my cosmetics case from my tote bag, and then plundered a suitcase for a nightshirt. I took a long, luxurious bath, brushed my teeth, and moisturized my face.

Lately, I'd avoided mirrors, but that night, I took a good look at myself.

I saw a thirty-four-year-old woman, no great beauty, but reasonably attractive. My skin looked pale, and there were shadows under my eyes, which, like my medium-length hair, were medium brown.

Everything about me was medium.

I had never done—or been—anything remarkable in my life.

With Craig, I'd thought I was living my dreams, but they'd all been shattered.

Now I could barely remember them.

A home and a husband. A baby or two. Singing in a choir. Maybe a small business, preparing and delivering special meals for people on various food plans.

It wasn't fashionable, but I'd mainly wanted to be a wife and mother.

My throat began to ache again.

I shook off the melancholy and headed downstairs, looking for Delores. I still had some savings, though the money was rapidly dwindling. I'd tell my aunt I was sorry about the misunderstanding; Marlie and I would move on to Sacramento as soon as we could. I'd find a job there and an apartment.

I found Delores in the living room with the TV on, seated in an easy chair, her injured foot propped on an ottoman. When she noticed me, she muted the set and started to get up.

"Sit," I said.

She frowned. Delores had never been married nor had she ever worked for anyone but herself, as far as I knew. She was set in her ways and not inclined to take orders, however benevolent the intention behind them.

"I'll make you some tea," I volunteered. I felt sorry for her, with that broken ankle, and wanted to make up in some way for letting her down by leaving.

A few minutes later, I returned with two steaming cups. "Milk and sugar," I said, setting hers down on the end table next to her chair. "Just the way you like it."

"You remembered," she said, surprised.

"I remembered," I said, suppressing a sigh, taking the other chair and tucking my legs up beneath me.

"Is Marlie all right?" Delores asked, blowing on her tea to cool it.

"She's asleep," I answered. "Whether she's all right or not is another question. She misses Craig something terrible, of course, and she's got this idea that if she just hooks up with her mother in Reno, everything will be peachy again."

Delores nodded. "Poor little thing."

Emotion swelled inside me, pushing aside the numbness I'd worked so hard to maintain. "How am I going to help her?" I whispered, more to myself than to Delores, who had never been any sort of confidante. "She's cast me as the wicked stepmother and I don't know how to reach her."

"Stop trying," Delores said.

I was confused, and a little angry. It was just the sort of advice I'd expect from her. "Huh?"

"Marlie's angry and afraid. She's got to put those feelings somewhere, and you're handy. Accept that. Push up your sleeves, stand toe-to-toe with that child, and *love her,* no matter what."

It was good advice, and I knew it. I just wished Delores could have found it in her heart to love *me,* especially after Dad died and I felt so broken and alone.

"Why didn't you come to Craig's funeral?" I asked. The words were out of my mouth before I'd framed them consciously.

For a long moment, Delores and I just sat looking at each other.

"I knew my old wreck of a car wouldn't make it that far," Delores said finally. "Anyhow, I figured I'd be in the way."

She could have flown. She could have taken a train or a bus.

She'd had a similar excuse when I invited her to my wedding.

"Okay," I said, standing up.

"You'll stay?" Delores ventured.

"No," I answered. "Probably not."

"Well," Delores said, "that figures. I thought maybe I could count on you, since we're family."

I didn't trust myself to answer kindly, so I took my tea, climbed the stairs, and shut myself up in my old bedroom.

Chapter Three

❄ ❄ ❄

"It's a mutiny," Delores announced dramatically, and with a touch of glee, the next morning in the kitchen, setting her old-fashioned phone receiver back in the cradle. "Mary Ellen Hershmeyer won't sing if Jenny Rivers is going to be in the same group. If I move either one of them to another team of carolers, I'll have the same problem. They're *both* difficult."

I set the omelet I'd made for her on the table. Thick flakes of snow drifted past the windows, but it was cozy and warm inside Delores's kitchen. "Why don't you just fire them both and hire new people?" I asked. Marlie was still sleeping, and I was half hoping she'd join us for breakfast and half dreading it.

Delores crutched her way to the table and sat down. "The competition would snap them up," she said. "I can't afford to lose them."

I took that in without comment. The whole thing was a moot point anyway, since I planned to pick up a copy of the *Sacramento Bee* after breakfast and check out the employment ads and rentals. Maybe Delores would let Marlie and I stay until I found something, if I helped her with the management aspects of Barrels of Carols.

Singing was definitely out, though.

I'd tried to sing, a couple of times in the shower, and always broken down.

I looked back over my checkered job history and found nothing that would equip me to make peace between these two women and get them to sing in harmony, literally and figuratively, but I was resourceful. I'd had to be, after Craig died, when I found out we were not only broke but in debt. I'd set aside what little insurance money he'd had for Marlie, sold everything we owned of any value, and paid off bills. I could probably keep a couple of carolers from going for each other's throats.

"How long are you going to be laid up with that ankle?" I asked, feeling a twinge of guilt.

"I should get the cast off toward the end of January," Delores said.

I took a sip of coffee. I'd made toast, but just then even a nibble seemed too much to swallow.

The pipes rattled overhead and both Delores and I raised our eyes to the ceiling, tacitly acknowledging the obvious.

Marlie was out of bed.

Inwardly, I braced myself for whatever mood my stepdaughter was in.

She might be nice. She might be toxic.

With Marlie, it was a crapshoot, and the odds were even, so things could go either way.

Delores tasted the omelet. "Not bad," she said.

"If it's all right with you," I said, wanting to get things settled, "Marlie and I will stay on for a couple of weeks, just until I can find a job and an apartment in Sacramento. In the meantime, I'll earn our keep managing the carolers."

Something sparked in Delores's eyes. Maybe it was triumph, maybe it was annoyance. "It's cold out there, Sarah," she said, and I knew she wasn't referring to the snowy weather, but the real world. "Sacramento is expensive. And what's so terrible about singing a few Christmas carols?"

"Nothing," I said wistfully. "I've just forgotten how."

"You're feeling sorry for yourself," she accused.

I flushed. "Whatever you do," I said, "don't say anything kind."

"I say what I mean," Delores retorted, "take it or leave it."

"I'd like to leave it," I answered, "but for the moment, I'm fresh out of options."

"I know that," Delores said. "If you had a choice, you wouldn't be here."

Well, at least we understood each other.

"You go to that carolers' meeting," she added. "We'll just take this one day at a time."

Great, I thought. A baptism of fire.

"Joe will help with the musical part," Delores prompted when I didn't say anything. "And the meeting is at the new community center. You know, Sarah, one of your problems is that you're always focused on what you *can't* do, instead of what you can."

I swallowed more coffee and ignored the motivational tidbit. "Won't he be at school? Joe, I mean?"

"His classes are all in the afternoon," Delores answered. "He usually spends mornings working on his book, but he's willing to make an exception for this meeting, God bless him."

I was intrigued, in spite of myself. Every shred of practicality I possessed warned me not to get too interested in Joe Courtland. As soon as I found a place for us to land, Marlie and I would be leaving. Besides, between Craig's death, the things I'd discovered since, my rocky relationship with Marlie, and the loss of a whole way of life, I was an emotional train wreck.

"Joe's writing a book? What is it—a novel?"

"Memoir," Delores said, looking proud. "He already has a publisher, too. Big New York outfit. He spends practically every spare moment at his computer."

"Impressive," I commented, glad the conversation had taken a different turn. "What kind of memoir?"

"It's about the last year of Abby's life." Delores's eyes glistened with tears. "She was an amazing person, Joe's wife."

Joe's wife. Why did those words make the little muscles in my throat tighten and twist? And how had Abby Courtland managed to amaze my aunt, when I couldn't get her to show up for a wedding or a funeral?

"When did she die?"

"Three years ago," Delores said. "I thought I wrote you about it. Abby and I were great friends. We used to go to garage and estate sales together, when she wasn't working, and pick up stuff to sell online. She really had an eye for bargains."

I set my elbows on the table and rubbed my temples with my fingertips. Three years ago, when Abby Courtland's life was winding down, I'd caught Craig in his first affair. We'd been in quiet crisis, and while I remembered receiving a few brief and scattered letters from Delores during that turbulent time, I couldn't have described the contents for the life of me.

Marlie circumvented any possibility of a further exchange by banging down the stairs and bursting into the kitchen like a one-girl commando unit. Her hair, the same pale butternut shade as Craig's, was pulled into a ponytail, and she looked ready for anything in her jeans, hiking boots, and bulky beige sweater. Her blue eyes were wide and rested.

I recalled the teddy bear.

A young woman by day, a child in secret. What else was going on with Marlie that I didn't know about?

"Do I have to go to school today?" she asked.

"Not much point in starting now," Delores observed, glancing at me a moment after she'd spoken, as though wondering if she'd spoken out of turn. Apparently, she decided she hadn't, for she immediately went on to say, "This is Tuesday, so there's only a half day of classes tomorrow, and then it's Thanksgiving. Monday ought to be soon enough."

Marlie scouted out cold cereal, a bowl and spoon, and the milk on her own. "I could just wait until after Christmas," she ventured. "To start school, that is."

"Fat chance," I said.

"I heard you telling Aunt Delores we wouldn't be staying," Marlie said. "So why do I have to go to class in the first place?"

Aunt Delores? Where had that come from?

"Because you do," I told her.

34

"We could move to Reno," Marlie put in, probably imagining that she was being helpful—and conveniently ignoring what I'd just said. "There are a lot of jobs there, in the casinos."

"Oh, right," I replied.

"I'm calling my mom to ask if I can move in with *her* then," Marlie snapped.

Delores raised both hands now, palms out, like a referee. All she lacked was the whistle. "Hold it, both of you," she said. "Sarah, you'll have your hands full with that motley crew of carolers, so you'd best think about that. Marlie, I've got twenty people coming for Thanksgiving dinner, day after tomorrow, so that means some heavy-duty advance cooking. I was hoping you'd help me."

"I don't know how to cook," Marlie said, but for once there was no rebellion in her tone. Only a sort of forlorn hope.

"Time you learned," Delores said.

Marlie beamed.

If *I'd* suggested cooking, the kid would have already been on her way to the bus stop.

I finished my coffee, pushed back my chair, and rose to carry my cup and plate of toast to the sink. I was running the disposal when I heard a dog bark, and when I turned to look, Joe and Dodger had just entered the kitchen.

Joe's dark hair was dusted with snow, as were the shoulders of his leather jacket. He smiled at me, and I felt a curious pitching sensation in the bottom of my stomach.

"I'm here to offer you a ride to the meeting," he

announced. His eyes twinkled. "Unless, of course, you still think I might be a serial killer."

"Where are the boys?" Delores asked, leaning in an effort to peer around Joe.

"Having a snowball fight in the front yard," Joe answered.

Dodger padded over to Delores, who stroked his head fondly with one hand.

"It's a little early, isn't it?" I asked. Earlier, Delores had mentioned that the meeting was scheduled for ten o'clock.

Joe shrugged. The twinkle was gone and his gaze rested soberly on my face. Again, I wondered what was going through his mind, what kind of person he'd thought I was. "I figured you might like to look around a little, see how the town's changed since you went away."

"What about the twins?" Marlie wanted to know. "Maybe they could stay here and help Delores and me make pies."

"They have school," Joe said.

Marlie blushed slightly. "I don't have to start until Monday," she said, with just the vaguest note of defensiveness. Since Joe was a teacher, she probably expected a truancy lecture.

"Makes sense," he replied. His brown eyes never left my face. "Come on," he said. "Let's take the tour."

Since I actually wanted to go, and could think of no graceful way to refuse even if I hadn't, I nodded.

We both said good-bye to Delores and Marlie, then Joe and I trooped outside, with Dodger on our trail.

The twins ceased their snowball warfare to grin at us.

"What?" Joe asked with mock annoyance, bending over to snatch up some snow. He lobbed some at each of his sons and their giggles rang out in the crisp, cold air. Dodger barked merrily, trotting around the boys in gleeful circles.

"Sarah's your girlfriend," one of the twins teased. Sam, I thought, though it could have been Ryan. They were mirror images of each other, after all.

"Kissy, kissy," added Ryan, who might have been Sam.

Joe laughed, squatted to make an arsenal of snowballs, and splattered both kids.

They fought back, and when all three of the Courtland men were splotched with snow, the fight finally broke up. Everybody piled into the van and we set out for the elementary school.

" 'Bye," one twin called out five minutes later, when we pulled up outside the familiar brick building. I'd never actually attended Bent Tree Creek Elementary, since I'd been in high school when I came to town, but I always wished I had.

"Kissy, kissy!" shouted the other twin.

"Remember," Joe told me with a serious mouth and laughter dancing in his eyes, "they're only eight."

"They're wonderful," I said.

Dodger barked a farewell from the backseat as the boys disappeared into a crowd of other children milling on the playground.

"I think so," Joe agreed as we pulled away.

"What's your secret?"

He concentrated on maneuvering slowly around a line-up of cars, moms and dads dropping off their kids for school, waving at a crossing guard standing on the sidewalk. "My secret?"

"Ryan and Sam seem so well-adjusted."

"They have their moments," he replied. We were clear of the snarl of school traffic by then, so he spared me a questioning glance. "It hasn't been easy for them, with their mother gone."

My eyes burned in the back. "No," I said. "I was about their age when I lost mine."

Joe was quiet.

I wished I hadn't mentioned my childhood. For one thing, it was a long time in the past. For another, Joe hadn't asked.

"You and Marlie are having some problems, I guess," Joe said after a decent interval.

"You could say that," I answered.

He grinned. "I just did."

"She hates me." The instant the words were out of my mouth, I wished I could jump out of the car and plunge my head into a snowbank. Illogical, I know, but that was how I felt.

"I doubt that," Joe said. "Losing her dad must have been tough. For both of you."

I was silent for a while. Joe and I hadn't known each other long enough to be having this conversation, but at the same time it seemed perfectly natural, as though I'd somehow been waiting for the chance to meet this small-town schoolteacher and tell him everything, and now it was finally here.

"It was pretty bad," I replied.

"Your husband was a pilot?"

I shook my head. "He owned a printing franchise," I answered. "His—friend was a pilot."

If Joe noticed the brief emotional hitch in my statement, he didn't comment.

"Abby was a software designer," he said.

"Delores told me you're writing a book about her."

"Delores talks too much sometimes," Joe responded, with no inflection at all. I wondered if I'd touched a nerve.

"It's quite an accomplishment, writing a book," I said. "She's proud of you."

"She's been a great friend, to me and to the boys. And while Abby was sick, she was a friend to her, too."

I swallowed. Delores had liked Abby, and she clearly cared for Joe and his boys. She liked Marlie. What was it about me that rubbed her the wrong way?

There was a long silence, then Joe broke it with, "It's none of my business, Sarah, but where the hell have you been all these years?"

I bristled. "Excuse me?"

"Delores is your aunt. She's been through some rough times over the last while. Why didn't you ever come to visit her?"

I practically had to bite my tongue. "Delores and I— were never close," I said.

"So I gathered," Joe said, and he sounded terse. He was in Delores's camp, so I shouldn't have expected otherwise, but I was strangely hurt just the same.

Another silence fell.

"That's the high school where I work," Joe said as we passed the building.

An opening. I grabbed it. "Do you like it? Teaching, I mean?"

Out of the corner of my eye, I saw Joe nod. "Yeah," he said. "What about you, Sarah? What kind of work do you do?"

I felt a slow, creeping sense of embarrassment. "I mostly did volunteer stuff when I was married," I said. "I helped out around the print shop, too, sometimes."

"And now?"

"Unemployed," I admitted.

"Okay," Joe persisted, "if you could do anything you wanted, anything in the whole world, what would it be?"

I thought carefully. "I've been doing the temp thing for the last year and a half," I said. "About all I'm good at is cooking."

Three teenage girls waved from the snowy sidewalk, their breath making plumes as they giggled.

"Delores says you sing like an angel."

"Does she?" I asked.

Joe slanted a look in my direction.

Seeing the schoolgirls had started me thinking about Marlie. The way things were going, she and I would end up about as close as Delores and I were. Not an encouraging thought.

I checked my watch. "Do you think we could stop by the supermarket?" I asked.

Joe glanced at me again, then nodded. "Sure," he said, but he sounded nonplussed. Maybe he thought I was going to stock up on groceries while he cooled his heels in the van with Dodger.

We pulled into the parking lot of a large store.

"I'll be right back," I said, getting out of the van.

I was as good as my word. Five minutes later, I returned with a poinsettia plant in a plastic pot. I had some rental and employment magazines, too, wedged under one arm.

Joe eyed the bright red leaves curiously. "Is that for Delores?"

"No," I said, wishing I'd bought her one so I'd come off as a devoted niece, but it was too late. I told Joe where I wanted to go.

He didn't exactly grimace, but I don't think it was a place he would have chosen to visit on a wintry morning.

"Hold on," he said. With the engine still running, he left Dodger and me behind to dash into the supermarket himself. He returned with two pots of poinsettias, setting one in the back and handing the other to me. "Give that to Delores," he said. "Tell her it's from you."

I felt a sting, but I didn't say anything.

We were back on the road in a moment, climbing the hill outside of town, crossing the narrow wooden bridge over the creek that had given the town its name. We traveled a mile or so east, then turned a corner.

The metal gates of the cemetery stood open, trimmed in snowlace.

I directed Joe to the place where my dad was buried.

He stopped the van.

I studied the snow-dusted headstone through the van window, my hand frozen on the door handle.

Dodger leaned in from the backseat to lick the side of my face.

Joe shut off the van, opened his door, and strode off

through the snow, Dodger bounding behind him. The pink poinsettia was a colorful spot in all that dazzling white. I watched as man and dog stopped next to a grave in a newer part of the cemetery.

Abby's final resting place.

What would he say to her?

Definitely none of my business.

Joe crouched, dusted off a place in front of the marker, and set the poinsettia down.

I drew a deep breath, exhaled, fogging up the glass in the passenger window, and got out of the van.

My father's headstone was a simple marble one.

PETER J. SULLIVAN. BELOVED BROTHER AND FATHER.

"I'm back," I said, holding out my own pot of poinsettias like an offering.

The snow slowed.

"Delores is doing great. Except for a broken ankle."

Tiny flakes whirled around me.

I dashed at my eyes with the back of one hand, just in case I'd shed a few stray tears without noticing.

"She wants me to sing," I heard myself say. "And I can't."

I stood in silent misery for a while, then bent to make a place for the flowers to stand, digging a little hole in the snow with my hands.

When I straightened and turned from the grave, I almost collided with Joe. I hadn't heard him approaching and I gasped, startled.

"Why can't you sing?" he asked, looking bemused.

"It's complicated," I said.

Joe sighed, glanced back toward Abby's grave, bedecked with pink poinsettias. "If it wasn't for the boys and music," he said, "I would probably have lost my mind."

"You must have loved her very much."

He was quiet for so long that I had plenty of time to wish I hadn't opened my mouth. Joe's feelings for his wife were personal ground and I'd stepped over the line. I certainly wasn't willing to open up about Craig.

"I did," he said, helping me into the van, then sliding open the side door for Dodger.

A few minutes later, we were on our way back into Bent Tree Creek.

"I'm sorry, Joe."

He glanced at me. "For what?"

"For prying."

"Because you said I must have loved my wife? That's not prying, Sarah." He paused. "For a long time, nobody but Delores would let me talk about Abby. It was as if people wanted to pretend she'd never existed—even her closest friends. I wasn't ready for that."

I wanted to touch his arm, let him know I understood, but I was afraid. "Is that why you're writing the book?"

"Partly," Joe answered without looking at me. "I wanted the world to know how brave Abby was, and how smart, and how funny. Even when we both knew the disease wasn't going to turn around, despite all the treatments we'd tried, she was always trying to make me laugh. She used to download jokes off the Internet, have them ready when I got home from work." He shook his head, sighed. "Most of all, I just want the boys to have a written record of what their mother was really like."

"They have you, Joe. You can tell them stories about her. Show them pictures."

He smiled sadly. "I do all that," he said. "But one day I'll be gone."

My reaction must have shown in my face.

"Everybody dies, Sarah," Joe said. "Sooner or later."

I tumbled into my own thoughts after that and didn't surface again until we reached the community center. It was a long, low-slung log building on the edge of town and there were at least twenty cars parked out front.

"Brace yourself," Joe warned, with a wan grin. Once again, he opened the sliding door for Dodger, who jumped out and headed for the entrance. Evidently, dogs were welcome at carolers' meetings.

A portly man opened the door just as we were about to enter, sparing a scowl for Dodger, who slipped past him and dashed inside.

"Hello, George," Joe said affably.

George was decked out in full Victorian caroler garb, holding a top hat in the crook of one arm, and he even sported mutton-chop whiskers. He looked as though he'd just stepped through a time warp between Dickens's England and modern-day Bent Tree Creek.

"Harummph," he said.

"This is Sarah Wagner," Joe told him. "She's Delores's niece, and she'll be in charge this season."

I smiled gamely and put out my hand. Joe didn't know I wasn't in this for the long run—unless he'd noticed the giveaway magazines I'd scored at the supermarket.

George softened a little and we shook. "Come in," he said, sounding resigned. "Come in."

I looked around. There were long tables, probably used for banquets and bingo, and lots of folding chairs. A piano stood in the far corner, a cat curled on the padded bench. I blinked, trying to decide if the feline was real or stuffed.

Dodger approached, sniffing, and the cat arched its back and hissed.

Definitely not stuffed.

"Everyone's testy this morning," George informed us in a stage whisper, "and mob psychology is about to take over."

"Terrific," I said with a forced smile.

Joe rested a hand lightly on the small of my back, steering me in the direction of the war zone. With Craig, I would have resented the gesture, felt as though I were being pushed. It was different with Joe, comforting somehow.

I stiffened my spine.

I'd half expected everybody to be wearing a costume, like George, but the dozen or so people sipping coffee from plastic cups were not so festive. The outfits ran the gamut from jeans and turtleneck sweaters to pricy boutique couture, and the buzz in the air indicated that either an argument was brewing or I'd interrupted one already underway.

Joe introduced me.

"How's Delores?" someone asked.

I scanned the crowd for the speaker. An incredibly thin woman dressed in a pink velvet jogging suit waggled her fingers at me and repeated her question.

"She's getting around well enough," I said brightly, wishing I knew more. "Still on crutches, though."

A heavy woman elbowed her way to the front. "Jenny Rivers," she said, "is trying to tell me I can't sing alto. *Me.* I was working for this company when she was still having her picture taken on Santa Claus's lap!"

"I didn't say you couldn't sing alto, Mary Ellen Hershmeyer," interjected Ms. Rivers. I remembered them then; even when I was singing with Barrels of Carols, years before, they'd had a running feud going. "I said you couldn't sing *period.*"

"I auditioned just like everybody else!"

"Hold it," Joe said. "Do you want to scare Sarah off before you even have a chance to get reacquainted?"

The change in the warring women was striking.

Both of them stared adoringly at Joe.

He was popular with the feminine gender, as I'd suspected.

Internally, I withdrew a little further.

"Maybe *you* should take this job," I told him, out of the corner of my mouth.

"I've got a deadline," he said smugly. "The book has to be in by New Year's."

I heaved a sigh.

George waved a sheaf of papers, glowering again. "Delores faxed over the performance schedule. She said you forgot it."

I hadn't even started the job and I already had a demerit.

I opened my mouth, but before I could draw a breath to speak, Joe piped up again.

"Why don't you pass out the schedules, George?"

George did so, and I got the last one. I scanned it, but

recognized only a few names: George's, Joe's, Mary Ellen's, and Jenny's. To my relief, Mary Ellen and Jenny had already been placed in different groups.

Problem solved. Or so I thought.

"I've *always* been on the blue team!" Mary Ellen protested. "This says I'm on red, and an alternate on green!"

Jenny looked smug.

"Is the blue team better than the red team?" I whispered to Joe. I didn't recall any particular hierarchy, but it had been a long time.

He chuckled. "I wouldn't know," he whispered back. "I always play for the green side."

Mary Ellen marched over and waved the schedule under my nose. *"I want to stay on the blue team!"* she informed me furiously. "I'll quit before I'll move!"

"Good riddance," said Jenny.

"Everyone," I said shakily, "please be calm. We'll straighten this out, I promise."

A murmur arose and quickly escalated to a dull roar.

Joe gave a shrill whistle through his teeth.

A blessed silence ensued.

"Let's start with the costumes," I said. "Does everyone still have theirs from last year?"

Another furor broke out.

Apparently, the costumes were a controversial subject, too.

Delores hadn't prepared me for any of this, except for alluding to the war between Mary Ellen and Jenny. I glanced hopelessly at Joe.

"Mine still fits," he said.

"That's more than Jenny can say," Mary Ellen sniffed.

"Like you haven't doubled in size since Labor Day," Jenny retorted.

"Do something," I told Joe.

He smiled endearingly. "Sorry," he said. "You're on your own."

Chapter Four

✳ ❄ ✳

Joe dropped me off at Delores's after the meeting, which was a complete disaster, and left to teach his afternoon classes. The house was redolent of pumpkin pie, and Marlie sat huddled at the bottom of the stairs, burning minutes on my pay-as-you-go cellphone.

Her guilty look told me all I needed to know about who was on the other end, but her eyes snapped with preemptory rebellion, and her cheeks were flushed.

I hung up my coat on the hall tree and made for the kitchen without a word. If there was one thing I'd learned about dealing with Marlie, it was to choose my battles.

Delores hailed me from her home office as I passed.

"How'd it go?" she asked, catching one of the crutches leaning against her desk before it could crash to the floor. Behind her, the screen of her antiquated computer flickered.

I suppressed a sigh and smiled weakly. "Fire me now," I said, only half joking, "before I run you into bankruptcy."

Delores smiled. "Jenny and Mary Ellen?"

I nodded.

"They do this every year," Delores said. "Don't let it get to you."

I leaned one shoulder against the doorjamb. "Why do they hate each other so much? They both seem like nice enough people, taken separately."

"They are," Delores affirmed. "Both of them are drama queens. Performers, you know."

I inclined my head toward the front of the house where, presumably, Marlie was still filling her Real Mother's ears with accounts of Sarah atrocities. I figured a house was due to fall on me at any moment, and all that would be visible of my smashed body would be a pair of ruby slippers and some striped socks. "Speaking of drama—"

Delores nodded knowingly. "It's only a reaction to baking pies," she said.

"You've lost me," I admitted.

"Getting ready for a holiday, baking pies—things like that bring out the sentimentality in a person. Especially when that person is only twelve and trying to get her bearings in a new place."

I checked the hallway to make sure we wouldn't be overheard. Marlie's voice was a low, rapid murmur in the distance.

"Bambi doesn't want her," I said quietly.

"I know that," Delores replied, adjusting her reading glasses, "and so does Marlie. The child is trying to get a rise out of you, Sarah."

I huffed out a frustrated breath. "What *kind* of rise?" I countered. "She knows I love her. If I didn't, I'd pack her stuff and put her on a bus to Reno."

"What does Bambi have that you don't have?" Delores prodded.

I was confused by the question. Make that *stumped.*

Delores tried again. "How long has she lived in Reno, this Bambi woman?"

I frowned. "Since Marlie was little."

"Same house?"

"I wouldn't know," I said, starting to feel defensive.

"Maybe it isn't Bambi Marlie wants," Delores reasoned. "Maybe it's to settle down in one place and be part of a community. To belong somewhere—even if it's backstage at a seedy nightclub."

"That," I said, "was a low blow."

"Think about it," Delores said blithely, and turned back to her computer.

Dismissed, I went on to the kitchen and, let me tell you, I was steam-driven. I poured a cup of cold coffee, stuck it in the microwave, and assessed the row of pies cooling on the long countertop.

"I'll pay you back for the minutes," Marlie said tersely from behind me.

I didn't turn around, but stood watching my cup turn around and around inside the whirring microwave, as if it required supervision. "Oh, really?" I asked. "How?"

"I'll get a job."

"You're twelve."

The microwave dinged and I heard a chair scrape back at the table. "I could get a paper route or something," Marlie said.

I took my coffee out, blew on it, and finally faced my stepdaughter.

Color flared in Marlie's checks, brighter than before,

and her eyes looked almost feverish. "I asked her if I could come there for Christmas," she announced, "and she said yes."

I sat down, the picture of calm, and blew on my coffee again. I'd only heated it for something to do; now I was incapable of swallowing. "How do you plan to get there?"

"I thought maybe you could borrow Delores's car and take me. It's not so far from here."

I studied her, looking for signs of dementia. Or possession. Marlie had a great little mother-daughter fantasy going, but she was a smart kid and she knew there was no place for her in Bambi's life.

"Not in this lifetime," I said tightly.

"Then just give me the money for a bus ticket!"

"Call your mother back and ask her to send one," I challenged.

"I will!" Marlie yelled.

She almost collided with Delores in the kitchen doorway.

"What was that all about?" Delores asked.

"The usual."

Delores looked exasperated. "Excuse me," she said, "but I don't have any idea what 'the usual' is between you two."

"We fight a lot," I said.

"That's obvious," Delores answered. "Why?"

The front door slammed in the distance.

"Where's she off to?" Delores asked.

"My guess is, she won't go any farther than the front porch. She's calling her Real Mother to ask for a bus ticket."

There went the last of my minutes. Not that anybody was hanging around by their telephone, waiting for me to call.

"To Reno?"

"That's the last known address," I affirmed.

"Aren't you worried?" Delores glanced nervously at the clock above the sink.

"No," I said. "Bambi won't spring for a bus ticket."

"Well, what if the kid buys one on her own? It's almost time for the four o'clock."

My stomach twitched nervously.

"Go looking for her," Delores urged. She looked so anxious that I got up from my chair and made for the front of the house.

Marlie wasn't on the porch or anywhere in the yard.

I ran back inside, up the stairs, and checked her room.

The teddy bear was gone.

"Damn!" I cried under my breath, then ran back down to the first floor.

Delores was waiting there, holding my coat in one hand and a set of car keys in the other. "I hope the old beater starts," she said. "I put in a call to Joe, but I got his voicemail."

"For a woman on crutches," I said, struggling into the coat and snatching the keys, "you accomplished a lot in two minutes."

"I'm going with you," Delores said, and headed for the kitchen and the door to the garage.

I wasn't inclined to argue.

It took three tries before the engine of Delores's old car cranked to life. If she hadn't pushed the button to roll up the garage door, I probably would have backed right through it.

The roads were slick and we had to stop twice for pedestrians.

The bus was pulling out when we got to the Mega-Pumper.

"Honk the horn," Delores said.

I honked.

The bus picked up speed.

"Honk again," Delores insisted, and reached for the horn when I hesitated a moment too long. "Flash your headlights, too."

I flashed.

One of the bus's signal lights came on and the vehicle lumbered to the side of the road.

I stopped the car, bounded out, and ran for the door, pounding on it with one fist.

The driver opened it, looking askance. "Lady," he said, "I got a schedule to keep. This better be good."

I climbed the steps, started down the aisle. I passed two alarmed-looking passengers before I found Marlie crouched behind a seat midway back.

I got her by the shoulder and pulled her to her feet, seething and, at the same time, dizzy with relief.

"She's kidnapping me," Marlie said, clutching her teddy bear. "I don't know this woman. I've never seen her before in my life!"

Everyone looked at me suspiciously and I might have been arrested if Delores hadn't spoken from outside the open door. "That kid is twelve," she told the driver, "and she's a runaway."

While I was a stranger, Delores had lived in Bent Tree Creek all her life. She had credibility.

"Get off the bus," the driver said to Marlie.

Her shoulders slumped, but she marched back up the aisle and down the steps. She wouldn't look at either Delores or me, and even though I wanted to shake her, I felt sorry for her, too. She looked so small, so young, and so defeated.

"I'll give back the bus fare," she said when we were all back in Delores's car.

"Where did you get it?" I asked. Obviously, Bambi hadn't come through with the funds.

"Out of your wallet," Marlie admitted, but there was a surly undercurrent to her tone.

"You are so grounded forever," I told her.

"Hush," Delores interjected. "You're just making things worse."

"Stay out of this," I snapped.

"I will not," my aunt said with spirit.

I muttered a swear word.

When we got back to Delores's place, Marlie jumped out of the car as soon as I pulled into the driveway and stormed into the house.

"That went well," I said, and laid my head on the steering wheel.

Tentatively, Delores patted my shoulder.

An hour later, I was sitting in the kitchen, trying to concentrate on the caroling schedule with half my mind on Marlie, who was upstairs, shut away in her room, when Delores bumpity-thumped in.

"I have an idea," she announced.

"Wonderful," I said.

Delores didn't catch the sarcasm. "Marlie told me, while we were making the pies, how you used to cook diet food for all your fat friends."

"My friends," I said, insulted, "were not fat."

"Whatever," Delores said. "Everybody's busy these days, commuting and the like," she rattled on. "Half the population is on a diet. I'll bet if someone would cook and freeze healthy, low-calorie meals, and offer to deliver them once a week, they'd have more orders than they could keep up with."

I took a sip of my coffee, which I'd forgotten, and it actually went down.

"This could work," Delores enthused.

I didn't comment. Yes, I loved to cook and I was good at it, but I didn't have the money or equipment or experience to start a business. There were probably a lot of regulations that had to be followed, too.

"Well?" Delores prompted.

"It would cost a lot," I said.

"You could start it on a shoestring," Delores insisted. She hobbled ably over to the cupboard and took down three plates. "Don't be such a Grinch, Sarah Jane Sullivan."

I was a little thrown by her use of my maiden name, though I couldn't have said exactly why. "I'm not a Grinch," I said, struck by the difference in her manner. *Who are you?* I wanted to ask, *and what have you done with my salty old aunt?*

Delores sliced into one of the freshly baked pies with a vengeance. "Marlie!" she yelled. "Get down here! We're going to eat pie!"

My face grew as warm as if I'd just been peering into a hot oven.

Miraculously, Marlie came.

"What's going on?" she asked.

"We're starting an industry," Delores said exuberantly. "It's history in the making!"

Marlie's eyes widened and so did mine.

Somehow, using only one crutch, Delores managed to serve our unorthodox lunch without spilling the food or falling. She tapped one temple with an index finger, after sitting down at the table. "Ideas," she said. "I've had some dandies in my time—Barrels of Carols was the first company of its kind in California—but this one takes the cake."

I stared at her, confounded.

She giggled—Delores *giggled*—at my expression. "Admit it," she said. "I'm brilliant."

"Are you on pain medication?" I asked without thinking first. I immediately blushed.

Both Delores and Marlie burst out laughing.

After a moment or two, I joined in.

"Am I still grounded?" Marlie asked when the mirth subsided a little.

"Until doomsday," I answered, sobering. "And by the way, if your mother is expecting to meet you at the bus terminal in Reno, you'd better call and let her know you're not coming."

Marlie looked down at the crumbs of pie remaining on her plate. "I was just going to drop in on her," she mumbled. "You know, as a surprise."

I started to speak, but Dolores grabbed my hand, squeezed, and shook her head.

"I guess I might as well go back to my room," Marlie said.

"Guess so," I responded.

She carried her plate and fork to the sink, then left the room, a forlorn little figure with stooped shoulders.

I softened, watching her go.

"All's well that ends well," Delores said quietly.

I was sitting alone in the kitchen, an hour later, going over the caroling schedules for the singing Hatfields and McCoys—the first event of the season would take place at a mall halfway between Bent Tree Creek and Sacramento, and the facility was so large that all three teams would be deployed—when a rap sounded at the back door.

I looked up, surprised to see Joe peering in through one of the frosty panes.

"Come in," I called, starting to rise and then sitting down again.

Joe entered after wiping his feet on the mat, and my gaze went straight to the job-and-rental magazines rolled tightly in his left hand. The set of his jaw was grim. "You forgot these in my van," he said, slapping them down on the end of the counter and keeping his distance.

I managed a smile. "Thanks."

"You're going to bail out on Delores, aren't you?"

"I came here with the understanding that it was temporary," I said. Why was I explaining? I was a grown woman, and if I wanted to move to a city where I didn't know anybody and start over from square one, that was my business.

"She needs you," Joe said. He broke away from the

counter, helped himself to a cup of coffee, and joined me at the table.

"Temporarily," I reiterated. I ran my gaze over his leather jacket; his broad shoulders filled it out nicely. "Are you going to take off your coat?"

"No," he replied. "I'm not staying."

That made two of us then.

"Marlie almost ran away today," I told him. It seemed I was always saying things to Joe that I hadn't intended.

He set his cup down slowly. *"What?* Why?"

"She wanted to go to Reno and move in with her mother, the pole dancer."

Joe's eyes widened, then narrowed. Finally, he sat back in his chair, thrusting out a sigh. "Damn," he whispered. "She wasn't hitchhiking, was she?"

"Next best thing," I answered and felt that too-familiar burning sensation behind my eyes again. "She swiped some money from my pocketbook and bought herself a bus ticket."

"Great," he said. Maybe he was thinking of all the things that can happen to a young girl, alone in a bus station, especially in a place like Reno. He drew in a breath, huffed it out in a resigned sigh. "Maybe Marlie needs some counseling, Sarah. I could recommend somebody."

"Maybe that would be a good idea," I agreed. Therapy would make a major dent in my cash reserves, but Marlie's welfare was my first consideration.

Joe smiled, for the first time since he'd stepped into the house, and I found it reassuring, though I couldn't have said why. "Betty Dorrance," he said.

"Betty Dorrance?"

"She's the guidance counselor at Bent Tree High," Joe explained. A light came into his eyes. "She works with the middle school kids, too, so there wouldn't be any costs involved."

Relief rushed through me, followed by mild indignation. Did Marlie and I look like charity cases to Joe? Never mind that we essentially *were* charity cases. Even the possibility of his thinking that chafed my pride, which had already been rubbed raw. "Okay," I said lamely.

Joe took his phone from his jacket pocket and speed-dialed.

He called this Betty woman so often that he'd programmed her number into his cell?

I frowned.

"Hi, Betty," he said. "It's me, Joe." Pause. Intensely masculine and somewhat intimate chuckle. "Yeah. That was fun."

What was fun? I wondered.

"Sure," Joe went on after listening again. "Maybe after the first of the year. I'm booked solid, with the caroling gigs, and then there's the writing." He glanced at me and turned solemn again. "Listen, Bets, I have this friend, and her stepdaughter is having a hard time right now—"

Bets?

I sat up very straight in my chair.

"Good," Joe said to "Bets." "Thanks. I will."

More talk on her end.

"Right, sure. I'll tell her," Joe said. After adding a good-bye, he snapped the phone shut and dropped it back into his pocket. "She'll see you both tomorrow, at twelve-thirty," he said. "Classes let out at noon."

I barely kept myself from asking if he and Betty Dorrance were dating.

Joe shoved back his chair. "I'd better get home before the kids try to cook dinner," he told me, and with that, he was gone.

The door had no more than closed behind him when Delores came in from the office or the living room or wherever she'd been. "Did I hear Joe's voice?" she asked.

I nodded.

She crutched it over to the fridge, opened the freezer door, and took out a casserole dish covered in foil. "Lasagna," she said. "If I'd known he was here, I would have invited him and the twins to have supper with us."

"Is he dating somebody named Betty Dorrance?" I blurted.

Delores studied me in silence for a long time, then grinned. "Now why would you ask me that?"

"I haven't the faintest idea," I admitted sheepishly, "since it's none of my business. He set up a counseling appointment with her for tomorrow, for Marlie and me."

My aunt turned a dial on the stove and stuck the lasagna into the oven. It seemed to me that she was enjoying my embarrassment a little. "They went out for a while, I think," she finally said. "But things got a little awkward, given that they work together and all."

I nodded and got up from my chair at last, taking some wilting lettuce, tomatoes, and green onions from the crisper in the fridge to start a salad. Maybe tomorrow, I thought, I'd stop at the supermarket and buy some groceries—after the session with Ms. Dorrance, of course. Shopping would be a marathon event, since it would be the day before Thanksgiving, and I sighed at the prospect.

"I don't think it was too serious," Delores said.

I looked at her, realized she thought I was sighing over Joe dating Betty, and felt my cheeks go warm. "I wasn't—"

Delores cut me off. "You can take my car," she told me. "To the appointment, I mean. There are some things I need from the store, if you wouldn't mind stopping on the way home."

"I wouldn't mind at all," I said.

We worked in companionable silence after that, two women engaged in the age-old pursuit of throwing supper together and, like Joe's smile, I found it comforting.

Marlie ate alone, in her room, by her own choice. I didn't mention the counseling appointment when I took her a plate—things were still too awkward between us— but it felt like I was keeping a guilty secret.

Later, while I washed the dishes, Delores sat at the kitchen table, reading a stack of manuscript pages. Every once in a while, she stopped to sigh, brush away a tear, or smile.

"Joe's book," she said, when she caught me stealing a glance at her. "He gave me the latest version a couple of days ago, but I couldn't get to it with all that was going on."

"How about some tea?" I asked, drying my hands on a dishtowel.

"I wouldn't mind that at all," Delores answered. "And there's one other thing you could do for me, if you would."

I turned around to face her again, waited, feeling unaccountably wary.

She flashed me a blinding smile. "Why don't you take one of those pies over to Joe? He likes my pumpkin pies."

I couldn't help smiling. "You wouldn't be trying to hook me up with Joe Courtland, would you?"

Delores put a hand to her bosom. "I don't know how you could even suggest such a thing," she said, but her eyes sparkled.

I shook my head.

After brewing Delores's tea and serving it to her, I put on my coat, chose a likely-looking pie from the line-up on the counter, covered it with a cloth napkin, and pointed myself in the direction of Joe's house.

"No need to hurry back," Delores called, reimmersed, by then, in the pages of Joe's book and taking a sip of her tea. "Stay and visit a while."

"Right," I said, but the irony I injected into the word was apparently lost on Delores.

It was snowing again when I stepped out the front door and made my way carefully down the walk to the gate.

Joe must have seen me coming, because he opened the front door well before I got there. He'd exchanged the clothes he'd been wearing before for sweatpants, a white T-shirt, and sneakers. Barking and boyish laughter billowed out from behind him in a chaotic wave of noise.

"I hope you weren't working," I said. "I mean, I wouldn't want to disturb you—"

Joe's grin could be used to guide ships through an

English fog. "I needed a break from the writing," he said. His gaze dropped to the pie after making a brief, searing stop, or so it seemed to me, at both my lips and the hollow of my throat. "Is that what I hope it is?"

I wondered how I could feel overheated in a gathering snowstorm. "If you hope it's Delores's pumpkin pie, yes," I answered. I held out the pie, but Joe only stepped back.

"Come in," he said.

I heard an instant Delores replay in my mind: No need to hurry back. Stay and visit a while.

I didn't want Joe thinking I was flirting, and my first choice would have been to shove the pie into his hands and bolt. I *was* curious to see the inside of the Courtland house, however. Before I left Bent Tree Creek for college, it was owned by two elderly sisters and purported to be haunted. It had fallen into disrepair, which only added to the spooky ambience, but now it looked more like a set for a fifties sitcom.

I stepped into a spacious hallway and immediately caught the scent of pizza. The boys were playing some rambunctious game that involved a lot of chasing and yelling, and Dodger yelped a merry accompaniment, putting me in mind of that old Christmas song, where dogs bark out "Jingle Bells."

"It's a madhouse," Joe said with a slightly harried smile. "I usually write in the mornings, when the boys are in school, but I'm a little behind." Immediately, he looked chagrined. "Not that you're interrupting or anything."

"I can't stay long," I assured him.

There was an uncomfortable moment.

"Yeah," he said. "We've been over that."

The noise, coming from a nearby room, escalated.

"Boys!" Joe yelled. "Put a sock in it!"

Silence.

Joe grinned at me, noted that I was gripping the pie with both hands. "I guess I startled you. Sorry about that. We're a little long on uproar and short on manners around here."

With that, Joe leaned around me to push the door closed against the cold and I caught the scent of his aftershave. Again, I felt that funny dropping sensation in the pit of my stomach.

He's writing a book about how much he loved his wife, I reminded myself silently.

Joe led the way into the living room, which was large and pleasantly cluttered. A fire crackled on the hearth and the boys, wearing feathered Indian headdresses and war paint, looked up at me with brilliant smiles. Either they were glad to see me or they needed somebody to scalp.

"Where's Marlie?" one of them asked.

"Is she old enough to baby-sit?" inquired the other.

The first chief favored the second with a scathing glare. "We're not *babies,*" he said.

"Go wash off the war paint," Joe told them. "The pizza's ready."

They dashed off, whooping.

"Did you ever read O. Henry's *The Ransom of Red Chief?*" Joe asked mischievously, as I followed him into a large formal dining room, seldom used by the looks of it, and into a kitchen that resembled something out of a design magazine.

"Yes," I said, distracted.

Joe set the pie on a granite-topped counter and opened one of two oversize ovens to pull out a pizza. He followed my gaze as I took the place in, wonderstruck.

"Abby liked to cook," he said quietly.

Of course, I thought. On top of being a wonderful wife and mother, a software designer, and a devoted friend to Delores and probably an inspiration, as well, Abby had been an accomplished cook.

"She wasn't very good at it, though," Joe added with a smile.

I was jolted. For a moment, it seemed he'd read my thoughts.

"Have some pizza with us?" he asked when I didn't say anything.

I shook my head. "I've eaten," I said. "But thanks." It might have been fun, I reflected, having pizza with Joe and the Red Chiefs. Then I quickly put the odd penchant aside.

"Sit down anyway," he urged. "You look as if you're about to make a run for the door." He laid three plates on a round table, set in an alcove, and watched me closely as he added silverware and paper napkins. "Are you afraid of me, Sarah?"

"No," I lied. "Now that I know you're not a serial killer, that is."

The joke fell a little flat.

"Then why don't you take off your coat, at least?"

I shouldered out of the coat, then nervously pushed up the sleeves of my sweater. Ryan and Sam zoomed in, sans feathers and makeup, and scrambled into their chairs.

Joe opened the door of the big Sub-Zero refrigerator, got out the milk, and poured a glassful for each of the twins.

"Pray," he said.

Both boys bowed their heads and squeezed their eyes shut.

"Thank you, God, for the pizza," said Ryan. Or Sam.

"Thank you for Dad and Dodger," said Sam. Or Ryan.

I'd perched on one of the stools at the breakfast bar, unsure whether to close my eyes and bow my head, or just wait it out.

"Amen!" both boys cried, in chorus, and dived into the pizza.

Joe put a slice on his plate and came to sit beside me at the breakfast bar. I felt the warmth of his skin as his bare arm brushed mine, and was unnerved all over again.

"You're sure you don't want to join us?" he asked.

"Positive," I said.

He began to eat, watching me. There was something sensual about that, but I wasn't about to explore the idea. At least, not while I was in his presence; he was way too perceptive for that to be safe.

"Delores is reading the chapters you gave her right now," I said, trying to make conversation.

Joe smiled, chewing.

I couldn't think of another thing to say, but I was feeling plenty.

"People used to say this house was haunted," Joe remarked.

"I remember," I said, grateful for the opening. "You've done a beautiful job restoring it."

"Abby gets most of the credit for that."

Dodger whined and pawed at the back door and Joe got up to let him out. He stopped at the Sub-Zero again, on his way back, and returned with two glasses of wine.

"She must have been amazing," I said. I hoped I didn't sound wistful, but I probably did.

"She was a woman," Joe replied easily.

A woman so special that her husband wanted to memorialize her in print. A paragon, evidently.

"Tell me about Craig," Joe urged quietly when I didn't comment.

I glanced uneasily at the boys.

Dodger scratched again, this time from outside the door.

"I'll get it," I said, stalling.

Dodger came in, bringing a chilly, snow-trimmed breeze with him.

I closed the door.

Joe patted the seat of the stool I'd just left.

So much for the idea of snatching my coat from the railing separating the kitchen from the alcove and getting out of there.

I went back to the stool, and to the subject of Craig, first taking a sip of my wine. "He was smart. He was good-looking. He had an adventurous side."

"Would you write a book about him?"

Suddenly, I wanted to cry. I felt like an intruder in that lovely, lively house. "Only as a warning to unsuspecting women," I said.

"Ouch," Joe responded. "That bad?"

The boys were busy discussing the virtues of pizza and paying no attention whatsoever to us.

"Not horrible," I answered.

"But—?"

"He was with another woman the day he died. And it wasn't the first time."

"Ouch again," Joe said.

The telephone rang and he excused himself and reached for the cordless receiver, lying a few feet away. Said hello. Listened, frowning.

"When?" he finally asked.

The boys picked up on the tension and stared worriedly in Joe's direction.

More listening.

"No," Joe finally said, "no—it's all right. I'll be there as soon as I can."

After a gruff good-bye, he hung up.

"What is it?" I asked.

"One of my students is in the hospital," Joe said quietly, watching the boys for a long moment before turning to me again. "I don't suppose you could—?"

"Look after Ryan and Sam for you? Of course I will, Joe."

"Thanks," he said. "Help yourself to some pizza if you get hungry later. It could be a long night."

I nodded.

Joe got off the stool and crossed to the table, where his sons sat, looking up at him.

My heart ached. They'd been small when their mother died, but they knew a crisis when they encountered one, and they also knew the call had been bad news.

"Sarah's going to stay with you," he said. "I'll be home later."

"Is Grandma okay?" one small voice asked.

Joe ruffled both boys' hair. "Yes," he said. "Grandma's fine. So is Grandpa and everybody else you love. This is something different, and I don't want you worrying, okay?"

"Okay," chorused the Red Chiefs, but uncertainly.

After Joe left, I called Delores to explain that I wouldn't be home right away, and to make sure things were all right on the Marlie front. Delores promised to leave the front door unlocked for me.

I joined Ryan and Sam at the table.

"So," I said, "which one of you is Ryan and which one is Sam?"

Grins erupted.

"He's Sam," they answered, pointing to each other.

"No fair," I said.

Half an hour later, when the boys were coloring at the table and I was doing dishes, the phone rang again.

I picked up the receiver. "Courtland residence."

"I'll be late," Joe said. "It's pretty bad. If you don't want to stay, you could bundle the boys up and take them over to Delores's—"

Ryan and Sam were watching me and their ears were practically standing out from their heads.

"I think they're better off right here," I said in the brightest voice I could manage.

The twins went back to their joint coloring project.

"You're probably right," Joe said wearily. "I really appreciate this, Sarah."

"Joe, what exactly is going on?" I kept the question low.

"Some kids from my third period class were spinning

brodies in a supermarket parking lot tonight, in an old car. They crashed into a light pole, and one of them is in pretty bad shape."

I closed my eyes. Kids, cars, parking lots, and ice. Still a bad combination, though I'd done it myself in high school and Joe probably had, too.

"Things are fine here," I said.

"Thanks again, Sarah."

We said our good-byes and rang off.

The twins did some more coloring.

I read a magazine article.

"We're supposed to go to bed at eight o'clock," said Sam or Ryan.

"Shut up," the other said.

I checked the time.

"Better boogie upstairs then," I told them. It was 7:55 already.

"Will you read us a story?"

I smiled. "Only if you'll tell me whether you're Sam or Ryan," I said.

"I'm Sam," was the reply.

"He is not," countered his twin. "He's Ryan."

I laughed. "Scoot," I said.

They went upstairs, with Dodger for an escort, and I wandered into the living room. The fire was almost gone, so I added a couple of chunks of wood and jabbed at the embers with a poker until a new flame caught.

A baby grand stood in the corner between two windows.

I approached, ran my hand lightly over the gleaming veneer.

Something swelled in my throat and got stuck there. Maybe it was a song.

Dodger came back downstairs and gave a pitiful whine. I let him outside and waited, shivering, while he did his business.

Delores's lights glowed warm and golden across the street.

The dog and I went back into the house.

Sam and Ryan were standing midway down the stairs, wearing pajamas and their feathered headdresses. Their faces were scrubbed and serious.

"Dad's reading us *Harry Potter and the Chamber of Secrets,*" one of them said. "We'd hate to miss a chapter."

I drew closer, squinting. Sure enough, their names were embroidered on their pajama tops. Ryan on the left, Sam on the right.

Of course, they could have switched PJs.

Get a grip, Sarah, I thought, they're kids, not FBI agents on a secret mission.

The twins turned and mounted the stairs, so I followed, with Dodger traveling right behind me.

The boys shared a large room, with two gabled windows overlooking the backyard. Dodger jumped onto one of the padded window seats, yawned magnificently, and settled in.

Ryan and Sam crawled into twin beds, headdresses and all, squirmed to get comfortable, and waited. The book lay on the night stand between them, with an envelope to mark the place.

I picked up the thick volume, admiring the room. Like the kitchen, it was fit for a photo spread, with frolicking lion cubs painted on one wall and circus clowns for lamps. A whole universe graced the ceiling—not mere stars and moons, either, but whole spiraling galaxies, in Hubble colors.

"Wow," I said.

"Mom used to sit on my bed when she read to us," Sam said hopefully.

"No, she didn't," Ryan argued. "She sat on mine."

"How about a compromise?" I asked, dragging over a chair from one of a pair of matching desks and placing it square in the middle.

The Red Chiefs settled into their pillows.

I found the place where Joe had left off and began to read.

Chapter Five

❄ ❄ ❄

I was asleep on the living room couch when I felt a hand touch my shoulder. I opened my eyes and blinked. Joe came slowly into focus, looking tired.

"Hey," he said.

"Hey," I answered, stretching.

His eyes seemed to darken, but that was probably a trick of the light.

I sat up and Joe dropped beside me with a sigh.

"Everything okay at the hospital?" I asked, bracing myself for the answer.

He grinned wearily, interlaced his fingers—the fingers of a musician, long and deft. "Yeah," he said. "Mike will be okay. In traction for a few weeks, though. He was lucky as hell, and he might even come to realize it by the time he's forty or so. Right now, he's grousing because he won't be able to play basketball this year."

I smiled, wanting to touch him, but not quite daring. "Mike's lucky in another way. He has you."

For a moment, Joe looked sad. "Life is tough for Mike, and a lot of kids like him. His dad ran off with a flight attendant he met on an airplane a few months ago and his mother is still reeling from the shock. I called Mike Senior to tell him about the accident, and he said to say hi for him." Joe's mouth tightened at the memory. "That was all. Just, 'say hi.'"

"What was your reply to that?"

Joe grinned and shoved a hand through his hair. "I can't repeat it in the presence of a lady," he said. "Were the boys good tonight, or was it a normal evening?"

I laughed. "They were great. Presuming, of course, that wearing Indian headdresses to bed fits in with the house rules."

"I'm just grateful there wasn't an uprising," Joe replied.

I stretched, looked at my watch. After midnight. "Yikes," I said. "I'd better get home. Lots to do tomorrow."

Like the appointment with Betty Dorrance. It was going to be hard, sharing family secrets with Joe's ex—or not-so-ex—girlfriend.

He caught hold of my hand when I would have risen to my feet. "There's something else I need to say," he told me with mischievous portent. "Two things, actually."

I got a nervous feeling, oddly festive. "What?"

"Thanks, for one," he replied. He paused, studying me with a sort of benign solemnity. He drew a deep breath and huffed it out, like a weight lifter about to hoist a very large barbell. "And 'I'm sorry,' for another. I shouldn't have given you a hard time about Delores. Would you consider letting me buy you dinner to make up for it?"

I swallowed. My heart fluttered and I barely stopped myself from putting a hand to my chest, a clear indication that I was rattled. "You don't have to do that," I said. "You're Delores's friend. It's natural that you'd be protective of her."

He got up, threw more wood on the fire, ambled to the piano.

Played the first few bars of "I'll Be Home for Christmas."

My heart ached.

I *wouldn't* be home for Christmas, and neither would Marlie, because we didn't *have* a home. We were indigent relatives, camping out in guest rooms.

Joe watched me thoughtfully. Played the "you can plan on me" part. The notes sounded plaintive somehow. Tinkling as they fell, like tiny icicles dropping from an eave.

"Friday night?" he asked. "After the mall gig?"

I relented. "Friday night," I agreed, feeling about sixteen and already mentally rifling my suitcases in search of something to wear.

As if he were reading my mind, Joe said, "Of course, I'll be in full Victorian regalia, so we might make an interesting couple."

I laughed. "I'm sure they've seen stranger things in the food court," I said.

He leaned ever-so-slightly closer and, for one deliciously terrible moment, I thought he was going to kiss me. In the end, though, he withdrew and thrust himself to his feet.

"I'll get your coat and walk you home," he said.

"It's only across the street," I pointed out when he

came back and held the coat for me to slip into. "You don't have to go to all the trouble of escorting me. Just watch from the porch."

"Not good enough," he teased. "I could lose my status as a Victorian gentleman."

"We can't have that," I said.

Although the snow had stopped, it was much colder, and there was a thin glaze of ice on the street. I had reason to be glad, and thankful, that Joe had insisted on chivalry, because I would probably have slipped and cracked my tailbone if he hadn't. He stopped me from falling at least twice.

On Delores's porch, under the soft glow of the porch light, there was another potentially romantic moment. Joe curled a finger under my chin and lifted, so that we were looking straight into each other's eyes.

In the end, he merely brushed my lips lightly with his own, and yet I still felt as though I'd just gripped a live wire.

"Good night," he said gruffly. "And thanks for taking such good care of the wild men while I was at the hospital."

I merely nodded, not trusting my voice.

What was happening to me?

I'd never felt quite the way I did that night, ever before. Not even in the early days with Craig, when I'd been smitten and swept away. This was different—quiet, somehow, and substantial.

I brought myself up short.

It *isn't* love.

It *can't* be.

I turned and fumbled with the doorknob, after an

awkward good night to Joe, and let myself into the house. For a few seconds I leaned against the inside of the door, trying to collect my scattered emotions.

Through the door, I heard Joe whistling as he walked away.

Have yourself a merry little Christmas . . .

Delores's office light was on, despite the late hour. I took off my coat, hung it up, and headed in that direction.

"Everything all right?" Delores asked, turning in her desk chair to peer at me over the tops of her reading glasses. "You look a little peculiar."

"Just tired," I lied. "Joe's student—Mike—is going to be fine, except for being in traction for a while."

"Poor kid," Delores said.

I recalled what Joe had told me about his telephone conversation with the boy's father and felt a corresponding pang. It seemed too depressing to recount, and I decided it could wait and changed the subject instead.

"What are you doing up? It's late, you know."

"Waiting for you," Delores said. "And—" one of those flourishing pauses that serves as a conversational drumroll, "building a website." She held up a software box. "Abby's own program. She gave me a copy when it was released, and I dug it out after you went over to Joe's."

"Why on earth would you be building a website, especially after midnight?"

"It's quiet," Delores said. "Come look."

I crept closer. Peered at the screen. There was a blue background, and what looked like a plate of lasagna revolving, planetlike, around the head of a frenzied woman. The heading read, TOO FAT? TOO BUSY TO COOK? CALL SARAH!

My mouth fell open.

"It's still in the rough stage," Delores said.

"Delores, I—"

"Give it a chance," Delores interrupted quietly. "And, while you're at it, why don't you give Joe Courtland a chance, too?"

Without thinking, I touched my lips lightly with the tips of my fingers.

Delores smiled. "Kissed you, did he?" she asked, pleased.

I felt myself blush. "Not really."

"Whatever," said Delores the body language expert.

I knew I ought to go to bed. Let the day be over. But something made me hesitate and ask, "Did you ever think about getting married?"

"Yes," Delores said without hesitation. "When I meet the right man, I'll snag him, sure as you're born." She gazed at me, as if wondering whether to go on or hold her peace. "Did your dad ever tell you that I was in love once?"

I shook my head, feeling strangely stricken. Delores was my aunt and yet I knew so little about her.

"His name was Chad," she said very softly.

I waited, almost holding my breath.

"He was killed in Vietnam. One day before he would have come home. I was bitter over that, for a lot of years."

I didn't answer immediately, because I was doing some internal scrambling. Delores must have had a reason for telling me such a personal thing, and I couldn't help wondering if I'd been the recipient of some of that bitterness. That was a lot of supposing, but there *had* been an explanatory note in her voice, if not an actual apology.

"I'm so sorry," I said at long last. I would have turned away, but Delores stopped me.

"I wasted too much time grieving," she said. "I shut people out, because I was afraid to care too much. The way I cared for Chad—it ran too deep."

If we'd had a different kind of relationship, I would have hugged her. "Good night," I said gently.

"Don't be so scared of loving again that you miss the next chance, Sarah."

Something fluttered inside me, like a bird trying to fly out of a tight spot. "Are you talking about Joe?" I asked.

"Maybe," Delores said.

"He's still in love with Abby," I pointed out.

"So what?" Delores retorted. "Love isn't a finite thing, Sarah. It stretches."

"One size fits all?" I replied with a touch of irony.

"Oh, go to bed," Delores said with a dismissive wave of one hand. "You're a regular Scrooge."

"Gee, thanks."

"Go to bed." Aunt voice. I kind of liked it.

I did as I was told, but it was a very long time before I fell asleep.

I woke the next morning to more snow and the fragrance of something delicious wafting upstairs from the kitchen. After a hasty shower, I put on jeans and a sweatshirt, pulled my hair back in a ponytail, and joined Delores and Marlie. They sat in the midst of a forest of cold cereal boxes.

"What smells so good?" I asked.

"My sweet potato casserole," Delores said. She was wearing another pair of sweatpants cut to accommodate her cast and a festive sweater with a reindeer on the front. Christmas lights twinkled in its antlers. "We'll need a boatload of it to feed all the people converging on this place tomorrow."

Marlie actually smiled at me from the table, where she was scarfing up little multicolored Os, swimming in milk. "My first *real* Thanksgiving in a long time," she said.

I frowned. "I beg your pardon? Last year we went out to a lovely restaurant. The year before that, the Mastersons and the Gillards joined us. Turkey, dressing, pumpkin pie, the whole bit." Craig had gotten drunk on wine and the Gillards had left early, bickering under their breath. I wished I hadn't brought up last Thanksgiving at all, and my face must have reflected it, because Marlie cut me a break.

"Delores and I are going on a reconnaissance mission," she said.

I looked pointedly at my aunt's cast.

"The Jinglers are trying to get the jump on us," Delores said. "I want to see what we're up against."

"Who—or *what*—pray tell, are the Jinglers?" I pictured a family of elves in curly-toed shoes and green velvet waistcoats, for some reason, and almost laughed.

"That new caroling outfit," Delores answered darkly.

"How do you plan on getting there? You can't drive with that foot."

"We're riding the senior citizens' bus," Marlie answered with a gleam of triumph in her eyes. "So there."

"You're not a senior citizen," I said, shaking multicolored Os into a bowl of my own. "Anyway, we have an appointment with a counselor today."

The room went still.

"What counselor?" Marlie demanded.

"Her name is Ms. Dorrance. She works at Bent Tree High."

"I'm not going."

"That's what you think."

"Couldn't it wait until after Christmas?"

"You stole money from me and hopped a bus to Reno yesterday, remember? Don't look now, kid, but that constitutes a personal crisis."

"It's all a moot point," Delores put in. "Betty called half an hour ago. She's running a temp, so she stayed home sick."

"Dammit," I said.

"Cranky," Delores remarked to Marlie. "Would you like to go with us, Sarah Jane, or would you rather stay here and bah humbug?"

I sighed. What I needed was coffee, so I poured a cup to wash down my cereal. "You two go ahead. I've been worrying about the carolers—I need to make sure the green, red, and blue teams are all on the same page with their schedules. That means I'd better call each and every one of them to make sure, and it will probably take a couple of hours."

"Sucks to be you," Marlie said.

I glared at her. "I just remembered something," I replied. "You're grounded."

"Make an exception," Delores wheedled. "It's the day before Thanksgiving and, anyway, I need somebody to help me spy on the Jinglers." She picked up her key ring from the counter and waggled it at me. "If you change your mind, you can hop in my car and join us. We'll be at the Center Street Mall, checking out the competition."

Marlie finished her breakfast and carried the bowl and spoon to the sink, where she rinsed them and put them on the drain board. Delores had never invested in a dishwasher; she'd always said ordinary household jobs were good for the soul.

"Amazing," I said, when my stepdaughter had left the room.

Delores just looked at me, the vision of innocence. "What?"

"The way the two of you just ganged up on me."

"It's not a big deal, Sarah."

"Marlie doesn't have any spending money," I felt compelled to add.

"It doesn't cost anything to look," Delores replied. "It's a good idea to call all the carolers," she added after a few moments of thoughtful silence. "You can use the phone on my desk, if you like. And you might want to set up an email account on the computer, too, since most people prefer to communicate that way whenever possible. The crew is in my address book, online, so you won't have to write them all individually. You can just use that group thingy."

I nodded. "Thanks," I said.

Delores left the kitchen and I ate my cereal alone.

Presently, I heard the honk of a horn and the slamming of the front door. Delores and Marlie were off on their secret mission in the senior citizens' van then. Would it have killed them to say good-bye?

I poured more coffee, went into Delores's office, and settled myself at the desk. The Barrels of Carols phone list was in plain sight—probably my aunt's doing—and I started making calls.

No one was at home.

After the tenth attempt, I logged onto Delores's Internet account, added an email address for myself, and sent out a group dispatch, with all pertinent details of Friday's gig at the shopping mall.

Everyone was to be on time.

Everyone was expected to be in costume.

I thought of Joe, saying he'd be dressed as a Victorian gentleman, and smiled.

The smile faded as my gaze fell on his manuscript, resting on a corner of Delores's desk. I reached for it— drew my hand back—reached for it again.

I read the title page:

Because You Were Here.

My eyes burned and my throat closed.

I turned to the dedication:

For Ryan and Sam. So you'll remember.

I put the manuscript aside. Joe's book was going to be published and thousands of people would read it, but now, in the quiet, happy clutter of Delores's office, sneaking even a small peek seemed an unconscionable intrusion, as though I'd been about to read his mail, or his diary.

I decided to do something constructive while I waited for the carolers to call or email. I'd go upstairs and unpack my suitcases. Find something decent to wear on Friday night.

I settled on a boot-length black skirt and a pink cashmere sweater, both of which needed airing and pressing.

I shook them out and hung them from the shower rod in the bathroom, then went downstairs again. The phone hadn't rung, but there was always the possibility of email.

I logged on again.

A computer voice informed me gaily that I had mail.

Hi,

Joe had written.

Want to come over for coffee? I need an excuse not to write.

I glanced at the manuscript, then hit the Reply button.

Shame on you. You have a deadline.

His response was almost instant:

Have pity. I'm really stuck.

I laughed.

Okay,

I typed.

Is there any pumpkin pie left?

No,

Joe replied.

But come anyway.

He was waiting on his porch when I came out of Delores's front door. Huge, fat flakes of snow were falling and, for a moment, I could have sworn Joe and I were both figures in a giant glass globe.

"Cross where the road's sanded," he called, grinning, "it's still slick. I almost put the van in the ditch when I took the boys to school this morning."

I crossed the street over a bridge of streaked dirt.

"You should be writing," I said.

He nodded in agreement, his eyes warm. "But I'm not."

I started up his walk and Dodger came to meet me, overjoyed by my visit. I felt an instant and incongruent longing for a dog of my own.

"Delores and Marlie went shopping," I told Joe. "At least, that's their cover story. They're actually checking out the caroling competition at the Center Street Mall."

He stepped back, in the same way he had the night before, inspiring a brief, sweet flash of déjà vu. "Delores," he said, "is flouting doctor's orders. She's supposed to stay off her feet."

"That's Delores," I answered.

Joe closed the door and took my coat.

Déjà vu all over again.

There was a fire popping industriously in the living room hearth, and Joe's laptop stood open on the coffee table. "Have a seat," he said. "I'll get the coffee."

I perched on the couch and stole a glance at the laptop screen.

I'd expected to see a page of his manuscript, but he was online, which made sense because he'd just emailed the coffee invitation a few minutes before. There was a message open, and I read it, though not intentionally. I just happen to be a really fast reader.

> Dear Dad—We want a mom for
> Christmas. Sarah doesn't have a husbund
> so maybe you cud get her. She's pretty
> and she sounds nice wen she reads.
> Love, Ryan and Sam and Dodger.

Tears filled my eyes and I scooted guiltily along the couch to get out of snooping range. I probably looked pretty normal when Joe came back, carrying two mugs of coffee. There was a doughnut box wedged under his right elbow.

Joe glanced at the computer.

I must have looked chagrined.

He smiled.

"I didn't mean to look," I said, spilling my guts.

"I believe you," he answered, juggling coffee and the doughnut box.

"They spell pretty well for eight-year-olds," I said.

"Abby taught them to read when they were three," Joe replied.

"Oh."

He handed me a mug, sat down, and simultaneously closed the laptop and popped the lid on the doughnuts. "Is this the part where you start feeling cornered and cancel Friday?" he asked.

I shook my head. "I think it's sweet," I said. "What are you going to tell Ryan and Sam?"

He sighed. "Not to mention Dodger," he quipped. He stared into his coffee for a long time, then turned his head to look directly into my eyes. "I think I'll say, 'Maybe next year.'"

My stomach pitched.

I reached for a doughnut, to have something to do. They were the powdery kind and the fallout sprinkled itself across the knees of my jeans.

Joe chuckled. "Relax, Sarah," he said. "I was only teasing."

I nodded, anxious to let him know that I hadn't, not for *one moment,* thought he was serious.

After that, we talked about the quarreling carolers, and Delores's broken ankle, and whether or not he should let the boys take karate classes.

I stayed about half an hour, told Joe to get back to work, and crossed the dirt streak to Delores's place to check for phone messages.

There were seventeen emails waiting and almost as many voicemails.

I waded through the calls one by one and the last sent me scrambling for Delores's car keys.

She and Marlie were at the police station and I needed to get down there, right away.

It took several grinding tries to get Delores's old car

started. The tires screeched and grabbed on the sanded ice covering the road, and I zoomed off.

The police station was on Main Street, a brick building with cardboard turkeys and pilgrims taped to the windows from the inside.

I parked illegally and dashed up the walk to the front entrance.

Delores and Marlie were sitting in the reception area. Marlie's head was down and Delores had an arm around her shoulders.

"What on earth—?" I blurted.

Shhh, Delores mouthed.

I stared at them both, but I managed to wait.

Marlie finally looked up. Her eyes were red from crying. "I got arrested for shoplifting," she said. "It was awful."

"Shop—?" I couldn't even say the whole word. I choked on it, right in the middle.

"She wanted a present to send to her mother," Delores said. "You know, for Christmas."

Heat flooded my body. "*Wonderful,*" I said. "I'm sure a mug shot will serve just as well. She can show it to all her friends and say, 'This is my daughter, the budding criminal'!"

"Sarah!" Delores said, shocked.

I already regretted my outburst, but I was still too furious and too shaken to retract any of it. Not that things like that can ever really be taken back.

"I hate you," Marlie told me.

"I'm not too wild about you, either, right now," I retorted. "Are you free to go, or do I have to post bail?"

"She can go," Delores said softly, bemused.

Tears of frustration filled my eyes.

"Let's go home," Delores told Marlie, helping her to her feet, as though Marlie were the wounded one.

Marlie rushed past us and out the door.

"I would appreciate it," I said, as calmly as I could when Delores and I were alone, "if you wouldn't act as though she's some kind of victim of happenstance. She has to take personal responsibility for this."

Delores's cheeks turned pink and her eyes flashed. Then the starch seemed to go out of her. She reached for her crutches, but let her hands fall to her sides. "I would have given her the money—it was just a bottle of cheap perfume—if only she'd asked," she said.

"So would I," I answered, my tone clipped because I was fighting back more tears, this time ones of despair. "But the point is, she *didn't* ask."

"Maybe she thought you'd say no," Delores suggested.

"Not good enough. She *stole* something, Delores. That's serious."

"I know," Delores said, looking defeated.

"Come on," I said gently, handing her the crutches. "I'll help you to the car."

Marlie huddled in the backseat, reminiscent of a criminal handcuffed in the rear of a squad car. I ignored her, opening the front passenger door for Delores and holding her crutches while she got in and buckled up.

When we got home, I saw that Joe's van was missing from his driveway. What that had to do with anything, I don't know, but I noticed just the same, and I felt bereft because of it.

Inside the house, Marlie immediately dashed upstairs

and into her room, slamming the door resoundingly behind her.

"Where were you?" Delores asked. "When I called from the police station, I mean?"

I held her crutches again, so she could get out of her coat. "Over at Joe's, having coffee," I said stiffly. Between that second and the next, I lost control. The tears came, and five minutes wasn't going to be long enough to cry them all.

Delores stared at me, worried.

"Is it my fault?" I blubbered.

My aunt put an arm around my shoulders, gave me a steadying squeeze, the kind that says, "buck up". "The shoplifting?" she asked.

I nodded miserably.

Delores chuckled throatily, on the verge of crying herself, I suspected, and gave me another squeeze. "No," she said.

"I shouldn't have said what I did. About the mug shot, I mean."

"No," Delores agreed, "you shouldn't have. But you did, and it's over. And it's not as if you didn't have reason to be angry."

"I don't know what to do," I confessed.

Delores smiled. "Of course you don't," she said. "Kids don't come with instruction manuals. Just take a little time to settle down and give Marlie a chance to stew in her own juices a while, then the two of you can have a nice, calm little chat."

"I don't know how 'calm' it's going to be," I said, squaring my shoulders. "Right now, I'd like to wring her neck."

"Think, Sarah," Delores counseled. "Marlie wanted to give her mother a present. She went about it in the wrong way, that's a given. You handle it in the *right* way."

"No problem," I replied. "Now I just have to figure out what that is."

Chapter Six

❊ ❊ ❊

T hanksgiving was a blur.
　　Marlie took care to stay on the opposite side of
　　any room we both happened to be in. We hadn't
discussed the shoplifting incident yet—I was still cooling
off—and it stood between us, a strange, concentrated
energy full of portent.

Dinner was served as a buffet, turkey and all the trim-
mings. Delores officiated in a red velvet skirt and white
ruffly blouse, and guests came and went all afternoon,
open-house style. Jenny made an appearance, and so did
Mary Ellen, though they were careful to arrive at different times, thus avoiding another encounter.

Joe and the twins showed up late, having made a visit
to the hospital to see Joe's student Mike, and the boys
sported not only their feathered headdresses, but matching buckskins, too.

"An interesting twist on the usual pilgrims, wouldn't
you say?" Joe asked, putting his mouth close to my ear in
a way that had nothing to do with red-headed Indians *or*
Puritans in search of religious freedom.

I laughed, and felt a little better.

Dodger pinched a panful of apple cobbler, wolfed down the goodies before anybody could stop him, and promptly threw up on the kitchen floor.

All in all, it was a regular American Thanksgiving.

I was standing on the front porch, trying to get some perspective on things, when Joe slipped outside to join me, carrying a plate with a huge slice of pumpkin pie on it.

"You okay?" he asked.

I told him about Marlie's brush with the law.

He gave a low whistle of exclamation. Waited.

"I'm a lousy mother," I said.

"Not," Joe replied, and offered me a bite of his pie, generously slathered with whipped cream.

I shook my head.

He persisted.

I ate the pie.

"Can I read your manuscript?" I asked and instantly blushed at my audacity.

Once again, Joe surprised me. "I'd like that," he said. "All ready for tomorrow?"

I wondered if he was referring to our date or the first caroling gig. Plus, I was still thinking about the manuscript. How it would make me feel to read it, whether it was a good idea or not.

Did I mention that I analyze things too much?

"I guess," I said. "I don't think my future lies in herding carolers from mall to mall. Who knew they were such an unruly breed?"

Joe laughed. Then he turned serious. Set his pie down

on the porch railing, half-eaten and forgotten. "Where *does* your future lie, Sarah?"

"I wish I knew," I answered after a long moment of fruitless introspection. I'd had a lot of those lately.

He opened his mouth to say something, but just then, the door opened and Marlie was there, holding out my cellphone.

"It's my mom," she said, daring me to back down and refuse to take the call. "She wants to talk to you."

I glanced at Joe, then accepted the phone.

Joe moved to the other end of the porch, after reclaiming his pie, and gestured for Marlie to go with him.

"Hello?" I said, feeling jittery. "This is Sarah."

"Hello," Brenda replied. "How's Marlie?"

I looked at my stepdaughter, standing with Joe, slanting a look my way.

Right answer? She was arrested for shoplifting yesterday. Before that, she ripped me off for the price of a bus ticket and tried to run away.

"Adjusting," I said instead.

"I heard about the bust," Brenda said. Then she laughed. "What a kick."

I stiffened. "Personally, I didn't think it was all that funny."

"So she said," Brenda replied. "Listen, this new guy I'm dating is a lawyer. And he says there are custody issues here."

I'd been waiting for this to arise, on some level, ever since Craig's funeral. Brenda was Marlie's biological mother and if she wanted to take over raising her daughter, there wouldn't be much I could do about it. I didn't have the money to fight her in court, and I had every reason to believe Marlie would take Brenda's side, not mine.

I closed my eyes. "I suppose he's right," I said.

"If she comes to stay with me, I'll get her Social Security payments," Brenda went on.

I quelled a surge of verbal violence. "Yes," I answered, keeping my voice as even as I could. "I've been banking the money for her. So she can go to college."

Brenda sighed. "If you keep her, I could be liable for child support. Way back to the time Craig died. That's what Dick says, anyway."

"I won't ask for that, Brenda," I said.

"You say that now. Would you be willing to sign release papers, if I gave you full legal custody?"

I felt as though I'd just taken a snowball in the face, both exhilarated and stunned to fury. "Yes," I said, very slowly and very carefully.

Brenda heaved a sigh of relief. "Good," she said. "Because Dick won't marry me if I'm liable for the kid."

I bit back a nasty comment about Dick. "Send the papers. I'll sign them."

There was a shift in Brenda's tone. She sounded almost childlike. "You'll explain to Marlie that it isn't because I don't want her?"

"Do you, Brenda?"

Long silence.

"No," she admitted. "I guess not."

"That's what I *won't* tell her," I said.

I gave Brenda Delores's address, then we said our awkward good-byes and rang off.

Joe went back in the house, leaving Marlie and me alone on the porch.

She sank into the swing where I remembered Delores sitting on summer evenings, and I joined her, but not too quickly.

"How'd you like to be legally my kid?" I asked. My voice probably quavered, because I was terrified of her answer.

Marlie's eyes widened. "You want me? After I stole that perfume and ran away and everything?"

I slipped a light, tentative arm around her shoulders. "Yeah," I said with a little smile. "Even after that. But you'd better not do it again."

"You really want me?"

"Of *course* I want you." How could she not have known?

Maybe because you didn't tell her. It was my internal voice, but it sounded more like Delores.

"Even though I swiped the perfume for her instead of you?"

"Even though," I said. "And don't do me any favors by lifting another gift. Your life on the wild side, young lady, is *over,* here and now."

"I don't know if I can get you anything for Christmas," Marlie fretted.

I hugged her, and suddenly my eyes filled again. "I'd settle for a quota of civil words, every day. No big deal. Just a sentence or two."

She forgot she was twelve, apparently, and practically grown up, and laid her head on my shoulder. I felt a childlike tremor go through her and thought of the teddy bear again. "I'm sorry, Sarah. For stealing, and for being mean."

"I'm sorry for the mug-shot comment." I kissed her temple. "Let's call it even and start over."

She looked up at me. "Can I call you Mom?"

"I'd like that," I said, echoing Joe's earlier words about the manuscript.

"Can we stay in Bent Tree Creek? Forever and ever?"

I chuckled. "Don't push it," I said.

The door creaked open and the Red Chiefs appeared again, side by side, and very serious. Their gazes were fixed on Marlie.

"Dad says he'll pay you if you'll baby-sit us tonight," said Ryan. Or Sam. There were no names embroidered on the buckskins, so I couldn't be certain. "He wants to take Sarah someplace."

Marlie looked up, hopeful. "Is it okay—Mom?"

The "Mom" sounded a little awkward, but I knew she'd get the hang of it eventually. And it already felt good to hear, settling over my heart like a warm, soft blanket.

"Yes," I said. "It's okay."

The Red Chiefs cheered. Remembering the email they'd sent to Joe the day before, I wasn't sure if they were just pleased to spend the evening with someone closer to their own age or if they thought they'd be getting a mom for Christmas.

We all went inside, since it was getting cold.

Marlie, Dodger, and the Red Chiefs departed happily for Joe's place.

Delores collapsed in her easy chair when the last guest departed.

Joe and I cleaned up the kitchen. Rinsed and stacked the dishes to be washed later, and put the pans in hot water to soak.

"So," I finally worked up the nerve to ask, "where are we going?"

"It's a surprise," he said mysteriously.

"Not the cemetery, I hope," I said.

He flashed me that lethal, knee-melting grin. "Definitely not the cemetery," he promised. I was wearing black slacks and a fuzzy red sweater, and he looked me over appreciatively. "Probably better if you change into jeans, though. Dress warm."

I went upstairs, in a pleasant sort of fugue, and switched clothes. When I came down again, Delores was still in her easy chair in the living room, with the TV tuned to a rerun of *The Bishop's Wife*.

"Need anything?" I asked, bending to kiss the top of her head. It was an impulse; if I'd stopped to think first, I probably wouldn't have done it.

She smiled up at me. "Just a breather. Joe went by a few minutes ago—said he'd meet you out front."

I blushed slightly.

"Take it easy, Sarah," Delores advised gently. "It's not rocket science."

I nodded, not at all sure I could follow her advice, but willing to try. "There was a breakthrough with Marlie," I said.

"I suspected as much," Delores answered. "She looked like a different child when she and the boys and Dodger left for Joe's place."

"Sure you don't want a cup of tea or something? A pain pill, maybe?"

She sighed. "I don't need a pain pill, and if I try to swallow one more thing, even a mouthful of tea, I'll burst for sure. I ate way too much turkey."

I dropped another kiss on her crown. "Leave the rest of the dishes. I'll do them later."

She smiled. "Good for the soul," she said.

"Good for the soul," I agreed.

Joe and I ended up at the skating rink.

"What?" I joked, when we pulled up in his van. "One broken ankle in the Sullivan family isn't enough?"

"Have a little faith," he said. "And by the way, I like the sound of that. You referring to Delores as family, I mean."

I was a little stung. "I've always—"

"Have you?" Joe interrupted.

"I guess not," I admitted.

"Let's skate," he said.

I couldn't help thinking of the skating scene in *The Bishop's Wife,* even though Joe and I were inside a rink, practically deafened by Christmas music, instead of gliding over the surface of a pond, under a bridge. I was Loretta Young, he was Cary Grant, and there was no David Niven waiting impatiently at home.

Even better.

We stayed for a couple of hours, then went back to Delores's—she'd fallen asleep in her chair by then—and made ourselves turkey sandwiches in the kitchen. Restored, we did the dishes together, and there was a lot of laughter.

I felt refreshed. Hopeful, for the first time in a long while.

When the kitchen was spotless, Joe said good night and left.

Marlie showed up a few minutes later, glowing. "He gave me ten dollars," she said. "Just for reading two chapters of *Harry Potter* and making sure the munchkins didn't burn down the house."

"Life is good," I said, lingering at the kitchen table, sipping reheated coffee.

"Do you think we could go shopping?"

"I'm pooped," I replied, "and we'll be at the mall tomorrow. I've got to keep all Delores's carolers in line."

Marlie grinned. "They behaved pretty well today," she said. Most of them had come by to say hello to Delores and have dinner, in small, convivial groups.

"You and Joe are going on another date, aren't you?"

I smiled. "I guess if you can call dinner in a food court a date, yes. Don't read too much into it, sweetie. I barely know Joe."

"I like him."

"Me, too."

"There's a really cool bedroom over there," Marlie said, indicating the Courtland house with a poke of her thumb. "It has a window seat and everything. Ryan and Sam said it would be mine, if you and I ever moved in."

"Marlie—"

Just then, Delores hobbled through the door on her crutches. She yawned. "What a day," she said.

"What a day indeed," I agreed.

I slept soundly that night, and when Friday dawned, I was ready for it.

I made turkey hash for breakfast, and after Delores, Marlie, and I had eaten, I pressed my skirt and pink cashmere sweater and took extra care with my hair and makeup.

I told myself it had nothing whatsoever to do with my date with Joe. Oh, no. It was all about dressing for success.

I'm so full of it sometimes.

Delores wanted to go along, just to get out of the house, she claimed, so she and Marlie and I got into her old car and set off. Joe's van wasn't in his driveway, although I really didn't notice all that much.

The mall was half an hour away via overcrowded, icy roads, and when we got there, parking was a challenge. I let Marlie and Delores off at the main entrance and cruised until I found a space, practically in the next county.

When I finally got inside and located the official meeting place, which was the gigantic Christmas tree in the central atrium, I felt as though I'd stepped into *A Christmas Carol.*

I was trying to be subtle, but my gaze went straight to Joe. He was wearing pin-striped pants and a waistcoat, and he took my breath away. Ryan and Sam stood on either side of him, again in the buckskins and headdresses.

I smiled. The Christmas of the Red Chiefs, I thought.

Delores materialized at my elbow. "I usually have them warm up with something lively," she said, gesturing toward the assemblage of costumed carolers.

I drew a deep breath, let it out.

Showtime.

"Okay, everybody," I called, pretending I knew what I was doing. "How about a round of—"

" 'God Rest Ye Merry Gentlemen,' " Delores whispered.

" 'God Rest Ye Merry Gentlemen'!" I piped.

There was a lot of shuffling and rattling of sheet music, along with some throat clearing. A crowd gathered as the singing began, and I was so proud that my eyes watered, even though I couldn't take any credit for the way my carolers sounded.

I put the blue group—I'd caved and let Mary Ellen Hershmeyer sing with them, even though I could have used an alto in the red group, where Jenny Rivers reigned—at one end of the mall. The green group, led by Joe, went in the middle and the red got the far end.

I confess I hung around the green team a little more than necessary, acting as though I wasn't watching Joe. By then, Marlie and the Red Chiefs were roaming the mall, supervised, from a discreet distance, by Delores.

During the first break, Joe took Marlie, the boys, and Delores back home. I noticed that Marlie was carrying a small shopping bag and acting mysterious, and I knew she'd bought a present for Brenda. I was all right with that, I decided—I'd even help her mail it.

Joe was back well before the second two-hour shift started.

I tried to spread the wealth and pay a little attention to the red and blue teams, but my mind was on green, big-time.

Everything would have gone fine if Jenny and Mary Ellen hadn't met in one of the restrooms and gotten into a hair-pulling match.

"Trouble," Joe whispered, close to my ear, as screams of fury echoed from the ladies' room.

Horrified shoppers stopped, stared.

I dashed inside.

The querulous carolers were rolling on the floor, in a colorful tangle of crinoline petticoats and fancy skirts.

I muttered a prayer and waded in to separate them.

"Go home immediately," I said breathlessly when I finally had them both at arm's length.

Jenny blinked at me. Sniffled. Her bonnet was askew and she'd torn the mutton-chop sleeve of her costume. "Are we fired?"

"I need this job," Mary Ellen whimpered.

"I'd never have guessed," I told her. "And I'm not sure whether I'm going to fire you or not. I should, though. Right here and now."

"But it's *Christmas*," Jenny protested.

"Then why don't you act like it?" I shot back, folding my arms. "You ought to be ashamed of yourselves. Two grown women, in a cat fight. I've got to tell you, I am disgusted."

"We've been fighting for years," Mary Ellen confessed.

"You were always a bully," Jenny accused.

"Oh, grow up!" I cried. "Both of you!"

"Can we have another chance?" Mary Ellen asked.

"Not today," I said. I knew I had to be firm. This was serious. "You're just lucky I broke up the fight instead of mall security. You might both have been arrested then, and believe me, Barrels of Carols doesn't need the kind of publicity that would result from *that*."

"I'm sorry," Jenny said.

"Me, too," Mary Ellen said reluctantly.

I wavered.

What would Delores do?

"Go home," I said.

I was bluffing, of course. If they'd gone back to the red and blue groups and started singing again, there wouldn't have been anything I could do.

They hung their heads.

Jenny opened the restroom door, held it for Mary Ellen. They both went out.

I waited a full thirty seconds before I followed.

Joe was standing in the corridor, looking concerned.

"Management bites," I said.

"You don't know the half of it," Joe said. "Suzie Moore just developed laryngitis in the middle of 'It Came Upon a Midnight Clear.' That means we're short a soprano."

"No," I said.

"Yes," Joe countered. "Some of the Jinglers are hanging around, too. They offered to loan us a singer. I've got to say I doubt their motives—the TV newspeople are here. They like to kick off the holiday season with Suzie's solo."

I put my hands on my hips. "Those *sneaks!*"

Joe's eyes shone with amusement. "The TV people?"

"The Jinglers!"

"How are you at 'O, Holy Night'?"

"I beg your pardon?"

"The song," Joe said.

"Oh."

"Yes, oh."

"Somebody else can do it," I said.

Slowly, Joe shook his head.

"You, for instance."

Again, he shook his head.

"Why not?" I asked.

"Because it would be enabling. You're a dysfunctional caroler. Sooner or later, you've gotta sing, and now's as good a time as any."

"One of the other women—"

"If you think the brawl Jennie and Mary Ellen just had in the bathroom was bad, you dangle a televised solo in front of the rest of them. It'll be a bloodbath. The Jinglers will step in with their own team. In fact, I'll bet they're skulking all over the mall, disguised as ordinary shoppers, hoping something like this will happen."

"No wonder you're a writer," I said. "You should try your hand at fiction."

"I intend to," Joe replied, "but right now, my career plans aren't the issue. Sarah, you've got to sing that song."

I was still deliberating fifteen minutes later, as we dined at TGI Friday's, Joe in his waistcoat and striped pants, me in my long skirt and cashmere. Or, I should say, *Joe* dined. I was too nervous to eat.

"What if I try to sing and nothing comes out?" I fretted.

His gaze was steady, but he didn't answer my question.

"I can't blow this, Joe," I said. "Delores is counting on me. If the Jinglers elbow her out tonight, and on television to boot, it could start a chain reaction. She could be ruined."

"Then *don't* blow it."

I looked down at my clothes. "I don't have a costume."

"You can borrow somebody's cape and bonnet. Amy

Davis is about your size. She can stand in back, for one song."

I bit my lower lip.

Joe signaled the waitress for the bill, paid, and led me out of TGI Friday's by the hand.

The TV crew was set up in the middle of the mall. The carolers were milling nervously, whispering to one another. Joe left me standing frozen at the foot of a tinsel-trimmed platform to speak with Amy. Sure enough, she forked over the bonnet and cape.

Joe buttoned me into the cape, plopped the bonnet on my head, and tied the ribbons in a big bow under my chin.

"You. Can. Do. This," he told me in a whisper.

I looked at the cameras, and the TV people.

I took in the gathering of eager shoppers, faces alight.

I stepped onto the platform. I heard nothing except the thrumming of my own heartbeat, and I thought I spotted a Jingler in the crowd, too. The man was cinched into a trench coat, houndstooth leggings, black ballet slippers, and a touch of makeup.

Someone handed me sheet music, but it was just for show. I knew every word of that venerable hymn. The question was, would any of those words come out of my mouth when I opened it to sing?

A TV crewperson bounded up, wired me for sound, and receded into the haze. I blinked in the brightness of the special lights.

Joe introduced me, and a pitch pipe sounded behind me.

I drew a deep breath, closed my eyes, and reached for the opening note.

O, holy night, the stars were brightly shining . . .

Was that my voice?

Hot damn, I *was* good.

When I finished, there was a sudden, wavering silence. Then a burst of applause.

I blinked, looked around for Joe.

He was smiling at me and clapping his hands.

I was bushed when I pulled into Delores's driveway that night, at the wheel of her car. Joe had a vanload of carolers to drop off at the community center, where a number of them had parked before setting off for the mall.

The garage door wouldn't open, so I shut off the engine, got out of the car, and approached the house.

Marlie waited on the porch, bundled in one of Delores's old coats, holding the shopping bag I'd glimpsed earlier. I heard the twins and Dodger playing some noisy game inside the house.

"I saw you on TV," Marlie said almost shyly. "It was good to hear you sing again, Sarah."

"Thanks," I answered, yawning.

"Delores said you saved the day."

"Delores," I replied, "talks in clichés." I glanced at the shopping bag. "We'll send the package on Monday, I promise," I added wearily.

"Send it?" Marlie looked puzzled. And very anxious. "I want you to open it now."

"Me?"

"It's *for* you," Marlie said.

I made my way up the porch steps. "Sweetheart, you shouldn't have spent your baby-sitting money on me. Besides, it isn't Christmas yet—"

Marlie's hands trembled slightly as she held out the bag. "It cost more than the ten dollars I got from Mr. Courtland," she admitted, "but don't worry. Delores floated me a loan."

I took the bag, as much in danger of dropping it as Marlie had been. Sat down with a plunk on the top step, snow and all. Felt the chill seep through the back of my coat.

Marlie perched beside me, her face eager.

I reached carefully into the bag and pulled out a snow globe. My heart shinnied into my throat. Inside the glass ball, a mother and daughter faced each other, holding hands, perched on tiny skates on a little blue circle of ice.

I gulped back a sob. "Oh, honey—"

"It plays 'You and Me Against the World,'" Marlie said, reclaiming the snow globe long enough to turn the little key on the bottom. The familiar Helen Reddy song tinkled in the crisp night air, as though flowing from a fairy piano.

I cried.

"Delores says it doesn't have to be that way," Marlie told me softly. "Just us against the world."

Joe's van swung into the driveway across the street. He got out, hesitated, then came toward us.

The music box wound down.

"Read the tag," Marlie said.

I blinked to clear my eyes. *To Mom, Merry Christmas, Marlie.*

I cried harder.

"Don't you like it?" Marlie whispered.

I put an arm around her and squeezed hard. "I *love* it, sweetheart. But I love you more."

Joe paused just on the other side of the front gate. "Am I interrupting a moment?" he asked.

"No," Marlie said happily. She bounced to her feet. "I'll get the boys and Dodger."

"Thanks," Joe said, but he still didn't open the gate.

Marlie rushed inside.

"Looks suspiciously like a moment to me," Joe pressed quietly.

"I'm a little soggy, that's all," I said with a sniffle.

"That's what you get for sitting in snow." He opened the gate, came through, walked toward me with his hands in the pockets of his winter jacket. He must have changed out of his Victorian garb before leaving the mall.

"I'm not talking about that part of my anatomy," I replied.

He sat down beside me, took the globe, turned the key.

The tune chimed between us, little quivering crystals of sound.

I glanced back and saw Delores, Marlie, and two Indian chiefs watching us through the living room window.

Joe must have looked, too, because he leaned in and confided, "We have an audience."

"I know," I said, and sniffled again. I'd been hoping he hadn't recognized the song, but he was a music teacher, after all. I could see by his expression that he knew it.

"I can wait," he said.

I turned to him. "Wait?"

"Until you're willing to let it be more than you and Marlie against the world."

I was speechless.

Joe handed over the snow globe and brushed my cheek with the backs of his fingers. A warm shiver went through me.

"It's too soon," he said. "But the truth is, Sarah, I knew the minute I saw you, standing there in front of the Mega-Pumper, scared to death and trying to be strong for Marlie's sake."

"You—knew?"

"That we were going to fall in love. I figure it will take about a year."

My mouth dropped open.

Joe put a finger under my chin and closed it again.

Kissed me softly on the mouth.

"Just say you'll stay. Give it—give *us*—a chance."

I clutched the snow globe in both hands.

Joe kissed me again, thoroughly this time.

Cheers erupted from the peanut gallery, muffled by the windowpanes.

"Stay," Joe said with a grin, his mouth still perilously close to mine.

"Okay," I said. Not the profoundest of answers, but I could see by the look in Joe's eyes that it would do nicely.

One year later . . .

I wore Jenny Rivers's caroling costume.

Joe wore his waistcoat and striped pants.

Ryan and Sam wore their headdresses, though they'd outgrown the buckskins over the summer and had to settle for suits.

Dodger had a new kerchief for the occasion.

Only Marlie and Delores looked like members of an actual wedding, in their perfectly normal dresses.

"Ready?" the minister whispered.

It was only three days until Christmas, so the little church in the square was decked out in fragrant evergreens and boughs of holly. The aroma was magical.

Joe looked down at me, raised his eyebrows in question.

"I'm ready," I said.

The minister cleared his throat.

People shuffled in the jammed pews.

"Dearly beloved, we are gathered here—"

I didn't hear the rest of the ceremony. I just said "I do" when Joe nudged me, and the next thing I knew, we were married.

We weren't taking a honeymoon, since Joe had just come back from a ten-city publicity tour for his book and was directing the holiday musical at the high school besides. I had my hands full with Call Sarah, the new company Delores and I had started back in the spring. We weren't exactly getting rich, making and delivering diet dinners, but we were breaking even, and I felt good about that.

Delores handed Joe an old-fashioned hotel key the minute we came out of the church, a broad smile on her face.

"I booked you a room at the B-and-B," she said. Her new boyfriend, Horace, stood proudly at her elbow. Horace had an RV, and the two of them were heading for Las Vegas on New Year's Day.

Joe grinned, tossed the key, caught it in a gloved hand. "Thanks," he said, and leaned down to kiss her smartly on the forehead.

The reception was held at Delores's place and it was a happy, noisy time.

I slipped out for some air and gazed at the house across the street, where Joe and I and the kids would be living.

I smiled, even as tears came to my eyes.

Abby's words, recorded in Joe's book, drifted into my mind.

Find somebody to love you, she'd said to him toward the end, when her strength was failing. *And to love my boys. That's all the tribute I want.*

"I'll take good care of them, Abby," I whispered. "I promise."

A slight, snowy breeze arose, curiously warm for a December evening.

The door opened and Joe stepped up behind me. Put his arms around me and kissed the back of my head.

"I love you, Sarah Courtland," he said softly.

I turned in his arms, felt the hardness and strength and warmth of him. I felt a funny tingling sensation in the soles of my feet, too, and grinned.

Roots.

I was putting down roots.

I felt them reach deep, through the floorboards of the porch, into the frozen earth beneath, green, growing tendrils, curling and spreading, finding their way.

"And I love you," I answered.

Joe pressed me closer. "What do you say we go over to the B-and-B, lock ourselves in our room, and have ourselves a merry little Christmas?"

Once Upon
a Christmas

⁕❉⁕

Catherine Mulvany

Special thanks to Torey Lehman, Tina Burts, Maggie Crawford, Meredith Bernstein, Janis McCurry, the Cherries, and last but not least, the Looney Binners.

Part I

"Be careful what you wish for . . ."

Chapter One

❄

Hailey Miller threaded her way through the crowded main hall of Crescentville High School even though she knew the detour would make her late for PE. What was a tardy slip when compared to a possible face-to-face with Kennedy MacCormack?

Halfway along the corridor she spotted him. Unfortunately, he wasn't alone. Blonde cheerleader Trisha Anderson had her bouncy D-cups pressed up against his chest.

Hailey frowned, irritated with Trisha for being there and irritated with her barely-graduated-out-of-a-double-A self for experiencing an undeniable twinge of boob envy.

Okay, dilemma time. Should she approach Kennedy as planned or just fade into the crowd unnoticed?

Trisha giggled at something Kennedy whispered in her ear, then batted her mascara-caked lashes. "You are totally bad."

Not to mention totally gorgeous, totally buff, and totally sexy. If this were a fairy tale, Trisha would be the witch who'd placed Prince Kennedy under a spell that only she, Hailey, the one true princess, could break. "I wish," Hailey muttered under her breath.

Kennedy glanced up just then and smiled at her.

Her knees went weak. Her heart stuttered.

"Hailey," he said in that husky baritone that made everything that came out of his mouth sound like the prelude to seduction. "Just who I was looking for."

And in that perfect moment of crystalline clarity, the prince recognized the one true princess.

"You were?" Hailey was proud of herself for not a) tripping over her own feet, b) dropping her backpack, or c) sounding as pathetically needy as she felt.

"You were?" A slight frown marred Trisha's flawless brow. She laid a proprietary hand on Kennedy's arm.

"Yeah." Kennedy smiled at Hailey, his chocolate brown eyes as sweetly seductive as the M&Ms to which Hailey was so hopelessly addicted. "You promised to loan me your physics notes so I could cram for the test this afternoon, remember?"

Trisha's snicker fell halfway between relief and mockery.

When the prince, a victim of the evil witch's most powerful incantation, failed to recognize the princess, the old hag cackled in glee.

Hailey buried her nose in her backpack, searching for the notebook.

"Hurry," Trisha said. "The bell's going to ring."

"It's in here somewhere." Hailey caught a flash of movement in her peripheral vision seconds before a massive impact sent her airborne. She landed butt first on the hall tiles with the entire contents of her backpack—including two stray tampons, a partially eaten bag of M&Ms, and a beat-up composition book—raining down around her.

Truck Lawrence, the apparent cause of the disaster, scowled at her. "Geez, watch where you're going, Miller."

"I wasn't going anywhere. *You* ran into *me,*" Hailey pointed out.

"Whatever." He lumbered off down the hall, muttering "must be that time of the month" just loud enough for Hailey and everyone else in the vicinity to hear. Laughter, ranging from furtive snorts to loud guffaws, rippled along the hallway.

Hailey snatched up the tampons, her cheeks on fire. *Shoot me. Shoot me now.*

Kennedy leaned over, and she thought for a split second he was going to help her to her feet or maybe just apologize for Truck's insensitivity, but all he did was extricate her physics notebook from the mess with a quick "thanks" before heading off to class, one arm slung around Trisha's shoulders.

A self-satisfied smile tilted the corners of Trisha's mouth as she glanced back at Hailey. Positioned as she'd been, Trisha would have had a clear view of Truck bearing down on Hailey, and yet she'd uttered not a word of warning.

Witch, Hailey thought. She squeezed her eyes shut, willing herself not to cry. Darn it, she was fifteen years old. Too old for tears.

The run-in with the troll had proved an unexpected setback. The evil hag and her minions had won this battle, but the princess vowed to keep fighting. She'd not rest until the spell was broken and the prince was free to follow his heart.

Hailey stepped off the school bus into knee-deep slush, courtesy of the snowplow her bus had followed all the way up the hill from the Crescentville, Oregon, city limits. Should have worn her boots. Better yet, she should have stayed home in the first place and saved herself a lot of grief.

Of course, she could have waited until basketball practice was over and hitched a ride home with Kennedy, but after the fiasco in the hall this morning, she figured that wasn't a good idea. He and Trisha probably had plans anyway—doing whatever it was popular kids did after school on the last day before Christmas break. Christmas shopping at the mall in Bend maybe. Or making out in the backseat of Kennedy's Mustang. She scowled at the snow-covered landscape.

The bus pulled away, the rear tires splattering her with a mixture of wet sand and gray slush. She said a word her mom probably didn't realize was in her vocabulary. Unfortunately, profanity didn't help. She was still cold and wet and facing a mile-and-a-half hike, most of it uphill, to Devil's Elbow, the cattle ranch on the eastern slope of the Cascades where she and her mom had been living since her mom had hired on as the MacCormacks' housekeeper six years ago.

Heaving a weary sigh, Hailey readjusted her earmuffs and tightened the straps on her backpack, then attempted to clear the slush from her glasses with the thumb of her mitten. All that did was smear the lenses, though. Giving it up as a lost cause, she stuffed her glasses in the pocket of her jacket.

Well, great. Not only did she have a miserable hike ahead of her, now she couldn't see two feet in front of her nose. Hailey started across the road toward the rustic log archway that marked the ranch's entrance, then quickly backtracked when a black pickup truck came flying around the hairpin curve just below her bus stop.

To her surprise, the truck clanked to a stop beside her, the tire chains flipping up yet more slush to soak her jeans. The passenger-side window slid down. "Want a lift?"

She squinted myopically toward the open window, trying to bring the speaker's face into focus. If she hadn't known better, she'd have sworn the voice was Kennedy's. But Kennedy was a blond. This guy had dark hair.

When she didn't respond, the driver, a broad-shouldered, dark-haired blur, leaned across the passenger. "Make up your mind, kiddo. We don't have all day. Got to get this boy up to the house before he starves to death. Hasn't had squat to eat all day except airplane food."

"Mac?" John "Mac" MacCormack was Kennedy's father, but the "boy" he was referring to wasn't Kennedy, which by process of elimination left Kennedy's nonidentical twin, the one who *hadn't* been kicked out of prep school last September. She leaned a little closer. "Thomas, is that you?"

"Hell yes, it's him," Mac said, sounding impatient.

"She can't see," Thomas told him. "She's not wearing her glasses."

"Where are your specs, kiddo? You didn't break 'em, did you? Your mom won't be happy if you broke 'em."

Thomas opened the door. "Pass me your backpack, Hailey. Then I'll give you a hand up."

She tossed him the backpack. "I didn't break my glasses," she told Mac. "I took them off, couldn't see through the slush blur."

Thomas grabbed her hand, hauled her into the pickup cab, then slid over to make room for her on the broad leather bench seat. The residual warmth from his body penetrated her clothing, but she couldn't stop shivering. Without a word, he kicked the heater up a notch.

As Mac bumped across the first cattle guard and headed up the hill, Hailey peeled off her soggy mittens, dug her glasses from her jacket pocket, and dried them on the tail of her shirt. "That's better," she said as her surroundings came into focus.

Mac was wearing his new Stetson and his good suede, fleece-lined jacket, but otherwise looked pretty much the same as normal, his long legs encased in Wranglers, his feet in cowboy boots. He tugged at the corner of his mustache and winked a greeting. "How'd you get so wet?"

"Bus attack," she said.

Thomas gave her the superior little half smile that always made her want to smack him. Apparently prep school agreed with him a little better than it had Kennedy. He looked happy and healthy. Very healthy. Lean but muscular. She could almost swear his broad MacCormack shoulders were an inch or two wider than they'd been when he'd flown east in September.

"Where are *your* glasses?" she asked.

126

"Got contacts," he said.

She smiled and nodded, trying hard not to feel envious. She'd been saving for contacts since eighth grade, but every time she got close to her goal, something happened to deplete her savings—like last summer when the radiator on her mom's car sprang a leak. Hailey had willingly offered the two hundred dollars her mom had needed for a replacement, and her mom was paying her back, naturally, but at twenty bucks a month, it would be a while before Hailey made that appointment with the optometrist.

She studied Thomas. "Contacts suit you," she said, which they did. She'd never noticed before what striking eyes he had, a steely gray color shot with blue flecks. In fact, she'd never really noticed how good-looking he was. Not Brad Pitt gorgeous like Kennedy, of course. Thomas's jaw was squarer, his cheekbones more prominent. Ruggedly handsome, he had thick dark eyebrows, a straight nose, and a surprisingly sensuous mouth—surprising since unlike Kennedy, Thomas was big on discipline and serious academic pursuits. Come to that, so was she, though with her it was more by necessity than because she was wired that way.

She sighed and fixed her gaze on the dash.

"How's school going?" Thomas asked.

"Fine." She shot a furtive sideways glance in his direction. There was no possible way he could know about her pratfall this morning, was there?

"The kid's got a perfect 4.0." Mac tapped the horn to spook the quail marching up the lane in single file, their topknots bobbing comically. The birds scattered, and Hailey found herself wondering if there was such a thing as an imperfect 4.0. Like maybe if you cheated on a test or hired someone to write your papers or did unmentionable things to the western civ teacher as a certain cheerleader was rumored to have done. Which reminded her of Trisha. Had she and Kennedy . . . ? Whoa! Was *that* what popular kids did after school?

"You decided yet where you're going to college?" Thomas sounded more like Ms. Levy, the CHS guidance counselor, than a seventeen-year-old who still wore a retainer at night.

"I'm only a sophomore," she reminded him. "What's the hurry?"

"Just making conversation," he said mildly. "You warm enough?"

She nodded, and he turned down the heater.

That was the thing about Thomas. On the surface, he was all big-brother solicitous, but that was just a cover for his true agenda—driving her insane. Asking stupid guidance counselor questions, for crying out loud, when he knew perfectly well her higher education options would be dictated by which schools offered the biggest scholarships. And that list wasn't likely to include Vassar or even Berkeley. *Rub my face in it, why don't you?*

She cast around for some way to annoy him. No use asking about his grades—perfect—or his free-throw average—also perfect. But there was one secret he'd let slip last time he'd been home, one secret Mac didn't know about. "You still doing the Dungeons and Dragons thing?" she asked, all wide-eyed innocence.

"What?" Mac's heavy, dark eyebrows snapped together in a scowl. His blue eyes flashed fire. "What Dungeons and Dragons thing?"

Thomas gave her a "thanks a bunch" look, immediately followed by an evil "I'll get even" smile. "It's a role-playing game," he told his dad.

"I know what the hell it is," Mac said testily. "You think just because I live in the sticks, I'm not up to speed? Bunch of adolescent misfits go on elaborate make-believe quests. It's all about hiding from reality."

"Actually," Thomas said, "in my case, it's all about sex."

Mac swerved to miss a jackrabbit that darted across the lane in front of them. His square jaw set at a stubborn angle. A muscle jumped in his cheek. He was silent for a ten count, then, "Sex?" he said in a strangled voice that sounded as if he was either about to burst out laughing or break down in tears. Maybe both at once.

Hailey allowed herself a smug little smile.

"See, there's this townie, Lucinda Meriwether," Thomas told his dad, "and she's really into the game."

"Dresses in black from head to toe, I bet," Hailey suggested helpfully.

Thomas shot her a quelling look, and her smug smile blossomed into a mocking grin.

"Don't tell me she's one of those Goth geeks." Mac swore under his breath as he dodged another suicidal bunny.

"Deal," Thomas said. "I won't tell you she's one of those Goth geeks."

"I'm guessing she is, though," Hailey said in the interest of full disclosure.

"Son of a bitch." Mac thumped the steering wheel for emphasis. "I'm shelling out big bucks so you can go to some highfalutin prep school all the way to hell and gone in Connecticut and you waste time dating a damned—"

"Hanging with," Thomas interrupted.

"Excuse me?"

"Not 'dating.' Hanging with. Lucinda considers dating an archaic ritual in which women are manipulated into prostituting themselves in exchange for dinner and a movie."

"Bullshit," Mac said.

Thomas grinned. "Yeah. But she's got the cutest way of curling her lip when she says it—all contemptuous and sexy as hell."

"Hey!" Hailey protested. "In case it slipped your mind, there's a lady in the truck, and I *so* do not want to hear this."

"Sexy as hell, huh?" Mac said.

"Uh-huh."

"I'm not listening." Hailey stuck her fingers in her ears.

"That's my boy."

The minute Mac turned away, Thomas gave her a victorious smirk. Score one for his team.

"Screw you," she mouthed. Unfortunately, Mac turned back around just then. Equally unfortunate was the fact that he was an excellent lip reader.

"Watch your mouth, kiddo. You grow up to talk like a mule skinner and sure as hell your mom'll blame me."

Kennedy hadn't shown up for Thomas's welcome home dinner. He'd called at 6:15 to say he'd been invited to a friend's house. A friend of the female persuasion, Thomas guessed, judging by the crestfallen expression that fell like a shadow across Hailey's face when she heard the news. Still hung up on Kennedy, obviously. Probably even more so now that they were going to the same school.

She'd disappeared after dinner, and he'd thought she'd gone to bed until he headed upstairs himself sometime after 10:00—1:00 in the morning Connecticut time— and found her perched on the top step, still dressed in the same faded jeans and dusty rose shirt she'd worn to school. Scribbling madly in a battered black-and-white composition book, she didn't notice him.

"Hey." He couldn't help smiling. She looked so sweet, so serious. "Thought you were in bed."

"Nope."

"Homework?" he said. "Haven't you heard? It's Christmas break."

She didn't even glance up. "Go away."

"The light's better downstairs," he said, a second or two before he realized that although the light might be better elsewhere, the view of the front door was optimal from her current perch. Kennedy wasn't home yet.

"The light's okay. Besides, it's quieter here." One flyaway strand of silky brown hair had escaped Hailey's ponytail. She shoved it out of her face, then gave him a pointed look. "Or at least it was."

"Is that a hint?"

"Go away, Thomas."

"Hey, you're not the boss of me." He sat down beside her, trying to get a peek at what she'd been writing. Diary? he wondered. Love letter? Christmas list?

She snapped the book shut and turned to him with a glare. "Mind your own business, why don't you?"

Her glasses had slid down to the end of her nose. He nudged them up with the tip of one finger.

A strange expression rippled across her face, gone before he could put a name to it. "What do you want, Thomas?"

You, he thought, surprising himself. Okay, yeah, he'd always liked Hailey. More than liked really, but . . . moss green with sprinkles of cinnamon. That's what color her eyes were. Moss green with long, thick lashes several shades darker than her chestnut brown hair.

"Earth to Thomas," Hailey said, and he realized he'd been staring.

He cleared his throat, feeling foolish. "Want? Me? I don't know. Adventure, I guess." He thought of all the places he'd never been, all the things he'd never seen. "How about you?"

She scowled at him for a moment in silence. "You always do that, darn it."

He shot her a curious sideways glance. "Do what?"

"Go serious on me. I mean, I was all ready to rip into you for interrupting my creative flow, and now I can't because you've effectively short-circuited my oh-so-righteous indignation."

"Are you speaking English? Because I'm not sure I follow."

"You never follow," she said glumly. "You lead."

"Okay, now I know I'm lost. Maybe it's just jet lag, but . . ."

"You're destined for greatness, Thomas MacCormack. Adventure." She heaved a sigh. "Adventure sounds great in the abstract, but I suspect the reality would scare me spitless. I'm not brave like you. What *I* truly want . . ."

She sighed again. ". . . is romance." She passed him her composition book. "See for yourself."

Thomas wasn't sure what he'd expected. Certainly not what he found written neatly in Hailey's perfect penmanship. He read one page, then another and another, not stopping until she poked him sharply with her elbow. "Well?" she said, sounding impatient and maybe a little scared.

He met her gaze. Her glasses had slipped down her nose again. He pushed them back into place, then handed the composition book to her. "Have you shown this to anyone else?"

"You're joking, right? Let people know I spend all my spare time writing fairy tales? Oh, yeah, that's gonna happen. I'd be the laughingstock of Crescentville High."

"But it's good stuff, Hailey. Really good. If you ask me, you're the one destined for greatness."

Her eyes widened. She stared at him.

Had he slipped up? Had she realized he had feelings for her? Not big brother feelings. More like I-want-to-jump-your-bones feelings. *That's why I was so gung-ho to go to school clear across the country,* he thought. *Because as long as he was in Connecticut, he couldn't do anything he'd regret.*

Now maybe if Hailey had been a different sort of girl, a girl like, say . . . Lucinda, they could have hooked up. No harm, no foul. But Hailey was definitely a happily-ever-after girl, and if there was one thing Thomas knew for sure, it was that MacCormacks didn't get happily-ever-afters. Not with the curse hanging over their heads.

Still, oh God, she was so sweet, so tempting, so innocently sexy with that long silky hair, that pouty pink mouth, and that graceful body. Without weighing the consequences, he leaned a little closer.

The front door banged open and Hailey jumped to her feet like a startled fawn. Her composition book flew out of her hands and went tumbling down the staircase to land in the entry at Kennedy's feet. "What have we here?" He bent to retrieve the book. "Lose something, Hail?"

"Give it back!" Hailey raced down the steps, snatched it from his grip, then ran toward the back of the house.

"What's *her* problem?" Kennedy shook his head and a thick lock of blond hair fell across his forehead. He brushed it out of his face and grinned at Thomas. "Hey, bro. I see they finally released you from the prison that is Crichton Academy."

"Yeah." Thomas descended the stairs slowly, not sure whether he was more relieved or disappointed by his brother's interruption.

"Sorry I wasn't here to welcome you home. I trust Hailey made up for my absence, though."

Meaning what? Surely Kennedy hadn't figured out how Thomas felt about her. Hell, Thomas had barely figured out how he felt about her.

Kennedy's laughing gaze met his. "That girl's something, isn't she?"

Thomas's gut tightened painfully.

His brother's grin widened. "Gotta wonder what secrets she's keeping."

"Secrets? Hailey?"

"She won't let anyone read that precious composition

book of hers. Not even her mom. Guards it with her life."

"Really?" The knot in Thomas's midsection relaxed.

Kennedy waggled his eyebrows and gave his brother a knowing smile. "My theory is she's into porn."

"And my theory is you're an asshole."

"The hell you say." Still smiling, Kennedy popped him a good one.

Thomas repaid him with interest, and before long they were rolling around on the floor, throwing insults along with punches. Half-pissed but enjoying every minute of it.

"Hey! Show a little respect!" Their dad glowered at them from the entrance to the living room. "Riggs is trying to decide whether or not to pull the trigger." In the background Thomas could hear the *Lethal Weapon* score.

"You've seen that movie a dozen times," Kennedy said. "You know he's not going to kill himself."

"It's a holiday tradition," their dad insisted.

Some people made gingerbread houses. Some went caroling. Mac MacCormack watched *Lethal Weapon,* his favorite Christmas movie.

Hailey poked her head into the kitchen. Tchaikovsky's *Nutcracker* played softly in the background. Her mom, looking like a teenager in jeans and a T-shirt, her fine, ash brown hair pulled back in a clip, stood at the stove stirring something in a big stainless-steel pot. "What are you making? Do you need any help?"

Her mom glanced up with a smile, her hazel eyes dancing. "Caramels as a surprise for Mac. And no, I've got it covered, but I wouldn't mind a little company. What have you been up to?"

"I was writing until Thomas interrupted me. Then Kennedy came barging in the front door and—"

"He does live here," her mother pointed out. She glanced at the clock on the stove. "Kennedy got home just now? Where's he been all this time?"

"I didn't ask."

"Then why are you scowling?"

"Because I have a pretty good idea." *The prince kissed the comely maiden, unaware that she was really the evil witch in disguise.*

"Cheerleader?" her mom said, which was a little unsettling since she'd never mentioned Trisha to her mom. She was pretty sure Kennedy hadn't, either.

"How'd you guess?"

"Boys like Kennedy always go for the cheerleaders."

Which definitely placed Hailey out of the running. She tried—and failed—to imagine herself jumping up and down and shaking her pom-poms.

"Blonde?" her mom said.

"Very. And blessed with big bazooms." She cast a furtive glance down at her own meager chest.

Her mom must have noticed because the corners of her mouth twitched in a combination of sympathy and amusement. "Don't worry," she said. "I was a late bloomer, too."

Like she hadn't heard that before. And yeah, Hailey knew she probably hadn't hit the pinnacle of sexual allure, but still . . . "I just wish Kennedy would look at me the way he looks at Trisha."

"Trisha. That would be the cheerleader."

Hailey nodded glumly.

"Don't worry," her mom said. "Kennedy appreciates you. If it weren't for your help, he'd be failing physics."

"Big whoop," she said. "Appreciating my brain is not the same as appreciating my girlfriend potential."

Her mom removed the pan from the heat, detached the candy thermometer, stirred in two cups of pecans, then dumped the mixture into a buttered pan to cool. "Want to lick the spoon?"

"Sure." Hailey took the caramel-coated spoon.

"Be careful. It's hot," her mom cautioned as if she were five instead of fifteen.

Hailey tested the caramel with the tip of her tongue. Hot. Very hot. So hot she had to suppress an "ouch." Well worth the pain, though. Her mom made the world's best caramel.

"You said you were writing earlier. How's it going?" Her mom glanced pointedly at the battle-scarred composition book.

Hailey shrugged and took another bite of the no-longer-hot-enough-to-blister-her-tongue candy. "Thomas thought it was good."

Her mother's eyes widened in surprise. "You showed it to Thomas?"

Hailey shrugged again. "He's a writer, too." Plus editor of his school paper. True, he didn't write fiction, but words were words.

"And Thomas thought your story was good?"

" 'Really good.' That's a direct quote."

"Hmm." Her mom nodded, then smiled. "Well then."

Hailey raised her eyebrows. "Well then what?"

Her mom suddenly became very busy at the sink. "Oh, nothing," she said.

Parent speak for "definitely something, but don't bother to ask what because I'm not going to tell you." Hailey sighed. Grown-ups.

Chapter Two

❄ ❄ ❄

Hailey saw little of either Kennedy or Thomas over the weekend. Mac took the boys skiing at Mt. Bachelor both days, which left Hailey and her mom free to complete their Christmas preparations.

On Saturday morning, they'd finished the last of the holiday decorations—fastening a fresh fir wreath to the front door, arranging her mom's prized nutcracker collection on the mantel in the living room, and hanging mistletoe in the archway that led from the living room into the dining room.

In the afternoon, they'd made one last run into Bend for supplies and last-minute gifts. Hailey'd squandered half her hard-earned cash on presents—a new nutcracker to add to her mom's collection, a sweater for Kennedy, chocolate brown to match his eyes, a used but pristine copy of *National Geographic*'s *Images of the World* for Thomas, and for Mac, a copy of *Die Hard,* in hopes that it might replace *Lethal Weapon* as his favorite Christmas movie.

On Sunday after church, they baked the Christmas

pies—pecan, Dutch apple, and banana cream. Actually, Hailey's mom did the mixing, rolling, stirring, and baking while Hailey concentrated her efforts on the tasting and sampling.

She was currently "cleaning" the whipped cream bowl, one finger swipe at a time. "So," she said in between licks, "what do you think Mac got you for Christmas?"

"Who knows?" Her mom shrugged.

Over the past year and a half, the relationship between Mac and her mom had evolved from purely employer-employee to something more. Hailey was fairly certain they weren't sleeping together, but they'd gone out to dinner several times, to the movies, and to a number of events at the high school, including Kennedy's games and her band concerts.

She wasn't sure how Kennedy and Thomas felt about their father dating her mother, but Hailey was definitely in the pro camp. Mac was a good guy, hot-tempered like his sons and a little rough around the edges, but honest and hardworking. By the sweat of his brow, he'd built a small, diverse empire in cattle, quarter horses, and real estate, and though he now had hired men who could have handled all the tedious chores—feeding in winter, irrigating in summer—he still did his share and more.

"What did you get him?" Hailey asked. "Aside from the caramels, I mean."

"A new fly rod he's had his eye on."

"But you have no clue what he might have bought for you?"

"None." Her mom frowned. "Funny thing is, he usually asks me for suggestions. Only this year he didn't."

"That's not a good sign. I'm thinking gift certificate."

Her mom made a face. "Or something nice and practical, like studded snow tires for the Buick."

Thomas hadn't realized how hungry he was until he walked in the front door and smelled baked ham, a Christmas Eve tradition in the MacCormack household ever since Sarah Miller had taken over as housekeeper. Prior to Sarah, his Grandmother Johnson—now happily retired in Arizona—had looked after them. Since Grandma J's idea of the perfect Christmas Eve dinner— or any other dinner, for that matter—was microwave pizza, Sarah's more traditional version had proved a pleasant change.

Kennedy came in right behind Thomas, dropping his gloves on the window seat and tossing his ski jacket at the hall tree. "Is that dinner I smell? Swear to God, I'm hungry enough to eat a horse."

Hailey poked her head through the doorway from the living room. "Sorry. You'll have to settle for a pig." She brushed a swath of silky brown hair back over her shoulder and grinned at them.

"Smart-ass," Kennedy said.

"Smart everything," she assured him.

It had been a long time since Thomas had seen Hailey in a dress and never in a dress like this one. The clingy hunter green fabric hugged her lissome curves and ended well above her knees to reveal a pair of truly spectacular legs.

Damn.

Thomas turned to hang up his coat, afraid that if he didn't look away from Hailey, he'd be tempted to push her glasses back into place. And if he got close enough to do that, he just might decide to kiss those soft pink lips.

Double damn.

"You look nice," Kennedy said, and Thomas was hard put not to smack him just on general principles.

Nice? *Nice?* What kind of flabby compliment was that? Hailey didn't look *nice.* She looked fantastic. He opened his mouth to say so, then shut it again when he saw Hailey's response to Kennedy's half-assed compliment. Her face glowed. No other word for it. And no mistaking the implication. Hailey had the major hots for his brother.

Triple damn.

"Hailey!" Sarah Miller called from the kitchen. "Come stir the gravy."

"You two better go get changed," Hailey said. "Dinner'll be ready in fifteen minutes." She slipped away.

Kennedy stood staring after her, a speculative look on his face.

"What?" Thomas said.

Kennedy pursed his lips for a moment. Then a smile lit his face. "Hailey. She looks nice. Really nice."

"Yeah," Thomas said. He turned abruptly and headed upstairs, afraid if he had to look at Kennedy's smile for two more seconds, he'd be forced to wipe it off with his fists. And if he ruined Christmas Eve dinner, his dad would be majorly pissed.

Fifteen minutes later, he was back downstairs, freshly shaved, his hair damp from the shower. He'd changed his clothes and his attitude. He was going to do his utmost to make sure this was a pleasant evening, dammit, even if it killed him.

I'm dying, Thomas thought half an hour later as he watched Kennedy flirting outrageously with Hailey. What the hell was going on? Hadn't Kennedy told him like a million times this weekend about the cheerleader he was dating? Trina or Tracy or something like that. So what was the jerk doing? Couldn't he see Hailey was hanging on his every word? Was he trying to break her heart or what?

Thomas scowled at his half-eaten dessert.

His dad, looking ruggedly handsome if unusually civilized in a Copenhagen blue cashmere sweater—Sarah's choice, no doubt, since his colorblind father inevitably picked unflattering shades—suddenly tapped his water glass with a fork. The low buzz of conversation died away. Hailey looked startled, Kennedy looked amused, and Sarah looked vaguely apprehensive. Thomas, who'd just told his father about his acceptance at Harvard, figured he knew what was coming.

"May I have your attention, please?" Mac cocked one heavy dark eyebrow. The corner of his mustache twitched. "I want all of you to share in this." He produced a small velvet-covered jewelry box and set it on the table in front of Sarah. "Merry Christmas, sweetheart."

"For me?" Sarah's cheeks went pink, then pale. Her eyes widened.

Mac laughed. "Who the hell else around here would I be calling sweetheart?"

"Watch your language," Sarah scolded.

"He calls me 'kiddo,' " Hailey said.

Kennedy smirked. "And I'm generally 'brain donor.' "

"Kennedy!" Sarah frowned.

"I never called him that," Mac protested.

"I beg to differ," Kennedy said. "Have you forgotten that incident this weekend?"

"Oh, okay, once. One damn time, but you deserved it, hanging off the chairlift like that. Could have killed your fool self."

"And Thomas is . . ." Hailey's sentence trailed off as she got a good look at his face. God only knew what she made of his expression. "Thomas?"

He didn't respond. He couldn't. If he opened his mouth, he'd spew for sure. Dammit, how could his dad do this? What was he thinking?

Sarah's narrow hands shook as she raised the hinged lid of the velvet box. The light of the chandelier sparkled off a large ruby in an intricate gold filigree setting.

Not an engagement ring then, after all. The tightness in Thomas's chest eased a little. His queasy stomach settled down.

"It's beautiful," Sarah said softly.

"Try it on," Mac urged.

When she hesitated, he plucked the ring from the box and slid it on the ring finger of her left hand. "But—" she started.

Mac gathered her hand in his. "Sarah, sweetheart, will you marry me?"

"What?" Hailey, Kennedy, and Thomas chorused.

A beatific smile lit Sarah's face. "Yes."

"Hot damn! Congratulations!" Kennedy said.

Hailey gave an incredulous little laugh. "Wow. My mind is officially blown now."

"No," Thomas said.

"Yes." Hailey laughed again.

Thomas ignored her, focusing instead on his father. "You can't do this. It's not right. You can't marry Sarah."

"What?" Kennedy stared at him as if he'd lost his mind.

Sarah's smile faded. Hailey narrowed her eyes.

His dad shot him a bemused look. "Why the hell not?"

"You know why the hell not. Our mother? Your mother? Your grandmother? The MacCormack family is cursed, the women anyway."

Kennedy rolled his eyes. "And *I'm* the one he calls 'brain donor'?"

"There's no such thing as a family curse, son," his dad said quietly.

Hailey was too wired to sleep. After an hour of tossing and turning, of punching her pillow and tugging at her covers, she finally admitted defeat. Mac had proposed to her mom. She still couldn't believe it. Mac and her mom. Unreal.

And as if that weren't enough to keep her brain buzzing, there was also Kennedy's uncharacteristic behavior. He'd flirted with her. Her. Uncool, four-eyed Hailey Miller.

At first she'd thought she was imagining it, that a look was just a look, a smile just a smile. Only then he'd caught her under the mistletoe. And not only had he kissed her, he'd Frenched her. Major tongue. Which, if she were honest, had pretty much grossed her out, but still, it meant something. According to what she'd read and to the little she'd picked up from snatches of overheard locker-room gossip, a guy didn't French a girl unless he was interested.

Kennedy. Interested in her. Not Trisha the Cheerleader. Her. Whoa.

Hailey sat up, switched on her bedside lamp, and fumbled for her glasses. Normally when she couldn't sleep, she worked on *The One True Princess,* but tonight her thoughts were much too scattered to focus on her fairy tale.

Maybe she should read for a while. Only problem with that was, she'd left her book downstairs in the den, and in order to retrieve it, she'd have to get out of her nice, warm bed. She lay there a few more minutes debating the issue before deciding to brave the cold. Then she tossed back the covers, slid her feet into her fuzzy black-and-white cow slippers, and wrapped the extra quilt around her shoulders for warmth.

Leaving her door open a crack for light, she tiptoed down the third-floor hall to the central staircase. Although the light didn't penetrate this far, she felt safe enough with the railing to guide her. She descended quietly, beckoned forward by the night-light burning in the second-floor hallway.

She paused on the landing, listening hard. She could almost swear she'd heard something—or someone— moving around down there on the first floor. But all was quiet now.

Hailey drew a deep breath. What was she thinking? That burglars had braved the icy roads to drive all the way out here to Devil's Elbow? Not likely. But if not burglars, what?

The princess gathered her magic cloak about her shoul-

ders and prepared to face the dragon she suspected lay lurking in the shadows at the foot of the tower stairs.

Hailey descended cautiously, pausing often to listen for sounds of an intruder. Silly, maybe, but in the darkness her imagination, always in high gear, spun completely out of control. Then just as she stepped off the last stair into the entry, she heard a sound. Unmistakable this time and definitely not her imagination. A sort of rustling.

"Is someone there?" The disembodied voice, too soft to recognize, came from the living room.

"Just me. Hailey." Slowly, she approached the entrance.

"Well, ho-ho-ho and merry Christmas!"

"Kennedy? Is that you?"

"Kennedy? Don't be ridiculous. It's Santa Claus, here to deliver presents for all the good little boys and girls."

She moved farther into the big room. Pale moonlight filtered in the big front windows, illuminating Kennedy's smiling face. She smiled back. "What are you doing?"

"I told you already. Delivering presents for all the good little boys and girls. Or actually, gift certificates." He hid a small white envelope among the branches of the tree, and once again Hailey heard the rustling sound that had first alerted her to his presence. He crossed the room to where she stood. "How about it, Hailey? Have you been a good girl?"

"I'm always a good girl." Stupid thing to say. Stupid, stupid, stupid, but she could scarcely breathe, let alone carry on a rational conversation.

The princess's heart fluttered against her ribs like a caged bird.

"Then you deserve a present, a very special present."
Kennedy moved closer, looming large in the darkness.

Hailey surprised herself by taking a quick step backward.

Kennedy followed, capturing her chin in one hand
and tilting her face up to his. "What's wrong?"

"Nothing. I . . . I just . . . I couldn't sleep. I came down
to get my book."

He inched closer yet. "And why was it, do you suppose, that you had so much trouble falling asleep?"

"I don't know. I always have trouble falling asleep on
the night before Christmas."

"Liar," he said. "You felt it, too, didn't you? That connection between us earlier under the mistletoe."

*The prince's eyes were finally open to the truth. At long
last he recognized the one true princess.*

"I . . . but . . . what about Trisha?"

"Who?" He laughed.

She smiled uncertainly. "She—"

He silenced her with a kiss. And what a kiss—sweet
and seductive. Fairy-tale-come-true and then some.
Locked in Kennedy's arms, Hailey felt as if she were dissolving, all fiery need and liquid heat. Her knees buckled. If he hadn't been holding her, she'd have fallen.

"I want you," he whispered.

And the prince declared his undying love.

"But—"

"Shh." He picked her up, cow slippers, quilt, and all,
and carried her through the archway into the dining
room, then through the kitchen, and out the mudroom
door.

"Where are you—?"

"Shh," he said again.

Despite two inches of fresh snow, he strode sure-footed along the brick path that wound its way among the pines behind the house, toward the enclosed gazebo at the top of the yard. Decorated with Christmas lights, it looked like something out of a fairy tale—at least from the outside.

Inside the large octagonal room, benches edged the screened walls, and cedar decking surrounded a hot tub.

Kennedy lowered her to a bench, removed the tub cover, and then flipped the switches that controlled the jets and underwater lights. "Ever been hot-tubbing in the middle of the night?" he said. "It's the ultimate in decadence."

"I didn't bring my suit."

He shot her a wicked grin. "Like I said, the ultimate in decadence."

Hailey gave a nervous little giggle. Surely he didn't expect her to strip naked. . . .

Oops. Apparently he did. At any rate, that's what *he* was doing, and thanks to the light reflecting up from the pool, she was getting a pretty good eyeful. Hailey drew a shaky breath. With broad shoulders, narrow hips, and long, muscular limbs, Kennedy's body was perfect in every detail. *The prince might have been a Greek statue come to life.* Hailey tried not to stare, but she'd never seen a naked male before and she found the sight fascinating. Fascinating and scary.

Kennedy turned to her then with a devilish smile, as if he knew she'd been watching his every move.

From the back he'd looked like a Greek statue, but

from the front . . . Hailey swallowed hard. Greek statues didn't sport erections. At least not the ones she'd seen.

She took a deep breath and told herself there was no reason to feel threatened, but darn it, he looked huge. Scary huge.

"Your turn," Kennedy said.

Okay, she could do this. She could.

Or not.

She managed to shrug off the quilt, but when she tried to stand, her legs refused to cooperate.

"What's wrong?" Kennedy said. "Need some help?" He closed the distance between them and suddenly she couldn't breathe, let alone undress herself.

Kennedy dropped to his knees in front of her.

The prince knelt at the princess's feet.

"Don't be nervous," he said. He captured her face between his hands and tilted her head so their mouths fit together perfectly. Then he kissed her, sucking gently at her lower lip until her embarrassment disappeared, swallowed up in a red haze of wanting.

She didn't protest when Kennedy removed her slippers and tucked them side-by-side under the bench. She didn't say a word when he stripped her tank top over her head, exposing her bare breasts to the cold night air. She didn't even make a sound when he pressed kisses to her puckered nipples.

But when he pulled her to her feet and started to peel away her pajama bottoms, she couldn't suppress a mew of protest.

"Hey," he said softly. "What's wrong?"

"We shouldn't be doing this. *I* shouldn't be doing this."

"Doing what?" he said. "Hot-tubbing? What's wrong with that?"

"What if someone sees?"

"It's the middle of the night. Who's going to see? Except me, of course. And you don't hear me complaining, do you?"

"No, but—"

"Who's there?" someone called from outside.

"Oh, shit," Kennedy said.

Thomas's first thought upon hearing voices from the gazebo was that Zeke and Cory Hatcher, the hired man's eleven-and twelve-year-old sons, were sneaking a smoke. He'd caught them hiding out in the gazebo doing just that several times last summer.

His second thought was that maybe Sarah and his dad were enjoying a little alone time, maybe celebrating their engagement with a bottle of champagne. Not that Sarah had much to celebrate. Any woman who married a MacCormack was living on borrowed time.

But the one thing he didn't expect to see in the eerie turquoise glow of the hot tub's underwater lights was Kennedy, bare-assed naked and pressed up against Hailey. "What the hell are you doing?" Thomas yelled.

Kennedy smirked. "What does it look like, genius?"

Thomas switched on the overhead lights and Hailey cringed away, turning three shades of embarrassed. "Thomas, I . . . we . . ." Her voice trailed off. Arms folded protectively across her chest, she huddled in silence, obviously miserable and mortified.

The pain took him by surprise. Hailey and Kennedy? God, that hurt.

Not that he blamed her. She was young and curious. Plus she'd had a crush on his brother since forever.

But Kennedy? What was his excuse? All he'd done all weekend was talk nonstop about his new cheerleader girlfriend. That didn't translate to "I'm crazy in love with Hailey" in Thomas's book. "You're not even wearing a condom," he said.

"But we weren't—" Hailey started.

Kennedy shrugged. "It was a kind of spur-of-the-moment thing."

Spur of the moment? What sort of lame excuse was that? He turned on Kennedy with a snarl. "You selfish bastard." Thomas tossed Hailey her quilt without once taking his eyes off his twin.

Hailey wrapped herself in the comforting folds of the quilt, wriggled her feet into her slippers, and headed for the door.

"What the hell . . . ?" she heard Kennedy say and turned just in time to see Thomas's fist split his brother's lip.

"Thomas, no! It was my fault as much as his."

"The hell it was." Thomas's gaze seared hers. "Get out of here," he said, then hit Kennedy again, hard enough to send him staggering backward into the hot tub. Thomas jumped in, too, clothes and all.

Embarrassed, ashamed, and wracked with guilt, Hailey turned again toward the door. All she wanted to do was race back to the house, bury her head under her pillow, and pretend none of this had ever happened.

"Damn you!" Thomas said behind her. At least she thought it was Thomas. He and Kennedy sounded so much alike, it was hard to be sure. "How could you do this to her?" Yes, definitely Thomas.

"Hailey was a willing participant," Kennedy said.

"You took advantage of a childish crush."

"Have you looked at her lately? She's no child."

"Son of a bitch." More smacking, thudding, splashing, and thrashing noises ensued, all of which Hailey ignored as she slipped out of the gazebo.

"So I planned to have sex with her. Big deal," she heard Kennedy say as she eased the door shut. "It's not like it counted. I mean, I was only practicing."

Hailey froze.

"Practicing?" Thomas's voice was as cold as the breeze rustling through the pines.

"Yeah, so when Trisha and I finally get it on, I won't look like an amateur."

Kennedy's careless words shattered her. Hurt, confused, and humiliated, she ran for the safety of her room.

Part II

" . . . you just might get it."

Chapter Three

❄ ❄ ❄

The present

Kira Jackson came to a dead stop in front of Hailey's retro-chic aluminum Christmas tree. Hailey fully expected her friend to say something scathing. After all, Kira, an interior designer, had some definite ideas about what was and what wasn't stylish. But all she did was shudder slightly and then close her eyes for a second, as if the sight of all that blatant artificiality made her faintly ill. Okay, maybe the plastic icicles and Styrofoam candy canes were a bit much, but . . .

Kira raked her hands back through her short strawberry blond hair. Surprisingly, though, the first words out of her mouth had nothing to do with Hailey's holiday decorations. "What did your stepfather say when you told him you weren't coming home for Christmas?"

"Not much." But oh, those silences.

Kira plopped down on one end of the sofa. "He probably expected it. I mean, with your mother gone . . ."

Hailey stared out across the rooftops of San Francisco

stair-stepping down the hill. On fogless days, she could sometimes catch a glimpse of the bay. "Dead," she said. "Mom's not gone. She's dead."

Almost two months now. Her mom had tried so hard to make it to Christmas, but by mid-October the cancer had gotten the upper hand. Hailey hadn't thought she could face Christmas at Devil's Elbow without her mother. That's why she'd agreed so readily when Kira had suggested the trip to Maui. Palm trees and poi had seemed like the perfect antidote to grief. Only now she wasn't so sure Hawaii was the best option.

She turned back to face Kira and saw that her friend's brown eyes were full of sympathy. Big old cow eyes of sympathy. Well-meant but . . . *I am not going to cry. I refuse to cry. I am totally cried out.*

"Hailey?"

Think about something else, she told herself. *Something unsad. Better yet, something annoying. Something like the twins.* "Thomas and Kennedy aren't going to make it home, either," Hailey said, "and Mac's really disappointed. He didn't say a whole lot, but I could tell."

The sympathy faded from Kira's expression. "They didn't attend your mother's funeral, either, as I recall."

"Kennedy did. Thomas was in Somalia. Last time he made it home to Devil's Elbow was a year ago Christmas."

"But he and his brother aren't going to be there this year. Why not?"

"Kennedy's making a film in St. Croix, and the network sent Thomas to Iraq."

"Iraq?" Kira gave an involuntary shiver.

"Thomas doesn't mind," Hailey said. "He thrives on

danger." Unlike her. Hailey crossed to the sofa and settled at the end opposite Kira.

"You introduced me to Kennedy last year when he was in town working on *The Golden Gate Massacre,* but I've never met his brother." Kira smiled and leaned a little closer. "Tell me, is Thomas MacCormack as gorgeous in person as he is on TV?"

"Gorgeous? Thomas? Most people consider Kennedy the gorgeous one."

Kira nodded in agreement. "And doesn't he just know it?"

Yes, Kennedy did have enough ego for a family of four, but an actor needed all the self-confidence he could muster in order to survive in Hollywood.

"Thomas is quite the hottie, too, though, don't you think? Very tough and edgy," Kira said.

Tough and edgy? Yes, definitely. Not to mention smart and sexy and totally ripped. Also, unfortunately, forever beyond her reach.

Ten years after the fact, Hailey could pinpoint the precise moment she'd fallen in love with Thomas. They'd been sitting on the stairs at Devil's Elbow, squabbling about something unimportant. Her glasses had slid down her nose and Thomas had reached out and nudged them back into place. Suddenly she'd been hyperaware of his every move, his every expression. And her instincts had said, "This is the one." Unfortunately, the hormones fueling her infatuation with Kennedy had drowned them out.

Not that it would have made any difference in the long run.

Hailey wanted the same thing she'd always wanted—

romance. Someone to love, someone to love her back, someone willing to work with her on the happily-ever-after part. But Thomas, as much as she might wish otherwise, wasn't that someone. He still believed in the MacCormack curse, a belief her mother's death had only reinforced. He had sworn never to marry, never to damn a woman with the MacCormack name.

And so with her Prince Charming off-limits, Hailey had looked elsewhere for romance. Once she'd even thought she'd found it. She and local radio talk show host Nick Simitzes had been engaged for almost two weeks before she'd overheard someone comment on Nick's resemblance to network correspondent Thomas MacCormack. Belatedly realizing what she'd done, she'd returned Nick's ring. Since then, she'd been more careful.

". . . unless you're not into that sort of thing," Kira said.

"Not really," Hailey responded, though the truth was, she didn't have a clue what Kira was talking about. "The point is," she said, dragging the conversation back on track, "with the twins out of the country, Mac's going to be all alone for Christmas."

"That's not good," Kira said. Then it dawned on her what Hailey was getting at. She frowned. "You're backing out on the *mele Kalikimaka* thing."

"Sorry," Hailey said. "I'd much rather go to Maui, but . . ."

"Well, hell," Kira said. "I was really looking forward to some serious beach time. I had this whole elaborate fantasy worked out involving me, a couple of long-haired surfers, and a bottle of coconut-scented tanning oil."

"Just because I'm backing out doesn't mean you can't go."

"Rattle around in that big empty condo all alone? No, thanks."

"Alone? What about your parents?"

Kira's eyebrows rose in an inverted V. "Didn't I tell you? My sister Monique, the one who's married to Sergio, the Brazilian soccer player, invited Mom and Dad to spend the holidays at their place in Rio de Janeiro."

"So why don't you go to Rio, too? I hear the beaches there are fantastic."

"My passport's expired," Kira said, "and I don't feel like shelling out big bucks to expedite the paperwork on a new one."

"Then come to Oregon with me. No surfers in Deschutes County last time I checked, but I'm sure we could scare up a few suitably hunky ski bums."

"Ski bums?"

"Hunky ski bums."

Kira grinned. "Sold." Then slowly, her grin changed to a puzzled expression as she stared fixedly in the direction of the Christmas tree. "All right, that butt-ugly scrap-metal tree is bad enough, but what's with the box underneath? Don't tell me you've decided to trade wrapping paper for ratty brown corrugated cardboard?"

Meaning what? Hailey followed Kira's gaze to the battered shipping box she'd stuffed out of the way under the tree an hour ago. "Oh, I'd forgotten about that. It was waiting outside the door when I got home." She crossed the room to retrieve the package. "The latest volume of the *One True Princess* series comes out next month. I assumed the box held my author copies. Only maybe not." She squinted at the label. "I can't read the return address and the stamps look weird."

"Maybe it's a foreign edition. Do they print the princess books in any languages other than English?"

Hailey frowned. "Not that I know of. Besides, the package seems too light for books." She set it on the coffee table, then headed for the kitchen.

Kira followed. "So it's a surprise," she said. "I love surprises."

"Whereas I hate them." Hailey sighed. "When I was a kid, Thomas and Kennedy were forever 'surprising' me with rubber spiders in my bed and gummy worms in my potato salad."

"Typical sick male humor." Kira, cursed with three older brothers, spoke from experience. "Got anything to drink?"

"Cokes and stuff in the refrigerator. Help yourself." Hailey dug the box cutter out of the junk drawer, then returned to the living room, where she cut through the packing tape and opened the flaps. Inside, nestled in shredded paper, lay a brass oil lamp inscribed with ornate Arabic lettering.

Kira wandered back into the room, a Diet Dr Pepper in hand. She peered over Hailey's shoulder. "Hey, it's an Aladdin's lamp. Did you order an Aladdin's lamp?"

"No, it must be an early Christmas present. The question is, from whom?"

"From Thomas?" Kira guessed. "Didn't you just tell me he's on assignment in Iraq?"

"Yes, Baghdad," Hailey said. She picked up the lamp and cradled it in her hands. It felt slightly warm, as if it had somehow retained a little of the desert's warmth. Or a little of Thomas's warmth.

"Rub it and make a wish," Kira said. "Isn't that how it works?"

"Only in fairy tales."

"So? Aren't you the one who makes a living writing fairy tales for preteens?"

"Yes, but—"

Kira waved aside her half-formed objection. "What's it going to hurt to give it a shot?"

"Nothing, but—"

"Then what are you waiting for?"

Hailey shrugged. "I don't know what to wish for."

"Ten million dollars would be nice."

"Too cliché. Everyone wishes for money."

"How about a Prince Charming to take you away from all this?"

"I like all this." Hailey spread her arms to encompass her elegant high-ceilinged apartment and the spectacular view of the city beyond her living room windows. "Besides, at twenty-five, I'm too old and jaded to believe in Prince Charming."

"Then wish me up a gorgeous, long-haired ski bum. Two gorgeous, long-haired ski bums. Blonds. Big, husky Swedes named Sven and Lars."

"Forget it. I'm not wasting my hypothetical wishes on boy toys."

Kira stuck out her tongue. "Okay, *be* that way." Her smile faded, to be replaced by a more thoughtful expression. "Seriously, though, if you could have anything you wanted, what would you wish for?"

Hailey's lighthearted mood wilted. "To wake up and find that my mom hadn't really died after all."

"Sorry," Kira said, looking guilt-stricken. "I didn't mean to remind you."

"Not your fault." Hailey blinked away tears. "The past couple months have been hard for me, but Mac . . ." She sighed. "I can't even imagine how difficult a time he's had. I think . . . I'm pretty sure he blames himself."

"Why? Your mom died of cancer, didn't she? How is that his fault?"

"The thing is, MacCormack wives never last long. Mac's mother died in a plane crash when he was small, and both his grandmother and his first wife died in childbirth. Thomas claims the family's cursed. He pitched a fit when Mac proposed to Mom. Said marrying her was as good as issuing a death sentence."

"But they were married, what? Ten years?"

"Nine," Hailey said.

"That's one slow-acting curse. *You* don't believe it, do you?"

"No, of course not, but . . ." She fell silent for a moment, thinking furiously. "I know what to wish for," she said at length. "I'll ask for something that will make Mac happy." She held the brass lamp in her lap and rubbed it slowly between her hands. Weird the way the metal felt so warm, almost as if it were alive.

She took a deep breath and closed her eyes. Silly, maybe, but if she was going to do this, she was going to do it right. "Genie of the lamp, hear me. I wish Kennedy and Thomas would surprise Mac by coming home for Christmas after all." She opened her eyes and turned to Kira. "There. Are you satisfied now?"

Kira stared at her, wide-eyed.

"What?"

Kira blinked. "Nothing," she said. "For a second, I thought . . ." She shook her head. "No, it was nothing. Just my imagination."

Hailey set the lamp on the coffee table. "*What* was just your imagination?"

Kira shot her a semiembarrassed grin. "It's dumb. Really. When you made your wish, I thought I saw something come out of the lamp."

Hailey laughed. "You mean like a genie?"

"No, like sparkles. Or fairy dust or something." She gave a little spurt of self-deprecating laughter. "Trust me, I know exactly how stupid that sounds."

"So what's the real explanation? Power of suggestion?" Hailey said.

"Must have been," Kira agreed.

Hailey's lemon of a rental car chugged up the last rise, and the ranch house came into view. But the "ta-da!" she'd been about to utter changed to a muttered "oh, no!" as she took in the signs of neglect. Frost-killed flower corpses littered the flower beds. Dead geraniums dangled from the hanging planters lining the verandah. Dry weeds encroached upon the driveway. Matted brown leaves covered the walk. "Home sweet home," she said.

"Geez, no wonder your stepdad's depressed," Kira said. "Talk about dreary. But hey, no fear. Wonder girl decorator's here. I'll have this place looking like Christmas central before you can say Donner and Blitzen."

"Donner and Blitzen," Hailey said.

Kira cocked her eyebrow in a disgusted look. "A slight exaggeration, okay?"

Hailey had to forgo the pleasure of further baiting her friend when the front door burst open and Mac came barreling out. The minute she stepped out of the car, he enveloped her in an exuberant bear hug that surprised her a little. Where was the sad, depressed shell of a man she'd spoken with on the phone last week?

He released her finally. "Good to see you, kiddo!" he said, beaming from ear to ear. "You'll never guess what's happened."

"You won the Megabucks jackpot."

"Better," he said. "Kennedy and Thomas are going to make it home for the holidays after all. They're both scheduled to fly in tomorrow."

"But I thought . . ."

"So did I," he said. "So did they. Funny how fate works sometimes, isn't it?"

"Funny." Kira's eyes twinkled. "Almost like a wish come true."

Hailey tied off the end of the evergreen swag she'd just draped across the verandah's rustic log railing. "How does that look?"

Kira, who stood ankle deep in the snow that had fallen overnight, frowned in concentration, her head cocked to the side as she studied Hailey's handiwork. "Needs something."

"Big red bows?"

"Nothing that blatant. I'm thinking pinecones."

Hailey glanced at her watch. If both flights had come in on time, Mac and the twins should be here soon. Hailey wasn't sure how she felt about seeing Thomas again after so long. Was she over him? She felt as if she were over him. Sort of. Maybe. But being thrust into close proximity again might reawaken old feelings.

"Or maybe clumps of berries," Kira said. "Red berries."

"Sure. Whatever." Hailey stood, brushing off the knees of her jeans. "While you're deciding, I'm going to check on my pies." Determined to make this a Christmas in the true Sarah Miller MacCormack tradition, she had been baking on and off all day—in between bouts of worrying about the upcoming meeting with Thomas and helping Kira with the decorations.

Thanks to Kira and Hailey's combined efforts and a little intercession from Mother Nature, the ranch house looked considerably more welcoming than it had when they'd arrived yesterday. They'd laid the dead geraniums to rest in the mulch pile, and the timely snowfall had buried the weeds. A creative application of Christmas lights and greenery had done the rest.

"Pinecones," Kira decided, "and some little gold sleigh bells."

"The ranch is pinecone central, but good luck on the sleigh bells."

"No problem. I'll pick up some in Bend when we go in to buy the last-minute groceries."

Mac had lots of staples on hand, but not all the special ingredients Hailey would need for the big holiday meals. No ham or turkey. No yams or celery or whipping cream.

"Which reminds me," Kira said. "Add eggnog to the master list, would you? It's not Christmas without eggnog."

"Mac and the boys don't like eggnog."

"I do," Kira said. "They're not the only ones whose Christmas traditions matter, you know." She paused, her head cocked to one side. "Speak of the devil . . . or is that devils, plural?"

Hailey hesitated, her hand on the doorknob, a sudden lump in her throat. The sound of an approaching engine heralded the appearance of Mac's big V-10.

"Planes must have come in on time after all," Kira said. "Funny, isn't it, how you wished the twins would make it home for Christmas and abracadabra, here they are?"

"Coincidence," Hailey said.

"You sure?" Kira joined her on the verandah.

"Positive." But Hailey spoke with a good deal more conviction than she felt.

Mac gave them a half dozen hey-we're-here beeps on the horn as he rumbled over the last cattle guard, then pulled up in front of the house with a flourish. The pickup doors opened and a veritable army of large men poured out. Or at least that was Hailey's initial impression. The army soon resolved itself into the three Mac-Cormacks; Hailey had forgotten how very much larger-than-life the twins were.

Kira sighed. "The man's got flair; I'll give him that."

Hailey thought Kira was referring to Mac's flamboyant driving style until she realized her friend wasn't gazing in Mac's direction. Apparently it was Kennedy, looking hunky and Hollywood, who'd snared her attention. He'd emerged from the passenger side and stood rolling the kinks out of his shoulders. Immune though Hailey now was to his charm, she had to admit the man was heart-stoppingly gorgeous—even with beard stubble. But . . . "Flair?" Hailey said sotto voce.

"The cane."

Cane? What was Kira talking about? And then Hailey spotted Thomas. He stood at the back end of the pickup, balancing awkwardly on a candy-striped cane as he fought the lock on the pickup's camper shell.

Mac noticed, too, and hurried back to help. "Let me get that, son."

It had to be a joke, right? A gag. Because why would Thomas need a cane? "Want some help?" she called.

"I think we've got it under control." Mac handed a couple of black leather cases to Kennedy, who'd wandered around to the back end. Then her stepfather shouldered an olive drab duffle and shut the camper shell.

"I can carry it myself," Thomas said. "My arms aren't broken."

"Neither are mine." Mac led the way up the steps to the verandah.

Kennedy followed him. Thomas, limping heavily, brought up the rear.

"Place looks great," Mac told Kira, who beamed at the praise.

"Thanks." Still smiling, she turned to the twins. "I'm Kira."

"Best friend and decorator extraordinaire," Hailey added. "I introduced the two of you on the set of *The Golden Gate Massacre*," she reminded Kennedy.

"Of course. I remember," he said, turning the full force of his charm on Kira.

She met his enthusiasm with a bland smile that said, "Don't waste your time, buddy. I've got your number."

"And this is Thomas," Hailey said. Up close she could see the bruise on his left cheekbone and the bandage above his left eyebrow.

"Hi, Thomas." Kira greeted him with a good deal more enthusiasm than she'd afforded Kennedy.

"What happened?" Hailey asked, trying to make the question sound casual, not as freaked-out worried as she felt.

"Damn suicide bomber." Mac looked grim.

"I was half a block from the blast," Thomas explained. "The explosion knocked me off my feet. Some debris fell on me—"

"Debris, my ass. More like a whole damn building," Mac interrupted.

Thomas ignored him. "I ended up with cuts, bruises, and a sprained ankle. Nothing serious."

"Be careful what you wish for," Kira whispered in Hailey's ear.

Hailey shot her a dirty look. She wasn't responsible for this. No way.

Mac opened the front door and ushered everyone inside.

Kennedy breathed deeply of the cinnamon-scented air. "Smells like Christmas."

"My pies!" Hailey sprinted for the kitchen.

"Since when does Hailey cook?" She heard Kennedy's amused query as she hustled down the hall.

Since my mom's not around, she thought sadly. Her eyes filled with tears, not just for her mom, but for Thomas, too. Nothing serious, he'd said, but she could tell by the way he held himself that he was in pain, his face pinched with it, the lines around his mouth and between his brows more pronounced than usual. *Ah, Thomas, what have I done?*

Nothing. She'd done nothing. Wished on a silly lamp. That was all. And just because her wish came true didn't mean a thing. Coincidence. It was all some huge cosmic coincidence.

She'd just opened the oven door to check the pies when Thomas hobbled into the kitchen, dwarfing the room with his presence. "Anything to eat around here?"

"Dinner's in two hours," Hailey managed to say, a miracle in itself since she was having a hard time just breathing.

Thomas smiled and all the barricades she'd built so carefully around her heart came tumbling down. "I'll die of starvation before that. All I've had to eat today is peanuts, pretzels, and a candy bar I bought in the airport. One of the airports. Not sure which one." He settled awkwardly on a barstool, hooking his cane over the top of the backrest.

"How about a sandwich? Would that hold you? Roast beef okay?"

"Perfect."

Hailey turned to dig the sandwich fixings out of the refrigerator, glad for an excuse to escape his penetrating gray-blue gaze. Why did he have to look so handsome, so sexy? Why couldn't he have lost his hair and developed a potbelly?

"You doing all right?" Thomas asked softly.

"What?" She spun around to face him.

"When I first came in, it looked as if you'd been crying, and I thought maybe being here . . . especially at this time of year . . . reminded you of Sarah."

"It's okay," she said. "Not as bad as I expected. I . . ." She paused. "Originally I planned to go to Maui. To get away, you know? Only then Mac told me you and Kennedy weren't going to be able to make it home, and . . ."

"And you worried about leaving Dad alone." The tenderness of his smile nearly proved her undoing.

"Mustard?" she said in an effort to steer the conversation back to the mundane.

"And horseradish, if there is any." He fell silent, but she could feel him staring.

She kept her gaze fixed on the sandwich she was assembling.

"When does your next book come out?" he asked.

She glanced up, making eye contact. God, he was gorgeous with that thick dark hair and that stubborn chin and that damnably sensuous lower lip. Even weary and battle-scarred, he was still her prince. "The end of January," she said, trying to sound as casual as he did.

"Another *One True Princess* story?"

She nodded, pleased that he'd remembered. "Last of the series. Right now I'm working on something new. *Cormac, the Adventurer* is the working title. It's about . . ." You, she almost said. "About a brave young boy determined to find out what lies beyond the tallest mountains, beneath the deepest seas."

"I can relate," Thomas said. But judging by his expression, he hadn't made the obvious connection: Hailey has made you the hero of her new series because Hailey has a major thing for you.

She passed him his sandwich. "Want some chips with that? We've got fruit, too. Apple? Orange? Banana?"

Thomas watched her face so closely that Hailey grew uncomfortable. She hadn't said any of that "you're my new hero" stuff out loud, had she?

"No thanks," Thomas said after a while, "but I wouldn't turn down a glass of milk."

"Moo juice, it is." Gratefully, she turned away to rummage through the cupboard for a glass.

"Hey, unfair! Quit hogging all the grub, bro. I'm hungry, too," Kennedy said from the doorway.

Hailey filled Thomas's glass, set it on the counter, then turned to Kennedy. "Roast beef okay?" What was she? A short-order cook?

"Roast beef, hell," he said, setting his legendary charm on stun. "What I really want is some of that apple pie I smelled when I first walked in."

"Not done yet," she said. "Besides, it's for dinner."

"Bummer."

"Bummer?" She smiled. "You sound like an eighties surfer dude."

"I'm playing an eighties surfer dude." His smile faded. "Correction. I *was* playing an eighties surfer dude. Or rather an eighties scuba diver dude who runs afoul of some smugglers."

"What happened?" she asked.

He looked grim, displaying no trace of his usual charm. "The bastards fired me is what happened."

"You're kidding. Why?"

He scowled off into the distance. "Production delays and budget overruns. I missed one too many early morning calls." The scowl deepened. "They say I've got a drinking problem, and until I get it under control . . ." He squared his shoulders in a stubborn mannerism she recognized. She'd seen him do the same thing times without number just before sinking a free throw. When Kennedy made up his mind . . . "I haven't had any alcohol in five days."

"Five days?" she said.

"Not a single drop since they axed me."

Five days, Hailey thought. She'd made her wish five days ago.

"Five days, huh?" Thomas frowned. "Maybe it's true what they say about twins being linked. Factoring in the time-zone difference, five days ago is when I had my thank-God-not-so-close encounter with the suicide bomber."

Coincidence, she told herself. Pure coincidence.

But before she had a chance to worry herself sick, Kira poked her head in the room. "So this is where you've all got to. Family reunion? Or is anyone welcome?"

"Join the party," Kennedy said. "Any more of the hard stuff, Hail?"

"I thought you'd given up drinking."

"Milk, he means," Thomas said.

"Whole milk," Kennedy clarified. "None of that namby-pamby one-percent garbage."

Mac strode into the kitchen. "So this is where you boys are. I might have known." He glanced around, a big happy grin on his face. "Just like old times."

Except Hailey was a pretty poor substitute for her mom. She set Kennedy's milk on the counter.

"Got any cookies?" he asked.

"You were right," Kira said as Hailey filled a tray with iced sugar cookies. "I thought pie *and* cookies was overkill, but I see now you knew what you were doing."

Kennedy helped himself to a couple of Christmas trees and a star. "Just like Sarah used to make."

"Used to." Two of the saddest words in the English language, Hailey thought.

She caught Thomas's sudden frown out of the corner of her eye, but she wasn't sure what it meant. Did he think she was wrong to try to replicate a Sarah-style Christmas? Or was he just irritated with Kennedy for hogging the cookies?

"Now if only we had eggnog," Kira said, "my holiday would be complete."

"Eggnog?" Mac, Thomas, and Kennedy chorused, looking mildly revolted.

Hailey retreated to her room a little after 10:00. The others were engrossed in *Die Hard,* Mac's second-favorite Christmas movie. But tradition notwithstanding, Hailey decided she needed a long soak in the tub more than she needed to watch Bruce Willis lock horns with Alan Rickman for the umpteenth time.

She'd just emerged from the bathroom, wearing a pink silk robe and flip-flops, when someone knocked on her bedroom door. "Come in," she said, expecting Kira, only of course it wasn't.

The door swung open to reveal Thomas, who looked as surprised as she felt. Maybe he'd forgotten how godawful she looked with wet hair and no makeup.

He, of course, looked gorgeous. The scrapes and cuts only emphasized his rakish good looks.

"Did you need something?" Embarrassed at being

caught at a disadvantage, Hailey spoke a little more abruptly than she'd meant to.

A slight frown creased Thomas's brow. "I saw the light along the crack under your door and assumed you were still up."

"I am still up."

"Dressed, I mean." His gaze drifted down her body, then slowly back up to her face.

"I'm dressed."

She wasn't sure how to interpret the look in his eyes. "In regular clothes," he said, his voice husky, "not going-to-bed clothes."

Clothes he was carefully not looking at. Did she look that horrible? Hailey shot a furtive glance down and immediately saw the problem. Her still-damp nipples were clearly outlined beneath the thin fabric. She might as well have been standing there naked. Damn.

Trying to be casual about it, she grabbed a crocheted afghan off the end of the bed and wrapped it around her shoulders. "Chilly in here."

"Yeah, I noticed," he said with a crooked smile.

Her cheeks grew warm and that irritated her. What was it about Devil's Elbow? Whenever she stepped through the front door, she immediately reverted to an awkward teenager. "What do you want, Thomas?"

"An aspirin?"

An aspirin. Well, what had she expected him to say? You? I want you, Hailey?

"I think I have some in my toiletries bag," she told him and retreated to the bathroom. She dug a miniature aspirin bottle from the side pocket of her bag. "Found 'em," she called, then turned to find Thomas standing right behind her, so close that she bumped into him, knocking him off balance. He staggered and grabbed at the shower curtain with his free hand. It held for a second, then ripped free.

"Whoops," he said, landing on the edge of the tub with more thump than grace.

"Are you all right?"

"The only thing hurt is my dignity. Who is this klutz? And what did he do with the real Thomas MacCormack?" His mouth curved in a rueful smile.

She studied him closely. "You're sure you're all right?"

He nodded. "Aside from a headache, which is why I came looking for an aspirin in the first place."

She handed him a couple of tablets. "If you don't mind drinking out of my glass—"

"Don't need water." He proved it by dry-swallowing the pills in two big gulps.

Hailey felt like gagging just watching him. "How anybody can do that . . ."

Thomas grinned. "One of my many talents." Using his cane for balance, he stood. "Thanks."

They stared at each other in silence. Then slowly, slowly Thomas leaned forward.

He's going to kiss me, Hailey thought, her heart rate accelerating.

And he did kiss her, just not on the mouth. His lips brushed her forehead instead in a brotherly salute that nonetheless sparked some extremely unsisterly physical responses.

Oh God. She was such an idiot. "Thomas?"

"Hmm?" He stared down at her, the expression in his smoky blue-flecked eyes unreadable.

"Nothing," she said. "Just . . . if those aspirin don't do it for you, we can try something else."

Thomas glanced at the alarm clock on his bedside table. Seventeen minutes after one, which was a whole ten minutes later than the last time he'd looked. His headache had dulled to a faint throbbing, but he still couldn't sleep.

If those aspirin don't do it for you, we can try something else. Hell, Thomas wouldn't mind trying a whole *Kama Sutra*'s worth of something elses with Hailey.

Hailey. Sweet, sexy Hailey. Brave as a lion and vulnerable as a kitten. With those soft pink lips and those big green eyes and that clean, soapy, just-out-of-the-shower scent, she was the perfect antidote to all the ugliness he'd seen in Baghdad.

He'd been in love with her for years, and if he was reading her right, she wasn't exactly indifferent to him. But he couldn't marry her. Marriage to a MacCormack was as good as a death sentence.

Which didn't mean he couldn't have sex with her, provided she was willing. Only if he used her that way, was he really any better than Kennedy?

No.

Unfortunately, that didn't stop him from wanting her.

Oh man, he was screwed. He was so damn screwed.

Chapter Four

Hailey was irritated with Kennedy and trying not to show it. He'd insisted on accompanying her and Kira on their last-minute shopping trip to Bend even though she'd all but begged him not to, and now, just as she'd feared, the excursion was taking twice as long as it should have because everywhere they went, Kennedy was mobbed by hordes of adoring fans.

"Should have worn a disguise, I guess," he said when they finally managed to escape from the mall. But Hailey could tell the conceited jerk was enjoying every second of adulation.

"Wear my sunglasses," Kira suggested once they were back in the lemon on their way to Barnes & Noble, the next stop on their itinerary.

"Your sunglasses have rhinestones on them," Kennedy objected.

"Bling is very in," Kira told him, straight-faced. She passed him the sunglasses.

Kennedy tried them on, then craned his neck, trying

to see his reflection in the rearview mirror. "I don't know," he said.

Hailey and Kira exchanged smirks.

"It's a trendsetting look," Kira said. "Hollywood anonymous."

"Now there's an oxymoron." Kennedy grimaced. "Nobody wants to be anonymous in Hollywood." He handed Kira her shades. "Thanks, but no thanks," he said. "Too girly. Besides, is signing a few autographs going to kill me?"

No, but I might, Hailey thought later as she was trying—unsuccessfully—to extricate him from a throng of admirers. She'd already paid for the DVD she'd come in for, a stocking stuffer for Mac. It was time to head for Safeway, dammit. Otherwise, they were doomed to microwave pizza for Christmas Eve instead of the traditional ham.

"He's driving me crazy," she complained to Kira.

"Hey, don't blame me. You're the one who conjured him up."

"I did no such thing."

"Okay, to be precise, you wished him up."

Hailey stared at her friend. "You don't honestly believe that!"

Kira shrugged. "I don't know, but if I were the one with the lamp, I'd be careful what I wished for. If there's a genie inside—and I'm not saying there is—but *if* there is, he's one twisted little rascal. I mean, all you did was wish that the twins would make it home for Christmas. You were trying to do something nice for your stepfather, and what happens? They make it home, all right, but not under the happiest circumstances. Kennedy gets fired—and for all we know, blacklisted—and Thomas nearly gets blown up."

"Coincidence," Hailey said.

"Maybe." Kira frowned. "Probably. But I did see something shoot out of that lamp. I think. I'm almost sure . . ." Her voice trailed off.

"Look, Kira, I write fiction. I know the difference between make-believe and reality."

Kira's frown deepened. "I'm just saying, if I were you, I'd be careful. For instance, don't go wishing for your mother to return from the grave." She paused. "You ever read Stephen King's *Pet Sematary?*"

"Kira!"

Thomas was checking the refrigerator for something to tide him over until dinner when he heard muffled swearing coming from the pantry. "Hailey?"

More indistinct epithets followed by an unmistakable "go away." Definitely Hailey.

He clumped across to the pantry, shoved the door open, and found himself staring at her backside. Not that he had any complaints. It was a very nice backside, round and firm in tight, faded jeans, but he had to wonder what had prompted her to get down on her hands and knees in the first place.

He watched her gingerly poke her right hand into the narrow space under the bottom shelf. "Lose something?"

She angled her head to glare at him over her shoulder. "Besides my temper, you mean?"

He laughed. And yeah, he knew it was probably the wrong thing to do, but he couldn't help himself. She looked so cute, all pink cheeks and fierce, scowling eyebrows.

Her expression went from cranky to thunderous. "You think risking smashed fingers is funny?"

"No, but—"

"Mac keeps a loaded mouse trap under here."

"Okay," he said, "but I still don't—"

"I dropped the red sword."

He stared at her, pretty sure one of them had crossed the border into la-la land, though he wasn't certain which one.

"Lieutenant Beanpole's red sword."

Again he stared.

"Lieutenant Beanpole," she repeated. "The tall, skinny nutcracker I got Mom for Christmas when I was fifteen."

"Okay."

"I was getting the nutcrackers down—Mom kept her collection in a big box on the top shelf—only I lost my grip and the box tipped. Half the nutcrackers fell. Luckily none of them broke, but I can't find the red sword. I've checked everywhere else. The only place it could be hiding is under the shelving. Hence the risk to life and limb. Or anyway, life and digit."

"Don't risk your fingers," Thomas said. "You need them for typing. Use this." Balancing on one leg, he handed her his cane.

"And once again, the prince rescued the princess from certain death," Hailey muttered.

"*What* did you say?"

"Nothing." Hailey did a sweep of the narrow space, producing a little red sword, a rusty mousetrap, and what looked like a set of tiny black wings.

Only who ever heard of a black-winged nutcracker?

Careful not to trigger the mousetrap, she nudged it back where it belonged, then gathered up her finds and scrambled to her feet. Grinning in triumph, she handed him his cane.

Their hands brushed, a fleeting touch, but enough to set Thomas's heart thumping double-time and to send a soft flush of color racing across Hailey's cheekbones. Her grin faded. She stared at him, her eyes wide, her mouth all soft, pink temptation, and he wanted to kiss her so badly he ached with the effort of restraining himself. Because face it, if he started, he'd never be able to stop. One kiss would lead to another. And another. And before he knew it, they'd be lying in a tangle on the pantry floor. So, "What are the wings off?" he asked, hoping to defuse the situation.

"Wings?" Hailey blinked, looking confused, as if he were speaking classical Greek instead of basic English. "Oh, you mean Sergeant Hasenpfeffer's mustache. You remember Sergeant Hasenpfeffer, don't you?" She pulled a chubby red-and-yellow nutcracker from a box near her feet. "The one with the bunny teeth?"

"And without a mustache," Thomas said.

Hailey frowned. "Apparently I was wrong in thinking there'd been no damage. Still"—she brightened—"a little glue and he'll be good as new."

If only hearts could be mended as easily, Thomas thought.

Hailey scrunched her pillow into a more comfortable shape and pulled the covers up under her chin, but it didn't help. Nothing helped. She couldn't sleep.

Thomas was avoiding her. Or at least avoiding being alone with her. When he'd found her in the pantry, she'd thought . . . well, she'd hoped maybe he'd kiss her. Or something. But the second things had started to sizzle, he'd bolted. And she couldn't figure out why.

Had she inadvertently said or done something to offend him? Maybe he was miffed because she hadn't thanked him yet for the lamp.

Or maybe . . . she frowned, wondering if his standoffish attitude had anything to do with their encounter last night in the bathroom. Had he known how much she'd wanted him to kiss her then—really kiss her, not just press his lips to her forehead? Maybe her all-too-apparent neediness had scared him off. Maybe he didn't feel the same way about her as she felt about him. Maybe he couldn't get past the fact that all those years ago she'd let Kennedy . . .

Dammit. What a mess! She'd been such a fool back then. Yes, Kennedy, the self-centered jerk, had used her, but he couldn't have "practiced" on her if she hadn't cooperated. She'd convinced herself she was in love with him, convinced herself *he* was in love with *her*, when the truth was, she'd been in love with the prince, a character who'd existed only in her imagination. As for Kennedy, he'd been in love with himself. Still was, as far as she could tell.

She listened to the wind whistling along the eaves and fought the sudden urge to cry. *Oh, Mom, I wish . . .*

No! Hailey sat up straight, shocked at what she'd almost done. Kira was right about not trying to raise the dead. Not that she believed such a thing was possible, but still . . .

Hailey did—theoretically, at least—have two wishes left, though. And no, she didn't really believe in magic lamps. Just because her first wish had come true—sort of—didn't mean a thing. Coincidence. That's all it was. Only just for the sake of argument, say the lamp really did have a genie. Seemed a shame to waste her two remaining wishes.

So okay, if she could wish for anything, anything at all, what would she wish for?

She had the answer in a heartbeat. Thomas. One perfect night with Thomas.

Only she'd wished for him to come home and almost got him killed. If she pressed her luck by wishing for one perfect night with Thomas, that one-perfect-night part might be a problem. Lots of ways an evil wish genie could put a twist on that. So better go with a safer wish, something unlikely to produce dire consequences.

Like maybe she could wish that Christmas dinner would go off without a hitch. No way an innocuous little wish like that could backfire.

Or she could wish for sunshine tomorrow. A sunny Christmas would be nice.

Or she could go the Miss America route and wish for world peace. Not much the genie could do to sour that one.

Or maybe she could wish that Thomas would quit avoiding her. Not avoiding would be good.

Better yet, she could wish that Thomas would take advantage of the not avoiding and kiss her. On the lips this time. Not much risk there. About the worst even a severely bent genie could do with that one was give her a cold sore, right?

Right.

Determined to give it a shot even if she did feel like a complete idiot, Hailey crawled out of bed and dug the lamp out of her suitcase. As she cradled it between her hands, she was struck once again by the warmth it seemed to generate. Closing her eyes, she gripped it tightly. "Genie of the lamp, hear me. I wish Thomas would kiss me. On the lips," she added quickly, not wanting to give the hypothetical lamp genie any wiggle room.

She opened her eyes in time to see a shower of sparks shoot out of the lamp. They died away almost immediately. She blinked, then stared hard at the spot where seconds ago the sparks had hung suspended in the air. Yes, she had a good imagination, but dammit, she hadn't imagined that.

Or had she? No question she'd been under a lot of stress lately. Weren't hallucinations an early warning sign of an imminent breakdown?

But then again, maybe the lamp really was magic.

She examined it closely, wishing she knew how to read Arabic. All that fancy lettering must say something. Illuminating words of wisdom from the Koran perhaps. Or "Hand Wrought by Omar, the Coppersmith." Or possibly even "Made in China." Unfortunately, she had no way of knowing.

She tucked the lamp back into her suitcase.

On the other hand, maybe she wasn't, strictly speaking, imagining anything. Maybe she was asleep. Maybe she'd dreamed the sparks. Of course, she really didn't feel like she was asleep, but . . .

Hailey pinched her arm hard enough to elicit an

"ow!" Then frowning, she sank down on the edge of the bed, rubbing at the tender spot. Okay then. She could probably cross dreaming off her list.

Which left only two possibilities. Either she was dealing with a paranormal event or traveling in the fast lane to the funny farm.

Someone knocked softly on her door.

Thomas, she thought. Bless you, wish genie.

She wrapped the afghan around her shoulders and padded barefoot toward the door, but before she reached it, the knob turned and the door opened a crack.

"Hailey? Are you awake?" Not Thomas. Kira.

Tamping down her disappointment, Hailey pulled the door open wide. "All bright-eyed and bushy-tailed. What's the problem?"

Kira, dressed in flannel pajamas and a yellow plush robe, stood just outside the door, her arms folded across her chest. "I saw something outside my window. A light. I think maybe there's a prowler."

"This is officially the sticks, Kira. We're over a mile and a half from the nearest public road. Prowlers are pretty thin on the ground."

"I saw something," Kira insisted. "If not a prowler, what about a cattle rustler? This is a cattle ranch, right? Perfect target for cattle rustlers. Maybe we should call the cops or the sheriff, or whoever you call when you're in the sticks."

"Or maybe we should check it out first, make sure we're not making mountains out of molehills."

"I know I saw something," Kira said stubbornly.

Hailey switched off the bedside lamp and led her

friend to the window. "Show me where you spotted this suspicious light."

Kira peered into the darkness. "Over there," she said. "In those trees."

"That's the path to the gazebo," Hailey said. "Probably Mac or one of the twins is up there using the hot tub."

"Oh." Kira sounded almost disappointed. "I didn't know there was a hot tub here at Devil's Elbow."

Probably because Hailey had never mentioned it. She tended to avoid the subject. Too many negative associations.

"To be on the safe side, though, we really ought to check it out." It had occurred to Hailey that if it was Thomas up there soaking his leg, what better opportunity would she get to let the wish genie do his thing?

"We?" Kira said. "Are you nuts? I'm going to go lock myself in my room. Wake up your stepdad. It's his ranch. Let him do the scary poking-around-in-the-dark stuff."

"Good point," Hailey said. "After all, Mac's the one with a gun safe full of fire power."

Kira went off to cower in her room. Hailey pulled on a sweatshirt and jeans, then headed down to the second floor.

Heavy snores, audible even through the closed door, told her Mac was not responsible for Kira's mystery light. Both Kennedy's and Thomas's rooms were quiet.

Hailey weighed her options. She could wake Mac and let him take over. Or she could check Thomas's room first. If he was gone, chances were he was the one Kira had seen. And if Thomas had gone up to the gazebo . . .

She knocked softly on his door.

No answer.

She knocked again, harder this time.

She was almost disappointed when the door swung open, putting an end to her hot-tub fantasy. Almost, but not quite. After all, Thomas in a pair of camo boxers inspired a whole new set of fantasies. Tall and bronzed and muscular, Thomas was a living, breathing, life-size G.I. Joe. G.I. Joe with beard stubble and a shaggy, nonmilitary haircut. "What?" He scratched his chest and blinked myopically in her direction.

"You still wear contacts," she said.

"Not at the moment," he said.

"I had Lasik surgery."

"Glad to hear it." He frowned, looking confused and sleepy and sexy as hell. "You woke me up to discuss Lasik surgery?"

"I woke you up because Kira thought she saw somebody prowling around outside."

He stifled a yawn. "Probably just Dad. He's had trouble sleeping since . . ."

Since her mother died, he meant. Hailey ignored the sudden twinge of pain. "Not Mac. I could hear him buzzing like a chainsaw as I went past."

"Kennedy then. Did you check his room? No, wait," he said. "What time is it?"

"Twelve-fifteen? Twelve-thirty?"

"I doubt he's back then. He was supposed to meet Trisha Anderson—remember her? Former CHS cheerleader?—when she got off work at eleven-thirty."

"Where does she work? A bar?" Hailey could see Trisha as a blowsy barmaid. Or better yet, a down-on-her-luck stripper. Karmic payback.

"Coanchor on the evening news," Thomas said.

So much for karma.

"Then by process of elimination, you're elected."

He shot her a crooked grin. "Elected to what?"

"If I'm going to check out Kira's mystery light, I need someone to watch my back."

"Better put in my contacts then," he said. "Can't watch your back if I can't see it."

Thomas and Hailey made a complete circuit of the main buildings, plus a short foray down to the hayshed, a thorough search of the unlocked horse barn, and a trip up through the trees to the gazebo. They found nothing. No suspicious vehicles. No mysterious footsteps. No evidence at all of intruders. Not that Thomas had expected to, but he didn't see the effort as a waste of time. Hell, he thought as he followed Hailey back to the house, he'd have walked all the way to Bend on his gimpy leg if it would have put her mind to rest. Truth was, he was getting pretty good at this tripod stuff, ought to have it completely nailed about the time his ankle healed.

Hailey opened the back door and he clumped in behind her.

She shrugged out of her coat and hung it on a hook in the mudroom off the kitchen. "Well," she said, "that was a big bust."

And, of course, all he could look at after that was the front of her sweatshirt, and holy shit, he'd bet his new Hummer she wasn't wearing a bra. "Uh-huh," he said.

Hailey frowned as if maybe she'd noticed his fascination with her chest and was getting pissed. "But Kira didn't just imagine that light," she said slowly. "She saw something. Or someone."

So apparently she hadn't noticed his preoccupation. Excellent. He sneaked another quick peek. Oh yeah. Definitely no bra.

"What do you think?" Hailey asked.

He whipped his gaze back up to her face. "About what?" Though he'd pretty much lost the thread of the conversation, he strongly suspected she wasn't requesting his opinion on the braless look.

"What do think Kira saw out there?"

The mysterious disappearing light. Right. "I don't know. Meteor shower? Airplane? Weather balloon? UFO?"

"Yeah, maybe," she said, sounding unconvinced.

"Or how about Santa Claus?" he suggested. "It *is* Christmas Eve."

That bit of silliness earned him a faint smile. God, she was so sweet, so beautiful, so forever out of his reach.

"Hailey," he started just as she said, "Thomas?"

"What?" they said in unison.

Hailey laughed. "You first."

"I was just going to say . . ." I've loved you since I was seventeen years old. I'll never love anyone else. ". . . thank you for going to all this trouble to make a real Christmas for Dad. These last few months have been pretty rough for him." He hesitated. "For you, too, I'm sure."

She nodded. "But this—all of us together again— Mom would have wanted this. It's for her as much as Mac." Her eyes suddenly filled with tears.

"Oh, dammit, Hail." He hadn't meant to make her cry.

"I . . ." she said, then fell silent, shaking her head and fighting for control.

Thomas couldn't stand to see her looking so sad and lost. He knew he shouldn't touch her. Touching her, holding her, was not a good idea, but . . . "Come here," he said and pulled her into his arms. Or rather arm, the one that wasn't glued to the damn cane.

She burrowed into his chest. He could feel her shaking and knew she was crying, but she made no noise at all, not even a muffled sobbing.

He felt completely inadequate. All he could do was hold her and murmur lame phrases—"Now, now," "There, there," and "It's all right"—likely none of which were even marginally helpful.

But gradually, her silent shaking eased. Then after a while—too short a while to suit Thomas, who'd very much liked the way Hailey had felt, so soft and warm next to his heart—she pulled away, wiping her eyes on the sleeves of her sweatshirt. "Sorry. Didn't mean to fall apart on you like that. It's just . . . I miss her so much."

They all did. Sarah had been the glue that held their mix-and-match family together. Without her . . . Thomas's eyes stung. He knew he'd lose it if he looked at Hailey, so he kept his gaze fixed on the floor. "Me, too," he said.

Most people wouldn't have noticed the gruffness in his voice, but Hailey wasn't most people.

"Oh, Thomas." She moved closer, close enough to trail her fingers down his cheek.

He closed his eyes, fighting for composure.

Hailey edged even closer, so close he could smell her clean soap-and-shampoo scent. "Thomas?"

He didn't say anything. He couldn't.

"There's no shame in grieving. Even big, tough guys are allowed to feel, you know." She wrapped her arms around his waist, laid her head on his chest, and held him close.

He stood there stiff and miserable, his throat tight, his chest aching. He felt, all right. He felt too damn much. Not just sharp pangs of loss in the wake of Sarah's death, but an equally sharp desire for Hailey herself. He craved her warmth and sweetness, his need so powerful that it terrified him.

I know it's wrong. I know it's hopeless, but I love her, Sarah. I love her so damned much.

"The way I loved your father."

An involuntary shudder rippled down Thomas's spine. Sarah's words. Sarah's voice. But that was impossible.

Wasn't it?

He detached himself from Hailey's embrace, common sense warning him to get the hell out of range before he did something he'd regret.

"Better?" Hailey smiled up at him, her eyelashes still damp and spiky from her crying jag.

He nodded, ignoring the turmoil in his chest. God, he wanted to touch her, to hold her, to—

"Then, if you wouldn't mind," she said, "could you help me with something?"

Help. Okay, sure. He knew that role. Always-eager-to-lend-a-hand Thomas. Ignoring the emotional storm raging inside, he nodded. Mr. Calm. At least on the surface. "What do you need?"

Hailey smiled. "Follow me."

Anywhere, he thought. To hell and back. But he didn't

193

say a word, just *clump-clumped* along behind her as she led the way through the kitchen and dining room. She didn't bother to switch on lights as she went. Maybe she figured the moonlight pouring in the windows provided sufficient illumination.

"What is it?" he asked. "What's the problem?"

"I just need to check something—see if it's working."

"If it's anything to do with electricity, you've got the wrong man. I'm hopeless with wiring."

"No wiring," she promised. "Though if it's working right, we may give off a few sparks. Stop right there." She positioned him beneath the archway between the dining room and living room.

He glanced toward the unlit Christmas tree. "Something wrong with the tree lights?"

"No." Hailey shot him a mischievous smile, then pointed up.

He was standing under the mistletoe. They were *both* standing under the mistletoe.

"Kiss me," she said.

And he knew it wasn't a good idea, especially after that whole tearful bonding thing in the kitchen, but dammit, it was Christmas Eve and here she was and here he was and it wasn't like she was saying, "Marry me so I can die in childbirth, lose my life in a fiery plane crash, or end up with a terminal disease." This was only a kiss, nothing more.

Yeah, but what a kiss. Instant sizzle, potent chemistry. Heat, heat, heat. Once they started, Thomas wasn't sure where he left off and Hailey began. It was as if their mouths, their bodies had melded together. Or maybe melted together. And that wasn't entirely hormone-induced hyperbole because apparently he really was melting—at least his knees were. One minute he was standing there under the mistletoe and the next, his cane went clattering across the room and he sank to the floor, still holding Hailey, still kissing Hailey, still wanting Hailey.

"Thomas," she gasped, and then kissed him some more, all the while unbuttoning and unzipping with feverish intensity. "Please." And she looked at him with those big luminous eyes and he knew he should say no. It was the right thing to do.

"No," said his brain.

But, "Yes," said his mouth.

Hailey finally managed to get his shirt off. She tossed it over her head, muttering, "Thank you, genie" under her breath.

"Who's Jeannie?" he started to ask, but before he could get the words out, Hailey stripped off her sweatshirt, proving he'd been right earlier. She wasn't wearing a bra.

Suddenly there didn't seem to be enough oxygen in the room. "You're beautiful," he said hoarsely. "Perfect." And she was, rounded in all the right places. He traced the silky curve from rib cage to waist to hip, drew his fingertips across her abdomen, then cupped one soft breast.

As he brushed his thumb across her nipple, she sucked in her breath, then uttered a faint moan. He went rock hard at the look on her face—equal parts surprise and pleasure. So her strangled "don't" didn't make sense.

"You don't want . . . ?"

"I do, but not this way. Not half-dressed." She kicked

off her shoes and socks, then wriggled out of her jeans and panties. "That's better," she said, and she wasn't wrong. Hailey dressed was a temptation. Hailey undressed was irresistible.

His chest tightened. He couldn't speak, couldn't breathe.

"Your turn," she said. "I'd strip those jeans off myself, but I don't want to hurt your ankle."

As if he would have noticed. Desire trumped pain any day of the week.

He removed the rest of his clothing, very aware of Hailey watching his every move. "I need a shave," he said. "You're going to get whisker burn."

"Promise?" Still smiling, Hailey pushed him down on his back and sat astride him right there in the archway under the mistletoe. "All I want for Christmas . . ." She showered kisses on his face—his forehead, his cheeks, his eyelids, his nose, his chin, his mouth, and very, very tenderly, his cuts and scrapes. "All I want for Christmas," she repeated, "is you, Thomas MacCormack."

Her expression brought tears to his eyes for the second time that evening. Because what she really meant was she loved him, and that admission broke his heart. They were on very dangerous ground here.

"Hailey, I—"

"Shh." She pressed a finger to his lips.

So he held his tongue and let her have her way with him.

This is not happening, Hailey thought. I am totally dreaming this.

And then she thought, If it's not real, if it's just a dream, then I can do whatever I want. I can indulge my wildest fantasies. Though truthfully, her wildest fantasies weren't all that wild. She wasn't into bondage or spankings or ice cube–enhanced blow jobs. None of that cheerleader/football player or maid-and-the-millionaire role-playing for her. All she really wanted was to come about three times in a row with Thomas inside her.

And oh! Oh my!

"That's once," she said, and rolled over so that he was on top.

"Hailey, you're killing me," Thomas said.

"I'm sorry." Concern drove a pair of lines between her eyebrows. "Did I accidentally kick your sprained ankle?"

"No." He smiled, then nibbled at her lower lip. "It's you. Us. This. It feels so damn good."

"But you said I was killing you."

"Yeah, but I'm destined to die happy."

She curled her fingers around his biceps and squeezed hard enough to get his full attention. "You shouldn't joke about dying," she said fiercely. "It's not funny. When I saw you with that cane, when I heard you'd been hurt in a bombing, I—"

"Shh," he said, kissing her gently.

"Don't try to distract me," she said. "I need to explain."

He waited, but no explanation was immediately forthcoming. "Explain what?"

She hesitated a second longer. "Explain my part in all this."

"And that would be what? Sexual exuberance? Unbridled passion?" He grinned. "You've got some major moves, lady."

"You're not too shabby yourself." She brushed the hair back off his forehead in a curiously tender gesture. "But that's not what I meant."

"Okay, then explain, because I'm not following, Hail."

"I wished it," she said, confusing the issue even more. "Not the nearly-getting-blown-up part or the Kennedy-being-fired part specifically, but still, it's my fault. If I hadn't wished you two home for Christmas—"

"Wishing doesn't make it so," he said firmly.

"Well, not usually, but—"

"Not ever," he said and kissed her again, not so gently this time.

Hailey wrapped her arms around his neck and kissed him back with a great deal of enthusiasm. Not so gently apparently worked as well for her as it did for him. She moaned a little deep in her throat when he finally came up for air.

"What?" he said.

"Don't stop."

He nibbled at her lower lip. "I thought you wanted to talk."

"Later," she said. "Much, much later."

"No, really." He shifted his position so he could concentrate on the nipples he'd been obsessed with ever since last night. "Communication is good. Tell me how this feels." He sucked one nipple into his mouth and teased it with his tongue.

"Ah," she said somewhat inarticulately, though her nonverbal response spoke volumes. She clenched at his shoulders and quivered beneath him as he brought her to the brink of orgasm.

"You don't play fair," she said, breathing hard, "but that's okay. Neither do I." She burrowed her hands between their bodies and found his erection. Up and down, she stroked. Up and down. And it felt so good.

Too good.

"No," he said.

Hailey blinked up at him. "No?"

"I want to come inside you."

She smiled, wriggled into position, and spread her legs.

"Oh, Hailey." He entered her slowly, prolonging the pleasure, loving the way she moaned and arched her body, trying to hurry the pace.

"Who's killing whom?" she muttered and nipped at his shoulder.

Good question. Unfortunately, by this time he was in no position to answer, having reached the place where he couldn't talk. All he could do was feel Hailey all around him, soft and wet and warm and eager. And sweet. So sweet. He groaned as he climaxed in a gut-wrenching rush of pleasure.

And almost immediately, he felt Hailey stiffen, then come apart as she experienced her own orgasm. "Oh," she panted. "My."

"I'm hoping that was understatement," he said.

She nodded, still breathing hard.

When her breathing finally slowed to a normal rate, she raised herself up to whisper in his ear. "That's twice." Which sounded so much like dialogue from a cheesy gangster movie that it made him laugh.

"Was that a threat? You're scaring me, woman."

"Good," she said. "Sex slaves are supposed to be scared."

"Sex slave? I'm your sex slave?"

"Hey," she said. "It's my dream."

Thomas cupped her face between his hands. "This isn't a dream," he said, suddenly serious. "This is real. You and me."

She explored his face with her fingertips, gossamer touches to his cheeks, his lips. "I know," she said. "I love you, Thomas."

"I—" he started.

"No." Once again, she pressed her fingers to his mouth. "Don't say it. Don't say anything you'll be sorry for later. I know this is a one-time shot. I know you believe in the stupid MacCormack curse. I know all that, Thomas. But . . ." She hesitated, her expression so sweet and serious and sad that it broke his heart all over again. "There's something else I know," she said. "I love you."

The front door creaked opened. A frosty breath of cold night air invaded the house, raising gooseflesh along Thomas's backside. Hailey stiffened.

That damn light, Thomas thought. Must have been Kennedy after all. They'd searched the gazebo, but hadn't followed the path any farther. Apparently, God only knew why, Kennedy had hiked on up over the hill to the old brush corral.

The door closed with an almost inaudible click.

"Thomas?" Hailey whispered. "I didn't hear a car. Who . . . ?"

"Kennedy," he whispered back. "With any luck, he'll head straight up to his room."

Or not.

The overhead lights flicked on and Kennedy strode from the entry into the living room. He was halfway to the fireplace before he noticed them on the floor under the mistletoe. A series of emotions chased themselves across his face—surprise and amusement quickly supplanted by something altogether darker. "Well, well, well," he said. "What have we here? St. Thomas, is that you?"

"Shut up," Thomas said.

Kennedy looked surprised for a second. Then he narrowed his eyes.

Not used to less than celebrity treatment these days, Thomas thought with grim amusement as he rolled off Hailey and tossed her some clothes.

Kennedy leaned against the mantel and struck a pose, arching an eyebrow, flaring his nostrils, and treating them to a supercilious smile.

Thomas wasn't impressed; he'd watched his brother practice all three mannerisms in front of the mirror.

"Got bored with the moral high ground, did you?" Kennedy said.

Balancing on one leg and knowing, unfortunately, exactly how stupid he looked, Thomas pulled on his boxers, then, grabbing his cane, advanced on his brother. "I told you to shut up."

"You always did come in a poor second, Thomas. Tell me, are you enjoying my leftovers?"

Thomas literally saw red in the millisecond before he lunged forward, swinging wildly at his brother.

Laughing, Kennedy stepped aside. Thomas overbalanced and went down in a heap, taking the Christmas tree with him. Fragile glass ornaments smashed into jagged fragments. One of the silver swags broke, sending loose beads skittering across the floor. The treetop angel took a header.

"Are you all right?" Hailey started to rush to his side.

"Stay back," he said. "You'll get glass in your feet."

"Ooh. How chivalrous of you!" Sarcasm laced Kennedy's words.

"Don't be an ass." Thomas grimaced as he plucked a sliver of glass from his shin.

Hands on hips, Kennedy shot him a gloating smile. "Not so tough this time, are you?"

"This time?" Hailey said.

Kennedy's nostrils flared again. "As opposed to last time, when he caught us making out in the gazebo and beat the crap out of me."

Slowly Thomas levered himself to his feet, ignoring the shards of colored glass embedded in his knees. "This isn't a competition."

Kennedy laughed again. "Don't fool yourself. With us, everything's a competition. I win a Golden Globe; you trump it with a Pulitzer. I get to third base with the housekeeper's daughter, and you've gotta hit a home run. Only apparently, the rules don't apply to St. Thomas. When I neglect to bring along a condom, it's a huge sin for which I'm beat to a pulp. When you do it, it's what? A mere peccadillo? Two Hail Marys and you're off the hook?"

"I'm on the pill," Hailey said.

"Interesting." Kennedy smirked.

Thomas scowled. "I didn't plan this, dammit."

"No, but I wouldn't be surprised to find out that Hailey did. Under that good-girl exterior beats the heart of a slut, you know. Or wait, I guess you didn't know."

"Bastard!" Thomas took another swing at Kennedy, but his brother danced out of range.

"You think I could have talked her out of her shirt back when we were teenagers if she hadn't been hot for me all along? Man, she was ripe for the plucking. I can't tell you how many times she 'accidentally' ran into me at school. Hell, her crush on me was the talk of CHS. I'd have had to have been blind, deaf, and stupid not to know how she felt."

"I was young and naïve," Hailey said. She had managed to get herself dressed, but her expression was naked—all pain and vulnerability. "I thought you were Prince Charming, not the Big, Bad Wolf. I thought I loved you. I thought you loved me. But you didn't. You just wanted to use me. You just wanted to 'practice.' "

"Like you weren't getting off on one-upping Trisha."

"I didn't. I never—"

"Ripe for the plucking," Kennedy repeated, then turned to Thomas. "And if you hadn't shown up when you did, I'd have plucked the ever-lovin' hell out of her."

All Thomas could think of was wiping that obnoxious smirk off Kennedy's face. He swung again and this time his fist connected with a satisfying impact. Blood spurted from his brother's nose.

"You son of a bitch!" Kennedy roared.

"Quiet!" Hailey said. "Do you want to wake up the whole house?"

Kennedy seemed not to hear her. Screaming incoherent threats, his face distorted by fury, he threw himself on Thomas and both of them fell heavily against the coffee table. The bowl of nuts flipped off, dumping its contents across the hardwood floor. The table gave way with a groan, collapsing under their combined weights.

A no-holds-barred punching match ensued, with Hailey doing her best to separate them. "Stop it," she kept saying. "Are you crazy?"

Pretty much, Thomas thought, as he did his level best to get a headlock on his brother.

Kennedy thrashed and twisted. They slammed against the mantel, knocking the lion's share of Sarah's prized nutcracker collection onto the stone hearth.

"Enough!" Hailey cried.

Thomas, who'd been about to bury his fist in Kennedy's gut, took one look at her tear-stained face and pulled his punch.

Seizing the advantage, Kennedy twisted free, one wild kick catching Thomas square in his bruised and swollen ankle.

Fierce pain blurred Thomas's senses for a moment. When he swam back to full consciousness, Kennedy was shouting, "Think you're so much better than I am, damn you!" and punctuating each word with short jabs to Thomas's stomach.

"Stop it!" Hailey shouted. "Stop it! Kennedy, you're going to kill him!"

At which point Mac appeared in the doorway, one hand holding his robe together while the other gripped a shotgun. "Knock it off," he bellowed, "or I'll fill both your backsides with buckshot."

They knocked it off.

Blood dripped from Kennedy's nose, the drops keeping time with the throbbing in Thomas's ankle and midsection.

Kira peered around Mac's shoulder. "Whoa," she said. "Is this Christmas? Or Armageddon?"

Chapter Five

✳ ❄ ✳

Hailey, open up," Kira said.

"Go away. Please." Hailey buried her head under the pillow. Childish, she knew, but she just couldn't face anyone right now, not even Kira. Christmas was ruined. Thomas and Kennedy were at each other's throats. Mac was furious. And it was all her fault. Her and her stupid wishes.

"Hailey?"

"I can't talk right now."

"Please?"

"No."

There was a long pause, as if maybe Kira were thinking about kicking the door down. "Okay," she said finally, "but if you change your mind, I'll be right next door."

Kira meant well, but there was nothing she could do to fix this. There was nothing anyone could do.

I messed up, she told herself. *I had my shot and I blew it.*

Because you tried to manipulate other people with magic. Face it, Hailey, life is no fairy tale.

Only it should be, dammit. If only . . .

She sat up suddenly. Maybe there *was* someone who could fix things, after all, the same someone who had caused all the problems in the first place. Her.

She shoved the pillow aside and dried her tears on the rumpled sheet. Theoretically, she still had one wish left. So what if she hocus-pocused everything back the way it had been? What if she used her third wish to unwish her second wish?

Tossing the covers off, she slid out of bed and dug feverishly through her suitcase. The way her luck was running, she half expected to find that the lamp had disappeared, but it was there, just where she'd left it. Carefully, she lifted it from her case.

The lamp had felt warm in her hands earlier. Now it was almost too hot to handle. Her fingers tingled unpleasantly at the contact. She suspected she'd end up with blistered fingertips if she didn't hurry.

"Genie of the lamp," she whispered. "Hear me. I wish that I had never wished for Thomas to kiss me."

Hailey was prepared for the shower of sparks this time. What she wasn't prepared for was the dizzying sensation that followed. One minute she was hunkered down next to her suitcase in her old room on the third floor, holding the lamp and wishing with all her might to set things right. The next, she was downstairs, standing under the mistletoe with Thomas.

"Kiss me," she said before she could stop herself, and then, "No, wait."

Thomas gave her a bewildered look.

She scanned the living room. "The tree's still standing," she said. "The coffee table's intact, and so is Mom's nutcracker collection."

The bewildered look on Thomas's face morphed into a has-this-woman-gone-completely-nuts look. "Okay," he said.

"Kennedy didn't catch us in flagrante delicto and go off the deep end, did he?"

"No," Thomas said. "I'm pretty sure I would have remembered something like that. Especially the in flagrante delicto part."

"Mac didn't threaten to fill your and Kennedy's backsides with buckshot?"

"No. Definitely not."

"And Kira didn't have hysterics when she saw that you'd bent the angel's wings and broken half the ornaments?"

Thomas glanced sideways at the Christmas tree, as if looking for evidence of shattered ornaments and deformed angel wings. "I'm guessing a good case of hysterics would have stuck in my mind."

"Okay, then." She pointed up. "Mistletoe. Kiss me. That's the rule."

"Hail, I don't think—"

"That's fine. No thinking required. Just some heavy-duty lip action and maybe a little tongue."

Thomas frowned. "This isn't a good idea. For so many reasons."

"Mistletoe," she repeated.

"I don't take orders from parasites."

She stared at him, open-mouthed with surprise. "Are you calling me a parasite?"

"No, Hail. Mistletoe. Mistletoe's a parasite. Given half a chance, it'll suck the life right out of whatever tree it has decided to call home."

"I knew that," she said, then frowned. "You didn't give me this much trouble the first time. Must have been the undue influence." She nodded sagely. "Undue wish-genie influence."

"What?" His face showed both confusion and concern. Probably convinced she was in desperate need of a good psychiatrist.

"Oh, hell," she said, and reaching up, pulled his mouth down within kissing range.

"What are you doing?" he asked, even though it was pretty obvious.

"Kissing you," she said and did.

Despite a reluctant start, Thomas soon got into the spirit. He had her sweatshirt half off before she came to her senses enough to call a halt to what threatened to be a repeat of the earlier disaster. "No," she said a little desperately.

Thomas looked so crestfallen that she smiled. "Well, yes, actually. But not here," she clarified. "Because when Kennedy gets back from his hike up to the brush corral—"

"Kennedy's at the brush corral? I thought he was supposed to hook up with Trisha Anderson. Seems odd he'd be back so early."

"Maybe Trisha stood him up. Maybe they had a falling out." Hailey shrugged, not much interested in Kennedy or his love life.

"That would explain the trip to the brush corral," Thomas said. "Kennedy always did like to walk off his disappointments."

"Must have been his light Kira saw in the first place," Hailey said, just now making the connection.

Thomas gave her an odd look. "If you knew Kennedy was out there, why did we spend half an hour searching the grounds for a prowler-slash-cattle rustler? And why didn't you say anything when I told you Kennedy had gone into Bend to see Trisha?"

"I didn't know then. All that happened before the second wish went ballistic on me."

"I see," he said, giving her that look again, the one that said he thought she had a whole bucketful of screws loose.

"No, you don't. You're just humoring me." She sighed. "But the thing is, it's complicated, and I don't want to deal with explanations right now. I have other plans." She wrapped her arms around his neck.

Thomas raised one eyebrow, a trick she'd never mastered. "And those plans would include . . . ?"

"A couple hours of hot, sweaty sex?" She aimed for a sultry smile, missed by a mile, and settled for a goofy grin.

But Thomas looked so serious that fear fluttered in her chest. He wasn't going to turn her down, was he? Because if he did, she was finished. Out of wishes and out of luck.

"Thomas," she said, trying not to sound pathetic. "I know you don't want to hear this, and God knows it was hard enough to say last time when my second wish had predisposed you to listen, but it's even more difficult for me now. So I'll just get it over with." She drew a deep breath, and she meant to tell him. Honestly. She meant to say, "Thomas, I love you," and all of the rest of it just as she had the first time, only he looked so sad and sober and *stricken* that she couldn't, absolutely couldn't, force the words past her lips. "I . . ." was as far as she got before her throat closed up on her.

Thomas leaned his cane against the doorframe, then balanced on his good leg and draped his hands over her shoulders. "Hailey," he said, making eye contact. A faint frown wrinkled his forehead. His mouth looked grim.

"Yes?" Oh my God. Was this the part where he told her thanks, but no thanks; you're not my type? Panic squeezed her chest. "Thomas?"

He rested his forehead against hers, then shut his eyes, as if he were in pain.

"Thomas?" she said again, her voice a strangled whisper.

"I love you, Hailey. I've loved you since I was seventeen years old. Maybe longer." He opened his eyes and what she saw there reassured her. Thomas was as scared as she was. "For me this isn't just about hot, sweaty sex, but . . ."

"I know," she said. "You think the MacCormack curse precludes a permanent relationship." She paused. "I don't care. I may think the curse is stupid, but I know you believe in it. So fine. I can accept that. I don't care if you can't promise me forever. I love you, and I want you. On any terms."

He gave a tentative smile. "Except not here."

"Definitely not here. Been there, done that. Disaster time."

Confusion clouded his eyes for a second, but he blinked it away. Thomas had always been good at keeping his eye on the objective. "Then where do you propose?"

"My room," she said. "With the door securely locked."

Thomas awoke with a smile on his face and Hailey in his arms. Not a bad way to start Christmas morning. He kissed the top of her head and she cuddled closer.

"What time is it?" she asked, her breath warm on his chest.

Thomas peered at the alarm clock on the bedside table. "Eight-oh-four."

"What?" Hailey sat up, agitated and seemingly oblivious to her naked state. Her bosom heaved, just as in romance novels.

Thomas lay back, preoccupied with the view and his body's nearly instantaneous response to it. "Still early," he said. "I bet we'd have time for another—"

"The turkey!" Hailey wailed. "I should have had the turkey in by six. What was I thinking?"

Obeying an almost irresistible impulse, Thomas reached up and toyed with the tip of one perfect breast.

Hailey gave a little gasp. "Thomas, what are you . . . ? The turkey . . ."

He scooted up to a sitting position, then used his lips and tongue to tease her nipple until she moaned. "What about it?" he said.

"What about what?" Hailey sounded confused.

He sucked a little on the other breast. "The turkey," he said.

She moaned again and reached for him. "The turkey can wait. I can't."

When Hailey finally made it downstairs at a quarter after 9:00, she found the turkey already in the oven and Kennedy and Kira sparring amiably across the breakfast table. "Hey," she said to Kira, "thanks. I didn't know you could cook."

"She's a woman of many talents." Kennedy flashed his trademark smile. "Best frozen waffles I ever ate."

Kira kicked him under the table.

"Hey!" Kennedy protested. "That was supposed to be a compliment."

"My mistake," Kira said, not looking the least bit sorry.

Kennedy gave her a mock-ferocious scowl.

Hailey poured herself some coffee.

"Forget my culinary skills or lack thereof," Kira said. "We were discussing Hitchcock's genius."

Kennedy raised his eyebrows. " 'Genius' was your word. Oh, I admit he made some good films, notably *Rear Window* and *North by Northwest,* but he's responsible for some real stinkers, too. If we're talking genius, what about Frank Capra? *It's a Wonderful Life* is a classic."

"Oh yes," Kira agreed with a smirk, "a masterpiece of melodrama and sappy sentimentality."

Kennedy, apparently speechless with outrage—at least temporarily—stared daggers at Kira.

"Spielberg?" Hailey suggested, hoping to avoid a full-scale war at the breakfast table. Kennedy admired Capra, but he worshiped Spielberg.

"Yes, what about Spielberg?" he said, taking the bait. "Unlike Kira's hero Hitchcock, Spielberg's both innovative *and* consistent. I'd work for scale to make a film with Steven Spielberg."

"Oh, please." Kira did an eyeroll. "Have you forgotten *The Goonies?*"

"What's wrong with *The Goonies?*" Kennedy demanded. "So it's not *Schindler's List*. It's not as lame as Hitchcock's *Topaz*. Not to mention his really early stuff."

Hailey perched on one of the barstools at the counter and took a sip of her coffee. Strong enough to revive the dead. Definitely Mac's recipe. He must have fixed a pot before he went out to feed.

"If you want to talk innovation," Kira said, "what about M. Night Shyamalan's *The Sixth Sense?*"

"Right, and then there's *Unbreakable,*" he said with a dismissive wave of his fork.

"I'm with you there, but *Signs* was good," Kira said, "all except maybe the hokey-looking aliens."

"And the premise," Kennedy said. "We're supposed to believe the invaders were smart enough to orchestrate the takeover of the world but too stupid to realize that Earth is three-quarters covered in water, the ultimate antialien weapon? Give me a break."

"Talking shop on Christmas?" Thomas, suffering from an acute case of bed head, spoke from the doorway.

"Kira started it," Kennedy said.

"I did." Kira beamed. "I was sucking up, actually, hoping your brother would recommend me to his rich Hollywood friends the next time any of them need a decorator." She paused, eyeing Thomas closely. "Nice hair."

He put a tentative hand to his head. "Is it sticking out?"

214

"More like up, down, and sideways," Kennedy said. "Ever heard of a mirror? Flat, shiny thing?"

Thomas shrugged. "Just because you're obsessed with your own reflection—"

"Wild hair notwithstanding," Kira interrupted before the twins could work up to a full-fledged battle, "the mountain air must agree with you, Thomas. You're looking very perky today."

"Perky?" Thomas did the one-eyebrow thing.

Kira grinned. "Healthy."

Oh, great. Kira must have heard them going at it last night. Or maybe this morning. Hailey pretended a sudden fierce interest in the surface of the granite countertop. Tiny pink speckles hid among the gray, black, and white ones. Funny she'd never noticed before.

"What's for breakfast?" Thomas asked.

"We're having waffles," Kennedy said. "There are more in the freezer. Help yourself."

Thomas limped his way across to the big side-by-side unit, opened the freezer, shut it, then peered into the refrigerator. "We have any eggs?"

"Top shelf," Hailey told him.

Mac came in via the mudroom door, presumably having left his boots behind since he was in his stocking feet. He struck a pose, hands on hips, doing his best to look stern. "Hell's bells, aren't you kids done eating yet? What's the holdup? Let's get this Christmas on the road. I want to open presents."

"But I'm starving," Thomas protested.

Hailey handed him a mug of coffee and a blueberry muffin. "This should hold you for a while."

"Thanks," he said with a smile that raised her temperature a couple of degrees.

"Come on. Come on," Mac said impatiently, and they followed him into the living room.

Still unwrecked, Hailey was happy to note. Then, noticing that everyone was staring at her, realized that she must have voiced her thought. "Bad dream," she said. "Very Grinchly. Christmas tree fell over. Presents got munched. Bad, bad dream. Nightmare, really."

"Must have been," Kira said. "I heard you thrashing around all night."

Hailey shot her friend a narrow-eyed look. The corners of Kira's mouth curled in a smug smile. Hailey wondered if maybe she and Thomas should have risked going at it under the mistletoe after all.

"Hailey, if you'll do the honors . . . ?" Hand out the presents, Mac meant.

Hailey distributed her gifts first—for Kennedy, sunglasses, a glue-on mustache, and a set of Billy Bob teeth. "So you can go out in public without being recognized," she told him. For Kira, she'd purchased a bottle of sunless tanning lotion and a CD of Don Ho's greatest hits; for Mac, an avid fly fisherman, assorted fly-tying material; and for Thomas, a St. Christopher's medal. "To keep you safe," she told him.

"But I'm not Catholic," he objected. "And besides, wasn't St. Christopher de-sainted?"

"De-canonized," Hailey corrected him, "but since this medal predates the de-canonization and was blessed by Pope Paul the Fourth besides, it should have some residual mojo."

Her throat went tight at the look on Thomas's face. "Thanks," he said softly. "In my line of work, I need all the mojo I can get."

"Great gifts, kids," Mac said. "Thanks." In addition to his fly-tying stuff, he'd received a float tube from Kennedy and new waders from Thomas.

"I think we should all change into our Christmas sweaters," Kira said brightly.

Hailey shot her an incredulous look. Mac had proudly presented them with hand-knit pullovers from a specialty shop in Sisters, well-meant but misguided gifts, proof that a colorblind man should not be allowed to do his own shopping. Hailey's sweater was particularly hideous, a bilious green covered in glittery snowflakes. "Maybe later," she said, "after I clean up this mess." The living room was a scene of devastation, littered with shredded wrapping paper and discarded ribbon. "I think I'm going to need a giant trash bag."

"Wait," Thomas said. "You haven't opened all your presents."

"Here's one from me." Kennedy handed her an envelope.

Gift certificate, she was guessing. Par for the course. "Thanks," she said, more polite than enthusiastic.

"And here's another one for Mac, too." Kira waved a small, shiny gold-wrapped package she'd rescued from among the folds of the tree skirt.

"For me?" Mac said.

"That's what it says." Kira handed him the package.

As Mac studied the tag, the color drained from his cheeks.

"Something wrong?" Hailey asked.

"It's . . ." Mac faltered, took a deep breath, and tried again. "It's addressed to me in Sarah's handwriting."

No one uttered a word for a full thirty seconds, then, "Open it," Thomas said.

"But I don't understand. How did she . . . ?" Mac stared at the package as if it were a time bomb.

"Open it," Kennedy said. "See what's inside."

Clumsily, Mac removed the wrapping paper to reveal a small decorative tin. With fumbling hands he raised the lid. "Caramels," he said unsteadily. "Homemade caramels."

Mac's favorite.

His gaze fastened on Hailey. "Did you . . . ?"

She shook her head. "Mom knew how much you loved her caramels. She must have arranged this before . . ." Her voice trailed off. Her mom must have filled the tin before she got sick because ghosts didn't have substance. They couldn't cook. Could they? Struck by a sudden suspicion, she turned to Kira. "You *did* put the turkey in this morning, didn't you?"

Kira stared at her as if she'd suddenly grown a second head. "Me? No way. I don't know giblets from goblets."

"Mac?" Hailey said.

"Hell no. Brewing coffee is the extent of my cooking expertise."

"Then who started the turkey?" Hailey demanded.

"You know who." Her mom's voice whispered in her ear. "And why. You and Thomas were somewhat preoccupied." A soft chuckle floated on the air.

Hailey glanced surreptitiously around the room, but judging by the bland expressions she encountered, she was the only one tuned to the paranormal network.

"You don't believe your ears, do you?" Her mother sounded amused. "Why not? Is a ghost any more incredible than a magic lamp?"

She must have looked a little shell-shocked because Kira, who was reaching into the nut bowl, glanced up, caught a glimpse of her expression, and frowned. "Are you all right?"

"The least you can do is thank me for saving Christmas dinner," her mom said.

"Thank you," Hailey said.

Kira gave her a funny look. "For what?"

"For what? For being concerned, of course. But I'm fine. Really," Hailey said.

"Good save." Her mom gave another soft chuckle. "And you're welcome."

A little unnerving, those chuckles.

"Your turn." Kennedy perched beside her on the sofa. "Open it." He tapped the envelope she'd been worrying between her fingers.

Surprised by his serious tone of voice, Hailey met his gaze. A muscle twitched below his left eye. He looked tense and worried. Kennedy MacCormack, king of I-don't-give-a-damn, freaking out over whether or not she liked her gift certificate?

Okay, this was weird, even weirder than ghostly voices, wish genies, and magic lamps.

Hailey ripped open the envelope. Not a gift certificate after all. A single folded sheet of paper.

Dear Hailey, she read. *This letter is long overdue. The ironic part is, I probably never would have written it if I hadn't been fired. It took a major career setback to force me to take a long, hard look at myself, and I'm ashamed to say, I didn't much like what I saw. I've been a jerk, a stupid, conceited, self-indulgent jerk.*

Hailey frowned. "Why tell me—"

"Finish it," Kennedy said.

Last night I met Trisha Anderson for drinks, and frankly, I figured we'd end up in bed, which we did, only it turned out she had an ulterior motive for hooking up with me. Seems Trisha has network ambitions. She only had sex with me so I'd introduce her to Thomas.

When I finally figured out I'd been used, I was royally pissed. Long story short, I came back to the ranch to walk it off. I tramped all the way up to the brush corral and back, but it took half a night's worth of tossing and turning before I finally realized my less-than-satisfying experience with Trisha was poetic justice. She used me the same way I tried to use you all those years ago.

Only the worst part is, my manipulation was even more unforgivable than hers because she doesn't give a damn about me, but I did—and do—care about you. I am sorry, truly sorry, Hailey, for the cavalier way I treated you and even sorrier that it took me ten years to apologize.

An apology. After all this time. Would wonders never cease?

"Forgive him." Her mother's voice again. Hailey glanced up, half expecting to see her mom, but it was Kennedy who sat there watching her.

"I acted like a skeezy rat bastard," he said softly.

"You did," she agreed.

"And I'm sorry as hell." He was telling the truth. Not

even Kennedy was that good an actor. "Can you ever forgive me?"

And the frog turned into a prince, not the one true prince, but a prince nonetheless.

"I already have," she said.

Kennedy smiled. "Friends?"

"Friends."

"And nothing more." Thomas, who'd come within earshot in time to hear the last bit of conversation, gave his brother a warning glance. "Now move it, so I can sit next to Hailey."

"Ooh, very territorial." Kennedy raised his hands in mock fear. "Chill. No need for violence. I'm moving."

Thomas slid into the spot Kennedy had vacated and handed her a beribboned package.

She smiled. "What? *Another* present?"

"Another?"

"I never thanked you for the lamp, did I?"

He tilted his head and gave her a puzzled look. "What lamp?"

"The Aladdin's lamp she got in the mail last week," Kira said. She'd found a plastic garbage bag and was stuffing it with discarded wrapping paper.

"I didn't send you a lamp," Thomas said, looking confused.

"But I thought . . . it looks Middle Eastern. I'm pretty sure the lettering is Arabic. And since you were in Baghdad . . ." Hailey frowned. "If you didn't send the lamp, who did?"

"Sarah," Mac said. "She ordered it online last fall." He faltered to a stop. Sadness shadowed his eyes for a moment or two, but then he smiled. "She knew you'd like it, something straight out of a fairy tale like that."

"Only I didn't realize the genie would turn out to be such a nasty little trickster." Her mom's voice again, clear as day.

Hailey looked searchingly at the others. "Did you hear that?"

"Hear what?" Thomas asked.

Kira, who was digging a wad of crumpled tissue out from under the coffee table, shrugged and said, "I didn't hear anything."

"Must have been my imagination," Hailey said.

Mac nodded. "You've always had plenty of that, kiddo."

Thomas nudged the gift on her lap with one finger. "Aren't you going to open it?"

She smiled. "Let me see if I can guess what it is first." She studied the package. "Hmm. Same size and shape as a shoebox. Could it be . . . glass slippers?"

Thomas laughed. "Open it, Cinderella, and find out."

Hailey tossed aside the ribbon, then peeled off the wrapping paper to reveal a battered shoebox.

Thomas chuckled at the expression on her face.

"Nikes? You bought me a pair of Nikes?"

"You can never have too many pairs of cross trainers," Kira said helpfully.

Kennedy, who'd been leafing through Goldman's *Adventures in the Film Trade,* his gift from Kira, paused to examine the box. "Size twelve, according to the label. And you're what? A seven? I'm guessing there's something besides shoes inside."

"It's an old shoebox of Dad's. Purely camouflage. Open it," Thomas said again.

She raised the lid, then stared at him dumbfounded. "All seven seasons of *Buffy* on DVD? Color me shocked. You hate *Buffy*."

Thomas grinned. "Yes, but you love *Buffy*," he said, "and I love you."

"I knew it!" Her mother's voice seemed to come from across the room this time.

Thomas's smile grew a little ragged around the edges.

He heard Mom's voice, too, Hailey realized. Had the others? She glanced toward Mac in his leather recliner.

He met her questioning gaze with a smile. "So you're a big fan of the vampire slayer, huh?" Mac seemed oblivious to any ghostly presence, though for just an instant, Hailey could have sworn she saw her mother leaning against the back of his chair.

"I'm a big fan of Joss Whedon," she said absently, which set Kennedy and Kira off on another spirited discussion of Hollywood's hottest directors.

Hailey turned back to Thomas. "You really love me?" she said. "This isn't just guilt talking?"

Thomas gripped her hand. "I meant it before and I mean it now, but it doesn't change anything. The curse . . ."

"Nonsense!" Across the room a glimmering form took shape, though apparently only Hailey and Thomas could see it.

Kennedy and Kira were busy dissecting Mel Gibson's work on *The Passion of the Christ* while Mac tossed in irrelevant comments like, "The *Lethal Weapon*s are great, but as far as I'm concerned you can have the *Mad Max*es. Postapocalyptic garbage."

Her mom's ghost gave a wistful smile. "Cancer killed

223

me, Thomas, not a curse. I don't believe in curses, but even if I did, I'd have married Mac anyway. Better a few years with the man I loved than a lifetime without."

"She's got a point," Hailey said.

"Thank you." Kira grinned at Kennedy in triumph. "See? Hailey agrees with me. Not only is Mel Gibson brilliant, he's a risk-taker."

"Maverick's my favorite of his films," Mac said. "First off, because it's a Western, and second, because I love the part where he and his Indian buddy scam the Russian."

"You heard Hailey," her mom said. "I have a point."

Thomas looked a little punchy. "I don't believe this. Ghosts aren't real."

"Then who are you talking to?" Her mom sounded exasperated.

"Hailey?" Thomas gave her a searching look.

"You're not crazy," she said softly.

"You are if you let Hailey slip through your fingers," her mom said. "She loves you. You love her. One plus one. You do the math."

"But—"

"I'm not going to argue with you, Thomas. I can't. My time is up. Just remember that I love you. All of you." She pressed a kiss to Mac's cheek, and then she was gone.

"Oh!" Mac's eyes grew round. "Talk about weird. I could swear . . ."

Kennedy broke off his impassioned dissection of *Apocalypta* in midsentence. "Did I miss something? What's going on?"

Mac gave him a bewildered look. "I thought I felt . . . and the scent."

Thomas ignored everyone but Hailey. Without a word he gathered her chilly hands in his big, warm ones. "Sarah's right. Curse be damned," he said. "Hailey Miller, will you marry me?"

Kennedy's jaw dropped in a vacant expression Hailey was fairly certain he hadn't practiced in front of the mirror.

Kira grinned from ear to ear. "All right!"

"Yee-haw!" Mac shouted.

Hailey searched Thomas's face for any hint of doubt, but all she saw was the tenderness in his smile, the love in his eyes. She drew a deep breath. "Yes," she said.

And the one true prince and the one true princess lived happily ever after.

Meltdown

❉

Julie Leto

To Suezette and Lulu and all the Sucias
who have been so generous to me all year round.
Besitos y abrazos, mi amigas!

To the Klapka family, for the inspiration
of our illustrious Thanksgiving holiday cruise.
This landlubber would not have enjoyed the open seas
if not for all the family fun!

And to the Leto family, for making Christmas
an experience to be anticipated and savored
all year round.

I have to acknowledge all the wonderful people at Pocket who have believed in me—Louise Burke, Maggie Crawford, Megan McKeever, and especially Amy Pierpont—for giving me this opportunity to be in this amazing project with such amazing authors. Though Marisela Morales, the star of my Pocket series, doesn't make an appearance in the story, I hope readers will enjoy the story of a very different Latina living and loving in my hometown.

Chapter One

❄ ❄ ❄

Simon Brennan stared up from the account sheets in front of him as his public relations manager fumbled with the video camera on the other side of his desk. For a split second, he allowed himself to fantasize about turning the device on her, about focusing the lens, close-up, on the parts of her anatomy that haunted his dreams. Pouty lips. Rounds breasts. Hips a man could hold onto. Dark eyes and lashes that could steal his ability to speak. Isabel Ruiz was the kind of woman most men couldn't resist.

Luckily for him, he wasn't like most men. As long as he kept his interactions with Isabel completely professional and didn't spend more than a few moments alone with her, he'd succeed at keeping his hands—and other body parts—to himself.

Which reminded him.

"Ms. Ruiz, perhaps we should do this another time?"

She jumped, nearly knocking over the tripod. He put down his pen and leaned back in his chair. Odd. Of all the staff at the Making Moms Foundation, Isabel normally oozed confidence, defined grace, and presented an "all-together" package. He'd often wished she'd have been flighty or annoyingly vivacious like the public relations women he'd worked with in the past. No such luck. This woman defined slick, gorgeous, and, in a word, rhythmic. Just watching her walk from the copy machine to her office inspired a soundtrack in his head, headlined by Gloria Estefan, Juanes, and Carlos Santana.

But this afternoon, her natural elegance seemed to have deserted her. Her fingers fumbled with the camera. She kept kicking the tripod until he was fairly certain the thing would topple if she so much as sneezed.

"Ms. Ruiz?"

Her head snapped up, her eyes wide as if she'd forgotten he was there. "What?"

"We can do this tomorrow."

"No, we can't. I leave on my cruise in four days," she said.

"I'm aware of your schedule," he replied, still unclear on her point. From the moment he'd signed off on her vacation request, he'd considered her absence a mixed blessing. Only a week after her return, the Making Moms Foundation would host their main fund-raising event of the year to celebrate and highlight the accomplishments the group had made in the three counties it served. He needed her expertise to ensure the event achieved its goal of not only honoring the mostly teenage, single mother recipients of the foundation's training and scholarships, but that the group raised enough money to remain in business. On the other hand, he didn't mind having a full seven days where he didn't have to act like the woman wasn't turning him on just by crossing a room. "I'm sure whatever project you're cooking up can wait until you return."

"It can't," she muttered. She flipped a button. The television monitor that had been glowing solid blue suddenly flashed with color—his face in high-definition resolution.

He groaned.

She jumped in victory. "Got it!" She dug into her briefcase for a file folder, which she slapped on his desk. She backed away quickly, but not fast enough for him to miss a whiff of the cinnamon-spicy perfume she wore each and every day. A scent so sensual, he had to clear his throat before he could speak.

"What's this?"

"That's your script," she informed him. "Take a few minutes to look it over. It's short."

He flipped open the folder and scanned the message. "This is the opening to the speech I'm giving at the holiday gala."

She smiled, her pearly teeth flashing against her ruby red lipstick and caramel latte skin. "Right."

"And why are we recording this?"

The perplexed look on her face in no way diminished her incredible beauty. He could clearly see why the board of directors had hired her for the public relations position. Who could possibly ignore a woman like her?

"We're going to practice," she informed him.

He closed the folder. "Ms. Ruiz, I know how to read a speech."

"Call me Isabel."

She'd made the request before. In fact, several members of his upper management team had asked him to surrender to a more casual form of address. He hadn't complied, preferring a professional distance between him and his employees. But for her? He could attempt to make an exception. This one time. What could it hurt?

"Isabel," he conceded.

Her smile vanished and in the ensuing silence, Simon heard the name echo in his ears, rolling off his tongue in a tone painfully close to longing.

He cleared his throat again. "Maybe I should stick to Ms. Ruiz."

"No!"

The word exploded from those ruby red lips of hers, ratcheting up the tension now simmering through his office. An unfamiliar tightening in his chest caused him to shift uncomfortably in his chair. Not to mention a clenching of muscle and skin a little bit lower on his anatomy.

She took a deep breath and then softened her voice. "I mean, I like the way you say my name. With a little accent thrown in," she quipped.

"I studied in Madrid one summer in college," he said.

Her eyebrows arched, intensifying the roundness of her hypnotic dark eyes. "You speak Spanish?"

Courtesy of his childhood baby-sitter, Magdalena. Or nanny, he supposed, though that term implied luxuries his mother couldn't have afforded until recently. He tried to visit Maggie every few weeks, if for no other reason than because she was the one part of his childhood that hadn't scarred him for life. He squelched an internal smile, thinking about how the old woman would probably offer incense to the saints if she knew he had a Latina in his life who made him forget, momentarily at least, who he was and what he was supposed to be doing. Fortunately for him, Maggie would never find out about Isabel. Not if he had any luck at all. Or any sense.

"You look surprised at my knowledge of languages," he said, returning to the topic at hand.

"I am," she said, leaning against the front of his desk as if drawn by his talent with languages. "So many of our clients are Hispanic. If I'd known you could speak their language—"

"You would have exploited that knowledge to enhance my image."

She frowned at his dismissive tone. That was another thing he liked about Isabel Ruiz. She wasn't afraid to show displeasure with him, even if she did so mostly through her facial expressions. He gave her credit. He was well aware that most of his employees were scared to death of him. Came in handy. Usually. But not with her. He didn't want her to be afraid.

"Your image is my job," she insisted.

"Actually, no. Your job is to tend to the image of the foundation. I'm just the CEO."

"And as CEO, you are the face of the Making Moms Foundation, sometimes more so than the volunteers or even the girls who come to us for help. Anytime you go somewhere or give a speech or an interview, you represent the good we do. And quite frankly, your image could use a little work."

Okay, maybe a little fear on her part might not be so bad.

"I come across exactly as I am," he insisted. "I'm a professional dedicated to ensuring that every dime dropped into our bucket goes to help the women who come to us."

She snagged her bottom lip with her teeth and crossed her arms loosely over her chest, which, unfortunately, served to enhance her fabulous figure. In a pearl white, short-skirted suit with a red, scoop-neck blouse underneath, she reminded him of a Christmas present he might be tempted to unwrap. Slowly. Carefully. Sensuously.

Okay, he was officially losing his cool. He needed her to leave. Now. He pushed the script aside and retrieved the printouts he'd been reviewing.

She cleared her throat. When he begrudgingly looked up, she gestured toward the chair in front of his desk. Despite his private personal demons, he recognized that she had a job to do. Even if he hadn't recognized that fact, she'd remind him. And remind him. And remind him. Until she got her way.

After he nodded in approval, she sat.

"I need to be frank with you."

He arched a brow. He could always count on lively management meetings when Isabel had an opinion—particularly one that clashed with his. "Aren't you always?"

She snorted. "Hardly."

Did he want to know what she hadn't been frank about?

Probably not.

About three feet of mahogany separated them and once again, her perfume drifted toward him, heating up the atmosphere with the lush, exotic spices.

"I can't imagine you ever tempering your opinion," he said.

"You have no idea just how opinionated I can be. But listen, this isn't about my opinion. This is about the board of directors."

"Our board of directors?"

"Yes, the same pleasant little group of altruistic philanthropists who provide for our paychecks," she clarified.

"I'm familiar with them."

"They think you're stiff."

If they didn't want him to be stiff, they shouldn't allow Isabel Ruiz to spend private, after-hours time with him.

"I'm merely professional," he said.

"Yes, and in banking, where your professional roots are, your demeanor was probably appropriate. But you're not in banking anymore. You're the figurehead of a charitable foundation."

"I'm still responsible for this operation's financial accountability."

"Did you fire Richard?" she asked, incredulous. "If you did, someone should tell him to pack up his stuff and go home."

Simon smirked. Yes, he did indeed have a more than capable chief financial officer to manage the accounts, but he preferred crunching numbers to glad-handing donors. Sure, he did his part when required, but the idea of changing his personality to fit some image didn't sit right.

"They'd rather me wear loud ties and tell off-color jokes to entertain the donors?" he asked.

"The world isn't always about extremes," she replied, her eyes alight with the mental picture he'd just given her. "I was hoping to find more of a happy medium."

"Which would be?"

She touched her red-tipped fingernail to her matching lips as she considered his question. "A sapphire blue tie to match your eyes. And an occasional smile?"

He frowned. "I smile."

"Right," she replied. "Good example. You keep smiling like that and the American Dental Association is going to pick you as their new spokesman."

His frown deepened into a scowl. "I don't want to be anyone's spokesman."

"See? That's the trouble. You *are* the spokesman for Making Moms."

"I thought that was your job."

"It is. Sort of. I mean, yes, I'm the official spokesperson for the organization, but you're the head honcho. You can't go to charity functions and scowl your way toward bigger donations."

"I don't scowl," he insisted, the lie bitter on his tongue.

She slipped her hand into her tote bag and retrieved her compact mirror. "Must I? Oh, wait," she jumped to her feet and turned the television monitor toward him. "Does that look like a happy man to you?"

Simon's glower deepened, despite his best efforts to prove her wrong. But a man had his limits. Sitting in such close proximity to a sexy woman like Isabel Ruiz while trying to keep his instincts in check was no easy task.

"No, I suppose not."

A grin bloomed at her small victory. "The first step toward changing is admitting you have a problem."

"I don't think I'm in need of a twelve-step program for happiness."

"It isn't just your facial expressions," she insisted. "It's your whole demeanor." She popped to her feet. "Stand up."

He stared, wide-eyed, at her.

She leaned forward gently, her lashes fluttering over her dark brown eyes. "Please."

He immediately complied, swallowing a mumbled complaint.

"Look at your shoulders," she said.

He glanced down. "That's a little difficult."

She tapped the television screen. "You're stiff as a board."

"Could you stop saying that?" he begged, though the words came off more as an order.

She crossed around the back of his desk and placed her warm palms on his shoulders. "See? Stiff."

Without warning, she dug her fingers deep into the sinews. He closed his eyes and willed his body not to respond to her ministrations, but after a minute, he couldn't help but allow the heat to ease through his jacket and shirt and seep into his bones.

"There you go," she said, her voice husky and irresistible, her fingers working deeper and deeper into his flesh. "Look at the television now."

Without stopping her massage, she pressed him back down into his chair. For a second, he did notice a certain relaxed air about him—a more concentrated look in his eyes, a more slackened appearance to his jaw, and he allowed himself a moment to enjoy the warmth she pressed into his skin. But the minute a deep-throated groan slipped past his lips, his cheeks reddened and instantaneously, ice shot back through his veins. He jolted in his seat and she stepped back with a surprised yelp.

"I see no difference," he said, his spine ramrod straight and his shoulders so squared, she might have cut herself on the edges if she hadn't pulled away.

She slapped him hard on the shoulders. "Well, it was there. For a minute." She crossed back to the front of the desk and leaned wearily on the edge. "Then you froze up again."

"I don't see why the state of my posture has anything to do with you or the board of directors. What exactly have they asked you to do?"

She bit her bottom lip again. God, he wished she'd stop doing that. The unconscious action drove him crazy. All he could think about was taking a taste of those lips himself, something he'd never, ever do.

Interoffice romances were beyond dangerous, something he knew firsthand. Indulging in such a dalliance while at Braselton, White and Schaeffer—the investment firm he'd worked at prior to joining the bank—had been one thing. Taking such a risk while employed by a non-profit was even more extreme—especially since this particular nonprofit had recently undergone a management shakeup due to the inappropriate behavior of the former chief executive officer. And Simon prided himself on his professionalism, his ability to get the job done without ever crossing the line. His demeanor was, after all, one reason why he'd been hired after the previous CEO had gone down in a blaze of shameless glory.

First his predecessor had been caught in an affair

with his married secretary. Then one of the volunteers. Several of the women enrolled in their classes complained about the way he leered at them. During Simon's interview process, the board of directors had made no bones about why Simon appealed to them. He was the polar opposite of their previous chief executive officer. And now they wanted him to change?

"The board has voiced no displeasure with my job performance," he said.

"When it comes to running the foundation with ultimate efficiency and instilling confidence in corporate sponsorships, you're the man. But our bread and butter, the homegrown, grassroots donors? You're scaring them away."

Simon crossed his arms defensively. "Our donations have taken a dip, but we're located in a hurricane zone. Big, private donations have mostly gone to relief efforts. All charities not recovery-related are taking hits." He lifted the folder he'd been working with earlier. "We're still in the black."

"And clearly, the board wants to stay that way. They've asked me to make you more warm and fuzzy."

Simon's jaw dropped, but he quickly closed his mouth and swallowed the expletive crackling on his tongue. He'd never heard of anything so ridiculous.

"I had no idea 'warm and fuzzy' was a job requirement," he quipped.

She narrowed her dark eyes at him. "Neither did the board, I don't think, until it became clear that the women we're trying to help have been too intimidated to even speak with you."

"That's an exaggeration," he insisted, but he couldn't

help feeling offended. "I visited the halfway house just yesterday."

"How many pregnant teenagers did you speak to?"

"Quite a few."

"How many words did you exchange?"

He shoved her file back at her. "I didn't count."

"Bet you could have on one hand," she retorted.

"You're perilously close to insulting me," he warned.

She rolled her eyes. "You think I'm enjoying this? You think I'm excited about having to go into my boss's office, a guy I don't mind admitting that I genuinely like working with, and telling him he's stiff and cold and unfriendly?"

"Do you really believe that?"

Isabel leaned closer, her hands braced on his desk. Unable to stop himself, he allowed his gaze to flicker over her cleavage. So curved. So alluring. Her skin reminded him of melted caramel and he could only imagine the glow that would burnish her flesh once she returned from her Mexican vacation.

She cleared her throat.

"Nice necklace," he said, covering.

She glanced quickly at the trio of diamonds dangling from her neck. "Gotta love good cubic zirconia."

He smiled, glad the topic had changed. "The joys of working for a nonprofit."

She slid her hip onto his desk. Suddenly, his large, spacious office seemed incredibly confined. The temperature rose several degrees as her perfume once again tempted him with scents that reminded him of red candles, gold cushions, and lingerie in deep, deep purple.

"One of those joys is connecting with people," she said softly. "Touching their hearts."

She reached out and pressed the tip of her finger to the place on his chest where his heart should be. It wasn't there. At the moment her touch connected with his shirt, his heart had dropped hard into his stomach.

He sat back in his chair, outside of her range. She stood and placed her hands on her hips.

"You do have a heart, don't you?"

"I'd still be working in banking if I didn't," he admitted.

The truth was rewarded by her sweet grin, though the twinkle in her eyes made him a little nervous. "Good, then I have something to work with. Before I leave for Mexico, I intend to have you all warmed up and ready for our holiday extravaganza." She retrieved the script she'd given him earlier and handed it back to him. "You up to the challenge?"

Querulously, Simon took the file folder with the script inside and flung it open. The sooner he did what she asked, the sooner he could get her out of his office. And out of his mind. At least until he went to bed, where she'd invariably torment him in his dreams.

"I'm always up to a challenge," he said, his voice perilously close to a growl.

Her response was a sassy smile. "Good, because so am I."

Chapter Two

※ ❋ ※

With a deep breath, Isabel pushed open the glass door leading into the health club Simon frequented on Saturday mornings. She expected to be greeted with the piquant scent of salty, stale sweat, but instead she inhaled the cool odor of ionized air. She stopped dead in the middle of the marble foyer and whistled softly at the impressive twelve-foot ceiling, pristine pearlized walls, and buttery leather couches adorning the entrance hall. She glanced over her shoulder, just to make sure the real world still existed behind her. Yup. The manicured landscaping and freshly paved parking lot brimming with BMWs, Mercedes-Benzes, and even one Dodge Viper remained on the other side of the door, out of reach in more ways than just the obvious. Isabel had once again stepped into the Neverland of the rich and healthy.

"Ms. Ruiz?"

A perky young woman in a royal blue polo shirt and crisp tan shorts greeted Isabel with a warm smile.

Isabel returned the grin. "I must stick out like a sore thumb around here, huh?"

The woman had the decency to look confused. "I'm sorry?"

Isabel waved her comment away. "Never mind. I'm here to meet Simon Brennan."

Ms. Perkiness nodded. "My name is Lisa. Mr. Brennan asked me to keep an eye out for you. Your guest membership is all set. He's over at the bikes."

With a skip that reminded Isabel of Dorothy's fateful adventure down the yellow brick road, Lisa led the way through the club, peppering their short walk with information about the equipment and the amenities, such as complimentary massages and aromatherapy, as if Isabel could afford the monthly fee this place charged. For the cost of burning off a few calories in this joint, she could probably afford the payments on a brand-new car. One of her job perks, however, was getting to hang out with the rich and locally famous, without all the pressure of actually having to live that lifestyle.

Though she wasn't exactly sure that hanging out with Simon Brennan on a Saturday morning could be considered a perk or pressure-free, not after the disastrous sessions they'd had since her vain attempt at media training. Instead of loosening up, the man was actually getting harder to connect with. Harder to read. As if he was hiding something from her.

Like a secret crush?

No, wait. That was what *she* was trying to hide.

She attempted to maintain her controlled façade when she spotted Simon, but since he was in the process of stripping out of his nylon workout pants to reveal cotton gym shorts that did amazing things to his backside, she failed miserably.

"Here she is!" Lisa announced happily.

Isabel pressed her tongue against the top of her mouth, just to make sure she hadn't swallowed it. She'd thought herself so incredibly brilliant when she'd suggested they schedule a workout together since all her other devices for softening the guy up had failed miserably. Her strategy this time aimed at getting to know him better outside the office milieu, thereby arming her with the knowledge she could use to coax out a new, relaxed Simon Brennan to present to the board of directors. Now, however, she agreed with her sister, Suezette, who upon hearing her plan, had instantly and professionally declared that her older sibling had lost her mind.

"You fantasize about the man and now you want to see him half-dressed and sweaty and breathing heavy? What are you trying to do? Torture yourself?"

Suezette couldn't have been more right. Isabel was teetering on the brink of sado-masochism.

She offered up a silent prayer, hoping there was some saint in the heavens who might save her from complete condemnation for the lusty thoughts zinging through her brain. Who'd have guessed he had such long, lean legs and such a perfect backside underneath those tailored slacks of his? Well, she'd actually done a whole lot of guessing about that exact subject, but now that she had confirmation, she doubted she'd ever regain the ability to speak.

She dragged her gaze up to his face, where Simon's

eyes, deep blue and dreamy, darkened sensually. For a split second. Maybe. Could have been her imagination. Or wishful thinking.

She pasted on a grin equal to Lisa's inexplicable enthusiasm. "Yes, here I am! Ready to get my heart rate up?"

Ha! He'd accomplished that goal simply by undressing.

Simon eyed her skeptically. "I had my doubts that you'd show."

His condescending tone spiked her ire. She dropped her bag and placed one fist on her hip. "Don't I look like I can handle your workout?"

Dios mío, when was she going to learn to keep her big mouth shut? The minute the challenge spilled from her lips, she dreaded the fallout . . . and just as she anticipated, Simon's gaze flicked down her body in full assessment mode. She willed herself not to squirm, but even though she'd yet to remove her oversize sweatshirt, the tank top and slim yoga pants she wore underneath seemed to tighten under his scrutiny.

"Hard to tell in that potato sack, but I'm sure you're physically fit."

He managed to be cool and insulting all at the same time. God, she had her work cut out for her.

Lisa disappeared, snagging Isabel's bag with a promise to assign her a locker and keep the key for her at the front desk. In a wave of defiance, Isabel ripped off the sweatshirt and tossed it over the handlebars of the nearest bike and then climbed on. "I'll show you physically fit, Brennan."

She focused on the control panel, ignoring the heated stare she was certain she'd imagined. Wishful thinking yet again. She was so not Simon Brennan's type. Not that she knew that for sure. She'd never once seen him with a date. He didn't have personal pictures in his office and he never, according to his secretary, took calls from women unless they were about business. Since he'd come to work at Making Moms, she'd never witnessed a single indication that the man had a personal life at all. Hence their meeting at his gym, which was the only place she figured she could get him to relax.

Yet according to some of the foundation's donors, many of whom knew Simon from his previous life in investment banking, he gravitated toward two types of women—delicate damsels in need of rescuing or icy ballbusters who sharpened their claws on imported jewels and soothed their consciences with Cristal champagne. Not that Isabel didn't like a sip of the bubbly from time to time, but otherwise, she was not in his league.

And frankly, he was out of hers. She preferred men who didn't mind exhibiting their emotions every so often. Not that she'd had much luck in finding the right guy to warm her bed. The sheets had been particularly chilly as of late. But she wasn't spending much time looking recently, either. Instead, she'd focused on going out with her girlfriends and having a good time, and frankly, she couldn't imagine that the word "fun" made a single appearance on Simon Brennan's list of long-term or short-term goals.

Despite the fact that she'd now witnessed the lean, tanned muscles of his legs without the camouflage of tailored pants, she chastised herself to keep her mind on her work. She'd come here today to connect with him through the kind of sweat and heavy breathing that wouldn't ruin her life and career and perhaps discover a little more about what made him tick. If she could uncover more about what he liked and who he was, she might yet find a way to bring the real man to the surface and push the staid, unyielding banker's persona out of the way of her advancing career.

Still searching in vain for a power button on the stationary bike, she pressed the speed control, the incline monitor, and the resistance level gauge, but nothing happened.

Resistance level. How apropos.

"How does this thing work, anyway?" she asked with a huff.

Simon cleared his throat, a sound which lured her attention away from the circuitry. His expression, masked by his classic scowl, failed to reveal anything useful. Like whether or not he'd been intrigued by how she looked in her snug tank top and yoga pants. Admittedly, she'd chosen the most modest exercise outfit she owned since today was supposed to be about business, but a little wide-eyed wonder at seeing her out of her office uniform would have gone a long way.

A long way toward the path of destruction.

He leaned over and set the machine for her, explaining the features with a crisp, emotionless tone. She opened her mouth to comment on his lack of enthusiasm, but decided they should have a few miles under their belts together before she started criticizing. Besides, when she leaned a little closer to make sure he'd set the ramp level equal to his machine, the whiff she'd gotten of his musky cologne sapped her ability to speak.

"On your mark," he joked.

She arched a brow. "Was that an attempt at humor?"

He smirked. "Not if you had to ask."

She bit the inside of her lip to keep from laughing, and then decided a good, old-fashioned chuckle of a response might do the man some good. Her experiment was rewarded with a small grin, one that nearly melted her insides. Before she oozed all over the bike, she concentrated on building a rhythm with her thighs. After approximately ten minutes, she realized she probably should have stretched before she started. Actually, she probably should have stayed home in bed and then met Suezette at their parents' for *café con leche* and sweet rolls, but there was no turning back now.

She closed her eyes, trying to block out the burn in her quadriceps, when Simon broke the lingering silence.

"How are you doing?"

"Just fine," she replied.

"These exercise bikes can be very demanding. If you want to slow down . . ."

She silenced him with a glare.

"Prickly when you're in pain, are you?"

"It's better than being prickly all the time."

He huffed. "I don't recall you telling me that the board thought I was hard to get along with."

She rolled her eyes. The last thing she needed was to deplete his self-confidence. Not that the man didn't have enough arrogance to get him through any shortage.

"They didn't. I just meant that you don't seem very open to my brand of image building."

"I like my image," he retorted.

She leaned forward on her elbows and turned toward him. "Tell me," she asked, "how exactly do you think other people see you?" Perception was a huge part of her job. She couldn't very well change the man's attitude toward the image he projected if they weren't even on the same page.

"I think people see me as efficient."

"True. What else?"

"I have a reputation for being fairly creative and resourceful."

"Definitely."

"I'm honest and inventive."

"All true."

"Then I don't see what the board's problem is."

"Do you think you're friendly?"

"I've never purposefully snubbed anyone, if that is what you're asking. I'm not a snob."

"No, it's not what I'm asking at all and I've never heard anyone use the word 'snob' and your name in the same sentence. But there is a long distance between a cold snub and a genuine, open-hearted welcome."

"I invited you to my health club. Do you feel unwelcome?"

Her legs were starting to shake from the exertion. "No, I just feel like once I'm done with this ride, I'll never be able to walk again."

He leaned over and made adjustments to her control panel. Immediately, the incline level dropped and the speed slowed. She almost moaned in appreciation, especially after he slowed his own bike down to the same degree.

"Better?" he asked.

She adjusted her body to the new speed. "Much. Thanks. So tell me, Mr. Brennan, is working out your idea of a good time?"

He stretched his arms up and took a deep breath, followed by a hard exhalation. "It beats sitting around on the couch watching football and eating potato chips."

Isabel shrugged. "I like potato chips."

"So do I," he admitted, "but if I indulged in all the things I liked simply because I liked them, I wouldn't be very healthy."

"Probably not," she conceded, but he might be a hell of a lot happier. "Depends on what you like, don't you think?"

He nodded. "I suppose."

"So?"

"What?" he asked.

"What other things do you like to do? You like working out. You like working. That can't be your entire repertoire."

"Actually, it pretty much is lately."

"What about before lately?"

His brow furrowed slightly. "Well, I used to be a member of a men's social club. We fished, went skiing, played the occasional hand of poker."

"Classic male bonding."

"Precisely."

"You're not active anymore?"

"I share a scotch with one or two of the guys every so often, sometimes take in a Bucs game."

"Nothing too taxing."

He sighed heavily. "Look, if you want me to admit that my life is boring, I'll do it. What about you? You're at the office for as many hours as I am. You can't tell me you have a raving social life."

"Actually," she said with a grin, "I do. I shop with my cousin every Saturday. I hit the clubs in Ybor with my sister on Saturday night. I do Sunday dinner with my family."

"What about Friday night?"

"That's date night," she answered quickly.

"You date?"

Shocked, she stopped pedaling. He did the same.

"Was that out of line?" He looked only half-repentant.

"Only if you think I'm not dateable or something."

"No, not at all. I simply . . ."

He stopped speaking and for this, she was glad.

Weird. He'd asked the very question she'd wanted to ask him, for purely personal reasons. She did, after all, have her personal fantasies to feed. But why would her boss be interested in such information from her? Unless . . . ?

"We're supposed to be talking about you, not me."

He resumed his ride. "Is that the rule?" he asked, flashing her what suspiciously looked like a smile.

"No," she replied, trying to balance her feet on the pedals and restart her ride. "But you're the one we should be focusing on. And you don't have to sound so surprised that men find me attractive enough to shell out the cash to cover dinner and a movie."

"That's not what I meant and you know it," he replied, a genuine grin taking some of the sting out of his words. "You're very attractive and gregarious. I imagine you have quite a few men banging on your door."

Isabel tried to concentrate on her exercise, attempting to ignore the trickle of sweat pooling between her breasts. Okay, was he playing it cool and flirting in a roundabout way or was he simply making small talk? Small talk, she noted, that focused on her instead of him.

"I enjoy my fair share of dates," she verified. "But like you said, I work a lot. I don't have time for anything serious. Besides, most of the guys I see get intimidated by my love for my job. They don't seem to understand that I take it home with me because I love it, not because I'm some shark woman obsessed with making it to the top, though I'm not afraid of heights, if you know what I mean. What about you? I'll bet the women you date have all sorts of preconceived notions about you, too."

With a few taps on the control panel, Simon resumed the more challenging ride he'd first programmed. Isabel was tempted to match his pace now that her muscles had loosened up, but she didn't want to upset the balance of this conversation, which had just entered some seriously interesting territory.

Unfortunately, he remained silent.

"Well?" she goaded.

"I fail to see how discussing my personal life will in any way help you achieve your objective."

She stopped riding and shook off a chill. The pedals continued to spin in her abrupt absence. "Whoa! You just went from one hundred to zero in a split second."

"Excuse me?"

"One hundred was friendly and relaxed. Zero is back to your closed-off, stodgy self."

He grimaced, but didn't offer a retort. Clearly, she'd touched on some seriously dangerous territory.

"My personal life is off-limits," he concluded.

She raised an eyebrow as she turned to resume her ride. "Are you gay?"

He expressed no shock at her question. "Would it matter if I were?"

"Not to me," she answered. He'd just be one more player with great potential traded to the other team, she supposed, but somehow she didn't think this was the case. She'd asked more out of logic than anything else. If Simon Brennan was gay, she was a blond WASP from the suburban Midwest. "But if you are, let me be the one to mourn on behalf of women everywhere."

A crack of a smile crept across his lips. "I'm not homosexual," he said firmly. "I'm simply a very private man. My preferences in women cannot possibly assist in your goal to change my image with the board. I'd prefer we not go down that road."

Isabel nodded. Great. One more path to the real Simon Brennan obstructed with a two-ton roadblock, but really, her interest in his dating preferences had been more personal than professional. She upped the velocity on her bike and, with shared smiles between them, took off at racing speed.

She'd find another way to get through Simon's walls of ice. She had to, or they could both kiss their jobs good-bye.

Chapter Three

❄ ❄ ❄

For the first time in her life, Isabel realized she'd bitten off more than she could chew. She went over the list of strategies one more time, turning her shoulder so that her sister, Suezette, who was sitting across the aisle from her on the air-conditioned bus bound for Chichén Itzá, couldn't see.

Unfortunately, her cousin, Lulu, who'd gone to the front of the bus to refill her margarita glass, caught her in the act.

"Oh, no you're not, *mi'ja*," Lulu chastised, her pale green drink sloshing over the side as the bus jumped a pot hole. "That had better be a list of all the brands of tequila we're going to buy when we get back to town and not something related to your work."

Suezette looked up wearily from the novel she'd brought with her to wile away the two-and-a-half-hour drive from Progreso, Mexico, to the Mayan temple. One margarita per hour was her self-imposed limit and she'd sucked hers down the minute the bus driver had put the vehicle in drive. "Leave her alone, Lu. She's got work to do."

Lulu pushed her five-foot-two, one-hundred-and-forty-pound body in between Isabel and the seat in front of her, then plopped down next to the window. The tropical Yucatán landscape dimmed beneath ominous black clouds overhead. Great, Isabel thought. We're going to travel all the way to Chichén Itzá and then get trapped in the bus on account of rain.

"I don't see how she can do any work when Mr. Too Sexy, Too Cool is back in Tampa," Lulu assessed.

Isabel decided to stop trying to hide her work and instead put her tote bag on her lap as a desk and spread out her folded list so she could review all the points. "I've got to come up with a new strategy to change Simon's attitude. The big charity event is only a week after I get back. That doesn't give me much time."

Suezette folded her book over her chest, her inquisitive eyes sparkling behind trendy, catlike glasses. "You ran him through the standard media training exercises, right?"

No matter what they discussed, Suezette always sounded like the scientist she was. If it wasn't for the fact that Isabel knew she'd die of jealousy, she'd fix Simon up with her younger-by-a-year sister and watch the intellectual, conservative sparks flair.

"Of course," Isabel answered.

On the other hand, Suezette might have her nose buried in books half the time and she might often speak in long strings of words that contained no less than seven syllables each, but when the time was right, the girl knew how to party.

Definitely not Simon Brennan material.

"No improvement?" Suezette asked.

Isabel shook her head. "It's weird. For split seconds here and there, I notice a difference. Like when I took him to Nordstrom and had him try on some new suits. I was unbuttoning his top button and for an instant, there was, I don't know, this natural warmth about him that nearly knocked me off my feet. His eyes seemed bluer. His skin pinker. A smile teased his mouth. But just before I could point it out to him, it was gone."

Lulu chuckled. "Men don't like getting caught with their dicks hard."

"Lulu!" Isabel shouted. "His dick wasn't hard."

"Did you check?" Suezette asked.

Her expression was so completely serious, the three of them dissolved into giggles. If only her sister and her cousin realized how insane the idea was. Simon Brennan attracted to her? Not likely. He'd had ample opportunities over the last week, particularly, to take advantage of her naturally flirtatious nature, but he hadn't made a single move.

"You guys have to help me," Isabel begged. Clearly, her cousin, a high school English teacher, and her sister, a research scientist at the Florida Aquarium, had no expertise in Isabel's field. But they were both women who had plenty of experience with men. Besides, she'd tried everything she knew. Maybe it was time to think outside the box.

Lulu took a long sip of her margarita. "I say seduce him."

Suezette's eyebrows popped up high on her head, as if the suggestion merited further study.

"Not an option," Isabel said, somewhat bitterly. "I can't do my boss and expect to keep my job."

Not that interoffice politics was remotely the reason why she wouldn't sleep with him. The man simply wasn't interested.

"Is there an expressed written exclusion against office romances?" Suezette asked.

"Not exactly," Isabel replied. The issue had come up several times in staff discussions, especially after their previous CEO got caught with his pants down. Or when some media story about affairs in the workplace hit the news. Otherwise, no one said much. Ninety percent of the staff was female and of that ninety percent, seventy-five percent were married, engaged, or seriously involved. Two of the women were married to men who also worked at the foundation, though all had been hitched prior to their employment. As one of the few single *chicas* on the staff, Isabel had tried hard to keep her personal and professional lives separate. She couldn't imagine the potential chaos if she went after the boss, especially while in pursuit of her ultimate, board-sanctioned goal.

"You can't toss out the possibility, then," Suezette concluded. "However, I don't think it's the most ethical first choice."

Lulu snorted. "Who gives a fuck about ethics? If she doesn't get this guy to let his hair down, she's going to lose her job anyway. Desperate times call for desperate measures, *verdad?*"

The bus slowed and through the windows, they watched the Mexican jungle thick with bright green foliage grow dark thanks to the ominous sky. Through breaks in the greenery, they spied stone pillars that looked thousands of years old, which was appropriate since they likely were.

"We're here," Lulu announced, downing the rest of her drink.

Suezette slid her novel back inside her tote bag. "Good. We can change the subject. Isabel, we have two days left on the cruise. I'm sure that by the time we reach port in Tampa, we can come up with a better idea to loosen up Simon Brennan than you sleeping with him in order to put a smile on his face."

Lulu squeezed by. She and Suezette immediately started talking trash about who was going to make it to the top of the ancient pyramid fastest, despite what felt like one-hundred-degree heat (and two-hundred-percent humidity) pouring into the bus from outside. Since they'd signed up for this excursion, Isabel hadn't been sure she was going to attempt climbing the gazil-lion narrow steps it took to get to the top. She'd only wanted to escape the cruise ship and her parents and her brother for a few hours and do something with just the girls. Now she realized she should have hauled her butt back to her stateroom to rack her brain until she figured out what to do about Simon.

She'd tried honesty. She'd been very clear with him during that first media training session, laying on the line the specific demands the board had made of her, and therefore, of him. She might have been less frus-trated with her lack of success if she'd felt like the man hadn't been trying. But he'd gone shopping with her, for Pete's sake. They'd gone to lunch. They'd worked out to-gether on his own turf—at his gym—where she'd hoped that endorphins and sweat would do the trick. All that excursion had done was shown her how delicious he looked in a tank top and shorts.

The fact of the matter was, Simon Brennan had issues. Personal issues. Deep, ingrained personal issues that had made him who he was and Isabel simply couldn't figure out a way to bust through since a) she wasn't a psychologist, and b) he'd made it entirely clear that his personal life was entirely off-limits.

Of course, maybe if they got horizontal . . .

"You coming?"

Isabel snapped out of a reverie that suddenly made her body even hotter than the air blowing in from the open bus door. Suezette and Lulu skipped down the steps, leaving her behind. She snatched the useless list, crumbled it with disgust, and shoved it into her bag. On the entire ride from the port at Progreso to the ruins of Chichén Itzá, she'd done nothing but think about Simon. Maybe if she could push him out of her mind for five consistent seconds, the answer to her dilemma would come to her. Beyond sleeping with him. Because frankly, the more she lingered on that possibility, insane as it was, the more she could think of nothing else.

Isabel couldn't deny that she was attracted to him; she'd always gravitated toward men who exuded power. Power often equaled control, though, and if there was one thing Isabel didn't want it was some man telling her what to do. In her culture, bossy boys were a dime a dozen—she certainly didn't need to go shopping outside the neighborhood to find one.

But at the moment, Isabel wasn't perusing the aisles for a relationship. She was toying more with the idea of one night—maybe two. Enough to coax the sexy, sensual side of Simon to the surface while at the same time satisfying the itch she'd had for her handsome boss since they'd first met.

With a shake, Isabel banished the thought from her brain, or at least pushed the possibilities back into her subconscious where they belonged. For the moment, she was going to enjoy the scenery and the history of the Yucatán. Her thoughts about Simon, as usual, would remain the star of her nighttime fantasies.

The Pyramid of Kukulkán proved just as magnificent as Isabel imagined. The timeworn stone structure, a four-sided triangle with a flattened top, jutted into the sky. Giant serpent heads, the detail of the carvings mostly lost to wind and rain, guarded the temple, while shooting up the middle on each side were ninety-one narrow steps that captured the gloom in the skies. Voices drifted down as tourists already at the top tested the wondrous ability to speak to those below without increasing their volume.

Yet despite the rumbling of thunder in the distance and the fact that they all hailed from Florida, the lightning capital of North America, and knew better than to climb to high ground right before a storm, Lulu and Suezette challenged each other to walk to the top. Isabel, on the other hand, left them to their contest, drawn by the site of a thousand columns and the mysterious ball field where archaeologists speculated the losers lost their heads.

Chugging on the water she'd bought on the cruise ship and wandering amid clusters of sunburned tourists, Isabel's attention ping-ponged between the architectural wonders around her and the pamphlet she'd picked up on the ship. After nearly an hour, she found herself walking down a long dirt pathway leading away from the main pyramid, El Castillo, toward a sacred cenote rumored to hold water as old as time itself.

Thick clusters of thin-trunked trees lined either side of the lane, the foliage condensed by large, leafy plants that glistened with moisture from the falling rain. Soon the drops morphed into a fine mist and, oddly, then into a thick fog. At first, Isabel thought she'd seen artisans sitting on the side of the road hawking their handmade wares, but now she was entirely alone, the path narrowed by the low-hanging clouds. Looking over her shoulder, she considered going back. No one seemed to be behind her. No one ahead. The suddenly cool haze, however, caressed her overheated skin. The slightly piquant scent of freshly hewn rock and recently turned soil filled her nostrils. Odd, since the place was over a thousand years old. She even thought, for a second, even in the dreariness, that she smelled the sun.

Once at the end of the path, the cloud of moisture blew aside long enough for her to read her now-damp pamphlet. She was at the sacred cenote, a naturally formed sinkhole filled with water. The limestone beneath her feet made the way rocky, but a few steps later, she found herself on the ledge of an impressive watering hole that reminded her of an exotic lagoon. In the gloomy light, the water shimmered emerald green.

"The Maya made offerings here," a voice intoned.

Isabel looked up. Despite the fact that she was oddly alone, the voice hadn't startled her.

"Excuse me?" she asked, scanning the landscape for who had spoken.

An old woman dressed in traditional Mexican garb

emerged from behind a thin tree. "The Maya. They made offerings here. To their gods."

Isabel recoiled from the dark water, which sparkled despite the lack of sunshine. "Human offerings?"

The woman smiled, her face at once leathery and lined. The grin changed her expression until she hardly looked real. "Perhaps. Two times the cenote has been dredged. The most wonderful pots and statues and talismans have been found. Like this one."

She turned her gnarled hand and in her weathered palm was a tiny gold mask, no larger than a silver dollar, but twice as glossy.

Isabel leaned forward. The face was primitive, but intriguing.

"Looks like Santa Claus," she offered.

The woman's face skewed in confusion. *"Quién?"*

With a wince, Isabel stepped back. "You know, Santa? The Christmas elf? Big guy in red? *Papá Noel?*"

The woman's eyes brightened a bit, but the confusion never quite left her opaque gaze.

"Never mind," Isabel insisted, then wondered how this native woman came to possess such a lovely artifact. Isabel thought it belonged in a museum, or at least a locked display case. The gold glistened as if it had just been forged and sculpted by the ancient artisans who had clearly done the work. "Did you get that from this cenote?"

The woman's smile indicated she might not have fully understood. "This is powerful magic."

"Magic?" Boy, could Isabel ever use some of that right now. Magic was, perhaps, the only strategy she hadn't considered in her dilemma with Simon Brennan.

"Ah," the woman said knowingly, "you have need of magic?"

"Who doesn't?" Isabel asked, trying to sound cynical, but not quite pulling it off.

"Take it," the woman offered, extending her palm toward Isabel.

Instinctively, Isabel shook her head. "I couldn't."

"Hold the amulet. Ask the gods for help. Then toss the tribute into the cenote. Your wish will come true."

The dark pupils of the woman's eyes seemed to swirl with a cloudiness much like the mist that again brushed Isabel's body, practically pushing her closer to the charm. Her fingers itched and she rubbed them against her thigh, trying to think rationally before she succumbed to such a crazy, desperate act.

Then again, what did she have to lose? If the woman was merely deluded, the worst that could happen would be that Isabel could be arrested for tossing a priceless artifact into a bottomless watery pit. She looked around again. Except for the woman, no one stirred. Once more, the fog had descended like a velvet curtain. Even if someone was nearby, they'd never see her.

Isabel took the coin and walked to the edge of the limestone. The gold warmed quickly in her palm. She closed her eyes and concentrated.

Instantly, Simon's face flashed in her mind's eye. Oddly, he was smiling. She remembered. She'd made a joke while they were working out. He'd laughed. The outburst had been so brief, she'd hardly registered it at the time. But his response had been open, genuine. Real. She caught a glimpse of the man she needed him to be, the man she knew he could be if he'd only relax. If he'd only let her in. Yes, this was her wish.

She tried to form the words in her mind, but another image curled out of the swirling colors behind her eyelids. Simon taking away the hand weights. Simon pushing her down onto the weight bench. Simon kissing her neck as he pulled down her tank and revealed her dark, hard-nippled breasts.

Shocked, Isabel's eyes flew open and she jumped back. The coin flew out of her hand, bounced once on the hard limestone, then whistled into the cenote. She gasped, which covered the sound of the splash in the green water below. The fog returned with a vengeance, enveloping her until she couldn't even see her hand in front of her face. Iciness shot up her spine, then rippled across her skin.

The mist began to choke her, and a feeling of dread overcame her, but she couldn't seem to get her legs to move, despite her brain screaming for her to run. Get away. Now. While she still had a chance to escape.

Or was she too late?

Chapter Four

❄ ❄ ❄

Someone grabbed her elbow. Isabel whirled around and expected to see the old woman, but instead saw Suezette, her round, brown eyes wide with worry. *"Mi'ja,* what the hell are you doing?"

Isabel blinked. The sun suddenly flashed against the white rock and nearly blinded her. She pulled her sunglasses off the top of her head and shoved them on. The fog was gone. The rain had disappeared. The mysterious old woman was nowhere in sight. And Isabel was no longer alone. Thirty to forty people milled around the edge of the cenote. How did they all get there so fast? And without her hearing them?

"I'm just looking at the water. What did you think I was doing?"

Suezette crossed her arms tightly over her chest. "You looked like you were going to jump."

Isabel laughed uncomfortably. "I did not."

Lulu joined them, her mood ebullient as she showed them a mask she'd just bought from one of the several dozen vendors Isabel now saw were lining the path.

Their wares were spread out before them on colorful mats and blankets. They were bargaining and hawking, their voices blending into an intense buzz that Isabel would have sworn she hadn't heard just seconds before.

"Isn't this just the coolest?" asked Lulu.

She showed the mask first to Suezette, who couldn't quite see the artistry, then turned to Isabel. Guiltily, Isabel fingered the mask, which was made of wood and looked extremely similar to the coin that she'd just tossed into the water.

"It's definitely unique," Isabel replied.

Lulu snickered, but remained unmoved. "I'm going to hang him up when I get home. He'll bring good luck. You watch. Here, I got one for each of you."

Her cousin and her sister, now complaining heartily about the heat despite the fact that they'd grown up in Florida and should be used to such temperatures by now, continued their discussion as if the world hadn't just turned upside down. Isabel spun around, trying desperately to find any sign of the Mexican woman who'd handed her the charm, yet knowing she'd find none. Had she actually tossed the coin into the pit while wishing for a forbidden liaison with her boss, or had it all been some sort of weird reaction to heat stroke?

Isabel scrambled into her bag for another bottled water. The one she found was lukewarm, but she didn't care. It would do until they reached the bus—more specifically, until they reached the margaritas that were being served so freely.

"You okay?" Lulu asked, placing her hand softly on Isabel's arm as they moved back toward the path.

She had to use all her self-control to keep from jumping out of her skin. "Yeah, I'm fine."

"This work crap really has you freaked."

Isabel forced a smile. "I've never lost a job because I couldn't get my boss to warm up."

Lulu shrugged and out of earshot of Suezette, who was now glancing over the masks being sold a few feet away, leaned in and gave her a wink. "I don't think your idea of sleeping with him was that bad."

"It was your idea, not mine," Isabel said.

"Then I especially don't think it was that bad," her cousin replied.

Isabel chuckled, but not because she thought the situation was funny. "It's just another way to lose my job, Lu."

"You might already lose it, right? If you don't bend the man to your will? I'd go for it, if I were you. A girl's gotta do what a girl's got to do."

"What if he's not interested?"

At this, Lulu broke into a hearty laugh that made her ample breasts jiggle provocatively underneath her tank top. "A man not interested in one of the *chicas de* Ruiz? Impossible."

Isabel smirked. Yeah, she, her sister, and her cousin had never exactly had a problem attracting men. Of course, neither she, her sister, nor her cousin ever went after a man like Simon Brennan. They tended to gravitate toward men who actually exhibited interest in them.

Lulu started back toward the path, catching up to Suezette as she finalized a purchase and then shouting to Isabel to follow. After one last glance into the cenote, Isabel caught up with her sister and cousin and decided she was better off forgetting about the old woman, the talisman, the wish she'd made—and especially the erotic image she'd formed in her mind shortly before tossing the coin into the water. Even if she had really met an ancient Mayan woman—which she wasn't sure she had—she had nothing to worry about.

Magic wasn't real. And even if it was, she doubted the ancient Mayan gods would have any interest whatsoever in her career, much less her love life.

No, when it came to Simon Brennan, she was on her own. And unless she came up with some brilliant scheme in the next forty-eight hours, she was also very screwed.

"Who is she?"

Simon looked up from his dinner and found his mother staring at him as if he possessed the secret of immortality. Wanting nothing more than a quiet meal alone and a chance to figure out what the hell he was going to do tomorrow when Isabel returned, he'd insisted the maître d' at his favorite restaurant give him a table as near to the back and away from the other diners as possible.

Unfortunately, no one he knew possessed disruption radar like his mother. Give her trouble to find, and she was like a bloodhound—particularly when it came to him.

"Jennifer," he said by way of greeting.

She rolled her thickly lashed eyes. "I wish you'd call me 'Mother' or 'Mom', or hell, I'd even settle for 'Mommy,' though it would sound a little funny now that you're over thirty."

Which made her barely forty-six, but who was counting?

Simon calmly set down his menu. "I haven't called you by any of those endearments since I was five and you asked me to lie to the landlord about you having cancer so he wouldn't evict us for unpaid rent."

She removed her cashmere gloves and smoothed her recently highlighted hair. For her most recent marriage, his mother had chosen to be a blonde. Maybe if she had more fun, the wedding vows would actually stick this time.

"I can't believe you remember that," she said with a chuckle. His mother always did find her larcenous ways hilarious, especially now that she was married to a man richer than God. A man, he now saw, who was sitting across the dining room at a table full of equally impressive-looking businessmen.

"I remember quite a bit of my childhood, unfortunately. Why else would I head up an organization to help girls who find themselves saddled with kids they don't know how to raise?"

She stamped her Manolo Blahnik in a way he was sure looked perfectly charming to anyone who didn't know her as well as he did. "Because that stodgy old bank you worked at before didn't like that their head VP had the hots for you and sent you packing."

"I resigned from Second National of my own accord, and you know it."

Simon grabbed his wine, eyeing the bottle the waiter had left on the table. He'd only had one glass so far. He had plenty left to get him through the rest of this exchange, but he'd keep the sommelier in sight—just in case.

Uninvited, Jennifer slid into the chair across from his.

He should have asked the waiter to remove it to ensure solo dining. He normally did when he didn't want to be interrupted by the myriad of movers and shakers who frequented this restaurant. However, his recent bout with Isabel-induced distraction had thwarted him in too many situations lately, and tomorrow the situation would only worsen. Isabel was scheduled to return from her cruise and if he knew his public relations manager, she'd come back twice as determined to mold him into the perfect spokesman for the Making Moms Foundation. Which meant they were going to have to spend a lot of time together. Alone. With her trying to dig into his psyche. With her smelling like night-blooming jasmine and exotic spices. And she'd probably come home with a tan, too, which on her naturally burnished skin would drive him completely wild with thoughts he had no business entertaining. He allowed himself a split second to consider the exact curvature of her tan lines when his mother cleared her throat.

"So are you going to tell me who she is?" Jennifer asked.

"Who are you talking about?"

Jennifer leaned forward, her blue eyes glittering with speculation. "The girl."

"What girl?"

"The girl who has you so tied up in knots?"

Simon leaned back from the table. "I'm not seeing anyone at the moment, no matter what you might have heard at your bridge game at the country club."

Jennifer laughed, and despite his devotion to being perennially annoyed with his mother, he couldn't help but notice how pretty she looked when she smiled. No wonder men couldn't resist her. "Like those South Tampa matrons would invite me to their tête-á-têtes. I do go play poker at the Tiny Tap on Thursdays, but no one in that crowd knows or cares about who the hell you are or who you may or may not be seducing."

Simon sipped his wine, struggling with the urge to throw back the entire glass.

Luckily, the lobster bisque arrived, giving Simon a reason to engage his mouth in something other than idle chitchat. Unfortunately, his mother didn't take the hint.

"I'll have my soup here, Matthew," she said to the waiter.

"Of course, madam."

"Isn't your new husband going to mind?" Simon asked, glancing across the room at his newest "step-father."

"I did my part already just by looking beautiful and serving martinis at the house," she replied, not without a hint of resentment. His first sip of soup dropped to the bottom of his stomach like a lead weight.

"Don't tell me there's trouble in paradise already?" he asked, hoping he was misreading his mother's tone. The thought of helping her through one more divorce destroyed his appetite.

"No, no," she insisted, though she wasn't entirely convincing. "He simply has no need for me, thankfully, when it's time to close the deal. I have no interest in business matters, Simon. You know that."

Jennifer wiggled her fingers in her husband's direction, and Russell Davis, a white-haired entrepreneur who'd met his mother after she'd plowed into his Porsche with her Mustang, matched the gesture with a smile that oozed love and devotion before returning his attention to the half-dozen businessmen huddling around him. Simon's appetite returned. Clearly, divorce court was not immediately in his mother's future.

But neither was the possibility that she'd leave him alone to enjoy the rest of his meal. His mother hated business dinners with a passion, but out of respect for her husband—who she at least genuinely loved so far as Simon could tell—she answered the call of duty on a regular basis. Tonight, however, she seemed inextricably focused on her eldest son. Lucky for him.

"Now," she said seconds after the waiter delivered her serving of classic French onion soup, "tell me about her or I'll harp on you all night until you do."

"What makes you think there's a woman?"

He hated to engage her, but he knew his mother well enough to know that the topic would not be dropped until her curiosity had been satisfied.

"Magdalena."

Yes, he could always count on his former baby-sitter to share the dish with his mother. Not that he'd said anything about Isabel on his visit Saturday to the assisted living center where he'd moved Maggie last year, but the woman had always possessed an uncanny ability to see right through him.

"She thinks I have a woman on my mind, does she?"

"She thinks it's about time you did, at any rate. How long has it been since you've been involved with anyone?"

"That's none of your business . . . Mother."

She arched a brow. Clearly, the endearment wasn't going to stop this line of questioning.

"And as your mother," she said with a sly grin, "I happen to want you to be happy. Is that a crime?"

Simon tasted his soup. The flavors of roasted corn and sweet shellfish soothed his nerves a bit, even as his mother waited patiently for him to finish his mouthful and sip his wine until he had no choice but to reply.

"No, it's not a crime. I know that you and Maggie care about me. But in case neither of you noticed, I'm old enough to make my own choices regarding my personal life."

"You've been old enough since you were seven, thanks to me."

The hint of recrimination in her voice stabbed like a knife. He gestured toward his mother's spoon, inviting her to eat in a way that verified she was now officially invited to share the entire meal. "I had to grow up early, that's true. But we all ended up okay in the end, didn't we?"

She smiled as she daintily sipped her soup. "Thanks to people like Maggie, pitching in and watching you and your brother in exchange for me taking her to the store with that wreck of a car I won in that pool tournament. It wasn't easy being fifteen, pregnant, and in love with a loser."

Simon chuckled and the reaction surprised him. He normally didn't look back on his childhood with much fondness, but since he'd come on board at Making Moms, he'd realized just how resourceful and determined his mother had been in ensuring her children had food on their plates and clean clothes to wear and love and laughter in their lives. Barely sixteen when she'd given birth to Simon, she'd had his brother just a year later.

Their birth father had hit the road shortly thereafter and Jennifer's parents had washed their hands of their wayward daughter. Jennifer Brennan's methods of survival hadn't been conventional or even legal half of the time— but they'd made it through fairly unscathed.

Except, for him, in the love life department. When it came to women, Simon felt his past keenly. Over the course of his adulthood, he'd gravitated toward women who either needed his help like his mother or were the polar opposite—ball-busting control freaks who could easily toss any man out of their lives like yesterday's garbage.

Probably explained his truncated attraction to Isabel. She was everything all those other women were not. She could take control when necessary, but she cared about people. She was beautiful, smart, and intriguing. And clearly, his mother had been right about one thing—because of Isabel, he had walked into this restaurant tied up in knots.

And he knew of only one way to loosen the ropes.

Chapter Five

❄ ❄ ❄

I t's nice that you visit her," his mother said, interrupting his train of thought.

It took him a moment to realize his mother had changed the subject. "Maggie?"

"She doesn't have anyone left now except her cousin and he's getting on in years, too," his mother explained.

Slick, his mother. She'd lull him into a sense of safety by talking about their old family friend, and then she'd pounce again with more questions about Isabel. He knew her too well, but saw no harm in playing her game.

"She's family," he said simply.

"And she knows you as well as I do. She said you were very distracted during your visit and asked her questions about Cuban culture. I take it the new object of your affection is from Cuba?"

Simon pressed his lips together tightly, but knew there was no use trying to deflect her questioning. "She's Cuban-American and she's not a girl I'm interested in, she's my public relations manager. I was simply curious about her cultural background."

279

"Why don't you ask her? Seems like perfect 'over coffee' conversation, especially around the holidays."

"She works for me."

"So what? You have several married couples working for the foundation. There's no rule there against fraternizing. Not even after your predecessor made a fool out of himself with his secretary."

"I don't want to talk about this."

"I know all the details. Russell was on the board of directors then. That's why they pursued you for the CEO position. Even if you did get involved with someone at work, they knew you'd do it with class."

Simon suddenly felt every morsel of food in his stomach turn to lead. "What part of 'I don't want to talk about this' did you not understand?"

"The part where you pretend you're not interested in a woman because that would be a sign of vulnerability. And God forbid you show any sign of human weakness."

"What's that supposed to mean?"

His mother pushed her soup bowl an inch away from her. "I mean that you have an image in your head of who you should be. Strong, beyond capable, always in control. That type of man doesn't allow himself to fall in love easily, Simon. And if there is one thing I know about, it's men."

The conversation thankfully ceased when, seconds later, both her soup cup and his disappeared and were quickly replaced by goat cheese salads they both raved over. They chatted about Jennifer's recent redecorating of her dining room and Simon's brother's promotion to head the football division of the sports agency he worked for. By the time the filet mignon was served,

Simon had finished several glasses of wine and the atmosphere was warm and relaxed in ways he hadn't experienced in years. Was this what Isabel wanted from him? And if so, why couldn't he be that man around her? Around the other people at Making Moms?

"So tell me more about this public relations manager of yours," Jennifer asked, a determined glint in her eye.

He opened his mouth to refuse again, but remembered the quote from Shakespeare and decided that too much protesting said more about his level of interest in Isabel than he cared to share.

"I'm surprised you don't know her, since your husband is a diamond-level donor to Making Moms."

Jennifer wiped the corners of her mouth with her napkin. "I deal mostly with the donation people and the board of directors. She's pretty?"

Trick question. "Anyone who has to deal with the press has to be, don't you think?"

She stabbed a bite of asparagus. "Very slick answer."

"She's gorgeous," he admitted.

"That's more like it. Where does she come from?"

He knew his mother hadn't morphed into a snob, so he answered honestly. "Here. I know she has a big family because there are pictures all over her office. She graduated from USF, so I assume she likes staying close to home."

"Home isn't a bad place once you have one that sticks."

"I wouldn't know about that," he muttered.

"Bullshit," Jennifer shot back. "I may have had to scramble, lie, cheat, and steal, but you and your brother always had a roof over your heads."

He looked askance. "You're right, I apologize."

Jennifer waved her hand dismissively. "Don't sweat it. But don't live in the past anymore, either, Simon Robert Brennan. You don't have to be the responsible one anymore. You don't have to be the man of the house. I'm so happily married, I scare myself. Your brother might be one step ahead of trouble half the time, but he's found a profession where his slick style is truly appreciated. Now, finally, you can focus on your own life. Have a little fun."

"I don't need your permission to have fun," he said.

Jennifer stared at him, her expression entirely serious. "Well, you sure as hell need someone's permission. Maybe that pretty public relations manager's."

Simon declined the waiter's invitation to the restaurant's dessert room upstairs and instead delivered his mother back to her husband. He escaped as quickly as he could and felt his stomach unknotting once the valet had delivered his car. Alone in the darkness, he replayed all his mother had said.

As much as he hated to admit it, Jennifer had been right about a few things. For one, he'd never quite overcome the need to protect his mother. He'd become the "man of the house," literally, by the age of two. He'd lied for her, cheated for her, worked hard in school so he could make enough money to keep his mother from having to marry rich losers just to keep her head above the poverty line. Now she'd found Russell and, as odd as it seemed, the man truly loved Jennifer and vice versa. Simon didn't have to worry about his mother anymore.

It's time for you to take care of you, she'd said.

Simple advice, really. But did Simon know how to put his needs first? His first instinct was to finally pursue a woman who could fit the bill for the long term—not just a short-term dalliance. As he drove through the streets of Tampa, he realized every woman he'd chosen until now had been nothing more than a temporary fix. What he truly needed was a real woman—down-to-earth, independent, intelligent—who would appreciate all he could offer and who would demand nothing less than the best of him for herself.

A woman like Isabel.

He's spent the week without Isabel and the experience had been tolerable up until the last few days. Then, on Thursday, while she'd probably been sunning in Mexico, he'd been thunderstruck by his inability to get her out of his mind. He'd found himself walking unnecessarily by her office. He'd reread several articles she'd left for him until he'd memorized nearly every word. He'd even found himself chitchatting with Beverly, her assistant, in hopes that she'd . . . what? Mention Isabel's name? Reveal some personal tidbit about her supervisor that would satisfy his suddenly insatiable obsession?

A few blocks away from his condo, Simon realized that home was the last place he wanted to be. He'd suffered at the office, but his hours at home had been even more unbearable. Especially at night. Especially when he was asleep. He hadn't entertained such erotic dreams since he'd been fourteen. His X-rated revision of their workout at his health club had sent him into a cold shower at two o'clock in the morning. Now, knowing that he was less than twelve hours away from seeing her again, the idea of heading home made him groan with frustration. He made a left turn instead of a right. He had some work he could pick up at the office. Maybe if he wore himself down with budget figures, departmental reports, and employee reviews, he'd get a few hours of undisturbed sleep and finally figure out if he was willing to risk his heart to pursue a woman he should, by all rights, consider off-limits.

Maybe, but not likely.

Isabel slammed the file drawer shut. The sound shook her before bursting through the deserted office like a sonic boom. Coming in to the office so late had been a lesson in frustration, but ever since the ship had sailed into port this morning she hadn't been able to think of anything but Simon. Simon winking at her. Simon smiling at her. Simon speaking to her in soft, rich tones that made her insides pulsate with needs she dare not name. The worst part was that her obsession wasn't stemming from the board's directive. She'd hardly thought about them at all. She wanted Simon to loosen up for purely personal, particularly sexual reasons.

Since she'd made her wish at the sacred cenote, the ability to think about Simon in a purely professional manner had completely deserted her. Every time she stared at the mask Lulu had bought her—the one that looked exactly like the coin she'd tossed in the water, though larger and in hand-painted colors rather than glimmering gold—her mind burgeoned with nothing but hot, erotic images of her and Simon. At the gym. In his car. On his desk.

"This is insane!" she screamed, slamming the file against the metal drawer.

"I agree. Pure insanity."

She started, but the warmness in Simon's deep baritone soothed away her fear instantaneously. Slowly, she turned to find him leaning against the doorjamb to her office, his tie abandoned, his arms crossed dashingly over his broad chest, his eyes glittering with something she'd never seen in them before.

Amusement? Casual comfort? Desire?

Man, she'd clearly gotten too much Mexican sun.

"What are you doing here?" she asked, inhaling deeply even as she tried to hide the calming move from his view.

"Trying to avoid you," he replied.

"Excuse me?"

He pushed off from the door and before she could retreat, he'd invaded her personal space—not close enough to touch without reaching, but close enough so that the sandalwood and musk in his cologne teased her nostrils and heated her already balmy skin. She glanced around, hoping no one else was here to witness this . . . what? Breach in office etiquette? Sexually charged moment? More like a one-hundred-and-eighty-degree personality change.

"You've been gone all week," he explained. "Five whole days, not counting the weekend. And yet, for some reason I either can't figure out or don't really want to, I haven't been able to get you off my mind."

She stepped back. Isabel wasn't one to retreat from any man, but she hadn't come into the office to pick up a few things before tomorrow's workday with any preparation of meeting the man that had somehow, in her absence, become the man of her dreams.

"Is that the same mind that you've so obviously lost?"

she quipped, hoping to offset this suddenly uncomfortable interaction.

The corner of his mouth quirked into a roguish grin.

Roguish grin?

"Okay," she said, pounding her fists onto her hips. "Who are you and what have you done with my boss?"

The grin spread to the other corner of his mouth and even reached his eyes, which sparkled sapphire in the dim office lights.

"Let me introduce myself," he said, reaching down to capture her hand, which she was sure shook as if she'd never touched a man before. "Simon Brennan, CEO of the Making Moms Foundation." He lifted her hand to his lips and brushed a kiss over her knuckles. The contact ignited a flash fire that instantly blazed across her skin. "And you are . . . ?"

Melting into a puddle on the floor?

"Confused," she whispered. He was so close, any higher volume would have been a waste of energy.

He cleared his throat and dropped her hand. Damn him.

"I was trying a new tactic."

He backed away, giving her the reprieve she needed to cross her arms protectively. "And this new tactic would be . . . ?"

He frowned. "I was going for charming. How'd I do?"

Man, oh, man, couldn't he tell? The crossed arms weren't just for comfort. She was quite certain her nipples were poking straight through her bra and blouse. His instant off switch, on the other hand, made her frown deeply.

"Not half bad, if you were the CEO of a brothel or

chain of strip clubs. I'm not sure 'wicked playboy' is the personality type the board of directors of a charitable foundation would appreciate running their show."

He nodded, though his smile had returned briefly, just after she'd said "wicked playboy." "Yeah, I was concerned about that. I guess we're going to have to keep working on the new, improved me."

How could she possibly improve on perfection? Okay, granted, the Simon Brennan she'd just experienced wasn't going to save her job or his, but she was certain that charmer could do amazing things in her bedroom.

She cleared her throat and marched back to her desk, trying to come up with something halfway professional or intelligent to say. Unfortunately, with her knuckles still trembling from the contact with his lips, she couldn't form even the simplest coherent thought.

"How was your trip?"

His words signaled a return to their normally cool and casual tenor, but his tone remained deep and bone-melting.

"Nothing to write home about."

"Not much reason to write home when your entire family was with you, right?"

Isabel smiled. Yeah, he had a point.

"My family actually isn't so bad. Don't tell anyone. We're very dysfunctional. We actually like each other."

He feigned shock. "How politically incorrect!"

She couldn't deny the opening. "What about your family? I'm assuming you have one?"

"I wasn't spawned in the icy waters in some mysterious polar region, if that's what you're asking."

The hint of humor in his voice, unexpected but welcome, kept her from feeling guilty about how her question sounded. "That's not what I'm asking. It's just that you don't talk about parents or siblings. You don't have pictures in your office."

He nodded and, surprisingly, slipped into one of the pair of chairs in front of her desk. Isabel sat beside him on the matching chair, allowing herself only a split second to notice how close their knees were to touching. "The pictures I have, and admittedly there aren't many, are at my condo, placed there by my mother. I also have a brother who lives in Los Angeles. In fact, I had dinner with my mother tonight. You might have heard of her? Jennifer Brennan Davis?"

"Her husband is one of our biggest donors." Isabel knew her eyes had widened to the size of saucers. "She's not old enough to be your mother!"

"That's what her parents said when she came home at fifteen, pregnant, and in love with a loser."

Isabel gripped the armrests of her chair. "You're just full of surprises tonight."

"Didn't expect that I was the child of a teenage mother just like the ones we help?"

"Even if I did—which I didn't—I never expected you to freely admit something so personal. Not that there's anything wrong with admitting your connection to the foundation's goals, but I'm just surprised at your candor."

He leaned forward, balancing his elbows on his knees so that mere inches existed between them. His fingers dangled perilously close to where the hem of her skirt flared over her lap. What would it feel like, she wondered, if he reached forward and explored the sensitive flesh of her thighs?

After a moment's hesitation, he looked up at her with hooded eyes. "I've had a lot of time to think about what you said to me before you left. And I think that opening up about my past, maybe just to you, might make it easier for me to relate to the women we work with here."

Isabel's chest tightened. He wanted her to be his confidante? Oh, this was a mistake of monumental proportions—for reasons too numerous to number and too personal to admit. How was she supposed to keep her hands and dirty thoughts to herself when he was about to unburden his soul to her?

And yet, she managed to clamp her mouth shut. He'd refused to open up to her when she'd made the suggestion to him last week, but he'd obviously had a change of heart. In fact, he was so warm, she was sure that one glance from him could turn any one of the cruise ship's famous ice sculptures into a dripping mess in ten seconds flat.

She prayed her voice wouldn't betray her once she opened her mouth to speak. "That sounds like a very enlightened idea."

He smirked. "It was yours, remember?"

"Sounds more promising when it comes from you," she replied. "Where do you want to start?"

Isabel nearly leapt out of her chair when she felt the tips of his fingers toy with the bare flesh on her knee. His gaze had drifted downward and this time she had no illusions about the tightness of her nipples. The chafing against the lace of her bra announced her arousal as clearly as the sudden, quick acceleration of her heartbeat, which pulsed everywhere from her neck to her wrists to between her thighs. She remained silent, unable to speak. And once he turned his lethal blue gaze on her, she realized that despite his promises about opening up to her, talking was the very last thing he wanted to do.

"I know I shouldn't be touching you," he admitted.

She managed to shake her head. Whether the gesture meant she agreed or that she didn't want him to stop, she couldn't determine—and frankly, didn't want to.

"Your skin is so soft," he said wondrously, then opened his hands so that his entire palm smoothed over her knees. "I always wondered . . ."

He hesitated and she knew he was waiting for a signal from her. Her mind swirled with the images that had been haunting her. Simon touching her. Simon arousing her. Simon learning the intricate nuances of her body, what made her tick, what made her rush over the edge. Here, in the quiet darkness, she could have her most secret fantasy, her most treasured wish, if only she'd surrender to the magic.

She leaned back in her chair, closed her eyes, allowed her body to meld into the fabric . . . and waited.

Chapter Six

✻ ❅ ✻

He didn't know what had come over him. Never in his life had he had so much trouble controlling his actions, his reactions, his thoughts, his needs. Yet from the moment he'd seen her in her office tonight, he'd been able to think of nothing else but tasting her, touching her, feeling her naked by his side.

Without removing his hands from her knees, he stood and kicked his chair away. She started at the sound of the crash, but he soothed her nerves by running his hands higher on her thighs.

"Relax, Isabel," he found himself saying.

Her smile broadened. "Oh, I'm relaxed," she assured him as she settled deeper into the chair. "You're the one who has trouble letting go, remember?"

"Not tonight."

He felt her quiver beneath his touch as he whispered those words into the shell of her ear. His fingers teased the top-most part of her thighs, but remained still while he initiated an exploration with his lips. He kissed her at the temple, on her forehead, on the tip of her nose. He nibbled along the base of her chin, then across to the lobe of her ear.

She sighed again, though this time the sound was a breathless quiver.

"You're incredibly beautiful," he said.

"Thanks for noticing."

He chuckled, brushing his mouth tentatively over hers. "You think I haven't noticed before?"

Weakened to a whisper, her voice would have been inaudible if his ear wasn't so close to her mouth. "You've never . . ."

"No, I've never. But I wanted to, Isabel. God, how I've wanted to."

His mouth closed over hers in an act of need and her mouth instantly parted for him. Their tongues clashed with such force, he clutched at her thighs to keep his balance. She slashed her fingers into his hair, wrapped her arms around his neck, and lifted herself higher so that the heat simmering from her center nearly scorched his hungry fingertips.

Could he? Did he dare? Moisture teased his hands. One inch. Maybe two. To know her need, intimately, meant only the slightest touch.

"Please, Simon," she coaxed between gasps.

He needed nothing more. He slipped past her satiny panties and found the treasure within.

She was hot. Wet. Needy. She cried out as he plied his fingers through her curls and teased the sensitive flesh with tentative fingers. He wanted more. He wanted to bury himself deep inside her, but they'd already gone so far, so fast.

She tore at the buttons of his shirt and then tugged the hem from his pants.

Could he deny her?

He pulled away, sat back on his heels. He tore his hands through his hair, as if yanking at the roots might restart his ability to think clearly. "This is crazy."

Her pout tortured him, especially when coupled with the bold rise and fall of her breasts. "Yes, Simon," she said, leaning forward and attacking the buttons on her own blouse with the same gusto she'd shown on his. "It is insane. It's spontaneous and wild and impetuous. But you want me and I want you. Why stop now?"

"I've had too much to drink," he muttered.

She froze. "If you know you've had too much, then you can't blame the booze," she snapped.

"That's not what I meant," he recovered. "The wine isn't making me want you, Isabel. I've been fighting my attraction to you from the first moment we met. The wine has just made it impossible for me to deny how much I want you anymore. How much I've always wanted you. You're the most desirable woman I've ever encountered and if I don't have you soon, I might lose my mind worse than I already have."

She tore her blouse aside, revealing a delicious pink lace bra that did little to hide the aroused state of her nipples, dark and hard beneath the light, frothy fabric.

"Then why are you stopping now?"

He shook his head, his mind blank. "I can't remember."

Her smile knocked the last of his inhibitions out of his body. His lips were on hers in seconds, his hands gravitating to her breasts of their own accord. The minute his palms connected with her skin, he rejoiced in his madness. If a man had to lose all semblance of rationality, this was the way to go.

She matched his hunger, scraping her nails down his bare back as he pushed beyond the lace and found her hardened nipples. When he flicked the sensitive flesh with his thumbs, she cried out in pleasure, spurring him to lower his head and take her into his mouth. Her skin was a potent combination of sweetness and salt. Her flesh reacted instantly to his kiss, and every level of hardness ramped up his need to push her farther. She sat up and cradled his head, offering fully what he couldn't help but take, spurring him to suckle harder and swirl tighter circles around her areola with his tongue. She released her hair from its barrette, and the moment the thick, dark strands caressed his face, he knew he'd found paradise.

Their remaining clothes disappeared as quickly as a condom appeared from inside her purse. He didn't question her readiness—or his own. He donned the protection, sat, and beckoned her with a crooked finger.

She'd doused the office light and locked the door so that the only glow came from the hallway outside, spilling in through the nearly closed blinds on her windows. She stepped daintily out of her panties, but didn't move.

"Isabel," he said.

She took a step nearer. "I want to savor this."

He smiled. "Trust me, I'll give you plenty to savor once you're here. I only wish I had a bed to offer."

Her grin crooked up on one side. "I don't know. I've

always wanted to try something a little less conventional."

He arched a brow. "Come here, Isabel."

She closed the distance between them. "Now that's the Simon I know. Demanding. To the point."

She glanced down at his jutting sex.

He chuckled at her joke, reaching out to take her hands and guide her the rest of the way. "And here's the Isabel I know. Sensual and decisive, making what she wants happen no matter the challenge."

As she climbed over his lap, he smoothed his hands down her sides and under her buttocks. He contained a groan, but just barely, as the heat inflamed his already burning body. She locked her hands on either side of his face and kissed him deeply as her sex enveloped his in one hot, languorous slide.

For an instant, Simon remained entirely still, his mind trying desperately to catch up to the fact that his body had achieved complete nirvana. The moment the realities connected, Simon wanted nothing more and nothing less than giving Isabel the greatest pleasure she'd ever known.

"Tell me what you like," he whispered, his mouth murmuring against the sweet curve of her breast.

He shifted in his seat. She cooed.

"Little . . . late . . . for that," she replied.

He teased her bottom with his fingers, buoying her sweet roundness with his palms. "Never too late."

She'd locked her hands onto the chair just above his shoulders. Her eyes, so dark in the dim light, glittered with unrepressed need.

"Take . . . it . . . slow."

With a deep breath, Simon realized she'd just asked the impossible. She was so tight, so hot. How could he? With her feet planted on either side of him, she started the rhythm at the tempo she preferred. The resonance wrenched at him so that every nerve ending, every inch of skin and muscle and bone, ached with pleasure. He braced his hands on her hips and allowed her to control the pace until she slipped her hands beneath her own breasts in bold offering, tweaking her nipples with her fingers. Enflamed, he pulled her forward and devoured her flesh as their mating hit a furious crescendo before they both slipped over the edge.

He didn't know how long it took for him to regain his ability to think and breathe, but the moment she started to move away from him, he wrapped his arms tightly around her and drew her close, even as she tried to escape.

"Don't run away," he demanded softly.

"I wasn't."

He didn't believe her.

"This can be the awkward part," he said. "But we don't have to play it that way."

Her smile seemed to light the room. "How should we play it?"

"Now or in the morning?"

Her face froze in horror. "Oh, Lord. The morning. Work! What if someone comes in early? What if . . . ?"

He kissed the tip of her chin and then captured her mouth until he achieved her silence. "We'll be long gone by the time anyone comes in to the office and when we show up again in the morning, we'll play it cool. As an expert in that area, I can teach you how to do that, if you'd like."

Her eyes widened at his playful tone and even he couldn't believe the natural way his voice sounded. How fluid his muscles felt, how relaxed his chest and lungs.

She shook her head. "We're headed down a dangerous road," she whispered.

He couldn't argue with that fact, but at the moment, he had no desire to discuss worst-case scenarios. "Maybe, but we can handle it. Tonight was our private moment. No one has to know we've become lovers. It's our secret."

She frowned at first, but after a long moment and a quick glance at her wall, where she'd hung her brand-new mask—clearly of Mexican origin—Isabel gave a determined nod. "What happened between us was simply magic," she said.

Oddly, the declaration wasn't wistful or romantic. Just matter-of-fact. While Simon agreed entirely with the sentiment, her tone perplexed him. He opened his mouth to question her further when she placed her hands over his eyes.

"Close your eyes. I need to get myself back together."

Since she punctuated the demand with a kiss, he didn't argue. He complied, peeking only once and grinning like a fool. He had no idea what had come over him tonight, but magic seemed a good enough explanation. The moment he'd seen her alone in her office in the shadowy hour before midnight, every rational reason he'd had for denying himself this woman melted away.

However, he knew that tomorrow morning would be a different situation entirely. The board had threatened his job, and hers, if he didn't loosen up in time for the charity ball, but he seriously doubted this was what they'd had in mind.

Chapter Seven

❄ ❄ ❄

Seven days. She'd survived seven days. In the office. Focused on her work. Ignoring how he looked at her. How his eyes never seemed to release her, how his smile seemed just a tad more wicked than ever before. But judging by the way Beverly, her assistant, clucked around her, focused entirely on their first fund-raiser of the holiday season and making only a cursory comment about the bright Mexican mask she'd hung in her office, she and Simon were successfully pulling this off. No one knew. No one even suspected.

They'd become lovers. Never in her wildest dreams, not even when she'd tossed the coin into the cenote at Chichén Itzá, did she ever imagine that the vibe between them could rev from zero to one hundred in the blink of an eye. Glancing at the mask now, in the once-again-empty office as she searched for the last-minute place card changes she needed to fax over to the beach hotel that was hosting their event, she wondered.

Was this real? Or was their affair only due to the mysterious Mayan magic?

"Isabel? Are you almost ready?" Suezette floated into Isabel's office in a stunning black ball gown they'd found together last year at Off 5th, their favorite outlet store in nearby Ellenton. Leftovers from Saks Fifth Avenue met their budgets, while making them feel like perfect fairy-tale princesses. Tonight, however, her sister looked more like a sexy wicked witch, all the way down to sleek, elbow-length gloves. Isabel stepped back from her fax machine long enough to whistle like a construction worker.

"If Papi saw you in that, he'd banish you to your room until you're thirty."

"I could wait," Suezette replied evilly, "thirty isn't as far off as it used to be. You look gorgeous yourself. The green suits you and clearly, you did not gain an ounce while on the cruise. Old Simon Brennan won't be able to resist you."

Isabel turned back to her fax machine, trying to cover the blush suddenly heating the skin beneath the lacy bodice of her emerald green gown. She punched in the phone number of the hotel. A pizza delivery place picked up. She tried again.

"Whaaaat?" Suezette asked, drawing out the word into a polysyllabic song.

Isabel pasted on her most innocent face. "I'll be ready to go in five minutes."

Suezette advanced like an attacking army, grabbing Isabel beneath her chin and forcing her to look her in the eye. "What aren't you telling me, big sister?"

Isabel hesitated. Mistake.

"Díos mío! You slept with him!" Suezette cried.

Isabel pushed her sister out of her way and fed the paperwork into the machine. "Technically, no."

Suezette's eyes widened like ebony saucers. "Did he or did he not have his penis inserted into your vagina at some point since we returned from Mexico?"

Isabel winced, then made a huge production of gagging. "God, Suezette, could you be a little *less* romantic?"

"I'm a scientist. Sue me. But we're not talking about romance, here, *mi hermana.* We're talking about sex."

"No," Isabel replied wistfully, "it was definitely romance. In a modern, *Sex and the City* way, admittedly, but romance nonetheless. It was wild, unexpected, and completely out of character for both of us."

Suezette arched a brow.

"Okay," Isabel conceded, noting that while she'd never before done the deed with her boss on a chair in her office, she had experienced a few brief flings in her adulthood. "It was out of character for one of us, namely him. I never imagined he could be so spontaneous. I wanted it, he wanted it, we did it. End of story."

"That's not the end of the story and you know it."

Her fax complete, Isabel retrieved the papers, slipped them hastily into a file folder, and stuffed them into her briefcase, which admittedly clashed with her gown. But tonight wasn't about her looking beautiful or sexy for Simon, it was about raising hundreds of thousands of dollars for Making Moms and honoring the young women who'd been through the programs this year and had successfully changed their lives for the better.

And about showing the board of directors the new-and-improved Simon Brennan. Hopefully, not the one who'd become her wild and unpredictable lover, but the man who'd finally learned how to smile.

Isabel grabbed her briefcase and purse, doused the

lights, and pointed her sister toward the door. They had a little less than an hour to get from Tampa to the beach in St. Petersburg, just across the bay. Luckily, rush hour was over and they were mostly going against traffic. During the ride, Suezette badgered her for details regarding her affair, but Isabel put her off by telling her instead about the mask, the old woman, the coin, the cenote, and then, reluctantly, the wish.

Suezette's scientist's eyes stared at her long and disbelieving.

"I know it sounds crazy," Isabel conceded.

"Do you? Because if you don't understand the full breadth of your insanity, I'm hauling your butt over to a psychiatrist friend of mine so he can perform some tests."

Isabel grinned wickedly. "I can only imagine what I'd see in those inkblots right about now."

Sensual images skittered through her mind, most along the line of an illustrated *Kama Sutra*. She and Simon had hooked up every night since their night in the office and each encounter had been as impetuous and unpredictable and sexually satisfying as the first. Once, they'd done it in his car while parked in the garage of his condo. Private garage or not, the act of making love to him and not the stick shift had spawned a night of laughter and pleasure she knew she'd never forget. Just last night, they'd surrendered to their passion in a private room at his favorite restaurant. Granted, he'd ordered the waiter to leave them alone right after dessert was served, but the risk and the adventure of their tryst pushed them beyond any limits either one of them might have had with other lovers. Isabel had never felt so free—and yet so constrained.

She had this hot, fabulous lover and no one could know.

"So you believe in this magic?" Suezette asked, her voice even-toned.

"I don't know if I *believe,* per se," Isabel hedged, "but right now, what I believe doesn't matter. I mean, the result would be the same, right? You've always told me that the subconscious is the most powerful part of the brain. Maybe I just willed Simon to drop his inhibitions and go after what he wants—which just so happens to be me."

"Makes more sense than some Mexican Santa Claus magic," Suezette said. "The Mayans had no symbolic personification in any way resembling the Dutch-inspired figure of . . ."

Her sister's voice trailed away.

"Why did Lulu buy me the mask anyway?" Isabel asked.

Suezette shifted uncomfortably in her seat, tugging at the seat belt. "She . . . uh, admired the artisanship."

"Uh-huh," Isabel said doubtfully, "you keep telling yourself that. The truth is, you have no idea why she bought that mask for me except she was compelled to do it. One minute you and Lulu were giving me grief for disappearing and the next she was shelling out her tequila money for a funky piece of Mexican art that just so happened to be an exact replica of the coin I'd tossed in the cenote before you two even walked up. I, for one, have no interest in asking too many questions, but I know freaky when it happens to me. For now, though, I'm just going to go with the flow."

"But what will be the end result?" Suezette asked. The worry in her sister's eyes unnerved her. She'd been too high on sexual pleasure and fulfilled fantasies to think much more beyond the next time she and Simon would share a secret glance or exchange a surreptitious touch. She supposed, eventually, the thrill would fade. She'd return to being the creative, effective public relations manager while he'd bask in the glory of being the most popular, effective, and respected CEO the foundation had ever had. Every so often, they'd hook up and maybe, perhaps, explore the expanding connection between them. But they'd keep things cool. Casual. No strings. Just like all her other lovers.

But Simon wasn't like her other lovers, was he?

Isabel chased away a chill by changing the radio station. "Well, hopefully, the end result will include the board of directors giving me a bonus for all my hard work. Tonight, they'll meet their new CEO, a man people won't be able to help but give their trust and money to. Our coffers will be filled for the upcoming year and I'll have had enough orgasms to get me through the cold winter."

Suezette reached forward and turned off the radio altogether. "You're prediction is completely illogical and based on none of the facts. You're already talking about magic as if it's real, for Pete's sake! I can't see anything but a huge disaster in your future."

"Now who sounds like the woo-woo queen?" Isabel muttered.

"I'd prefer you putting stock in supernatural intervention than seriously believing this affair with Simon Brennan will last beyond the initial thrill," Suezette declared.

"You don't know what's going to happen between us."

"Has he made promises? Given you any solid proof he intends to follow through on his desires in a permanent way?"

Isabel nearly let the steering wheel slip from her hands. "Whoa, who said I wanted more than a fling from him anyway? I've never had more than a fling in my entire life."

Suezette rolled her eyes. "And that's another part of the problem, isn't it? While you've admittedly lusted after this man for a significant amount of time, you also respect him deeply. As a man and as a CEO. That's the kind of guy girls like us fall for, Isabel, not the kind you take to bed and forget was supposed to call the next day because you've already moved on to someone new."

Isabel couldn't form a convincing counterpoint. Isabel's track record with men spoke for itself. She sought out the guys who knew how to dance, how to party, how to show her a great time. They were buddies. Diversions. Not one of them had ever come close to invading her heart. It wasn't as if she was closed off to the possibility of love, it was just that once she fell, she knew she'd be looking at a lifetime commitment. Knowing all she did now about Simon's past, about the man he was and the man he could be, the precipice steepened.

"I can't think about that tonight," Isabel decided. "I have to concentrate on making a great impression on the board."

Suezette snorted. "If they find out about your affair with their golden boy, they'll fire you."

"There's no rule against our involvement," she insisted.

"No written rule," Suezette clarified. "But those people aren't going to want another scandal on their hands. Unless Simon Brennan slips a ring on your finger, the board of directors isn't going to consider your personal relationship with your boss a good thing."

Isabel's gaze flicked to the temperature setting on her car's air conditioner. Shivers should not be running up and down her spine, but the icy marathon existed nonetheless. Rings? Marriage? To Simon? To *anyone?*

"They can't dictate my personal life. So long as we're discreet, they have no say. Besides, they might not even care so long as he's finally the CEO they want."

"Or they might just like him so much that they decide to solve any potential problem by getting rid of you." Suezette shook her head. "You're thinking with your *concha* and not your head, Isabel. You could lose your job. Your reputation. Maybe something even more valuable to you."

Her sister didn't name that elusive something, but she didn't need to. Both of them knew that above all else, Isabel protected her heart. She'd never once taken a chance on a relationship that could truly work out for the long haul, preferring to tread lightly in the love department. But now, thanks to the magic and the man, she was in deep.

Perhaps too deep to escape.

The rest of the trip progressed in silence, allowing Isabel time to concentrate on the fact that her fun little fling with Simon could result in her losing everything she'd worked so hard for. Rising up the ranks of the public relations game, particularly in the philanthropic field, hadn't been easy. First, she was young. Second, she was attractive. Normally, that wouldn't necessarily be a point against her, but coupled with her Latina coloring and curvaceous curves, Isabel had learned that a lot of women—and men—mistrusted her altruistic motives. And therein lay the other part of her problem—Isabel hadn't accepted the job at Making Moms exclusively to help the less fortunate. Ambition drove her to be the best in her field. She never accepted being anything less than the best.

She'd had to work hard to build trust and cultivate her reputation as a consummate professional. Was this affair going to blow her career all to hell?

And if it did, would the explosion be worth the price? Because now that Isabel allowed herself to be completely honest, she knew she was risking something infinitely more valuable than her reputation or her career—she was risking the whole of her heart.

The minute Isabel stepped over the threshold into the main ballroom, Simon noticed two things. First, she would clearly be the most beautiful woman in the room tonight. She'd pulled her hair back in a tight chignon, but instead of making her look severe, the style enhanced the exotic sophistication he always associated with her. Her emerald green dress, sewn from sensuous lace that smoothed over her abundant curves, picked up the decorative color scheme all around them, and made her look like a delicious Christmas treat. Keeping his hands to himself would be a challenge of epic proportions.

The second thing he noticed was the tiny frown tugging at the edges of her ruby red lips. Either something was wrong with the planning of the event—which

Simon knew to be utterly impossible—or something was wrong with her. And by her, he really meant "them."

When she spotted him, the frown intensified.

Definitely *them.*

"If you'll excuse me, Mr. Vandermere," Simon said as politely as possible to the chairman of the foundation's board of directors who'd been regaling him with a tale about his most recent yachting excursion. "I see Ms. Ruiz. I need to go over a few details with her before the bulk of our guests arrive."

Vandermere gave a knowing smile. "Of course, my boy. See to business. We all have a great deal riding on tonight's event."

Simon gave a polite nod, then made a beeline across the room for Isabel. When he reached her, she didn't look happy to see him. He felt his smile dim and his spine straighten as anger threatened. What was he suddenly angry about?

"Simon," she said formally, "this is my sister, Suezette."

An attractive, short-haired brunette about two inches taller than Isabel extended her opera-gloved hand. "I've heard a great deal about you," she said as a greeting.

Simon spied a wary look in the woman's brown eyes, but he took her hand nonetheless and gave it a friendly shake. "I've seen your picture in your sister's office. You're even more stunning in person."

Suezette arched a brow, then smiled thoroughly. "Okay, you pass. Now point me toward the champagne and I'll get out of your hair."

Isabel's severe look softened and she not only directed her sister toward the bubbly, but also made sure she found Beverly and several other volunteers she clearly already knew. Simon watched Isabel ease through the crowd, warmly greeting volunteers, recipients, donors, and dignitaries with a grace he could only describe as amazing. Suddenly, he remembered the ultimate goal he had for tonight—to show the board of directors and the countless people involved with Making Moms that he wasn't an intimidating, stiff board more concerned with facts and figures than with genuinely helping the young women who reached out for assistance. Whatever had been bothering Isabel earlier simply had to wait until they'd both achieved their prime directive for the night.

She was weaving her way back to him with that same concerned look on her face when a tall, burly, white-haired man stepped into his path. It took him a split second to recognize his own "stepfather."

He offered his hand genially. "Russell, so glad you could make it tonight. I hope you have your checkbook warmed up and ready."

Surprisingly, his mother's normally amiable husband stared at Simon's hand with complete distaste. "I'm not giving one penny at this shindig unless you do something about your mother."

Simon felt his friendly expression freeze in place. Three decades worth of lying, cheating, covering, and protecting his mother rushed back at him until bile seemed to rise in his throat. And yet he'd done enough specialized training with Isabel to keep those emotions from ruining tonight's event. He placed a hand softly, but firmly, on Russell's squared shoulder. "Let's go out into the hall and work this all out."

Russell shrugged off the gesture. "I will not! You'll take care of that woman right here and right now, or I'm walking out with my donation firmly in my pocket, got that?"

Simon glanced around. Oh yeah, he got it. And judging by the shocked looks on the faces around him, so did everyone else.

Chapter Eight

※ ❄ ※

Isabel took a deep breath and blocked out the glittering pageantry around her. The cheerful holiday music. The crowd chattering with wondrous enthusiasm for all that was Christmas, from the mistletoe curled into the flower arrangements to the gold garland strung across the stage. She heard the awed voices of the women Making Moms served, amazed by the beauty of the hotel and the decorations and the music and the elaborate buffet. All for them. All for their children. The effect allowed Isabel to fully concentrate on why she was here tonight. Not for herself, but to represent the foundation. To raise money for next year's operating budget. To honor the women who came to their group for help.

And, of course, to show the board the new-and-improved Simon Brennan. The man who might, thanks to her unorthodox methods, end up breaking her once-so-guarded heart.

Isabel opened her eyes. The gleam and sparkle of the streamers and the sequined and bejeweled ball gowns lightened her mood, reminding her of the coin she'd tossed into the cenote. Real or not, the magic spawned by her trip to Chichén Itzá had had genuine results. For a very long time, she'd fantasized about making love with Simon and now she had. For months, she'd told herself that she'd held back from pursuing him because he was her boss, because he wasn't interested, because he was from a different world, where facts and figures were more important than having a good time.

But now that they'd both let loose, all bets were off. And if she had to risk her heart to see this through to the end, then what choice did she have? She couldn't allow fear to stop what they'd started.

She was falling in love with him.

Dammit.

For all his former stiffness and formality, Simon had, from the beginning, been exactly the kind of man Isabel could love. Proud of his work. Determined to succeed. Respectful of others, even if he wasn't being warm or friendly. Handsome. Sexy. Mysterious. Now that he'd re-vealed his true, generous self to her, now that she knew that his sexiness was part and parcel of who he was and not some fantasy illusion, she guessed there was no going back. She wanted him. And no one was going to stop her from getting her man.

No one, except, perhaps, the man shouting at the top of his lungs at Simon in the middle of the crowd.

She skewered through the kaleidoscope of bodies, soothing her wake with excuse me's to anyone within earshot. When she finally broke through, she found Simon standing toe-to-toe with his mother's husband, Russell Davis. Just a few feet away stood Arthur Vander-mere, the member of the board of directors who'd initially approached Isabel with her directive to change Simon's image. She was quite sure they didn't expect him to change from a staid, cool businessman to a hothead who engaged in public arguments at charity events.

"Russell, please," Simon said with a shaky but genuine smile. "I don't think these good people want their Christmas cheer served with a loud helping of family strife. Let's take this outside."

"I'm tired of this crap," Russell replied. "You're going to put a stop to it, do you hear me?"

Isabel scooted the rest of the way through the growing audience, positioning herself directly beside Simon. "Mr. Davis, I really do think we should retire to the hallway."

Simon leaned in. "Really, Russ. We're here to help the single mothers," he said quietly, "not validate their beliefs that all men can be counted on is for making a mess of things."

The crowd in close earshot all twittered with uncomfortable laughter, but after a few seconds, the chuckles grew. Even Russell Davis, who'd taken a moment to inhale a deep breath, now blushed deep red. "I'm . . ."

"Perplexed by my mother," Simon provided, more loudly this time. "Russell, if I could figure women out and bottle my knowledge, I not only wouldn't still be single, but I'd also be rich enough to fund Making Moms for the next ten years myself. Now, let's allow this gorgeous crowd to return to their party while we work out the traditional Christmas family conflict on our own."

The comment brought another round of laughter and once Isabel had the guts to look up, the approving look of Arthur Vandermere and several other board members standing nearby. Simon had made not one joke, but two. Not stand-up comedian worthy, of course, but pithy and quick, light-hearted, and, as Russell and he walked out practically arm-in-arm, entirely effective. The crowd returned to their merriment instantly.

Situation defused. By the once stiff, too-stern-to-approach CEO.

The man she'd help make.

The man she was falling in love with.

She scooted toward the door, but was wrangled by Vandermere.

"I see you've been successful in your objective, Ms. Ruiz. He handled that situation with an inordinate amount of patience and wit."

Isabel shook her head. "I didn't do anything, Mr. Vandermere. Simon Brennan is simply a consummate professional. Had you asked him yourself to soften his image, I'm sure he would have complied."

Vandermere clucked his tongue. "Brennan is a good man, but his background has long dictated his professional attitude. Take credit where credit is due, Ms. Ruiz. If he handles his presentation tonight with the same self-deprecating aplomb he just did to defuse what could have been an ugly situation, your job is ensured."

Using all the self-control she possessed, Isabel bit down a sarcastic retort, pasted on what she hoped looked like a grateful smile, and excused herself. Business was business. Sometimes you just had to suck up the pride and do your job. And she had done her job. And so had Simon.

She found him in the hall, huddled with his stepfather in a now quiet conversation. She tried to linger out of earshot, but Simon spotted her and waved her over.

Instinctively, she glanced behind her to make sure he meant her to intrude on their private moment.

He rolled his eyes and waved more emphatically. "Isabel, you know Russell Davis."

Isabel approached sheepishly and shook the man's hand. She'd become Simon's lover, yes, but now he was including her in what she guessed was a delicate family matter. The intimacy struck her hard, but she covered with an outstretched hand. "Yes, of course. I hope everything is under control now."

Davis looked completely contrite. "I'm sorry I disrupted the gala. I'm just so frustrated with that woman, I could spit fire."

"Welcome to the club," Simon cracked.

He and Davis shared a laugh, but Isabel didn't see the humor this time.

Simon noticed her frown immediately. "I'm talking exclusively about my mother, not women in general or you in any way, shape, or form. My mother is a remarkable woman and I know you'll love her and vice versa, but she can be . . . difficult."

Davis cursed softly. "That's an understatement. I just figured since Simon here has been handling her with kid gloves a lot longer than I have, he could rein her in before things got out of hand."

Isabel shot a quizzical glance at Simon.

"Mother thinks Davis is cheating on her," he explained, glancing at his watch, which prompted Isabel to do the same. According to the schedule, Simon had five minutes until he addressed the crowd. Tonight of all nights, he couldn't afford to be late or distracted.

Isabel eyed Davis warily. "I take it you're not."

Russell laughed. "No, ma'am. My Jennifer might be high-strung and high maintenance, but she's more than enough woman for any man. Besides, God help me, but I love her to pieces. So, Simon, you'll talk to her? She insisted she had to talk to you before she'd drop this nonsense."

Simon glanced down at Isabel and she saw an odd expression cross his face. A mixture of conflict and empathy and then decision. " 'Fraid not, Russ. You go to my mother and remind her that she's the one who told me I had to concentrate on taking care of me now, not taking care of her. It's time for all of us to stand on our own feet."

"She hates eating her own words," Russell pointed out.

Simon clapped his palm over the older man's shoulder. "But she'll hate losing you more. She loves you, Russ. And that probably scares the crap out of her."

Isabel inhaled sharply. If his guess was correct, she knew exactly how Jennifer Davis felt. Despite where they were and who might be watching, Isabel couldn't help but lean closer so she could touch Simon softly on the arm without anyone noticing. "Fear can do crazy things to a woman," she admitted.

Simon shifted his gaze, staring down at her with intense blue eyes that reflected such profound emotion that Isabel quivered. As if he were warm steel and she an electronic magnet, a vibrating switch flipped deep within her. She leaned closer to him, saturating herself with his heat, inhaling the heady mix of his cologne and igniting a flame she'd guessed might just be eternal.

"You should see what fear does to a man," he whispered.

A round of applause from inside the ballroom struck like a gong at the midnight hour. Russell Davis disappeared down the hallway.

Isabel checked her watch again. "It's showtime," she said, her heart pounding hard against her chest.

His perfect lips curved into a sexy frown. "I couldn't have done any of this without you, Isabel."

She rolled her eyes, trying desperately to keep her breath steady. "You defused Russell and impressed Vandermere without any help from me. Our chairman is in that ballroom right now, rooting for you. And so am I."

Simon leaned down and brushed a quick kiss along her temple. "That's all that matters."

With confidence in his step, Simon spun on his heel and strode into the ballroom, assuming she would follow. At first, she had every intention of doing so. Then she heard the MC introduce Simon to the audience. They applauded while she imagined him making his way to the stage, then she closed her eyes and crossed her fingers. They'd gone over his speech so many times, she'd committed the text to heart. When the crowd laughed after the third sentence, her entire body released the tension that had been holding her up since he left.

Ah, success.

"Isabel, what are you doing out here?"

Suezette slipped into the hallway, closing the door quietly behind her. "Your boy looks good up there. Why aren't you standing beside him?"

She shook her head, uncertain of why she hadn't been able to go inside. Nerves, maybe? Or perhaps a strong sense that now that they'd accomplished their objective, the reason for their romance no longer existed?

"Suezette, I need to leave," she said.

"What? The evening just started! I didn't get all dressed up to leave the party before the dancing gets hot."

Isabel pressed her lips tightly together and with her eyes pleaded with her sister to understand.

Suezette took her hands. *"Mi'ja,* what's wrong?"

Isabel forced a smile. "Nothing," she answered, breathless. "Everything. Please, Suezette, I just need to take a drive. Can you get a ride home with Beverly? I need some time to sort things out."

Hesitantly, Suezette nodded. Behind them, the crowd inside laughed again, followed by applause. Simon was clearly wowing the crowd with his new persona and despite their mutual success, Isabel couldn't stand to be in the building one more minute. She hugged her sister, instructed her to tell Beverly to take over for her, then dashed for her car.

The drive back to Tampa passed in a blur. Parking her car in the dark lot and sprinting into the foundation's building all happened so fast, Isabel barely registered her surroundings. Only once she was back in her office, staring face-to-painted-face with the mask from Mexico, did clarity finally break through.

She loved Simon. That part she knew. What she didn't know was what happened next.

She ripped the mask off the wall. The wire that stretched across the back pinged in protest. The magic had done this to her—turned her world upside down. She'd been going along just fine until then, partying with her sister and cousin, dating when the mood struck her, concentrating entirely on her job and only fantasizing about the man who'd now rocked her world. Tonight he'd looked down at her with love in his eyes, but how long would it be until he said the words? And then what? What if it all ended? What if no matter how much they cared about each other, some unknown force drove them apart? Her heart was now in jeopardy in ways she'd never known. All thanks to Mayan mumbo jumbo.

She never would have surrendered to her passion for Simon if the seed of magic hadn't been planted in her brain. Or at least she didn't think so. She would have quit before she'd surrendered to the swirl of conflicting emotions that assailed her every time she and Simon shared the same air. Wouldn't she?

Her attention spun to the chair in front of her desk, and as if she were watching a video screen, she pictured herself sitting there, anticipating the pleasure of Simon's touch as he slid his hands beneath her skirt. The memory sapped her breath. Her pulse points flared. She'd never known anything as intimate and earth-shattering as making love with Simon. And the fear of losing him, the fear of him not loving her with the same incredible breadth with which she now knew she loved him, sent her into a panic that showed no signs of abating. She had not prepared for this. She hadn't once anticipated the full force of her feelings. Quick, no-strings affair? Ha! She was at risk of a total meltdown, all on account of a man who'd shed his icy demeanor because of her.

Grabbing her keys from her desk, she dashed through

the office, unlocked the front door, and made her way in her emerald green ball gown down the lawn of Making Moms and then across busy Bayshore Boulevard to the waterfront on the other side. Through the balustrade that lined the sidewalk overlooking the bay, a crisp breeze snapped from the water and seeped straight into her bones. She hugged herself against the chill, her eyes immediately drawn by the lights over the city.

Tampa wasn't a big place, but it was home. The half-dozen skyscrapers standing sentry over her had dressed up for the holidays. With red and green lights, the glittering white bank building had morphed into a mammoth Christmas tree. The rest looked like ornaments, glowing and festive. Normally, she loved the holiday. She allowed herself a moment to imagine spending Christmas morning making love to Simon amid an assorted collection of torn wrapping paper and shiny bows. She imagined wrapping herself up in nothing but ribbons. Maybe finding a few naughty things to stuff in his stocking. She knew she could make this fantasy real, but for how long?

Behind her, cars roared down Bayshore Boulevard, mostly ignoring the speed limit. She looked at the street, at the water, at the mask she still held tightly in her hands. *Mayan magic, my ass*, she thought. *Nothing but trouble.* She hauled back her arm to toss the mask in the water when the sound of a car horn stopped her.

Simon's sleek sports car slowed to a stop along the curb. He rolled down the window.

"Why aren't you at the charity ball?" she asked, horrified.

"Funny," he quipped, "I drove all the way to your place, then back here to ask you the very same question."

Isabel watched, wide-eyed, as cars flew past him, honking at his audacity at stopping in the middle of the street. With a growl, he threw the car into drive, hopped the curb, and parked on the median, inches from the sidewalk. He waited for traffic to thin before throwing open his car door and joining her near the balustrade.

"You're going to get a ticket," she said, pointing at his illegally parked car.

"I can afford the fine. Why did you leave?"

He slid his hands over her elbows, holding her in place while his body heat chased away the cold. "I had something to do," she replied.

He took the mask out of her hand. "Like toss this into Tampa Bay? Why?"

God, she couldn't tell him. He'd think her a superstitious idiot—or worse.

"Isabel," he said, his tone deep and insistent.

"You're going to think I'm crazy."

He chuckled. "You've been sleeping with me for the last week. I already think you're nuts."

"You're becoming a regular Jerry Seinfeld."

"I'm better looking," he countered.

Her muscles unclenched. "This is true."

"It's also true that you scared the hell out of me by running out without a word. Now I find you standing on the side of a busy street, about to toss a five-dollar Mexican mask into the bay when you should be sharing the evening with me, basking in the glory of our success."

She couldn't tamp down a grin. "You wowed them, didn't you?"

He matched her smile, though his exhibited a tad

321

more humility. "Every member of the board was beelining toward me with wide grins on their faces when I realized you'd disappeared."

"You didn't blow them off, did you?"

He didn't look the least bit contrite. "Beverly made my excuses. Now tell me why you're here."

Isabel took a deep breath. If he thought she was crazy, so be it. She'd reached the point where she had to come clean.

"My cousin Lulu bought this mask for me in Mexico."

He stared at her quizzically. "I know."

"But you don't know why the mask is significant."

"No," he confirmed. "Care to share?"

She did. She recounted her experience, from the temperature on the stifling hot bus to the old Mayan woman and her coin to Lulu's spontaneous purchase of the mask. When she finished, she watched Simon for signs that he might soon dissolve into an uncontrollable fit of laughter.

He merely grinned. "So you think we wouldn't have gotten together without the magic."

"I know it sounds crazy . . ."

"It *is* crazy. Though I have to admit that if I were you, I'd probably think the same thing."

She smacked his shoulder. She didn't mind him being understanding, but patronizing? "You would not! You're too logical."

"Well, I used to be. Then this incredibly sexy and sensual woman wormed her way into my life and turned everything topsy-turvy."

"Hey!" she protested. "You made the first move, remember?"

"And the mask was in the room. Hmm." He tugged her close and pressed his humming lips against her neck. "Maybe we should fly down to Mexico and pick up a whole bunch to place in every room we're ever in?"

Despite the delicious feel of his mouth on her skin, she pushed him away. "I'm serious! What if the only reason we're together is because of some mysterious magic? What if the magic doesn't last and we're both left . . ."

Her voice trailed away.

"With broken hearts?" he provided. "That's the risk of falling in love, isn't it?"

Her chest constricted. "You're falling in love?"

He arched a brow. "Aren't you?"

She glanced down at the mask. "Yeah, I think I am. In fact, I think maybe I've been falling in love with you for a very long time."

The wind whipped up off the water again and the chill forced them closer together. Simon caught a strand of her hair before it flipped across her face, his fingers lingering against her cheek. His cufflinks glittered in the pink glow from the streetlight, reminding her of the coin. Of the magic. Of the fantasy come true.

"There was a moment," he confessed, "while you were gone on your cruise, when every tactic I'd once used with great success to keep you off my mind stopped working. I couldn't sleep without dreaming about you. I couldn't work without walking past your office. Maybe I'm just as crazy as you were, but maybe that wish of yours did break the ice for us."

Isabel glanced down at the mask, nestled tightly between them. "We could always test our theory."

"How?"

Isabel pulled away from Simon, lifted the hem of her skirt, and walked gingerly to the balustrade. She closed her eyes and once she felt Simon's body heat sidle up behind her, she tossed the mask into the bay.

She peeked an eye open. The mask floated on the surface for a split second, then the colors disappeared into the rough, black waves.

"Feel different?" he asked, snaking his arms around her.

She leaned her head back so she could look dreamily into his eyes. "Just as in love as before, I'm afraid."

His smile faded. The sparkling blue of his irises matched the storminess of the bay water splashing against the seawall just beneath them. "Don't be afraid, Isabel. I love you. It seems like I've waited a lifetime to be with you and I'm not going to let fear for our careers or anything get in the way of us being together."

Isabel's heart swelled, and she trusted Simon enough to finally trust her own feelings.

"Even without the help of a little Mayan magic?" she asked.

"I don't know about that," Simon said. "We could always honeymoon in Mexico. I've always wanted to walk up all those steps at Chichén Itzá."

Isabel didn't have time to express shock at his free and loose use of the word "honeymoon." His lips instantly captured hers and their kiss was long and lingering and full of promises—every one of which Isabel intended to keep. Only when horns honked from the passing cars did she register that they should probably take their private holiday party inside.

He opened the passenger door to his sports car with

exaggerated courtesy, kissing her hand as she folded herself into the car. He waited for a break in traffic, then jogged around and slid into the driver's seat. He started the engine, but pulled her into his arms before he made any move toward leaving.

The kiss stole her breath. Only when she leaned back against the leather seat did she notice that while she'd been in his embrace, he'd unhooked the top of her dress. Her breasts nearly spilled over the top of her bodice.

His eyes gleamed with wicked delight.

"I guess the stiff ice man really has melted," she commented as he sped off down the street.

He licked his lips, eyeing her like a hungry man. "How can any man not turn into a puddle with all your heat around?"

She clicked on her seat belt, adjusting the strap to emphasize the fullness of her breasts. "Seems like the temperature around here has risen suddenly, hasn't it?"

He shifted the car into fifth gear. "It's going to be an unseasonably hot Christmas so long as we're together, sweetheart."

Isabel eased back into the seat, closed her eyes, and enjoyed the feel of his hand snaking up her thigh. A hot Christmas and an even hotter lifetime. Just exactly what she'd wished for before she tossed the Mayan mask into the churning bay.

You Can
Count on Me

❄•✳❄✳•❄

Roxanne St. Claire

For Debbie Macomber and Linda Lael Miller,
great writers and great women, who not only pave the
rocky road, they shed light, hold my hand, guide
and inspire me every step of the way. Thank you!

Special thanks to Matthew Weigman of Sotheby's New York for providing in-depth details and valuable guidance into the structure—both physical and financial—of this great institution.

A great big *spasiba* to Susan Robb Weidner for generously sharing her remarkable Russian interpretation skills and cultural insights.

Chapter One

❄ ❄ ❄

*W*hoompf! The solid right uppercut landed smack on target, sending a jolt of pain up Raquel Durant's arm and a deep sense of satisfaction and release to her gut.

The punching bag didn't whimper.

"Is that my face you're pummeling or some mysterious evil-doer?"

Raquel wiped some sweat from her eyes with the back of her training glove and grinned at her boss. "Like you'd let me land one, Luce."

"But you're mad enough to try."

How was it that no matter what Raquel did to disguise her feelings, Lucy Sharpe could sniff out the truth? The woman was a human bloodhound. In the CIA they called that an "elicitation expert" and Lucy sure had been one of those before she started the Bullet Catchers.

"I'm frustrated, is all." Raquel pulled off her gloves. "I've been training for three years and I'm ready for field work. I know you need me upstairs doing the admin and research, but I'm goin' stir crazy." Lucy opened her mouth, but Raquel stopped her by waving a glove. "Not that I don't like spending my days in a mansion on the Hudson after the living hell that's called New Jersey, and not that I don't appreciate that you took a chance on me."

"Raquel—"

"And don't think I don't know how incredible the Bullet Catchers are, because those guys are great and treat me like their favorite little sister. But they—"

"Raquel—"

"—are all out in the field protecting ambassadors and running threat assessments on private islands and advancing security on the *Queen Mary 2* and generally kicking butt, and I'm stuck on the computer—"

"Raquel—"

"—finding them unlisted phone numbers and entering their flippin' expense reports."

She finally took a breath and waited for Lucy's thoughtful nod and promise that she'd know when the time was right—right before she delivered her first demand for Raquel to jump through hoops today. Then Raquel would ask "how high and how many," because Lucy engendered that kind of loyalty and devotion.

"Are you finished?" Lucy asked.

"No," Raquel admitted, dropping onto a workout bench with a defeated sigh, "but I feel better."

Lucy sat next to her and looked Raquel square in the eye. "You're ready."

Raquel blinked and drew back. "I am?" She coughed and changed her tone. "I mean, I *am*."

"I'm giving you Grigori Nyekovic's assignment. Because if I didn't, you'd sneak out of here pretending to take a long Christmas vacation, and then show up at his Manhattan apartment as the bodyguard he requested yesterday."

Raquel shook her head and let out a soft laugh. "How did you know I was thinking about that?"

"Because I saw the flush in your cheeks after you got off the phone with him."

"That could just have been the sexy Russian accent and all that folklore about his former KGB work."

Lucy smiled. "If hot guys with dangerous backgrounds melted you, you would have been a puddle at our first staff meeting."

"True." She paused for a moment, then grinned. "How hot?"

"He's very good looking. In that ice-blue-eyes, golden-hair, northern-Russian hunk way."

Raquel shrugged. Hot guys were a dime a dozen around here. "Thanks for the job, Luce. It sounds like a perfect starter assignment: a bodyguard for his eight-year-old daughter while he's in New York for the holidays. I mean, how hard can one little girl be?"

She could have sworn Lucy paled as she stood up and her dark, exotic eyes shuttered. "If he wanted a baby-sitter, he'd have called a nanny service. He called for a bodyguard and if you take the assignment, you take it as a full-fledged Bullet Catcher." She narrowed her eyes. "*Your* life is on the line, not the person you're guarding. As you know, we've never lost a principal."

The weight of the responsibility pushed on her, but Raquel stood, and notched her chin to look up at her six-foot-tall boss. "Nor will we this time."

"Good. Then go get your gear. He expects you in midtown today and you'll stay through New Year's."

Raquel felt the urge to slam the punching bag in joy. "I know Gregg is an old friend of yours, and your confidence means the world to me. I won't let you down and I won't let him down and I—"

"Raquel." Lucy held a finger over her lips. "Bullet Catchers don't talk. We listen."

"Right. Got it." She pumped both fists in solidarity and acknowledgment. "We listen." Jogging toward the door, she fought the urge to do a full-fledged boogie of happiness. Instead, she squared her shoulders and bounded up the stairs like the tough, trained security specialist she was.

"Raquel?" Lucy called from below.

"Yeah?"

"Keep your eye on that little girl . . . not her father."

"Come on, Luce. You know you can count on me."

Before Lucy could issue one more warning, Raquel slipped through the door and thrust a victorious fist in the air. *Finally!* Nothing, absolutely nothing, would screw up this opportunity.

Grigori set the jewel-encrusted treasure back into its cushy velvet box and looked up to study the plasma screen that beamed visitors' images from the lobby directly to his office wall. So this was Raquel Durant.

Lucy's choice for Kristina's bodyguard was utterly inspired.

For the first time since he'd returned from the auction house that morning, his attention remained on something other than the Fabergé egg collection he'd come to New York to acquire.

From their brief, banter-filled telephone conversations over the past year, he'd imagined Raquel Durant a blonde, but dark hair curled past her shoulders. It perfectly suited the subtext of passion he'd always picked up in the melody of her round vowels and snappy consonants. And he'd thought she'd be delicate, perhaps spare in size. Yet she moved like a woman made of taut, honed muscle, and her square chin looked proud, confident, and strong. That was, when it stopped moving.

She'd talked the entire time it took the guard to check her identification and announce her, even making the guard laugh.

She scanned the area behind the desk, giving Grigori a straight shot of her pretty face as her almond-shaped brown eyes took in the artwork that hid the security camera lenses. She looked directly into the camera, kicked up her generous mouth in a half-smile, and winked.

He damn near winked back.

Yes, Lucy's choice was inspired. Strong, smart, and unafraid. He didn't care that this was Raquel's first official assignment as a Bullet Catcher, and he'd told Lucy that when she'd called this morning.

He just wanted Kristina to be as safe and happy here as she was during the holidays in St. Petersburg, and an ambitious young woman determined to succeed in her bodyguard debut would work perfectly. He had to be in New York this Christmas; he had no choice. And if that left him spending a few quiet evenings at home with the bubbly Jersey-bred girl while he waited for the deal to go through, he could think of worse ways to pass the time.

He impulsively picked up the phone and dialed the nanny service, and asked the owner to cancel the baby-sitter for that night. Between the bodyguard and her father, Kristina wouldn't need another companion.

Satisfied, he returned his attention to the egg, his fingers absently tracing the delicate lines of gold enamel, the diamonds that surrounded the finely painted image. Lost for almost half a century . . . and finally almost ready to make the return journey *home*. If all went according to plan.

He heard the soft bell warning him the private elevator would open in ten seconds, so he pushed his chair back and was waiting there for her when the door opened.

"Mr. Nyekovic?" She thrust a hand toward him. "I'm Raquel Durant."

"Please call me Gregg." He held her hand and drew her out of the elevator. Her grip was as sincere as her smile, as if she put her heart into both. "How'd you know which camera?"

She frowned for a beat, then understood. "I saw the tiny lenses hidden in the flower petals of the painting. I just assumed the top one was the penthouse." She shrugged, tilting her head to the side in an endearing gesture of self-deprecation. "Lucky guess."

Not lucky, and they both knew it. "You'd make a good spy," he said with a smile as he led her into the entryway. "Here, let me take your coat."

"Thanks." She shook off a simple, dark broadcloth peacoat that wouldn't stand out in the streets of New York. Good choice for a bodyguard, especially because he bet her personal style leaned toward bright colors and hip fashions. Under the coat, the hint of feminine curves were covered in all black.

"I just got off the phone with Lucy," he told her. "I'm honored to have Kristina as your first assignment."

"She told you I'm a rookie?" She curled one hand on a narrow hip. "It won't be . . ." Her focus moved over his shoulder. ". . . an issue. And speaking of spies, I think my principal just spied on *me.*"

He glanced back toward the hall that led to the office and bedrooms. "She comes by it naturally, I'm afraid. And she's a bit shy. Let's give her a minute." He indicated a sitting room off to the side with a sly grin. "We'll draw her out."

"Is she used to personal protection?" Raquel asked as she followed his request to take a seat, but perched on the edge, ready to jump up.

"Most of the time she lives in London with my ex-wife," he said. "Her mother maintains a low profile and a high wall around her home, so Kristina is quite safe there. I have full custody of her for a few weeks in the summer and over the holidays, and we spend them at my family home in Russia, where she is also secluded." He shrugged. "But I have some business here, and I feel the need for more security."

"Did anything in particular happen to make you want a bodyguard?"

He shook his head. "Blame my former profession. I just thought it a smart precaution to contact Lucy." He gave her an approving look. "I'm quite delighted with her choice. I didn't want a hulking, six-foot-six human Rottweiler following her around the city."

"You've met some of the Bullet Catchers, then." Her laugh quieted the moment they heard the soft scuff of a shoe. "I think we got her," she whispered to him.

He leaned forward, closer to her. "All she needs is a little incentive."

Raquel nodded. "Have you taken Kristina to the American Girl store yet?" she asked, raising her voice. "I understand they have a wonderful Christmas display."

Three, two, one. Kristina appeared in the door and Grigori shot an "I'm impressed" smile to Raquel.

"Look who's come to see us," Grigori said gently. He stood and held a hand out, his daughter's wide-eyed gaze twisting his heart as it always did. "Kristina, I'd like you to meet Ms. Raquel Durant."

Kristina looked beyond him to Raquel. "I'd like to go there," she said, clutching a denim handbag with beaded butterflies under her arm and training her blue eyes on their guest. "To the American Girl store. Now."

Raquel covered a surprised laugh. "Well, I suppose we could arrange that." She looked at Grigori. "You're the boss, Dad."

"Where is it and what is it?" Grigori asked, also a little surprised by his daughter's bold request.

"It's a very large, painfully expensive doll store on Fifth Avenue near Rockefeller Center," Raquel explained.

Grigori raised his eyebrows. "You have all sorts of hidden expertise," he said.

"I have a nine-year-old niece."

"You'd like to go to this doll store right now?" he asked Kristina. She nodded, enthusiastic for the first time since he told her they had to spend Christmas in New York.

A little shopping trip might be just the ticket for his daughter to get comfortable with the idea of having a bodyguard.

"All right, then," he agreed. "Raquel will take you."

Kristina's gap-toothed grin was all the reward he needed.

A few minutes later, he guided them out the front door of the apartment, sucking in a deep lungful of cold city air and getting the faintest whiff of something musky, like vanilla and oak, from Raquel's hair. No floral scent for her, but something more grounded, more enticing.

"Would you like to go with us?" Raquel asked, buttoning her coat.

The offer was tempting, as was her easy smile. "I think it best if you two go together." He reached for his wallet and pulled out a hundred-dollar bill. "And let Kristina get one early Christmas present."

"Thank you, Daddy," Kristina said, reaching up to kiss him.

"Have fun, Kristyusha," he whispered, hugging her close, then ruffling her silky blond hair.

When the cab pulled away, he stood for a long time watching it disappear into the traffic and chaos of New York. His heart pulled a bit, wishing he had gone with them. His time with his daughter was so brief.

But his time with the treasure upstairs was brief, too, and he needed to submit a formal bid for the work of art.

He slowly returned to the elevator, letting himself in the hushed apartment that seemed empty without Kristina. And, he thought with a wry smile, without the vibrant Miss Durant. He should call Lucy Sharpe right now and commend her on her choice of bodyguards— and make perfectly sure it was *Miss* and not *Mrs.* Durant. He rounded the desk, lifting the phone just as his gaze fell on the empty nest of red velvet.

Nyet! The egg was gone!

Chapter Two

❄ ❄ ❄

The little girl was nearly as charming as her father, with her soft British accent, clutching her handbag like a security blanket, and staring in doe-eyed wonder at Christmas in New York City. During the short cab ride to Rock Center, Raquel reminded herself that the trick to protecting a VIP child was to appear to be a family member or caretaker, while staying focused on potential threats.

As they climbed out of the cab in front of Saks, Raquel laid a possessive hand on Kristina's small shoulder. "It's right across the street." Raquel guided her charge through a pack of tourists, scanning the crowd for anyone who appeared the least bit menacing.

But there was no menace. The New Yorkers looked preoccupied and visitors simply awed. The child fell in step with the crowd, bouncing in her pink sneakers as she spied the massive red-and-white logo draped in holly and lights.

"Look! There it is!" This female mecca evidently knew no international boundaries, since Kristina was a Russian child raised in England . . . and yet she was magnetically drawn to something called "American Girl." "I want every single doll they have."

Raquel smiled and patted the purse hooked over Kristina's shoulder. "Then you better have more money, kiddo, because what your dad gave me will get you exactly one American Girl doll and not a stitch of extras. But I suppose you could ask Santa."

Kristina pulled the purse higher. "I'll just make a list, then. What Santa doesn't get, Daddy will."

"Does he get you everything you want?" Raquel asked.

"If I ask nicely."

"Just like a man," Raquel muttered. Though she didn't believe anything about Grigori Nyekovic was like most men. And not just because Lucy should win the Understatement of the Year contest for calling him "good looking." But it wasn't his sculpted cheekbones, cleft chin, or that mop of blond hair that fell invitingly close to Dresden blue eyes that intrigued her.

It was something else altogether. An undercurrent of intensity that hummed around him, bubbling just under the surface with the promise that only the right person, the right *woman,* might tap some of that electricity. An easy six-foot-two, he was lean and rangy yet still powerful. As if he could pummel an opponent mentally, and be more deadly than if he'd shot the man between the eyes. Or kiss a female opponent senseless so she didn't even know what hit her.

All the KGB folklore about the man must be true.

"I know our names are almost the same, but I don't want a Kristen doll; I want Elizabeth."

Kristina's musings broke Raquel's train of thought like a punch: *Keep your eye on that little girl . . . not the father.*

She scanned the crowd again, alert.

"And maybe we could have tea," Kristina continued, her shyness dissolving more with each step closer to her destination. "Did you know they have a theater here? And you can buy clothes to match your doll's, and there's a bookstore with all their stories! And don't forget the pets and horses. All American Girls have them."

Raquel laughed. "You talk as much as I do."

"Then you're perfect for me," Kristina announced.

"Of course I am." Really, could Max Roper or Dan Gallagher or Chase Ryker or any of the alpha dogs that Lucy hired possibly handle this job as well as a woman? Not a chance. There were some jobs only a *female* Bullet Catcher could handle.

She pulled the heavy glass door open and guided Kristina from the swarm of Fifth Avenue pedestrians into a completely different human crush. Kristina's sneakers squeaked on the pale hardwood floor as the little girl twirled to drink in the displays of perfect little dolls and glorious accessories. All around, packs of excited young girls did the same.

This was definitely a job for a Bullet Catcher with estrogen.

As they entered the first-floor boutique, Kristina exclaimed, "It's like magic!"

"Where to first?"

"The historical dolls," Kristina announced. "Then we'll go upstairs to the American Girl Today collection—"

"Have you been here before?" Raquel asked.

"On the Internet."

Biting back a smile, Raquel kept a firm hand on Kristina's shoulder and guided her through the store, still carefully monitoring the crowd. With each moment, Raquel relaxed a little more. Her first task as a Bullet Catcher was a piece of proverbial cake.

And there was Lucy's voice again . . . *The easy ones'll kill you.*

Shaking it off, Raquel concentrated and before long, the hundred dollars was spent on an eighteen-inch blonde named Elizabeth who came with a book, a backstory, and a Revolutionary War gown.

"Can we have tea now?" Kristina asked. "In the café? Please?"

Raquel looked at her watch, deciding. "What do you think your father would say?"

Kristina shrugged. "Whatever I want." She was already heading toward the escalator that led to the café.

"I'm sure he doesn't let you do just anything," Raquel said, taking note of the faces of strangers coming down toward them. "It's probably just because he doesn't see you that often."

There was a long line outside of the café for tea. "Lot of ladies waiting here," Raquel said.

But Kristina stood on her toes, clutching her Elizabeth doll in one hand, her purse in the other, as she tried to see into the café. "I want to stay."

"Maybe we could call and make reservations to come back later in the week. Then we won't have to wait."

"Would my dad come?"

"That would be nice," Raquel said, meaning it more than she allowed herself to sound. "Why don't we get back home and make the arrangements?"

Kristina reluctantly agreed and they went back down the escalators, through a maze of boutiques designed to make any young female stop and browse—and Kristina was no different—and toward the front door to the Fifth Avenue exit.

"We'll catch a cab going uptown," Raquel said. "Button your coat," she reminded Kristina as they pushed the door open.

The mob moving in was as sizable as when they'd arrived. Somewhere a bell jingled, and the horns of New York's cabbies blared. Raquel guided Kristina through a pack of pedestrians just as something flashed behind her. A camera?

Raquel turned, her hand still touching Kristina's collar, and as she did she met the direct gaze of intimidating, determined, dark brown eyes. The light flashed again, blinding her.

"Hey!" Kristina screamed.

Raquel pivoted on one foot, blinking the blindness away as Kristina broke free and started running. Adrenaline stabbed like a knife as she lunged after the child.

"Stop!" Kristina yelled. "They took my doll!"

Raquel sidestepped an old man, nearly knocked over a woman, and seized Kristina by the coat, yanking her to a halt. She glanced at the confused faces of onlookers just as the brown-eyed man turned the street corner twenty feet away. She caught a glimpse of his profile, then he disappeared.

Kristina jerked her arm and tried to get free, fury darkening her delicate features as she tried to run in the same direction, but Raquel held tight.

"Someone took Elizabeth!" she screamed, tears rising along with two bright red spots of righteous indignation on her cheeks.

What kind of lowlife would take a little kid's doll? Tamping down her own irritation, Raquel put both hands on Kristina's shoulders and breathed evenly as though she could will the child to do the same.

"Calm down, Kristina." She eased her out of the crowd, closer to the building, where she could physically protect the child with her body. "Are you okay? Did he hurt you?"

The girl shook her head furiously, blinking at the tears. "That person, just took . . . took my do—do—doll!" She held up her empty hands as living proof. "My brand-new Elizabeth doll!"

Raquel glanced in the direction of the thief, then back at Kristina. "Are you hurt?"

"No . . . not . . . no." Her chin quivered and tears fell. "But Elizabeth!"

"It's okay," Raquel soothed her, resisting the urge to crouch down. That would put her off balance. She tightened her grip on the little girl's shoulder. "I'm afraid you just learned a very ugly lesson. Some people just take what they want, especially if it's valuable. It's wrong and awful, and . . . what's the matter?"

Kristina's anger had suddenly morphed into something deeper. Raw terror.

"What's wrong?" Raquel urged her.

The girl closed her eyes and clutched her empty shoulder. "He stole my handbag, too," she whispered.

The bastard. "Oh, hon, I am so sorry." Raquel leaned over. "I know you'll get another purse. I know you'll get another doll. I'm sure your daddy will understand."

She shook her head violently. "No, he won't!"

"Of course he will. He won't blame you, honey."

But Kristina just gave her a wide-eyed look of pure panic. "Don't . . . don't . . . don't tell him."

Raquel straightened. Why? Kristina had told her that her father basically got her whatever she wanted. "Of course we have to tell him," she said.

"No!"

Why would she be afraid of her father's reaction? If anyone would be in trouble, it would be the bodyguard who let Kristina get robbed in broad daylight on Fifth Avenue, not the innocent victim.

"Come on," Raquel closed her hand over Kristina's. "Let's go home and face the music."

But Kristina remained still and terrified. "Do you think my daddy will be home?"

Raquel's heart lurched. The child was truly scared of her own father. "I don't know, honey. But just remember, my job is to protect you."

From everyone.

When Kristina returned from her shopping trip with her new bodyguard, her face looked as stricken as Grigori felt. As soon as they entered the apartment, he momentarily forgot his troubles and dropped to one knee, taking his daughter's tear-stained face in his hands.

"Lapinka," he crooned. "What's the matter?"

Raquel stood sentry next to his daughter, and he looked up at her when Kristina didn't answer.

"We had an incident," she said quietly.

His gut tightened as he fixed a gaze on her umber-colored eyes. "What kind of incident?"

"Kristina's doll was stolen."

He blinked and drew back. Was there an epidemic of thievery going around? "What happened?"

"Someone grabbed her doll from her arms as we left the store," Raquel said. "It happened very quickly, after a camera flashed in my eyes."

He pulled his daughter closer. "Are you all right, Kristyusha?"

She nodded, but still didn't speak.

"You're shell-shocked," he said, stroking her cheek. "The only thing that matters is that you're not hurt. We can get a new doll—"

Kristina yanked away and ran down the hall, then disappeared into a room, slamming the door behind her. It happened so suddenly, he was still crouched on the ground.

"I'm very sorry," Raquel said, her voice and body language guarded.

He rose. "Your job is to keep her safe," he said. "And you did. I'm not paying you to protect her dolls."

"But she's a mess about this."

He had much bigger problems than a lost baby doll. "Yes, she's distraught."

"She thinks you're going to be very mad at her."

He frowned at her accusatory tone. "I can't imagine why. I doubt I've ever raised my voice to her."

Raquel's eyes, so friendly and open earlier, burned with suspicion. "She's terrified of how you'll react to this. She's been shivering in fear the whole ride uptown."

"I'm sure the incident was very upsetting, but she has no reason to be afraid of me," he insisted. "I'll go talk to her."

He started down the hall, but Raquel took his elbow. "Are you sure you've never raised your voice to her?"

The demand irked. "I am quite sure." He searched her face and she did the same. "What did she tell you?"

"It wasn't what she said, it was how she said it."

"And how was that, may I ask?"

"Most of the time, she painted you as a very generous and giving father, even spoiling her."

Grigori narrowed his eyes at her. Where was this going? "And then?"

"And then her doll was stolen and she was upset."

"She thought I'd be mad at her for something that wasn't her fault? That's ridiculous."

"She didn't get truly upset until she realized her purse was stolen, too."

"What?"

"The thief took both the new doll she was holding and her little shoulder bag."

He scowled in dismay. "A purse snatcher took the bag of a little girl?"

"Pathetic, isn't it? Who would steal a child's purse when there are thousand-dollar Chanel bags all over Fifth Avenue? There's certainly nothing valuable in a little girl's handbag."

A tiny, white light flashed in his head. "Certainly not," he said, but the words stuck in his throat.

He followed Raquel's surprised gaze over his shoulder to where his daughter now stood, wide eyed and, yes, terrified. The pieces were falling into place and the picture was not pretty.

"Kristina?" he asked softly. "What was in your handbag?"

Her lower lip quivered and her eyes got smoky gray. He knew what was coming, dammit. He *knew* it.

"I thought it was so pretty, Daddy. I thought it was a new ornament for the tree. I'm sorry. I took it."

Grigori closed his eyes and voiced his worst fear. "Some purse snatcher just hit the international jackpot."

Chapter Three

❄ ❄ ❄

Raquel waited in a well-appointed room that faced Central Park, her gaze on a ten-foot Christmas tree in the bay window, her thoughts bouncing around the bit of information she'd gleaned from Gregg's gentle interrogation of his daughter.

A multimillion-dollar ornament?

An Imperial Fabergé egg?

A *chance* purse snatching?

At the sound of a footfall behind her, she turned and the questions evaporated at the look of exhaustion and concern on Gregg's face.

"I think she's going to sleep now," he said, that Russian lilt in his voice a little more pronounced with the stress of the last hour. "I gave her some milk."

"She needs that," Raquel agreed. "And you, too. Sleep, not milk."

He smiled. "I have too many questions. I could use a drink, though. Something stronger than milk." He walked to a dark wood cabinet and wet bar that took up half the wall. "What do you drink?"

"Ice water," she replied. "I have questions, too. But you first." *Bullet Catchers listen.*

He reached into a tiny chilled compartment, pulling out a water bottle and something clear with Russian letters on the label. He dropped ice in one glass, added water, and handed it to her. When their fingers brushed, he punctuated the contact with an intense blue-eyed gaze.

"This cannot be an accident," he said somberly.

For a moment, Raquel thought he meant that little electrical charge when their hands touched.

"But," he continued, pouring his own drink with no ice, "Kristina said she took the egg on a whim after you arrived. She slipped into my office, found it, and hid it in her handbag. Then she forgot or didn't know how to tell me . . ." He shook his head. "No wonder she was frightened of my reaction." He nodded for her to sit.

"I'm sorry about that," Raquel said, setting her water glass on a table coaster without drinking. "She was genuinely scared and I thought . . . perhaps . . ."

"I beat my daughter." The corner of his lips lifted a little.

"I automatically jumped to her defense."

He warmed her with an appreciative blue stare. "That's your job."

Raquel reached for her drink. "I saw him."

"The thief?" He leaned forward, interested. "Tell me."

"I turned and saw very deep brown eyes, rugged and mean. It happened so fast, that was all I saw. Then someone flashed a camera, and Kristina screamed—"

"He was behind you?"

Raquel frowned, closed her eyes, and replayed the

moment. "Whoever flashed the camera might have taken the doll from Kristina's left hand and then I turned," she opened her eyes in realization, "and the guy with the brown eyes moved against my right, and I think he took the purse." She blew out a breath of self-disgust. "I can't believe I let that happen."

"You protected her," he said. "You had no way of knowing she carried a national treasure."

"And neither did the thief."

He nodded slowly. "That's what really bothers me. I assumed someone slipped in here while I was downstairs seeing you off, a lucky robbery at best. It never occurred to me that Kristina would have taken it. I never even thought of the possibility. So who else would have?"

"Who knew that egg was here?"

He leaned back against the sofa, crossing impossibly long legs and locking his hands behind his head. The gesture pulled the fabric of his button-down shirt just enough to highlight the planes of his chest and Raquel forced her attention to his face. Which was just as appealing a sight.

Hot guys with dangerous backgrounds did not melt her. They *didn't*.

"The representative from Sotheby's, Mark Duncan. He allowed me to take the egg for a close examination, since my purchase bid is about to go through."

"Who owns the egg?" While Raquel had waited for him to put Kristina to bed, she'd done a basic Internet search on her BlackBerry, which had given her a lesson in Fabergé and the fifty masterpiece jeweled eggs the famed Russian artisans had created for the czars.

"This is one of the original eight missing Imperial

eggs," he explained. "An anonymous family had four of the missing eight for more than fifty years. Amazingly enough, they didn't discover them until an old woman died recently and they found the eggs in her belongings."

"Wow. I never heard about this."

"No, it's been kept absolutely quiet by the owner and by Sotheby's, who's handling the sale. And that's precisely the way I want to keep it. If news of this theft gets out, every collector in the world will swarm in. And I . . ." He closed his eyes, his voice soft. "I want these eggs."

The quiet determination sent a shiver over her. She had no doubt that whatever this man wanted he got. "Are you an art collector?"

"Not in the least. I don't want to keep the eggs," he explained. "They belong in Russia. All of them, someday, I hope. I'd love to see them in St. Petersburg, since it is the home of Carl Fabergé. But I'll settle for Moscow, where ten are now. Nine more were recently purchased to be returned there."

"Which one did you have?"

He warmed her with a gaze. "Are you familiar with the collection?"

"I did some research." She pulled out the handheld Internet device tucked into her pocket. "I have to admit to scant knowledge of czarist Russian art."

"It was one of the simpler ones, known as the Danish Jubilee, made in 1903. It is encrusted with diamonds and a miniature likeness of the King of Denmark, commemorating a visit from a Russian czarina. It actually does resemble an elaborate Christmas ornament." He glanced at the tree.

"What's it worth?"

He shrugged. "Market price varies. Stalin sold a few for under five hundred dollars. The Coronation egg recently sold for about twenty-four million." He paused and held her surprised gaze. "I've bid five million."

She whistled out a slow breath. "KGB consulting must pay well."

He laughed softly. "I long ago gave up the spy business. Didn't Lucy tell you? I'm in real estate, investments, and some oil companies now. Pretty dull stuff."

Nothing about the tall, blond Russian was *dull*. "Other than your contact at Sotheby's, who knew you had the egg here?"

"No one."

"Someone had to know," she said. "Like the owner."

"If I ask Duncan, my contact at Sotheby's, that would alert him to the theft and he would call the authorities and the whole story will be out in two days."

"How long do you think you can keep it a secret?"

His look was dismal. "Not that long."

"We have to go to the police so I can go through files and photos. I think I could recognize those eyes."

"Not yet." His tone left no room for arguing. "If the news gets out that these four eggs have been located, I'll lose the other three, too." He took a deep drink. "It's not an accident or a coincidence. And if I can figure that out, then I should be able to find the thief."

She happened to agree, but one piece of the puzzle still bothered her. "Even if someone knew you had the egg, no one could have known that Kristina would pull a childish prank and take it, or that she'd impulsively decide to go shopping with it hanging over her shoulder. Nothing was planned this afternoon."

They looked at each other for a beat.

"A camera?" They both said it at exactly the same time.

"Have you had this place swept for bugs?" Raquel asked.

"Before I arrived. Old habits."

"I know. I work for a former spy." Raquel had already started combing the room visually. "They might have missed something. We should start in your office. The only explanation is that someone saw her take the egg and followed us. Let's go tear that room apart." She indicated for him to come along as she hustled toward the hall. "I'll find any bug or a camera. There has to be an answer in there—" She glanced over her shoulder when he didn't follow. "What? Aren't you coming?"

"Tear the room apart?" He smiled. "I like your style."

She was focused. Talkative. Energetic. Alive. Intelligent. Dynamic.

And flat on her back, under his desk, deep into her task, Raquel Durant was knock-down sexy. If Grigori hadn't just lost a priceless treasure, he'd seriously consider crawling down there to do some bug hunting with his daughter's bodyguard.

"Unless someone's hidden a device in this—" She reached up and slapped a plastic Dalmatian dog on the desk. "Then you're clean under here."

"I let Kristina set up her miniature house under there the other day," he said as he secured the last screw in the plasma screen. "There's nothing behind here."

Popping up from behind his desk, Raquel pushed a dark wave from her face and narrowed her eyes. "No way that camera in the lobby can be turned around to see in here, instead of down there?"

He shook his head. "No, I triple-checked that; it was my first thought."

She leaned back on her haunches, shoving all that hair off her face with two hands. "Who else could possibly have known you had the egg?"

"I keep going back to the owner who might not really want to part with it."

She pulled herself up. "Me, too. The guy at Sotheby's might have told him he let you take one. Who is it?"

"I don't know," he said, feeling the point of contention stab him as it had since the initial call from Sotheby's had come in a few weeks ago. "They refuse to be named."

"Is that common practice?"

"Not really, but it isn't illegal. Sometimes wealthy collectors want to stay entirely anonymous. In principle, that's why they have an intermediary like Sotheby's."

"And your guy there will absolutely not, even under pressure, give you the name?"

He lifted his eyebrows. "Pressure?"

"You know, brute strength? Threats?" She punched a fist into her palm. "Come on, weren't you in the KGB?"

He couldn't help smiling. "Lucy must portray quite an ugly picture of me. I was not a thug, Raquel. I was a spy. Most of the time I merely sneaked into places where I didn't belong, grabbed a little intelligence, and delivered it to someone else, then disappeared."

"Lucy doesn't portray any pictures," she assured him. "I've just read too much Tom Clancy. And I like to box—"

"You do?"

She slid into his desk chair, her rich brown gaze on him. "And I've got a plan."

He almost laughed at her bravado. "Let's hear it."

"Why don't we go to Sotheby's, into the office of the person you're working with—what's his name?"

"Mark Duncan."

"Okay, into Mark Duncan's office and I'll distract him, and you skim his Rolodex—or even better, you distract him and I'll skim his computer because I'm good at that—and get the name of the owner of the egg." She leaned forward on one elbow, a mesmerizing light in her eyes. "What do you think?"

"Don't forget the part where we make love on the way home in a limousine."

Her elbow slid off the desk. "Excuse me?"

"You make it all sound as easy as a James Bond movie."

She tapered those toasty brown eyes at him. "You're making jokes. I'm making plans. There's a five-million-dollar egg out there and I feel responsible for its loss. Doesn't look good on my brief résumé, if you know what I mean. You have a better idea?"

None better than sex in a limo with a vibrant . . . *boxer.* "Yes."

"What is it?"

"Let's bypass the middleman." He stood and rounded the desk, where he flipped open a laptop computer. "I know a little bit about the collector. Not a lot. I would have researched more if I thought I needed to know, but the sale seemed destined to go through."

"What do you know?" She cracked a knuckle, as if she were about to attack the keyboard.

"That the family, at least part of it, lives in New York City. I know that one of them is named Evan, because Mark Duncan let that slip once. Although that could be a last name. I know that the oldest living female in the family died sometime in October. And I know—"

She held up her hand. "I can find them."

Half an hour later, it looked like she had. In the time it took him to make them sandwiches, check on Kristina, who slept soundly, and pour them both fresh drinks, Raquel had surfed and searched and deduced and homed in on the family of Ross Kiplinger, a retired investment banker who lived in the Hamptons. His mother, Dorothy, a ninety-six-year-old dowager, had passed away on October 15 and his son Evan was the executor of Dorothy Kiplinger's estate.

Raquel thanked him for the sandwich and pointed it at the computer. "Here's an online invitation to the Christmas party he's having tomorrow night." She clicked to another screen. "Here's his cable bill." Tapped to another screen. "And here's his cellphone record."

"You're good," he said, settling on the desk to see over her shoulder.

"Well . . ." She took a bite and barely swallowed before adding, "I can't find his picture to save my life."

He resisted the urge to wipe a caraway seed from her lower lip. "Let's look at the phone bill."

By the time they finished eating, she was convinced they'd found their man. "According to this phone record," Raquel said, brushing crumbs from the sandwich off her lap while she studied the computer, "he first contacted Sotheby's on October twenty-third, then had eight additional conversations in the next two weeks."

"Duncan called me on November sixth."

"It has to be him."

"Possibly."

Determined, she clicked a few times and then drew back. "Well, look at this. A phone call to Moscow." She reached for his phone. "May I?"

Grigori nodded and she dialed, hitting speaker so they could both hear. The recorded voice answered in hushed Russian, and a tingle of pleasure shot through him. God, he missed spying.

"The Armory?" Raquel asked.

"The Kremlin Armoury Museum."

She lifted her shoulders. "Yeah?"

"The home of the largest collection of Fabergé Imperial eggs. To date." He grinned and leaned close to her. "So, I'd say *yeah.*"

Her eyes widened and she pushed away from the desk. And him. "Let's go talk to Evan."

He reached for her arm. "No."

"Oh, of course. I'm getting carried away." She eased out of his touch. "I'll stay with Kristina. I'm forgetting why I'm here."

So was he. "Actually, I think you should come with me tomorrow. I'll call the nanny service and lock Kristina safely at home. We're going to crash a Christmas party."

Her eyes lit up. "Great idea. What will we do there?"

"Whatever it takes to get that egg back."

"What if we're wrong and he didn't take it?"

"Well, you know . . ." He reached out and brushed that full, soft spot on her lower lip. The caraway seed was gone, but not the urge to touch her. "There's always the limo ride home," he said huskily.

"You know . . ." She flicked the tip of her tongue over the lush spot on her lip, right where he'd touched her, pinning him with a meaningful gaze. "I like your style, too."

Chapter Four

❋

"N yet." The word came out under his breath as Gregg looked up from the game of checkers on the floor between him and his daughter.

"No?" Raquel put her hands on her hips, somehow certain he was referring to the little black dress she'd purchased to party crash and not the fact that Kristina had just double-jumped him.

His smoky gaze meandered over the deep V neck, the long waist, and the skirt that skimmed her knees and finally settled on the black high heels, a hint of a smile threatening.

"Daddy, it's your move." Kristina tapped her checkers on the floor impatiently but Gregg didn't look away from Raquel, his expression both appreciative and apprehensive.

"What's the matter?" Raquel demanded. "I did exactly as you said and picked something that wouldn't stand out."

His mouth kicked up and finished the smile. "I suppose you can't help it."

He'd been doing that to her all day. Sending silent compliments as he gave her a crash course in spying and letting his attention drift over her face, her body. And, no doubt about it, she was doing the same thing. The only break in the tension was during the few hours when she'd gone to shop and he'd continued researching their target.

"You won, Kristyusha." Gregg stood, brushing the fabric of his dark pants and reaching for a cashmere sports jacket slung over the back of a sofa. "I'm afraid I'm much better at chess."

"I'll play chess with her, Mr. Nyekovic." The taut, brittle voice came from behind Raquel, who turned to meet the gray-eyed gaze of a pale, middle-aged woman wearing dull brown from head to toe.

"I'd like that, Joyce," Gregg said. "This is Ms. Durant. Raquel, this is Joyce Henderson from the nanny service I use here in the city."

Raquel greeted her and got a cool nod in return. With that permanently pinched face, she thought, won't she be a barrel of laughs for Kristina?

"Do you have a coat?" he asked.

"I found a cashmere wrap." She went to get her shawl and her evening bag while Gregg gave instructions to Joyce about snacks and bedtime, saying that they might be home very late. Raquel slid the cashmere over her bare arms against a little quiver of anticipation. Surely that was just because this was the kind of undercover, secretive field work the top-of-the-line Bullet Catchers did, and not because the nature of her bodyguard job had morphed into spywork . . . and her partner was a drop-dead-sexy former KGB agent who said her name with the most enticing Russian trill.

No. That would be losing sight of the objective—and Lucy wouldn't like that.

"Are you ready, Raquel?" But there was that trill again, and Raquel's stomach took a dip.

"I am."

He called for the elevator, looking hard at her as they waited.

"I'm ready," Raquel insisted. "I've gone over all the things you told me this morning. Have an escape route. Keep encounters brief. Don't invite attention. Be opportunistic. And, no, before you ask, I'm not nervous, because I've been training for this for years and I am determined to find that egg. So don't worry."

He laughed softly as the elevator arrived. "I was just going to say you look beautiful."

"Oh."

In the lobby, he spoke to the doorman, giving him a cellphone number along with instructions that no one, no matter who they were or who they knew, was to be let near the apartment.

"I've used Joyce once before," he said as he guided Raquel toward the front door. "I don't think that woman would let in Mother Teresa."

"And I don't think you'll have to worry about Kristina staying up late because she's having so much fun."

"I don't pick baby-sitters because they're fun," he said as a black stretch limo pulled up and stopped.

Raquel notched an eyebrow. "You were serious about the limo?"

"I'm always serious."

The driver hopped out and hustled around to open the door. "Evening, Mr. Nyekovic."

"Thomas." Gregg nodded and indicated for Raquel to climb in ahead of him.

She sank into a warm, plush seat that engulfed her as completely as the leathery fragrance and near darkness. Gregg followed and sat next to her, leaving little room between them and a wide, empty seat across.

"You don't think arriving in a limo will draw attention to us?" she asked.

"*Not* arriving in a limo would draw attention." He reached down to open the refrigerator. "Drink?"

"Water."

As he opened a bottle and split it for them, Raquel studied the spare movements of his long, lean fingers. Beautiful hands. Masculine, strong, but tender, too.

She looked away. "Speaking of escape routes—"

"Thinking of escaping already?" He handed her the glass with a devilish wink.

"I'm just wondering if you'll point one out, or if I'm on my own."

He sipped and turned his whole body toward her, his leg brushing her thigh and sending more delightful warmth over her. "Spies call it E and E. Escape and evasion. I'll try to indicate any ways out, but you should stay alert. The most important thing to do is act natural. There will be over a hundred people at this party; blending should be easy. I am a Russian businessman who lives partly in New York. Call me Carl."

She leaned back and gave him a teasing look. "As in Fabergé?"

He chuckled. "You think like I do, you know that?"

"Scary," she said with a dry laugh. "And who am I?"

He lifted a curl of her hair, brushing it behind her ear,

and then grazing her cheek with his fingertip. He outlined her jaw, her chin, and settled on that same spot on her lip where he'd touched her the day before. And the same heat and awareness shot low in her belly.

"You, Rakishka, are my gorgeous date."

The trill got her again. And the fingertip. "Rak-whatsha?"

He laughed. "A Russian habit. Raquel is so . . . formal."

She sipped her water, dousing the taut tendril of arousal pulling at her. "And how, in your cover story, did you and your date get invited to the party?" she asked.

"If we don't have to say, we won't. You'll find most people would much rather talk about themselves and may never ask. But if they do, my father was friends with his father. That way there is no direct link." He set his water in the well next to him.

"We need to keep every encounter and conversation brief, appearing to be wrapped up in ourselves. But our objective is to find a way into the personal areas—a bedroom or office—of Evan Kiplinger before he ever notices we are there. We might find something."

"The egg?"

"Wouldn't that be great," he said with a wry smile. "A clue, something."

"But we don't know who Kiplinger is."

He nodded. "That, of course, is our first objective when we arrive."

"And if we're introduced to him at the door?"

"We'll greet him. There'll be a crush of people. He won't be suspicious, he won't have time. All you need to do is act natural. No one ever suspects a person who is completely comfortable in their own skin. Be calm, but be hyperaware of everything around you."

She blew out a breath, her nerves starting to tingle. "Don't you think this could be a wild-goose chase?"

He reached for his drink and held it up to offer a toast. "Of course. But what better way to find an egg than chasing a wild goose?"

Gregg instructed the limo driver to circle the block twice, and Raquel realized he was waiting for the largest group of people to enter the Riverside Drive apartment building on the Upper West Side. When that happened, they got out and blended in.

One hand snug in his firm grip, she produced the printout of the invitation she'd snagged with some creative firewall cracking, and joined several couples the doorman escorted to the elevator. Some of the people were laughing and one woman was in the middle of a loud, elaborate story. Gregg guided her to the back of the car, placing her in front of him and sliding both arms around her waist. Wordlessly, he pulled her back snugly against his stomach and chest. He was stone solid muscle from shoulders to thigh, and her stomach tightened under his possessive hands.

So when he said they'd pretend to be "wrapped up in each other," he meant . . . literally. He pulled her even closer, his head dipping near her ear, his breath warm as he whispered like a lover, "You *will* tell me how you got that password code to print the invitation, won't you?"

She glanced over her shoulder. "Then I'd have to kill you."

He responded with a soft laugh and a quick squeeze.

They cruised in with the festive crowd to Evan

Kiplinger's sprawling apartment. He clearly didn't *need* the millions his grandma's heirloom eggs would fetch. He already owned a two-story showcase with a postcard view all cloaked in dim, flattering lights and jam-packed with a tony mix of the young, beautiful, and rich. Gregg never let go, touching her hand, her shoulder, her lower back, always close but just as alert as she was to their surroundings.

"I'll have to tell Lucy that you're ready for more advanced fieldwork," he said as they made their way to a giant martini-pouring ice fountain.

She beamed at him. "Thanks, Gregg."

"Carl," he whispered.

"Oh." She tilted her head to the side as though he'd just said a witty line. "My bad."

He handed her a martini. "You don't have to drink if you don't want to, but you should hold it."

"I want to," she admitted. "Big time. But I'll wait until we're done."

He leaned over to brush her hair over her shoulder, his lips near her temples. "Let's work the room and get an ID on Kiplinger."

She looked up at him with lover's eyes. "I'd love to."

"A very strong recommendation to Lucy," he said with that appreciative luster in his eyes. "You're good."

The thumping sound of Annie Lennox belting out a scat version of "Winter Wonderland" warred with voices and laughter. Gregg kept them skimming the edges of the rooms, talking softly while they did a visual of the floorplan. Downstairs appeared to be strictly living and lounging, so any office and the master bedroom must be upstairs. Fortunately there were front and back stairs, giving them a built-in escape route.

In a quiet corner in the dining room, Gregg leaned against the wall and turned Raquel to face him, planting a soft kiss on her hair. "Listen to me," he whispered. She looked up at him as though he'd said "I love you."

He kept the cover going by caressing her bare shoulder, one finger traveling over her collarbone and settling in the dip of her throat, his thumb casually dipping toward the rise of her breasts. "We are going upstairs."

She managed to keep her breathing even, but had absolutely no control over her pulse as he grazed her skin, then slid his thumbs under the thin spaghetti straps of her dress. She ran her hands up his arms, pausing at the solid curl in his biceps. "Front or back stairs?"

"Front." He pulled her closer, eliminating all space. "We'll look for an office first." He lowered his head, his mouth brushing her forehead. "Or a bedroom."

Just the word sent a blast of heat through her. He kissed her hairline, then she felt his whole body freeze.

"What?"

"Think I got the host at ten o'clock." He looked into her eyes, smiling. "Do not turn around."

Raquel reached up and caressed his jaw. "What does he look like?"

"Very short dark hair," he said, brushing his lips over her temple again. "Light eyes. Blue or gray. Dark jacket with a red kerchief in the pocket." He lifted her hair and placed his lips on her ear. "He's headed this way."

Goose bumps rose over her flesh. Just as he nearly touched her lips for a kiss, he looked up—a natural move to see if anyone was watching their public display of affection—then stopped just as their lips touched.

He didn't kiss her. "You can turn now. He's talking to the short blonde in gold pants. We're going to the right, behind him, up the stairs. Now."

He moved like liquid, and she stayed in step with him, putting every cell of her body into the act of blending in. Around the perimeter of the room, toward a hallway that led to a wide set of stairs. One hand on her back, he eased her forward, occasionally leaning into her ear to whisper ostensible endearments that were really directions.

At the top of the stairs she slid her arm around his waist, laughing playfully. To anyone watching, they were a juiced-up couple, drinking, flirting, and on the hunt for a private place to make out.

He opened the first door, to a study.

"Bingo," she whispered, flattening herself against the wall while he found a light.

"Stay by the door while I search."

Gregg scanned the room, then headed straight to a wall unit of bookshelves and cabinets. His search revealed nothing, although she still wasn't completely sure of what he was looking for. The desk was locked and he didn't take the time to pick it. A file cabinet opened and he searched the titles of the files quickly, but closed it with a decisive thud. The computer was off and they didn't have time to boot it up.

"Nothing," he said. "No connection to the eggs or Sotheby's. This may have been a dead-end idea."

"Let's keep going," she said.

Agreeing, he whipped the door open to the sound of

raucous laughter down the hall as a few people disappeared down the back stairs twenty-five feet away.

When a woman emerged from a room near the top of those steps, Raquel recognized her as the blonde who'd been talking to Kiplinger, who, not surprisingly, followed right behind.

"Our host dead ahead," Gregg whispered.

"Got it."

Another couple emerged, blocking their view of Kiplinger, and as they did the man turned enough to reveal a profile. Without missing a beat, Gregg pivoted in the other direction and as he did, the man looked down the hall at them, catching Raquel's gaze for one split second.

It was enough to turn her whole being into jelly as she followed Gregg.

"The man with the brown eyes," she said in a harsh whisper. "That's him! He's here."

"It would make sense," he agreed, an odd look on his face.

"It would?"

Without explaining, he yanked her down the stairs toward the front door. "We have to get out of here. He can't see us together."

He already did. But she knew better than to argue as Gregg tugged her toward the front entryway. The place rocked now, with deafening music and a crowd lubricated enough to be dancing in small groups or laughing loudly. She glanced over her shoulder and through a cluster of bodies, she saw Kiplinger and the blonde come around the corner first. No doubt Brown Eyes would be right behind.

Before she could even breathe, Gregg had both arms around her and pushed her hard into the wall. "Sorry this is a cliché," he muttered. "But it works."

He covered her mouth with his, the kiss so hard and without finesse that it took the little breath she had away. He opened his mouth and somehow managed to envelop her whole body with his. He was covering her and hiding his face. She knew that, but it didn't stop the heat lightning that flashed through her.

"Stay with me," he murmured into the kiss. The words were spoken like a demanding lover, but she knew it wasn't an invitation to spend the night. He started moving to his right, and she followed. He tunneled his fingers in her hair, a move that might appear sensuous but actually helped him guide her.

In two feet, he reached an open door and pushed her into the darkened space, keeping her completely covered by his body until he managed to close the door with his foot.

Only then did he break the kiss or look to see where they were.

A powder room.

"Why are we hiding from Brown Eyes?" she demanded, catching the breath he'd taken. "He stole the egg."

"Brown Eyes?" He shook his head in disgust. "His name is Mark Duncan and he works at Sotheby's."

She slumped against the wall. "The guy from Sotheby's stole the egg?"

"It looks that way."

"No way! An inside job." Pushing him aside, she reached for the door. "Let's get him."

"No." He held her in place. "Not here. I know what happened now. I know who stole the egg. I don't know how he knew Kristina had it, but we'll find out. I'll get it back."

"Are you crazy? He's right out there!" She was actually bouncing on her toes, almost shaking with her response to the news, the moment. *That kiss.*

He smiled at her in the dark. "You're ready to go a round with him, aren't you?"

"Hell yeah." She narrowed her eyes at him. "Why are you so worried about him seeing you?"

"Because I'll lose the element of surprise that I'll have when I walk into his office and get him where he works."

The door handle turned, and Gregg instantly kissed her again, pulling up the skirt of her dress and covering her backside with his hand.

"Oh, sorry, man," the intruder said, quickly slamming the door closed.

For a moment, neither one of them moved. His hand remained on her rear end, hot and large and possessive, his body pressed so hard into hers she could feel every muscle.

Slowly, he let her go, but kept her pinned with his gaze. One corner of his mouth lifted. "Nice work."

She finally exhaled. "Put that in my letter of recommendation."

"I will." Stepping away, he put his head to the door, listening. "I think he went looking for another bathroom. Let me check, then we'll slip out the same way we came in."

She smoothed her dress down. "Are you seriously going to let that Duncan guy walk away tonight and sleep at home with his five-million-dollar egg, thinking he got away with it?"

"He didn't get away with it. I'll get him tomorrow."

The adrenaline that had fired her veins dumped, leaving her with a little shiver of dissatisfaction. "So we're done here."

"Mission accomplished," he said with a decisive nod. "We found the thief. We should celebrate." He reached for her hand and looked into her eyes. "In the limo."

A wholly different kind of shiver danced through her body.

Chapter Five

❄ ❄ ❄

Gregg took off his jacket, raised the privacy glass, and exchanged a meaningful look with the driver. Obviously, he was in no rush to get home and wanted no interruptions. Just as the blackened glass reached the top, Raquel saw the driver nod in acknowledgment.

"You're still bouncing like a prizefighter," he said, opening the bottle of something with a black-and-gold label in Russian, the same stuff he had at home. He poured several ounces of clear liquid into two crystal tumblers.

Raquel had taken the seat across from him, but there was something in his movements, and his gaze, that told her she wouldn't be alone for long. She took the drink he offered and kicked off her shoes, tucking her feet under her legs. "Just a wild guess here: vodka?"

He laughed softly. "A sober beverage for people who want to remain sober. This is Juri Dolgoruki vodka, very gentle grain from Ryazan. The vodka of the czars."

"And ice is a no-no?"

He gave her an incredulous look, as if she were insane for even asking. That made her laugh and he raised his glass. "Your laughter is as beautiful to the ears as this liquid is to the mouth."

"An old Russian toast?"

"An honest observation." He took a drink, and she watched his throat move.

She still didn't sip, high enough on adrenaline and frustration and the spy games she'd just played.

"Someday," he said, studying the glass for a moment, "I will tell you the very long and very colorful history of this drink. But now, just sip slowly. The taste is much like spring water, really. Clean and natural and pure."

She took a delicate sip, dropped her head back, and closed her eyes. In a flash, she popped up, fire on her tongue. "And hot!"

"I like the pepper flavor. Would you prefer citrus?"

"And be a wuss who prefers vodka mixed with orange juice and ruined by ice? No, thanks." She closed her eyes again, head back. "What are you going to do about Duncan?"

"I will go to Sotheby's tomorrow."

"With the police?"

When he didn't answer, she lifted her head and looked at him expectantly.

"I'm done with that subject for now," he said, moving from his seat to hers.

She gave him a wary look. "How? It's a five-million-dollar egg and you were duped by the guy brokering the deal."

"I compartmentalize. I bet your boss does, too. It's the only way to be a spy."

"Well, I don't. I'm can't forget those brown eyes. He targeted me. He targeted Kristina!"

"I will have him tomorrow." He lifted a strand of her hair and let it fall against her shoulder, his fingertips grazing her skin. "Tonight, I want to play with you."

His tone was raw seduction, and more intoxicating than the spicy liquor warming her blood. "Play what?"

"Games."

"Spy games?

He chuckled softly. "Fun games."

From under partially closed lids, she watched him dip two fingers into his drink, drenching them in the peppery vodka. He touched the hollow of her throat and the icy liquid trailed down her breastbone.

He followed the trail first with just his gaze, then his finger, then his mouth, lowering his head to lick the rivulet just as it meandered into her cleavage. Her body rose to meet his mouth and she shuddered at the shocking blend of hot tongue and cold liquid.

"Don't tell me. This a Russian kissing game called Follow the Volga River?"

He kissed the warm flesh just above the neckline of her dress. "Russians don't play kissing games."

"Could have fooled me."

"We play drinking games." He wet his finger with vodka again and dribbled it into her cleavage, watching it disappear before he looked into her eyes. "Will you play with me, Rakishka?"

Very slowly, she threaded her fingers into his silky hair and guided his face up to meet hers, brushing back the golden lock that fell over his forehead. "Will you mention it in my recommendation letter?"

"No."

"In that case . . ." She tilted her head in consent and he kissed her. Not as hard as the brutal exchange at the party, and for some reason his gentleness simply increased the burn low in her stomach and right between her legs. He reached around her, deposited his glass in a drink well, and did the same with hers.

She moved into him, opening her mouth and tangling her tongue with his. He tasted spicy and sweet and completely different from when they kissed for cover. He eased one dress strap over her shoulder, murmuring her name.

"You weren't joking about making love in the limo, were you?" she asked as he feathered kisses over her shoulders and neck.

"I don't joke." He nibbled her throat as he reached behind her and eased the zipper of the dress all the way down, the sound as sexy as any words. "You do."

Street noises and horns and the occasional shout filtered into the limo, threatening to pull her from the moment. But he lowered the bodice of her dress, and all other senses evaporated with one hot kiss on the flesh that spilled out over her lacy strapless bra.

"How do you play?" she asked on a whisper.

He dipped his tongue under the fabric and grazed the tip of her hardened nipple. "Since I am a gentleman," he murmured into her skin, "I'll go first and show you."

He unfastened her bra with one flick and dropped it on the seat, sparks lighting his eyes as he lingered over her bare breasts. She shivered and arched toward him.

"Oooh," she sighed. "I like this game."

"I knew you would." He picked up one of the tumblers again and tilted the glass to let a tiny bit of vodka drip onto the rise of her breast. Raquel didn't know which was the sexier sight—the clear liquid sliding over her skin or the hungry, lusty look on his handsome face.

She offered him a taste of her breast, which he took, suckling her to a painful peak. She tightened her grip on his head as her hips rose to meet his. He was hard, everywhere. Hard thigh muscles, a stiff and ready erection, granite-hard chest. He licked a circle around her nipple, making the vodka disappear as fast as any uncertainty she might have had about what was going to happen in the limo.

She opened his shirt to touch his chest, flattening her palms against the hard planes and digging into the nest of rough hair. He kissed her again, his tongue taking ownership of hers, exchanging the drink mouth to mouth. He inched her dress over her hips and thighs until it fell in a silky hush to the limo floor.

"You only need to say *nyet,* Rakishka, and I will stop the game. *Nyet* or *da.*"

Arousal twisted inside her, the need to move in rhythm against him as relentless as the rush of her own pulse in her ears. *"Da,"* she said softly. *"Da, da, da."*

He half laughed, half groaned and finished taking off his shirt so their chests could touch, their warm breath heating up the inside of the darkened car as she moved against him in only panties. He kneeled over her, maintaining the contact and rhythm of their hips while he dribbled another stream of vodka, this time low on her stomach. When his tongue scorched her, she swore softly, burying her fingers in his flaxen hair and nearly whimpering at the touch of his tender, clever mouth.

He inched the lace of her panties lower, and the next drop of liquid slivered into the tuft of hair between her legs, only to be shockingly swept up by his tongue. He swirled and dipped and tortured and, true to his word, *played* with her until she nearly came. She pulled him up hungrily.

"When is it my turn?"

With one long, deep kiss, he widened his legs in invitation. "Now."

She reached for her vodka, dipped her finger in the liquid, and placed a drop on his lower lip. With a flick of her tongue, it was gone.

He smiled. "Good."

She wet two fingers and dribbled the vodka directly on his breastbone, letting one trickle head down to that enticing six-pack. She licked it off.

"Even better," he whispered.

She handed him the glass to hold, unzipped his pants and freed him, stroking the mighty, hard flesh and eliciting a groan of pleasure. She pushed his pants open and reached for her vodka, holding the glass aloft with one hand and thumbing the wet, velvety head of his pulsing erection with the other.

"This could be messy," she warned.

"Some games are," he replied.

She drizzled a tiny bit of the icy clear liquid, tossed him a bold look, then dropped to her knees to taste the salty, hot flavor of vodka and man. He relaxed into her, stroking her hair, whispering words she'd never understand while she sucked him deep into her mouth.

He grew even harder and larger, his breath ragged as he fought for control. "Sweet Jesus, stop before I can't."

She released him and gave him a saucy grin. "Does that mean I win?"

He pulled her back up, kissing her hard and open-mouthed, palming her breasts with a slow, blissful caress.

"We tied. We'll finish the game at home," he promised huskily. "I want you too much and for too long to be satisfied in a car."

Laying her head on his chest, she shuddered. "Gregg, once I'm near Kristina, even if she's asleep, I'm her bodyguard again. No games."

He took her face in his hands and lifted it up to meet his gaze. "I'm going to make love to you tonight, Rakishka. Your client is safely asleep in her room and I want you to wake up in my bed." When she didn't answer, he added, "That is not a game."

Her heart skipped as she closed her eyes. Not a game she wanted to lose, anyway.

At the rustle of sheets, Grigori turned, seeing Raquel's silhouette against the earliest whisper of dawn.

"Don't leave," he said, reaching for her hand. He was aroused again and hungry for more of her.

"I don't want Kristina to find me in here, and neither do you."

That was true. "It's not even five. She doesn't wake before seven."

"I don't want to take that chance." She squeezed his hand and he pulled her back down on the bed for a kiss. "I'll come back."

"Tonight?"

She nodded. "As long as Kristina is safe and asleep, and you are comfortable."

"Kristina is safe and asleep now," he said, dragging her hand to his hard-on. "But I am not comfortable. See? Very uncomfortable."

She gave him a quick, heartless squeeze. "Live with it. You have a big day today. Criminals to bring down. International treasures to locate." She sighed, enviously. "I don't suppose I can go with you and rough him up?"

She slipped away, so he propped his head in one hand to watch her step into the sliver of black panties he'd taken off with his teeth. "You can come anywhere with me, as long as Kristina is home with that nanny."

"Joyce? Sheez." Raquel shook her head, sending her dark hair tumbling over her shoulders. "Did you see the look we got last night? She smelled the vodka."

"She smelled sex. And didn't approve of either one."

"Let alone at the same time."

He laughed softly, drinking her in as she put her bra on and bent over to pick up her dress. Her breasts weren't big, but they were luscious. Warm. Soft. Responsive. His whole lower half ached.

"You know, Rakishka, I should spend more time in New York."

She shot him a questioning look. "Yeah? You have a helluva place to live here."

"We could take more limo rides."

"And play drinking games." She pivoted suddenly to offer her back. "Zip, please."

He let his fingers travel down the soft skin of her backbone, his fingers grazing the snap of her brassiere. It would be so easy to take it off and touch her again. "Would you like that?"

"If I'm in New York. Bullet Catchers travel a lot. Zip."

"My home in St. Petersburg is stunning, and I have an apartment in London." He grazed his knuckle over her flesh.

"Sounds like quite the jet-setting life. Lucy's friends all have these fabulous places in St. Moritz and Johannesburg, Paris and Hong Kong. One of the reasons I want to be a Bullet Catcher is for the travel. You can't believe the places these . . . guys . . . Are you going to zip me?"

"I'm admiring your back." He reached around to fondle her breast. "And your front."

She eased him away. "Zip!"

With a grunt of resignation, he zipped the dress. "You talk a lot in your sleep, too, did you know that?"

She shrugged. "What did I say?" She reached down to slide her delicate feet into shoes she'd kept on just long enough to make him crazy last night.

"I'm not telling you."

She bent over, fastening the buckle. "What is this, another game? Stump the Bodyguard?"

"I'll tell you tonight. You have to promise to come back."

"I'll come back," she said, throwing a playful look over her shoulder. Then her gaze turned serious. "I like you."

He closed the space in one move and pulled her back flat on the bed and leaned over her. "I like you, too."

She grinned. "So that works out well."

But did it? The only serious relationship he'd ever had was a total disaster. Except for Kristina, it had yielded nothing but pain and heartache and misery. For his wife.

She stayed on her back, looking up at him. Her black hair spilled over the white sheets, her eyes dark from the shadow of last night's makeup, her lips swollen from his kisses and rough beard.

"I'm going to tell you something just so that it's out there," he said, tracing those swollen lips with one finger. "I'm utterly pathetic at anything except friendship and sex."

She studied him for a moment, then flicked his fingertip with her tongue. "Guess what? With me, you can have both." She curled her hand around his neck, pulling him down to her face. "Right now, as a matter of fact."

This time she kept her high heels on, and it did drive him crazy.

The glass vastness of Sotheby's New York headquarters was even more beautiful and dramatic draped in Christmas decor. Giant wreaths and frosted windows beckoned passersby into the famed auction house.

Raquel peered through the cab window as Gregg paid the fare, studying the ten-story building. Was the missing Fabergé egg back inside? Was Duncan? Or had he run away with his stolen property?

Taking her gloved hand, Gregg led her across the sidewalk toward the building. He hadn't discussed his plan with her, but had agreed to leave Kristina with the same baby-sitter and let Raquel come along. She wanted the experience of seeing Gregg confront Duncan and he seemed to understand that.

She wasn't here as his bodyguard, certainly, but she'd tucked her Glock 19 compact in a harness she wore under her pullover sweater and heavy coat, just in case.

Something in the set of Gregg's jaw and the determination in his step told her that he might be armed, as well.

Sotheby's lobby was bathed in the sunlight pouring through the hundred-and-fifty-foot atrium. As they approached the first of a complex web of escalators, Raquel looked up to the top, still holding Gregg's hand as she craned her neck to see the breathtaking and imposing vision. All the way up nine floors, a skeleton of glass and steel showcased elaborate "storefronts" of exquisite auction items.

"His office is on the fifth floor," Gregg said as they stepped onto the escalator. "We'll skip the elevator to keep our eyes open for him."

Instead of lingering over the second-floor displays of Chinese classical paintings, European antiques, American silver, and nine hundred bottles of rare Romanée-Conti wines recently discovered in a countryside cellar in Burgundy, Raquel searched the eyes of every person who passed by, seeking the menacing gaze the color of polished mahogany. Clusters of shoppers and guests passed them in the opposite direction, but no one looked familiar as they took the next escalator up to three.

"Is he located in the area for twentieth-century decorative arts?" she asked as they passed an auction room on the third floor, heading for the next escalator.

"Actually, they have a Russian art department here and in London. They handled the last major Fabergé sale of the Forbes Collection." His gaze scanned the crowd on the next escalator. "But this sale won't be anything like that. Probably because I bid so far over the asking price that the owners agreed immediately. At least verbally."

"Is that why Duncan was allowed to let the egg leave here?" They rounded the fourth floor, past a vast wall of Dutch Masters paintings, mostly blocked by viewers.

"Yes. He told me it was approved by the head of the—"

Gregg froze and looked up the escalator to the fifth floor. She followed his gaze to the barricade erected along the top, surrounded by several police officers, plainclothes and uniformed.

He squeezed Raquel's hand tighter, muttering something in Russian.

"Maybe he's already been busted," she said.

"Stay here." He jogged up a few frozen escalator steps and a policeman at the top held out his hand to stop him.

"This area is closed," he warned.

"I have urgent business," Gregg said, slowing but not stopping.

Raquel stayed at the bottom, itching to follow him, but waited to see how he dealt with the cop, who continued to glare at him. When Gregg got a few steps higher, he said something to the policemen, but Raquel couldn't hear.

The cop shook his head at first, then indicated for Gregg to wait for a moment, then walked away to talk to someone else.

Two women moved away from an art exhibit behind Raquel to check out the action.

"I wonder if they'll bring him down on the escalator," one mused. "That'd be quite a show."

"Never," the other said, still staring at the barricades. "They'll put him in the elevator."

Raquel looked from one to the other. "Who?"

One of the women gave her a look of knowing superiority. "A dead man. Someone was shot up there. Or shot himself. That's what we heard."

Raquel's chest tightened as Gregg came back down the stalled escalator. When he reached the bottom, she didn't even have to ask. The look on his face told her exactly who the dead man was.

Chapter Six

❅ ❅ ❅

Grigori didn't say a word as he tugged Raquel through the crowds, out of the lobby, and back into the street to hail a cab. When he yanked the door closed, he spat out the address to the driver and finally let his temper out, slapping his palm on the seat and growling a string of the blackest Russian curses he could think of.

"That means what?" she asked, a sarcastic edge in her voice. " 'I should have listened to Raquel last night and nailed Duncan when we had him and gotten the egg back'?"

He stared ahead. "We made the right decision last night."

"Then why are we going back to Kiplinger's apartment? Isn't that the address you just gave the cabbie?"

"Because it's the only lead I have at the moment."

"Why not stay at Sotheby's? We should talk to management. They may not know that the egg has disappeared."

He snorted softly. "On my watch. I signed a document stating that I had it in my possession. Now Duncan is dead. If I can't prove he stole it, I'm responsible for it."

"But it was stolen from you."

He ran a hand through his hair and stared at a troupe of hip-hop dancers dressed in Christmas colors, gathering a crowd at the southeast corner of Central Park. Even through the closed glass, he could hear the pounding bass of their sound system, thumping like blood into his heart.

"It wouldn't be the first time," he muttered.

"Excuse me?"

"It wouldn't be the first time my reputation was at stake," he said, turning to look into her eyes, the shape and color of warm, roasted almonds.

She watched him, waiting for an explanation.

And why he suddenly wanted to give one, he had no fathomable reason. She was just a woman. His daughter's bodyguard. His friend's employee. Last night's lover.

She reached over and closed her strong, narrow hand over his. "Tell me."

No, she was far more than just last night's lover, and he'd known that instinctively the minute he'd entered her. He ignored the tightness in his pants that thought caused.

"I was a double agent in the KGB. Did Lucy tell you that?"

She arched one lovely eyebrow. "I assumed that since you are on such friendly terms with a former CIA agent, you straddled the fence. And what does this have to do with Fabergé eggs being stolen?"

"Nothing." He closed his eyes. "Everything."

Again, she waited, uncharacteristically quiet. The only sound was the blast of warm, dry air from the car heater and the horn of an impatient cabbie stuck in the Columbus Circle traffic.

"I did what I thought was right at the time," he said softly. "But now, the world is different. Fifteen years ago I was a young agent, barely twenty-eight years old. I chose a course of action which, as it turned out, was the right one. But not everyone knew that at the time."

He didn't need to explain his role in ending the cold war. There were dozens of agents who made bold decisions and stopped a coup that would have changed the course of history; many who were more heroic and more deserving of credit. There were dozens of others who also had to betray their homeland in order to restore order and civilization and sanity in that country.

"All that matters," he said, "is that black time in Russia's great history is over. And my goal now is to do whatever I can to replenish what was good and great about our country."

"Like returning Fabergé eggs?"

"I have enjoyed tremendous success in business and can afford to do that. But," he sighed deeply, "I live under the cloud of suspicion that always darkens the path of a traitor."

Her fingers tightened on his hand. "You were a traitor?"

He gave her an incredulous look. "What would you call a double agent?"

"Since I'm on the side of the good guys, I'd call you smart and brave."

He smiled. "There are those in Russia who wouldn't agree."

"And by returning the eggs to their rightful home, you are assuaging the guilt you feel for what some might call betraying your country. Even though it was the right thing to do."

He looked out the window, then turned to her. "You are right, Rakishka." Amazingly, shockingly right. Though he'd been married to Nathalia for three years, she'd never even begun to understand his complex motivations. She thought it was about his *ego*. He squeezed Raquel's hand.

"What's your plan?" she asked. "To explain to Evan Kiplinger that you lost the egg that Duncan let you borrow, and that you believe Duncan stole it back to keep for himself?"

"I'm not sure yet." He was suspicious of Kiplinger, but for different reasons. "The whole arrangement has been odd from the beginning—not handled with the fanfare and openness of the Forbes sale of Fabergé eggs, and worthy of far more press coverage since these eggs have been missing for decades."

"That's what you want, though, right? You don't want word to get out that the eggs were discovered until you've finalized the purchase and have them back in Russia."

"Yes, but it's been too easy. Even taking the Danish Jubilee egg home was a little too easy. I'm suspicious."

"You were born suspicious. You're a spy."

True. They pulled up to the door of Kiplinger's apartment, and Grigori paid as Raquel pulled on her gloves.

"Think he'll let us up?" she asked after he announced himself to the doorman and they waited for the apartment to be called.

"If not, we'll figure a way in."

Her eyes widened. "We will?"

"Of course we will." He grinned at her and a little fire lit in her brown eyes. "You'd like that, wouldn't you?"

"It'd be educational." She winked at him as the doorman approached.

But there was no such education, as they were given permission to enter almost immediately. Any remnants of last night's party had been cleaned by an efficient staff; the elevator and the pristine hall showed no sign that well over a hundred people had celebrated into the wee hours the night before.

Grigori knocked twice before the door was answered.

The man he'd guessed was Kiplinger stood in front of them, a forty-something with receding, dark hair and wide, gray eyes that went from wary to surprised as he looked from one to the other.

"You were here last night," he blurted out. "Both of you. Why didn't you introduce yourselves? I recognized your name as the highest bidder."

Highest? Grigori's gut clenched. There were other bidders on the eggs? "I never had the chance. You were busy with Mark Duncan." He let purposeful implication in his voice. "Have you seen him today?"

Kiplinger paled. "I've just heard he shot himself."

"Is it Sotheby's policy to contact a client when an employee dies?" Grigori asked.

"They called to assure me that they had the eggs."

"All of them?" he asked.

"Except for the Danish Jubilee. Duncan brought that one back last night."

Relief warred with disbelief in Grigori's head. "You have it?"

Kiplinger looked dubious. "I thought he told you."

"He told me nothing. And since he's dead and I'm here," Grigori pushed the door a little and narrowed his gaze at Kiplinger, "why don't you tell me."

Kiplinger didn't budge. He glanced at Raquel, then back at Grigori. "I've had an attractive offer to split the sale. Someone wants to buy the Danish Jubilee egg and not the other three. I'm considering it."

"I'll beat whatever offer they make." Grigori inched forward and looked down at the man. "Let me see the egg."

The man lifted his chin, attempting defiance, but the fear in his eyes gave him away. "I'm having the egg taken by armored vehicle to Sotheby's today, as soon as the police clear the scene. You can make an appointment to see it there."

"I don't believe you have it," Grigori said.

"I have it." He tucked his hands into the front of worn jeans. "The other buyer was here this morning looking at it."

"Prove it."

"Look, I can't let you in here just to look at it. I've never even met you before."

"I'm Grigori Nyekovic. This is Raquel Durant." Grigori slid a small SIG-Sauer out of his pocket and pointed the ugly black snub at Kiplinger's stomach. "Now we've met. Let me see the egg."

Kiplinger took one step back, holding up two hands. "All right, man. I'm not going to die for a stupid piece of porcelain that was in my grandmother's basement."

A stupid piece of porcelain worth five million dollars. And on the gray market? Probably six or seven. "Smart man," Grigori said as he led Raquel into the apartment.

"It's upstairs," Kiplinger said, throwing another wary glance at the gun. "You can put that away."

He didn't, but lowered the weapon.

They took the back stairs this time, and Kiplinger led them into the bedroom where he had emerged with Duncan the night before. Grigori shared a look with Raquel, who followed in silence. She might talk a lot, but she obviously knew when to be quiet.

Kiplinger opened a closet door and revealed a common home jewelry safe, then entered a digital code and popped the door open. He pulled out a plain brown box and set it on the bed.

"Here it is." He lifted the lid and under some tissues lay the four-inch-long porcelain egg.

"May I?" Raquel asked. At Kiplinger's nod, she lifted the egg, the tissue rustling as the brilliant white and gold emerged, the handpainted image of a Danish king glistening on the side.

"Oh, it's so light," she said. "I expected it to be heavier."

Grigori took a step closer. "It's not light. Here." He took it in one hand and stabbed Kiplinger with a black look.

"What?" Kiplinger asked. "What's the matter?"

Grigori raised the gun to Kiplinger's face, clicked the safety, and threw the egg on the hardwood floor. The shatter of porcelain was only slightly louder than Raquel's gasp.

"Where's the real one, you bastard?"

"That fucking bitch stole it." Evan backed away from

Gregg's gun, stepping on a piece of broken porcelain. Raquel held her breath, half expecting Gregg to shoot as waves of fury and frustration rolled off him. "I left her for twenty seconds to answer the phone, and she stole the egg."

"Who?" Gregg demanded, lifting the gun higher.

"The other buyer. The one Duncan sent over here so early this morning."

"What's her name?"

"I—I—"

Gregg stuck the gun into Evan's neck and the poor guy looked ready to wet his pants. "What's her name?"

He closed his eyes and Gregg knocked his jaw with the barrel of his pistol, smacking Evan's teeth together. "Five seconds. What's her name?"

Evan blinked.

"Four."

"It was—"

"Three."

"Let me think!" he whined, glancing for help at Raquel, who gave him a harsh stare.

"Two."

"Jacobson. Mrs. Jacobson."

"What's her first name?" Gregg demanded.

"Hallie or Haley or something like that." He blew out a breath, half shuddering. "Duncan told me she was legit. I believed him."

Raquel headed straight for the door. Gregg didn't ask where she was going, his burning focus on Evan. When she stepped into the hallway, she heard him demand more information, a moment of silence, then Evan grunted in pain.

She dashed into the study they'd found the night before, relieved to see the computer on. Immediately, she logged onto the Bullet Catchers proprietary site and began searching their massive database for the name of Hallie or Haley Jacobson.

She heard another cry of pain. Would Gregg kill the guy trying to get the truth? The thought sent a shudder through her. The look in his eyes when he'd realized the egg was fake had been deadly. She had no doubt he was capable of killing.

"I don't know where she lives!" Evan's whimper floated down the hall, barely audible over the clicking of computer keys.

They had Jacobsons in the database, but none with a similar first name. While she waited for a search, she pulled open a drawer and started leafing through Evan's papers. Nothing. She tried a few more back doors into different criminal databases, and while the computer worked on them, she flipped through the electronic address book. Nothing. She skipped the standard FBI database—it was so easy to elude that one—and dipped into her secret stash of names and aliases, typing in every spelling of "Hallie" and "Jacobson" she could imagine. Nothing.

She checked parole, probation, U.S. Marshal's lists, and all of New York State. Damn it all, everything came up blank! If this was a real person, she certainly didn't have a criminal file.

Swearing at precisely the moment she heard a body fall to the floor with a grunt, she tried another Bullet Catcher search engine for anyone who'd ever filed a legal motion. Divorce, adoption, credit issues, even malpractice would show up. Anyone who'd ever been listed through a legal service would appear.

Footsteps neared the door and Gregg called her name.

"I'm in the study," she said just as a match for Hallie Jacobson flashed on the screen.

Gregg stood in the doorway, not even slightly out of breath.

"Did you kill him?"

He half smiled. "Not even close. What are you doing?"

"Trying the nonviolent method. I found a match."

He stepped behind her. "For what?"

"Hallie Jacobson. She's listed in . . . child-care provider background checks."

A tiny ping popped in her head.

"What?" The tone in his voice told her the same alarm rang in his brain.

She started typing madly, her heart rate up. A list of known aliases came up right away. Hallie Jacobson . . . Henrietta Jacoby . . . Janice Henries . . . *Joyce Henderson.*

The nanny.

They both whispered, "Kristina."

"You can grab a cab," Gregg said as they tore out into the street. "I'm going on foot. It's faster through Central Park."

She shot him a look. "I can keep up. Run."

They dodged pedestrians and traffic as they darted toward the park. Evan's description matched the woman who was baby-sitting Kristina, and so did her alias. Raquel wanted to dig, to call, to send in backup, but

Gregg was crazed with the realization that his daughter was in danger.

There wasn't time to do anything but *get home.*

There certainly wasn't time for either one of them to kick themselves for leaving Kristina with an art thief. Raquel pieced the puzzle together as they reached Central Park. "Duncan and Joyce probably run some kind of high-end art theft ring," she said as they hustled around a snow drift on the asphalt drive.

Gregg nodded as though he'd been thinking the same thing. "She poses as a nanny to the people he lets 'borrow' the treasures."

"When they are stolen, people probably pay because they don't want to get in trouble."

"Wouldn't the police track them, though?" she asked. "I mean after she's at the site of a crime two or three times?"

"Not if parents think their little ones are responsible for losing the item. It's a setup."

Raquel bounced on her feet at a light and as soon as there was a break in the traffic, they ran across. "But she didn't put that egg in Kristina's bag."

"I know," he said grimly. "But she was scheduled to come that night. I canceled her when you arrived. I decided I would have a better evening at home with you."

She ignored the compliment and wound around a pack of tourists. "You said she sat for you once before. Could she have urged Kristina to take something for her, or preplanned it somehow?"

"I had her once before." He closed his eyes in disgust and realization. "Right after I made the offer to Duncan for the eggs. I don't know if she had that much influence over Kristina." They'd reached the block on Fifth Avenue where he lived, and neither of them was winded yet. "We're about to find out."

"I hope so."

He guided her into the elevator. "Oh God," he groaned as he banged the button to the penthouse. "Please let her be there."

Raquel silently said the same prayer. "You go straight to Kristina," she said optimistically. "I'll kill the nanny."

His smile was tight. "Get the egg first."

Her *first* assignment. A little girl. And she was off "observing" Gregg instead of guarding Kristina. Guilt and anguish punched her in the chest. Some fine Bullet Catcher she was.

When the elevator doors opened to his foyer, the apartment was dark and quiet.

"Kristina?" Gregg called, the first hint of panic in his normally cool voice.

He bounded down the hall to her room and Raquel headed in the other direction. The lights on the Christmas tree were the only ones on in the whole place and the curtains were all drawn closed.

"She's not in her room or on that side of the apartment," he said, coming into the main living area and meeting her after she'd checked the kitchen and dining room.

"I'll check with the security guard and doorman."

"I'll check the security tapes for when they might have left."

Raquel's gaze scanned the room, looking for any clue. Gregg turned back to his office, then froze, his gaze on the tree. Raquel followed the direct line from his icy blue eyes . . . to a single ornament.

"Oh my God," she whispered. "Is that it?"

He reached for the oversize egg, carefully removing it from the branch. "No. It's another cheap imitation." He opened it and pulled out a single piece of paper. He read it and handed it to Raquel, as though it pained him just to touch the paper the words were written on.

Her ransom is your silence.

Chapter Seven

❄ ❄ ❄

I'll wait here," Raquel said. "She might call or contact you."

Gregg didn't look up as he loaded another clip into a second weapon. "Fine."

"Where are you going to start?"

"I have my resources," he said briskly.

His silence was infuriating her. "Won't you talk to me?"

He finally glanced at her, but said nothing.

"You blame me," she stated simply.

"No, I blame me." He holstered the weapon and grabbed a cellphone, checking the battery.

"But I was her bodyguard."

"And I am her father." He flipped the cellphone closed. "I let her down."

"You had no way of knowing that a vetted nanny could possibly be involved in art theft, Gregg. You hired a bodyguard." Who was off on another job instead of paying attention to the principal.

"I should never have brought her here." He brushed by her into the hall. "She should be safe in London with her mother. I should never have . . ." His voice trailed off and he turned away, striding down the hall to his room.

The bed was still unmade, sending a stark and powerful reminder of their lovemaking the night before. "You should never have what?"

He grabbed a leather bomber jacket from the closet and shoved his arms into the sleeves, finally looking at her. Pain darkened his blue eyes and a frown slashed his forehead. "It doesn't matter."

"Yes, it does."

"All that matters is that she knows we're closing in on her. She may have killed Duncan, for all I know. And she could easily kill Kristina." His voice cracked and he shook his head as though to clear it. "She's all I've got."

The man who thought he could only offer friendship and sex was clearly capable of more. And it hurt to see him think he might lose it. Raquel left him alone, wandering into the kitchen for the tenth time, her whole being wired for sound. She cracked her knuckles and tried to think. They'd get nowhere placing or taking blame. Let him go off like some KGB cowboy. She'd stay here and do what she did best. *Dig.*

Maybe she should have stayed back at the Bullet Catchers, getting unlisted phone numbers and tracking GPS readings to find missing persons. Suddenly, the clearest of answers presented itself in her head. Of course! She almost smacked herself when the thought occurred to her. That's how Duncan knew where the egg was!

"Gregg," she called out, rushing toward the center hall. "I just thought of how the—"

The elevator doors closed with a silent *whoosh*.

She battered down her disappointment that he'd left

without saying good-bye. He was consumed by terror for his daughter and fury for his enemies. She'd seen that look before in the eyes of a Bullet Catcher on a mission: the need to protect, the urge to kill an offender, the bone-deep determination to save a life, even if it cost one. Even it if cost *yours*.

Could she really be one of those people?

God knows she was failing her first test. Ignoring the wave of self-disgust, she set up her laptop in Gregg's office, connecting to his wireless and staring at the screen while she considered where to start.

She could find anything that had a satellite transmission anywhere in the world. Hadn't she helped Alex Romero locate a cache of stolen weapons in Hong Kong last year? Hadn't she tracked down a kidnapped principal using nothing but a cellphone signal when someone stole her out from underneath Max Roper? She could find anything . . . if it transmitted something. That was her gift. It kept her chained to an office, and she was sick of using that gift when she wanted the satisfaction that came with physically thwarting a bad guy, but her real superpower was tracking. And if she didn't use it now, what good was she?

Mark Duncan had probably planted a simple tracking device in the egg he let Gregg borrow. That was done all the time now with rare art that was being shipped. The chips were so small now that they were virtually invisible. But would Joyce know it was there? And would she remove it?

An hour later, she'd tracked the history of a signal that had originated in the quadrant where Sotheby's was located, moved to the area where Gregg lived, and then followed its path to a Fifth Avenue location. That *had* to be the egg. It had traveled to a location just above the Bronx, then another in Brooklyn, then another down in the Financial District, where the signal terminated yesterday.

She called Gregg's cellphone and he answered on the first ring. "Did you hear anything?" he asked, anxiety deepening his Russian accent.

"No, but I have some leads." As she explained her theory and the signal she'd tracked, she grazed her fingertip over a small framed picture of Kristina on Gregg's desk. In it, she still had baby teeth, but her hair was the same—long and pale like her father's, her gaze completely sweet and guileless. Raquel's heart melted. "I have three areas that I suspect were the location of the egg in the last forty-eight hours. The signal emits a general location, so I don't have a precise address." She read each to him. "Where are you?"

"South, in midtown."

"Perfect. You go down to the Financial District, and I'll go up north to Mt. Vernon. We can meet in Brooklyn later."

"No. Stay there."

She bristled. "Why? If Joyce wants to contact you, she'll call your cellphone. Surely she has the number."

"I just want you to stay there."

She recognized the protective tone, but her function wasn't to stay safe—it was to keep Kristina safe. She angled the photograph into the light. "Time is wasting, Gregg. We need to split up and look for her."

"Nyet," he insisted.

"Da," she shot back.

"Stay at home, Raquel." He used that trill in her

name, just enough to melt her heart a little bit more. But melted hearts were not the stuff of Bullet Catchers.

"Call me on my cell." She hung up and grabbed the picture. On her way out, she checked the clip of her little Glock, then headed due north toward the Bronx.

Raquel's cab cruised the residential streets of Mt. Vernon, lined with barren trees and rows of brick homes with snow drifts around empty front porches. Wire Santas and reindeer sat like skeletons left out in the cold, ready to light up when darkness fell. There couldn't be more than four houses within the quadrant that the signal had emitted and that made her feel confident about doing a door-to-door search.

Then Terrace Avenue widened and, to the north, Raquel saw a half-dozen multistoried brick apartment buildings, with easily forty or more units in each. Her heart dropped in disappointment.

Kristina could be in any one of them.

Or not.

Taking a deep breath, she instructed the driver to cruise the streets that surrounded the complex while she got her bearings. Once she'd located the entrances to all six buildings, she let the cab go and started reading the mailboxes. None of Joyce Henderson's or Hallie Jacobson's known aliases were listed. The closest she could find were Joseph Hendricks and H. Jackson. There was no answer when she buzzed Hendricks, and Jackson sounded like a sick old man who wouldn't let in strangers. She managed to get into one building, cruised the halls and showed Kristina's picture to two very nice ladies playing canasta, but got nowhere.

"Try the playground, honey," one said. "It's behind Building Four. Lots of children there now that school is out."

She hustled to the back of Building Four, where about a dozen children and mothers and sitters were bundled up against the cold and making do with beat-up playground equipment. None had seen Kristina.

Just as she was about to leave to try and get in another building, two middle-school–age girls came running out in bright parkas, their ski caps pulled low. Giggling, they were intently blowing white puffs of cold air, their fingers in a V shape to imitate smoking.

When one of them opened her jacket and revealed a handbag, Raquel froze at the sight of yellow beaded butterflies over blue denim. "Where did you get that purse?" she demanded.

The girl stopped, eyes wide. "My neighbor gave it to me."

Raquel forced herself to sound casual. "Really? I have a niece who'd love one like that." The girls looked slightly more interested and Raquel jumped on it. "Can you tell me which apartment your neighbor lives in? I'd love to find out where she bought it."

Lame, but they were young. How suspicious could they be?

"She's in Building Two, over there. Um, she's upstairs of me in two-oh-one." She squinted heavily mascaraed eyes at Raquel and leaned closer. "She's kind of a bitch."

Raquel grinned, certain she'd found Joyce Henderson. "I can handle that."

At Building Two, she waited until a young mother emerged with her hands full of kids, held the door for her, then slipped into the drafty entryway. She dashed up two flights of stairs, and navigated the hallway to the painted metal door bearing the numbers 201. It was locked. She drew her gun, kept it hidden, and knocked.

No answer.

"Joyce?" she called. "Are you in there?"

She heard a definite sound of movement from inside, but still no answer.

"Open the door or I'm calling the police."

Another movement, and suddenly the door opened a crack. The colorless face of the nanny peeked out. "Why on earth would you do that?"

"I know she's in here," Raquel said from between gritted teeth. She lifted the gun for Joyce to see. "I know you have her and I know you have the egg."

"I don't know what you're talking about," she insisted, allowing the door to open another inch. "I left that child with a nanny replacement that the service sent over. They told me you had ordered someone else for the afternoon."

"Bullshit."

Joyce looked offended. "Go away."

Raquel couldn't take a shot, Kristina could be anywhere. Purposely holding the woman's gaze, she took a half step back, then another, as though she were leaving. Just before Joyce closed the door, Raquel lifted her leg and kicked the door with all her strength, popping Joyce right in the face. As she tripped backward, Raquel pushed into the apartment.

"Kristina!" she called.

Joyce jumped her from behind and Raquel flipped her on her back in one smooth move. Grabbing the woman's scrawny neck, she pulled her up off the ground with one hand and stuck the Glock in her stomach. "Get her."

Turning red, she shook her head. Raquel jammed the gun harder and the woman nodded and mouthed, "Okay."

Raquel loosened her grip enough for Joyce to lead her into a back bedroom and to a closet. Raquel's heart tumbled around. "If anything happened to that girl, you are *so* dead."

Joyce opened the closet door and there was Kristina, sitting among the shoes and some clothes on the floor. Her eyes were wide with terror, her cheeks tear-stained.

"Oh my God." Raquel gave Joyce a solid push and bent over to get Kristina. Joyce tried to slam the closet door closed, but Raquel kept her balance, spun on one foot, and landed a solid punch right in the woman's face.

She fell over like a cardboard cutout, completely unconscious.

Raquel grabbed Kristina and pulled her out to freedom. "Let's go, honey," she said, pushing her out of the room. "I'll get someone back here for her." Her only goal was to get Kristina to safety. Nothing else mattered.

The child stumbled and started to cry, so Raquel scooped her into her arms and rushed out the door, navigating the stairs down to the first floor. As she rounded the final landing, Raquel shifted Kristina so she could see the front door and stopped dead in her tracks at the sight of a man entering the building, his gun drawn, his vicious brown eyes locked on her.

Mark Duncan was definitely not dead.

Chapter Eight

❄ ❄ ❄

T hank God you found her," Duncan said, his gentle tone belying the look in his eyes. "You can take her now, Ms. Durant."

"But—I thought you were . . ."

"Dead. I know. It was all part of the sting."

She frowned at him, Kristina wiggling to look at the man. He turned quickly toward the stairs. "I'm with the FBI art crimes department and we appreciate your assistance." He jogged up the first few steps. "I'll go get the perpetrator."

He disappeared on the next landing, leaving Raquel slack-jawed and in serious doubt that he was telling the truth.

But all that mattered was that she had Kristina, alive and well.

She eased the child to the ground. "Let's go home now, honey."

Kristina's eyes widened. "What about Daddy's pretty egg?"

"That man is going to get it," Raquel assured her,

glancing up the steps and hoping that was true. "Our only job is to get out of here and get home safely."

"Daddy will cry if we don't bring home the egg."

Raquel almost laughed at the idea. "He'll cry if I don't bring *you* home." She took her hand and tugged her toward the door. "That man who just passed us will get Daddy's egg and the bad lady who took you." God, she hoped so.

Kristina shook her head. "He's bad, too. He was the one who took us from home and brought us here."

"Are you sure? You didn't see him."

"I heard his voice," she said. "It was him."

Oh God, what should she do? Let Duncan and Joyce get away—with the Fabergé egg? Or run like hell and get her principal to safety? A good Bullet Catcher would do the latter.

But a great Bullet Catcher would do both.

The two girls from the playground buzzed themselves in.

"Hi!" The one who had carried Kristina's purse said brightly. "Did you find her?"

"I did." Raquel squeezed Kristina's hand a little. "Girls, how would you like to earn twenty dollars apiece?"

They looked at each other again. "Cool."

"I need you to watch this little girl for ten minutes. Is your apartment nearby?"

One pointed to the first door. "I live right here. What do you need?"

Raquel kneeled down next to Kristina and brushed her hair back. "Ten more minutes of baby-sitting, and I promise you the trip of a lifetime to the American Girl store."

Her eyes lit up. Raquel handed her over to the teenagers. "You have to stay in that apartment with the door locked, and don't let *anyone* in for *any* reason, no matter who they say they are. Just me. Or, if Kristina recognizes him, her father. That's it."

They nodded solemnly, one taking her hand while the other unlocked the apartment door. As soon as Raquel heard the deadbolt inside, she pulled out her Glock and ran up the stairs.

The apartment door was still open. Did they get out somehow? Holding the gun straight ahead in a two-handed death grip, Raquel entered the apartment. She kicked the door closed, ready to shoot someone behind it. No one.

Damn it all, they'd escaped.

Sure enough, the back window with a fire escape was open. She stared at the easy exit, lowering her weapon with a deep sigh.

"Guess I'm just a good Bullet Catcher," she said softly. "Not a great one yet."

A hard, vicious hand clamped over her mouth and the cold barrel of a gun jabbed her in the neck. "If you don't tell me where that fucking egg is, you'll be a dead one."

Grigori used a universal code to unlock the apartment complex door and slipped into the entryway well ahead of the FBI agents who already surrounded the block. He hadn't heard from Raquel and she didn't answer her cellphone, which spurred him to move fast and take chances.

She'd be delighted to know that the investigative work

he'd done for the last few hours—including the discovery that Mark Duncan had shot someone in his office and successfully faked his own death for half a day—had led him directly to the location that Raquel had given him after her first round of searching.

He heard a burst of childish laughter from the first apartment on his right, and stopped. God, that sounded like Kristina. He paused, but it was quiet and he knew from the investigation that Joyce Henderson, aka Hallie Jacobson, rented on the second floor, in 201. He continued toward the stairs, listening for any sounds.

From upstairs, the sudden thud of a body hitting a wall chilled his blood.

Maybe Raquel was finally beating the crap out of Duncan . . . or the other way around. He took two more steps, then a sudden squeal came from the apartment, and Kristina's voice exclaimed, "Oh, I can't believe you have that!"

He barreled toward the first-floor apartment and banged once, calling her name.

"That's my daddy!" he heard her cry, and in a moment, the door flung open and he was greeted by the bright eyes of his daughter—completely and utterly safe—as she darted toward him, holding her handbag out as if it were the grand prize of a lifetime. "Look! Look what I've found!"

He instantly ran to her, stashing his weapon so he could embrace her with all the love and adrenaline that coursed through his veins. "Kristyusha!" He squeezed her tiny body into his chest and closed his eyes in a silent prayer of relief. Then he looked over her at the stranger's face. "Where's her bodyguard?"

The teenage girl lifted two overly plucked brows in surprise.

"He means Raquel," Kristina explained. "Look, Daddy. Look." Again she held the bag out. "I have it."

"Yes, you found your bag, *lapinka*." They had so much more at stake and there was no way to explain that to a child. "But I have to go find—"

"Your egg!"

"Yes, but more importantly, I have to find—"

"Your egg!"

He nodded, forcing himself not to scare her by running after Raquel. "I'm not as worried about the egg right now as I am about Raquel." He looked up, about to ask the interim sitter if she would watch her again when Kristina reached into the bag and raised her little hand in triumph.

"The egg," he said, staring at it. "How did you—"

"When we got here, I found my handbag in Miss Joyce's closet. When she was talking to that mean man, they weren't looking, so I stuffed the egg back in here. Then Tiffany . . ." she turned and pointed to the teenager, ". . . came up and wanted something and Miss Joyce was trying to get rid of her really fast so she gave her the bag. But I didn't know it until now."

He took the egg, knowing immediately from the weight that this was no cheap knockoff. "How did you get out of Miss Joyce's apartment?"

"Raquel beat Miss Joyce up. She punched her in the face really good and knocked her over."

"I bet she did." And then she found someone to take care of Kristina and went back for his *other* treasure. His heart twisted as he eased his daughter toward the teenager. "Ten more minutes, please. And, no matter what—"

The older girl held up her hand. "I know. Keep her locked in the apartment." She looked over her shoulder at another teenager in matching makeup and long, dark hair. "We'll take care of her and your ornament."

Kristina looked up, her gaze serious. "It's not an *ornament,* Tiffany. It's a national treasure." She gingerly took the egg from Grigori. "I'll protect it, Daddy, just like Raquel protected me."

He kissed her on the forehead and ran up the stairs to save his newest treasure. The one that had just taken on monumental value in his heart.

Unfortunately, Joyce wasn't dead. Duncan had clobbered her, though, and when he pushed Raquel into the bedroom with repeated demands for the egg, they'd almost tripped over the woman who lay in misery on the floor.

She moaned something about the kid's purse.

"What purse?" Duncan barked at her, punctuating his anger by sticking the gun deeper into Raquel's neck.

"Maybe the kid put the egg back in her purse," Joyce said, her voice husky from pain. "She was playing with it when I first got her here. I went to the bathroom. Maybe she found it and hid it back in her purse. It's the only thing I can think of."

"You idiot," Duncan said, throwing a disgusted look at her. "You screwed this up so bad. What the hell were you thinking, taking that stupid kid?"

"Ransom," she moaned. "They had us, Mark. We needed a way out."

"*You* needed a way out." He focused his attention on Raquel. "Where'd you put that kid?"

She'd die before she told him.

He smacked her head with the gun, rattling her teeth and sending fire through her head. But she just stared daggers at him. He'd have to kill her before she let anything happen to Kristina.

"Did she have this purse with her?" he demanded, squeezing her arm so hard she thought he'd break the bone. "Where the hell is she?"

She just looked at him.

"Talk to me!" He thwacked the side of her face with the gun and Raquel stumbled to the side, but kept her jaw clenched.

Bullet Catchers don't talk. They listen. That didn't mean she had to get the holy shit beat out of her.

Hot anger singed her blood and Raquel found her footing, blinking at a drop of blood that slithered into her eye. Damn this man. He would *not* be her undoing.

"She's downstairs, isn't she?" he asked. "You didn't have time to take her anywhere, so she's in the building somewhere."

She glared at him, mentally bracing for the next blow.

"Bitch," he muttered, pushing her so hard she fell on the bed. As he turned away, Raquel propelled herself to a stand, pulling back her right fist. He sensed the move and inched around just as she let go of the punch, landing a wicked temple shot on the side of his head.

While he was off balance, she let loose, kicking the gun out of his hand and landing another blow to his jaw. He raised a fist to her face, but she blocked the punch with her left hand, exploding a right cross between his eyes. He reeled backward from the impact, but lunged before she had a chance to reach his gun.

She slammed him with another straight right, then a hook-and-uppercut combination, eliciting a groan as he bent over, his face heading straight for her knee. To finish him off, she kicked him in the stomach, whipping him backward so that he fell on Joyce's body.

Breathing hard, Raquel scooped up the gun he'd dropped, cocked it, and aimed it at his heart.

"That definitely goes into your recommendation letter."

She spun around at Gregg's words, her heart jumping at the look of raw approval and admiration on his face. Right behind him, three more men poured into the room, shouting, "FBI! Freeze."

She ignored them and walked straight into Gregg's open arms. "Kristina is fine," she whispered. "I promise you that."

He held her tightly. "I never doubted you."

"Yes, you did." She welcomed his embrace and warm kiss on her hair. "You told me to stay at home."

His smile was bittersweet. "I have a feeling I could never tell you to do that." He kissed her bruised cheek, then found her mouth for a long, soulful kiss. He touched her bleeding forehead gently. "Let me take you to the hospital."

She shrugged. "Nah. It just needs—"

"Vodka."

"That'll work." Smiling, she wrapped her arm around his waist and gave him a squeeze. "Let's get Kristina and go home."

For Christmas, at least, she'd stay with him. How

could she not? Then, in the new year, she'd start her life as a Bullet Catcher. A good one, anyway.

"Oh, by the way," he said as they headed for the apartment door. "Kristina has the egg."

Raquel stopped, her jaw open. Then she laughed. "A great one, after all."

Grigori Nyekovic
835 Fifth Avenue
New York, NY 10021

December 31, 2006

Ms. Lucy Sharpe
CEO, The Bullet Catchers
1 Clifton Point Road
Astor Cove, NY 10536

Dear Lucy,

Three weeks ago, when your newest staff member, Raquel Durant, was assigned to provide personal protection to my daughter, Kristina, we agreed that I would observe your employee's performance and provide you with a complete assessment of her capabilities. Since we are longtime friends, one-time enemies, and will no doubt work together in the future, I will be entirely forthright in this evaluation. I know you appreciate candor.

Over the course of the past three weeks, I have had the opportunity to witness the range of unique and remarkable talents that Ms. Durant brought to her assignment. She possesses sharp wits, the capacity to anticipate and thwart any threats, amazing resourcefulness in obtaining information, and a tremendous aptitude and willingness to learn new skills and techniques. She embraced a range of physically challenging activities, and with every one, she demonstrated an ability to use her well-developed physical prowess along with her keen intellect, her exceptional mental focus, and her clear vision of the overall goal of her assignment.

For these reasons and countless others—including her infinite capacity for selfless acts of heroism—Raquel Durant will make an exceptional Bullet Catcher.

Very best regards,
Grigori Nyekovic

P.S. Thank you for agreeing to extend Raquel's assignment so that she can accompany Kristina and me to Russia for the unveiling of the four Fabergé eggs in St. Petersburg. Upon our return, I plan to spend most of the next year based in New York and will require the constant companionship of a security specialist. I am looking for someone who is willing to work very closely with me as I undertake several consulting jobs, some requiring extensive international travel, for the CIA. I'll need someone intelligent, strong, alert, fearless, protective, and trustworthy.

No doubt that describes all of the extraordinary individuals who work for you. But I also request someone who has finely tuned verbal skills, top-shelf technological capabilities, and a mean uppercut. I would appreciate your limiting your selection to the most beautiful woman on your staff, one who has shown outstanding skills at competitive Russian social activities and exceptional undercover work.

P.P.S. You knew I'd fall in love with her, didn't you?

About the Authors

Linda Lael Miller lives in Washington State.

Catherine Mulvany, also the author of the paranormal romantic suspense novels *Run No More* and *Shadows All Around Her,* lives her own fractured fairy tale of a life in the wilds of the Pacific Northwest. To learn more, visit www.catherinemulvany.com.

Julie Leto is a *USA Today* bestselling author who has penned more than fifteen books for Harlequin's Temptation and Blaze lines. She resides in Tampa, Florida.

Roxanne St. Claire left her public relations career to write full time. She lives in Florida with her husband and children.